Masterpieces

OF
Mystery

The Grand Masters Up To Date

Selected by ELLERY QUEEN

COPYRIGHT NOTICES AND ACKNOWLEDGMENTS

Grateful acknowledgment is hereby made for permission to reprint the following:

The Third Floor Flat by Agatha Christie; reprinted by permission of Dodd, Mead & Company, Inc. from THREE BLIND MICE AND OTHER STORIES by Agatha Christie; copyright 1928 by Agatha Christie, copyright renewed 1956 by Agatha Christie Mallowan.

Man in Hiding by Vincent Starrett; copyright © 1964 by STARRETT MEMORIAL LIBRARY; reprinted by permission of Michael Murphy, Literary Executor: Vincent Starrett Estate.

A Dog in the Daytime by Rex Stout; appears as "Die Like a Dog" in THREE WITNESSES by Rex Stout; copyright 1954 by Rex Stout; reprinted by permission of The Viking Press.

The Three Widows by Ellery Queen; copyright © 1950, 1955 by Ellery Queen; reprinted by permission of Scott Meredith Literary Agency, Inc.

Danger Out of the Past by Erle Stanley Gardner; copyright 1955 by Erle Stanley Gardner; originally published as *Protection*; reprinted by permission of Thayer Hobson and Company.

The Other Hangman by John Dickson Carr; copyright 1940 by William Morrow and Company, Inc., renewed; reprinted by permission of Clarice M. Carr.

Death Certificate by George Harmon Coxe; copyright 1947 by George Harmon Coxe; reprinted by permission of Brandt & Brandt.

Stan the Killer by Georges Simenon; copyright 1944 by Georges Simenon, renewed; reprinted by permission of the author.

A Clue from Bing Crosby by Baynard Kendrick; copyright 1958 by Fosdeck Publications, Inc.; reprinted by permission of Paul R. Reynolds, Inc.

Gideon and the Shoplifting Ring by John Creasey (J. J. Marric); © 1969 by John Creasey (J. J. Marric); reprinted by permission of Harold Ober Associates, Inc.

Dead Man by James M. Cain; copyright 1936 by James M. Cain, copyright renewed; reprinted by permission of Harold Ober Associates, Inc.

Postiche by Mignon G. Eberhart; copyright 1935 by Mignon G. Eberhart; reprinted by permission of Brandt & Brandt.

The Homesick Buick by John D. MacDonald; copyright 1950, copyright renewal 1977 by John D. MacDonald; reprinted by permission of the author.

The Contradictory Case by Hugh Pentecost; copyright 1951 by Judson Philips; reprinted by permission of Brandt & Brandt.

The Missing Sister Case by Ross Macdonald; copyright 1953 by Kenneth Millar; reprinted by permission of Harold Ober Associates, Inc.

The Case of the Pinchbeck Locket by Eric Ambler; copyright 1945 by The American Mercury, Inc., renewed; reprinted by permission of Peter Janson-Smith Ltd.

The Destructors by Graham Greene; from TWENTY-ONE STORIES by Graham Greene; copyright © 1955 by Graham Greene; reprinted by permission of The Viking Press.

CONTENTS

INTRODUCTION

As of the time of this writing there are 20 Grand Masters of mystery, as voted by the Mystery Writers of America (MWA), and you will find stories by all 20 in this eighteenth volume of MASTERPIECES OF MYSTERY.

It occurs to us that if MWA and other mystery organizations in the world finally decide to found a Mystery Hall of Fame, it will be necessary to install the masters of the past who would certainly be acknowledged to have been Grand Masters in their day.

With 20 Grand Masters now, suppose we strive for the magic number of 60 (the number of stories about Sherlock Holmes), thus adding 40 more names to the definitive roster of Grand Masters.

We would have to start with Voltaire, awarding him an Honorary Grandmastership for his creation of Zadig, the progenitor of Dupin, Holmes, et al. Voltaire might be called the Great-Grandfather of the Detective Story.

Next, in chronological sequence, we would nominate François Eugène Vidocq as another Honorary Grand Master, especially for his influence on Poe. Vidocq might be called the Grandfather of the Detective Story.

The pedestal of highest honor would go unquestionably to Edgar Allan Poe—what could be termed the Grand Grandmastership—as the Father of the Modern Detective Story.

So our current 20 Grand Masters would now be 23. Let us add 12 more names of the Old Masters who come immediately to mind:

> Charles Dickens
> Wilkie Collins
> Emile Gaboriau
> Anna Katharine Green
> A. Conan Doyle
> Israel Zangwill
> Arthur Morrison

E. W. Hornung
Jacques Futrelle
Maurice Leblanc
Gaston Leroux
R. Austin Freeman

We now have 35 of our 60 members of the Mystery Hall of Fame. We nominate the following 25 of those mystery writers who are no longer with us, to round out our magical 60:

Mary Roberts Rinehart	Edgar Wallace
G. K. Chesterton	Earl Derr Biggers
Baroness Orczy	S. S. Van Dine
A. E. W. Mason	Anthony Berkeley
William MacHarg	(Francis Iles)
Arthur B. Reeve	Harvey J. O'Higgins
Sax Rohmer	Roy Vickers
E. C. Bentley	Dashiell Hammett
Ernest Bramah	Margery Allingham
Melville Davisson Post	Nicholas Blake
Freeman Wills Crofts	Raymond Chandler
H. C. Bailey	Cornell Woolrich
Dorothy L. Sayers	Charlotte Armstrong

In the eighteen volumes so far, we have given you examples of the work of 50 of the 60 Grand Masters of all time, and in this volume we give you stories by the 20 Grand Masters of our own time.

Happy reading!

ELLERY QUEEN

THE THIRD FLOOR FLAT

By AGATHA CHRISTIE

Agatha Christie, Dame Commander Order of the British Empire, was born Agatha Clarissa Miller in Devon, England, on September 15, 1890. Her American father died when she was a child and she was raised by her mother. She wrote scores of short stories, plays, and novels and introduced such world-famous characters as Hercule Poirot and Jane Marple. She was married to archeologist Sir Max E.L. Mallowan in 1930 and for many years accompanied him on his annual digging trips to Syria and Iraq. Dame Agatha received the Grand Master Award in 1954. She died on January 12, 1976.

"BOTHER!" said Pat.

With a deepening frown she rummaged wildly in the silken trifle she called an evening bag. Two young men and another girl watched her anxiously. They were all standing outside the closed door of Patricia Garnett's flat.

"It's no good," said Pat. "It's not there. And now what shall we do?"

"What is life without a latchkey?" murmured Jimmy Faulkener.

He was a short, broad-shouldered young man, with good-tempered blue eyes.

Pat turned on him angrily.

"Don't make jokes, Jimmy. This is serious."

"Look again, Pat," said Donovan Bailey. "It must be there somewhere."

He had a lazy, pleasant voice that matched his lean, dark figure.

"If you ever brought it out," said the other girl, Mildred Hope.

"Of course I brought it out," said Pat. "I believe I gave it to one of you two." She turned on the men accusingly. "I told Donovan to take it for me."

But she was not to find a scapegoat so easily. Donovan put in a firm disclaimer, and Jimmy backed him up.

"I saw you put it in your bag, myself," said Jimmy.

"Well, then, one of you dropped it out when you picked up my bag. I've dropped it once or twice."

"Once or twice!" said Donovan. "You've dropped it a dozen times at least, besides leaving it behind on every possible occasion."

"I can't see why everything on earth doesn't drop out of it the whole time," said Jimmy.

"The point is—how are we going to get in?" said Mildred.

She was a sensible girl, who kept to the point, but she was not nearly so attractive as the impulsive and troublesome Pat.

All four of them regarded the closed door blankly.

"Couldn't the porter help?" suggested Jimmy. "Hasn't he got a master key or something of that kind?"

Pat shook her head. There were only two keys. One was inside the flat hung up in the kitchen and the other was—or should be—in the maligned bag.

"If only the flat were on the ground floor," wailed Pat. "We could have broken open a window or something. Donovan, you wouldn't like to be a cat burglar, would you?"

Donovan declined firmly but politely to be a cat burglar.

"A flat on the fourth floor is a bit of an undertaking," said Jimmy.

"How about a fire escape?" suggested Donovan.

"There isn't one."

"There should be," said Jimmy. "A building five stories high ought to have a fire escape."

"I daresay," said Pat. "But what should be doesn't help us. How am I ever to get into my flat?"

"Isn't there a sort of thingummybob?" said Donovan. "A thing the tradesmen send up chops and Brussels sprouts in?"

"The service lift," said Pat. "Oh, yes, but it's only a sort of wire-basket thing. Oh! wait—I know. What about the coal lift?"

"Now that," said Donovan, "is an idea."

Mildred made a discouraging suggestion.

"It'll be bolted," she said. "In Pat's kitchen, I mean, on the inside."

But the idea was instantly negatived.

"Don't you believe it," said Donovan.

"Not in *Pat's* kitchen," said Jimmy. "Pat never locks and bolts things."

"I don't think it's bolted," said Pat. "I took the dustbin off this morning, and I'm sure I never bolted it afterwards, and I don't think I've been near it since."

"Well," said Donovan, "that fact's going to be very useful to us tonight, but, all the same, young Pat, let me point out to you that these slack habits are leaving you at the mercy of burglars (non-feline) every night."

Pat disregarded these admonitions.

"Come on," she cried, and began racing down the four flights of stairs. The others followed her. Pat led them through a dark recess, apparently full to overflowing of perambulators, and through another door into the well of the flats, and guided them to the right lift. There was, at the moment, a dustbin on it. Donovan lifted it off and stepped gingerly onto the platform in its place. He wrinkled up his nose.

9

"A little noisome," he remarked. "But what of that? Do I go alone on this venture or is anyone coming with me?"

"I'll come, too," said Jimmy.

He stepped on by Donovan's side.

"I suppose the lift will bear me," he added, doubtfully.

"You can't weigh much more than a ton of coal," said Pat, who had never been particularly strong on her weights-and-measures table.

"And anyway, we shall soon find out," said Donovan cheerfully, as he hauled on the rope.

With a grinding noise they disappeared from sight.

"This thing makes an awful noise," remarked Jimmy, as they passed up through blackness. "What will the people in the other flats think?"

"Ghosts or burglars, I expect," said Donovan. "Hauling this rope is quite heavy work. The porter of Friars Mansions does more work than I ever suspected. I say, Jimmy, old son, are you counting the floors?"

"Oh, Lord! No. I forgot about it."

"Well, I have, which is just as well. That's the third we're passing now. The next is ours."

"And now, I suppose," grumbled Jimmy, "we shall find that Pat did bolt the door after all."

But these fears were unfounded. The wooden door swung back at a touch and Donovan and Jimmy stepped out into the inky blackness of Pat's kitchen.

"We ought to have a torch for this wild night work," explained Donovan. "If I know Pat, everything's on the floor, and we shall smash endless crockery before I can get to the light switch. Don't move about, Jimmy, till I get the light on."

He felt his way cautiously over the floor, uttering one fervent "Damn!" as a corner of the kitchen table took him unawares in the ribs. He reached the switch, and in another moment another "Damn!" floated out of the darkness.

"What's the matter?" asked Jimmy.

"Light won't come on. Dud bulb, I suppose. Wait a minute. I'll turn the sitting-room light on."

The sitting room was the door immediately across the passage. Jimmy heard Donovan go out of the door, and presently fresh muffled curses reached him. He himself edged his way cautiously across the kitchen.

"What's the matter?"

"I don't know. Rooms get bewitched at night, I believe. Everything seems to be in a different place. Chairs and tables where you least expected it. Oh, hell! here's another!"

But at this moment Jimmy fortunately connected with the electric-light switch and pressed it down. In another minute two young men were looking at each other in silent horror.

This room was not Pat's sitting-room. *They were in the wrong flat.*

To begin with, the room was about ten times more crowded than Pat's, which explained Donovan's pathetic bewilderment at repeatedly cannoning into chairs and tables. There was a large round table in the center of the room covered with a baize cloth, and there was an aspidistra in the window. It was, in fact, the kind of room whose owner, the young men felt sure, would be difficult to explain to. With silent horror they gazed down at the table, on which lay a little pile of letters.

"Mrs. Ernestine Grant," breathed Donovan, picking them up and reading the name. "Oh! help. Do you think she's heard us?"

"It's a miracle she hasn't heard *you*," said Jimmy. "What with your language and the way you've been crashing into the furniture. Come on, for the Lord's sake, let's get out of here."

They hastily switched off the light and retraced their steps on tiptoe to the lift. Jimmy breathed a sigh of relief as they regained the fastness of its depths without further incident.

"I do like a woman to be a good, sound sleeper," he said approvingly. "Mrs. Ernestine Grant has her points."

"I see it now," said Donovan; "why we made the mistake in the floor, I mean. Out in that well we started up from the basement." He heaved on the rope, and the lift shot up. "We're right this time."

"I devoutly trust we are," said Jimmy, as he stepped out into another inky void. "My nerves won't stand many more shocks of this kind."

But no further nerve strain was imposed. The first click of the light showed them Pat's kitchen, and in another minute they were opening the front door and admitting the two girls who were waiting outside.

"You have been a long time," grumbled Pat. "Mildred and I have been waiting here ages."

"We've had an adventure," said Donovan. "We might have been hauled off to the police station as dangerous malefactors."

11

Pat had passed on into the sitting room, where she switched on the light and dropped her wrap on the sofa. She listened with lively interest to Donovan's account of his adventures.

"I'm glad she didn't catch you," she commented. "I'm sure she's an old curmudgeon. I got a note from her this morning—wanted to see me sometime—something she had to complain about—my piano, I suppose. People who don't like pianos over their heads shouldn't come and live in flats. I say, Donovan, you've hurt your hand. It's all over blood. Go and wash it under the tap."

Donovan looked down at his hand in surprise. He went out of the room obediently and presently his voice called to Jimmy.

"Hullo," said the other, "what's up? You haven't hurt yourself badly, have you?"

"I haven't hurt myself at all."

There was something so queer in Donovan's voice that Jimmy stared at him in surprise. Donovan held out his washed hand and Jimmy saw that there was no mark or cut of any kind on it.

"That's odd," he said, frowning. "There was quite a lot of blood. Where did it come from?"

And then, suddenly, he realized what his quicker-witted friend had already seen.

"By Jove," he said. "*It must have come from that flat.*"

He stopped, thinking over the possibilities his words implied.

"You're sure it was—er—blood?" he said. "Not paint?"

Donovan shook his head.

"It was blood, all right," he said, and shivered.

They looked at each other. The same thought was clearly in each of their minds. It was Jimmy who voiced it first.

"I say," he said awkwardly. "Do you think we ought to—well—go down again—and have—a—a look around? See it's all right, you know?"

"What about the girls?"

"We won't say anything to them. Pat's going to put on an apron and make us an omelet. We'll be back by the time they wonder where we are."

"Oh, well, come on," said Donovan. "I suppose we've got to go through with it. I dare say there isn't anything really wrong."

But his tone lacked conviction. They got into the lift and descended to the floor below. They found their way across the kitchen without much difficulty and once more switched on the sitting-room light.

"It must have been in here," said Donovan, "that—that I got the stuff on me. I never touched anything in the kitchen."

He looked round him. Jimmy did the same, and they both frowned. Everything looked neat and commonplace and miles removed from any suggestion of violence or gore.

Suddenly Jimmy started violently and caught his companion's arm.

"Look!"

Donovan followed the pointing finger, and in his turn uttered an exclamation. From beneath the heavy rep curtains there protruded a foot—a woman's foot in a gaping patent-leather shoe.

Jimmy went to the curtains and drew them sharply apart. In the recess of the window a woman's huddled body lay on the floor, a sticky dark pool beside it. She was dead, there was no doubt of that. Jimmy was attempting to raise her up when Donovan stopped him.

"You'd better not do that. She oughtn't to be touched till the police come."

"The police. Oh! of course. I say, Donovan, what a ghastly business. Who do you think she is? Mrs. Ernestine Grant?"

"Looks like it. At any rate, if there's anyone else in the flat they're keeping jolly quiet."

"What do we do next?" asked Jimmy. "Run out and get a policeman or ring up from Pat's flat?"

"I should think ringing up would be best. Come on, we might as well go out the front door. We can't spend the whole night going up and down in that evil-smelling lift."

Jimmy agreed. Just as they were passing through the door he hesitated.

"Look here; do you think one of us ought to stay—just to keep an eye on things—till the police come?"

"Yes, I think you're right. If you'll stay I'll run up and telephone."

He ran quickly up the stairs and rang the bell of the flat above. Pat came to open it, a very pretty Pat with a flushed face and a cooking apron on. Her eyes widened in surprise.

"You? But how—Donovan, what is it? Is anything the matter?"

He took both her hands in his.

"It's all right, Pat—only we've made rather an unpleasant discovery in the flat below. A woman—dead."

13

"Oh!" She gave a little gasp. "How horrible. Has she had a fit or something?"

"No, it looks—well—it looks rather as though she had been murdered."

"Oh! Donovan."

"I know. It's pretty beastly."

Her hands were still in his. She had left them there—was even clinging to him. Darling Pat—how he loved her. Did she care at all for him! Sometimes he thought she did. Sometimes he was afraid that Jimmy Faulkener—remembrances of Jimmy waiting patiently below made him start guiltily.

"Pat, dear, we must telephone to the police."

"Monsieur is right," said a voice behind him. "And in the meantime, while we are waiting their arrival, perhaps I can be of some slight assistance."

They had been standing in the doorway of the flat, and now they peered out on to the landing. A figure was standing on the stairs a little way above them. It moved down and into their range of vision.

They stood staring at a little man with very fierce moustaches and an egg-shaped head. He wore a resplendent dressing-gown and embroidered slippers. He bowed gallantly to Patricia.

"Mademoiselle!" he said. "I am, as perhaps you know, the tenant of the flat above. I like to be up high—the air—the view over London. I take the flat in the name of Mr. O'Connor. But I am not an Irishman. I have another name. That is why I venture to put myself at your service. Permit me."

With a flourish he pulled out a card and handed it to Pat. She read it.

"M. Hercule Poirot. Oh!" She caught her breath. "*The* M. Poirot? The great detective? And you will really help?"

"That is my intention, Mademoiselle. I nearly offered my help earlier in the evening."

Pat looked puzzled.

"I heard you discussing how to gain admission to your flat. Me, I am very clever at picking locks. I could without doubt have opened your door for you, but I hesitated to suggest it. You would have had the grave suspicions of me."

Pat laughed.

"Now, Monsieur," said Poirot to Donovan. "Go in, I pray of you, and telephone to the police. I will descend to the flat below."

14

Pat came down the stairs with him. They found Jimmy on guard and Pat explained Poirot's presence. Jimmy, in his turn, explained to Poirot his and Donovan's adventures. The detective listened attentively.

"The lift door was unbolted, you say? You emerged into the kitchen, but the light it would not turn on."

He directed his footsteps to the kitchen as he spoke. His fingers pressed the switch.

"*Tiens! Voilà ce qui est curieux!*" he said as the light flashed on. "It functions perfectly now. I wonder—"

He held up a finger to ensure silence and listened. A faint sound broke the stillness—the sound of an unmistakable snore.

"Ah!" said Poirot. "*La chambre de domestique.*"

He tiptoed across the kitchen into a little pantry, out of which led a door. He opened the door and switched on the light. The room was the kind of dog-kennel designed by the builders of flats to accommodate a human being. The floor space was almost entirely occupied by the bed. In the bed was a rosy-cheeked girl lying on her back with her mouth wide open, snoring placidly.

Poirot switched off the light and beat a retreat.

"She will not wake," he said. "We will let her sleep till the police come."

He went back to the sitting-room. Donovan had joined them.

"The police will be here almost immediately, they say," he said breathlessly. "We are to touch nothing."

Poirot nodded.

"We will not touch," he said. "We will look, that is all."

He moved into the room. Mildred had come down with Donovan, and all four young people stood in the doorway and watched him with breathless interest.

"What I can't understand, sir, is this," said Donovan. "I never went near the window—how did the blood come on my hand?"

"My young friend, the answer to that stares you in the face. Of what color is the tablecloth? Red, is it not? and doubtless you did put your hand on the table."

"Yes, I did. Is that—" He stopped.

Poirot nodded. He was bending over the table. He indicated with his hand a dark patch on the red.

"It was here that the crime was committed," he said solemnly. "The body was moved afterwards."

Then he stood upright and looked slowly round the room.

15

He did not move, he handled nothing, but nevertheless the four watching felt as though every object in that rather frowsty place gave up its secret to his observant eye.

Hercule Poirot nodded his head as though satisfied. A little sigh escaped him.

"I see," he said.

"You see what?" asked Donovan curiously.

"I see," said Poirot, "what you doubtless *felt*—that the room is overfull of furniture."

Donovan smiled ruefully.

"I did go barging about a bit," he confessed. "Of course, everything was in a different place to Pat's room, and I couldn't make it out."

"Not everything," said Poirot.

Donovan looked at him inquiringly.

"I mean," said Poirot apologetically, "that certain things are always fixed. In a block of flats the door, the window, the fire-place—they are in the same place in the rooms which are below each other."

"Isn't that rather splitting hairs?" asked Mildred. She was looking at Poirot with faint disapproval.

"One should always speak with absolute accuracy. That is a little—how do you say?—fad of mine."

There was the noise of footsteps on the stairs, and three men came in. They were a police inspector, a constable, and the divisional surgeon. The Inspector recognized Poirot and greeted him in an almost reverential manner. Then he turned to the others.

"I shall want statements from everyone," he began, "but in the first place—"

Poirot interrupted.

"A little suggestion. We will go back to the flat upstairs and Mademoiselle here shall do what she was planning to do—make us an omelet. Me, I have a passion for the omelets. Then, M. l'Inspecteur, when you have finished here, you will mount to us and ask questions at your leisure."

It was arranged accordingly, and Poirot went up with them.

"M. Poirot," said Pat, "I think you're a perfect dear. And you shall have a lovely omelet. I really make omelets frightfully well."

"That is good. Once, Mademoiselle, I loved a beautiful young English girl, who resembled you greatly—but alas! she could

16

not cook. So perhaps everything was for the best."

There was a faint sadness in his voice, and Jimmy Faulkener looked at him curiously.

Once in the flat, however, he exerted himself to please and amuse. The grim tragedy below was almost forgotten.

The omelet had been consumed and duly praised by the time that Inspector Rice's footsteps were heard. He came in accompanied by the doctor, having left the constable below.

"Well, Monsieur Poirot," he said. "It all seems clear and aboveboard—not much in your line, though we may find it hard to catch the man. I'd just like to hear how the discovery came to be made."

Donovan and Jimmy between them recounted the happenings of the evening. The inspector turned reproachfully to Pat.

"You shouldn't leave your lift door unbolted, Miss. You really shouldn't."

"I shan't again," said Pat, with a shiver. "Somebody might come in and murder me like that poor woman below."

"Ah! but they didn't come in that way, though," said the Inspector.

"You will recount to us what you have discovered, yes?" said Poirot.

"I don't know as I ought to—but seeing it's you, M. Poirot. . . ."

"Précisément," said Poirot. "And these young people—they will be discreet."

"The newspapers will get hold of it, anyway, soon enough," said the Inspector. "There's no real secret about the matter. Well, the dead woman's Mrs. Grant, all right. I had the porter up to identify her. Woman of about thirty-five. She was sitting at the table, and she was shot with an automatic pistol of small caliber, probably by someone sitting opposite her at table. She fell forward, and that's how the bloodstain came on the table."

"But wouldn't someone have heard the shot?" asked Mildred.

"The pistol was fitted with a silencer. No, you wouldn't hear anything. By the way, did you hear the screech the maid let out when we told her her mistress was dead? No. Well, that just shows how unlikely it was that anyone would hear the other."

"Has the maid no story to tell?" asked Poirot.

"It was her evening out. She's got her own key. She came in about ten o'clock. Everything was quiet. She thought her mistress had gone to bed."

17

"She did not look in the sitting room, then?"

"Yes, she took the letters in there which had come by the evening post, but she saw nothing unusual—any more than Mr. Faulkener and Mr. Bailey did. You see, the murderer had concealed the body rather neatly behind the curtains."

"But it was a curious thing to do, don't you think?"

Poirot's voice was very gentle, yet it held something that made the Inspector look up quickly.

"Didn't want the crime discovered till he'd had time to make his getaway."

"Perhaps—perhaps—but continue with what you were saying."

"The maid went out at five o'clock. The doctor here puts the time of death—as roughly—about four to five hours ago. That's right, isn't it?"

The doctor, who was a man of few words, contented himself with jerking his head affirmatively.

"It's a quarter to twelve now. The actual time can, I think, be narrowed down to a fairly definite hour."

He took out a crumpled sheet of paper.

"We found this in the pocket of the dead woman's dress. You needn't be afraid of handling it. There are no fingerprints on it."

Poirot smoothed out the sheet. Across it some words were printed in small prim capitals.

"I will come to see you this evening at half-past seven.—J.F."

"A compromising document to leave behind," commented Poirot, as he handed it back.

"Well, he didn't know she'd got it in her pocket," said the Inspector. "He probably thought she'd destroyed it. We've evidence that he *was* a careful man, though. The pistol she was shot with we found under the body—and there again no fingerprints. They'd been wiped off very carefully with a silk handkerchief."

"How do you know," said Poirot, "that it was a *silk* handkerchief?"

"Because we found it," said the Inspector triumphantly. "At the last, as he was drawing the curtains, he must have let it fall unnoticed."

He handed across a big white silk handerchief—a good-quality handkerchief. It did not need the Inspector's finger to draw Poirot's attention to the mark on it in the center. It was

18

neatly marked and quite legible. Poirot read the name out.

"John Fraser."

"That's it," said the Inspector. "John Fraser—J.F. in the note. We know the name of the man we have to look for, and I dare say when we find out a little about the dead woman, and her relations come forward, we shall soon get a line on him."

"I wonder," said Poirot. "No, *mon cher,* somehow I do not think he will be easy to find, your John Fraser. He is a strange man—careful, since he marks his handkerchiefs and wipes the pistol with which he has committed the crime—yet careless, since he loses his handkerchief and does not search for a letter that might incriminate him."

"Flurried, that's what he was," said the Inspector.

"It is possible," said Poirot. "Yes, it is possible. And he was not seen entering the building?"

"There are all sorts of people going in and out at that time. These are big blocks. I suppose none of you"—he addressed the four collectively—"saw anyone coming out of the flat?"

Pat shook her head.

"We went out earlier—about seven o'clock."

"I see." The Inspector rose. Poirot accompanied him to the door.

"As a little favor, may I examine the flat below?"

"Why, certainly, M. Poirot. I know what they think of you at headquarters. I'll leave you a key. I've got two. It will be empty. The maid cleared out to some relatives, too scared to stay there alone."

"I thank you," said M. Poirot. He went back into the flat, thoughtful.

"You're not satisfied, M. Poirot?" said Jimmy.

"No," said Poirot. "I am not satisfied."

Donovan looked at him curiously. "What is it that—well, worries you?"

Poirot did not answer. He remained silent for a minute or two, frowning, as though in thought, then he made a sudden impatient movement of shoulders.

"I will say good-night to you, Mademoiselle. You must be tired. You have had much cooking to do—eh?"

Pat laughed.

"Only the omelet. I didn't do dinner. Donovan and Jimmy came and called for us, and we went out to a little place in Soho."

"And then without doubt, you went to a theater?"

"Yes. 'The Brown Eyes of Caroline.' "

"Ah!" said Poirot. "It should have been blue eyes—the blue eyes of Mademoiselle."

He made a sentimental gesture, and then once more wished Pat good night, also Mildred, who was staying the night by special request, as Pat admitted frankly that she would get the horrors if left alone on this particular night.

The two young men accompanied Poirot. When the door was shut, and they were preparing to say good-bye to him on the landing, Poirot forestalled them.

"My young friends, you heard me say that I was not satisfied? *Eh bien,* it is true—I am not. I go now to make some little investigations of my own. You would like to accompany me—yes?"

An eager assent greeted this proposal. Poirot led the way to the flat below and inserted the key the Inspector had given him in the lock. On entering, he did not, as the others had expected, enter the sitting room. Instead he went straight to the kitchen. In a little recess which served as a scullery a big iron bin was standing. Poirot uncovered this, and doubling himself up, began to rootle in it with the energy of a ferocious terrier.

Both Jimmy and Donovan stared at him in amazement.

Suddenly with a cry of triumph he emerged. In his hand he held aloft a small stoppered bottle.

"*Voilà!*" he said. "I find what I seek."

He sniffed at it delicately.

"Alas! I am *enrhumé*—I have the cold in the head."

Donovan took the bottle from him and sniffed in his turn, but could smell nothing. He took out the stopper and held the bottle to his nose before Poirot's warning cry could stop him.

Immediately he fell like a log. Poirot, by springing forward, partly broke his fall.

"Imbecile!" he cried. "The idea. To remove the stopper in that foolhardy manner! Did he not observe how delicately I handled it? Monsieur—Faulkener—is it not? Will you be so good as to get me a little brandy? I observed a decanter in the sitting room."

Jimmy hurried off, but by the time he returned, Donovan was sitting up and declaring himself quite all right again. He had to listen to a short lecture from Poirot on the necessity of caution in sniffing at possibly poisonous substances.

"I think I'll be off home," said Donovan, rising shakily to his feet. "That is, if I can't be any more use here. I feel a bit wonky still."

"Assuredly," said Poirot. "That is the best thing you can do. M. Faulkener, attend me here a little minute. I will return on the instant."

He accompanied Donovan to the door and beyond. They remained outside on the landing talking for some minutes. When Poirot at last re-entered the flat he found Jimmy standing in the sitting-room gazing round him with puzzled eyes.

"Well, M. Poirot," he said, "what next?"

"There is nothing next. The case is finished."

"What?"

"I know everything—now."

Jimmy stared at him.

"That little bottle you found?"

"Exactly. That little bottle."

Jimmy shook his head.

"I can't make head or tail of it. For some reason or other I can see you are dissatisfied with the evidence against this John Fraser, whoever he may be."

"*Whoever he may be,*" repeated Poirot softly. "If he is anyone at all—well, I shall be surprised."

"I don't understand."

"He is a name—that is all—a name carefully marked on a handkerchief!"

"And the letter?"

"Did you notice that it was printed? Now why? I will tell you. Handwriting might be recognized, and a typewritten letter is more easily traced than you would imagine—but if a *real* John Fraser wrote that letter those two points would not have appealed to him! No, it was written on purpose, and put in the dead woman's pocket for us to find. There is no such person as John Fraser."

Jimmy looked at him inquiringly.

"And so," went on Poirot, "I went back to the point that first struck me. You heard me say that certain things in a room were always in the same place under given circumstances. I gave three instances. I might have mentioned a fourth—*the electric-light switch, my friend.*"

Jimmy still stared uncomprehendingly. Poirot went on.

"Your friend Donovan did not go near the window—it was by

resting his hand on this table that he got it covered in blood! But I asked myself at once—*why did he rest it there?* What was he doing groping about this room in darkness? For remember, my friend, *the electric-light switch is always in the same place—by the door.* Why, when he came to this room, did he not at once feel for the light and turn it on? That was the natural, the normal thing to do. According to him, he tried to turn on the light in the kitchen, but failed. Yet when I tried the switch it was in perfect working order. Did he, then, not wish the light to go on just then? If it had gone on you would both have seen at once that you were in the wrong flat. There would have been no reason to come into this room."

"What are you driving at, M. Poirot? I don't understand. What do you mean?"

"I mean—this."

Poirot held up a Yale door-key.

"The key of this flat?"

"No, *mon ami*, the key of the flat above. Mademoiselle Patricia's key, which M. Donovan Bailey abstracted from her bag some time during the evening."

"But why—why?"

"*Parbleu!* So that he could do what he wanted to do—gain admission to this flat in a perfectly unsuspicious manner. He made sure that the lift door was unbolted earlier in the evening."

"Where did you get the key?"

Poirot's smile broadened.

"I found it just now—where I looked for it—in M. Donovan's pocket. See you, that little bottle I pretended to find was a ruse. M. Donovan is taken in. He does what I knew he would do—unstoppers it and sniffs. And in that little bottle is ethyl chloride, a very powerful instant anaesthetic. It gives me just the moment or two of unconsciousness I need. I take from his pocket the two things that I knew would be there. This key was one of them—the other—"

He stopped and then went on:

"I questioned at the time the reason the Inspector gave for the body being concealed behind the curtain. To gain time? No, there was more than that. And so I thought of just one thing—*the post,* my friend. The evening post that comes at half-past nine or thereabouts. Say the murderer does not find something he expects to find, but that something may be delivered by post later. Clearly, then, he must come back. But the crime must not be discovered by the maid when she comes in, or the police would take possession of the flat, so he hides the body behind the curtain. And the maid suspects nothing and lays the letters on the table as usual."

"The letters?"

"Yes, the letters." Poirot drew something from his pocket.

"This is the second article I took from M. Donovan when he was unconscious." He showed the superscription—a type-written envelope addressed to Mrs. Ernestine Grant. "But I will ask you one thing first, M. Faulkener, before we look at the contents of this letter. Are you or are you not in love with Mademoiselle Patricia?"

"I care for Pat damnably—but I've never thought I had a chance."

"You thought that she cared for M. Donovan? It may be that she had begun to care for him—but it was only a beginning, my friend. It is for you to make her forget—to stand by her in her trouble."

"Trouble?" said Jimmy sharply.

"Yes, trouble. We will do all we can to keep her name out of it, but it will be impossible to do so entirely. She was, you see, the motive."

He ripped open the envelope that he held. An enclosure fell out. The covering letter was brief, and was from a firm of solicitors.

DEAR MADAM,

The document you enclose is quite in order, and the fact of the marriage having taken place in a foreign country does not invalidate it in any way.

Yours truly, etc.

Poirot spread out the enclosure. It was a certificate of marriage between Donovan Bailey and Ernestine Grant, dated eight years ago.

"Oh, my God!" said Jimmy. "Pat said she'd had a letter from the woman asking to see her, but she never dreamed it was anything important."

Poirot nodded.

"M. Donovan knew—he went to see his wife this evening before going to the flat above (a strange irony, by the way, that led the unfortunate woman to come to this building where her rival lived)—he murdered her in cold blood—and then went on to his evening's amusement. His wife must have told him that she had sent the marriage certificate to her solicitors, and was expecting to hear from them. Doubtless he himself had tried to make her believe that there was a flaw in the marriage."

"He seemed in quite good spirits, too, all the evening. M. Poirot, you haven't let him escape?" Jimmy shuddered.

"There is no escape for him," said Poirot gravely. "You need not fear."

"It's Pat I'm thinking about mostly," said Jimmy. "You don't think—she really cared."

"*Mon ami,* that is your part," said Poirot gently. "To make her turn to you and forget. I do not think you will find it very difficult!"

MAN IN HIDING

BY VINCENT STARRETT

Charles Vincent Emerson Starrett was born in Toronto, Canada, on October 26, 1886. He was taken to Chicago when he was a child and for many years conducted the "Books Alive" column in the Chicago *Tribune*. His *The Unique Hamlet* (1920) is generally considered to be the best Sherlock Holmes pastiche ever written. Starrett also produced essays, biographical and bibliographical works, and critical studies of a wide range of authors. *The Private Life of Sherlock Holmes* (1933) is probably his best known work. He was one of the founders (with Christopher Morley) of the Baker Street Irregulars. Starrett died in 1974.

DR. B. EDWARD LOXLEY (jocularly called "Bedward" by the Chicago gossip columnists), the wife-murderer for whom hundreds of police had been scouring the city for three weeks, sat quietly at his desk in the great Merchandise Exchange reading his morning mail. The frosted glass door of his outer office read simply: *William Drayham, Rare Books. Hours by Appointment.* After three weeks of security he was beginning to feel a little complacent. For three weeks he had not left his hiding place in the huge business complex and he had no intention of leaving it for the time being—except feet first.

It had all been carefully thought out beforehand. The office of "William Drayham" had been rented two months prior to the killing of his wife, and Loxley had quietly taken possession and created his new personality as a dealer in rare books. He had been accepted by all his neighbors in the sixth-floor corridor. The elevator starter was getting to know him. He breakfasted, lunched, and dined at several restaurants in the building, was shaved by a favorite barber, and was—he had every reason to believe—an accepted fixture. His neighbors were inoffensive and unimaginative workers who did not for a moment question his identity, and the words *Rare Books* on the door were formidable enough to frighten away casual visitors.

Lora Loxley, murdered by suffocation, had been buried for nearly three weeks and even the newspapers were beginning to play down the sensational story. The feeling was growing that Dr. Loxley himself might also have been murdered and a desultory search for his body continued whenever the police had nothing more urgent to occupy them. Since Loxley's office window overlooked the river where, in addition to the normal traffic, police boats occasionally plied, he was able to watch the activities on the river with amused appreciation. He had now spent two lonely Saturdays and Sundays watching the weekend traffic with a pair of binoculars, waiting for any active renewal of police attention. He was on excellent terms with the watchmen in his part of the giant building, and they were now accustomed to seeing him at the most unlikely hours.

The Merchandise Exchange was actually a city within a city. It contained everything a man in hiding needed—restaurants, laundries, barber shops, tobacconists, dentists, newsstands, banking facilities, a gymnasium, even a postal station. He was already known by name in the restaurants and barber shops. He bought all the newspapers, morning and evening. Occasionally he dictated a letter to one of the public stenographers, ordering or declining rare books. As William Drayham he had a sufficient banking account downstairs for all his immediate needs. The rest of his wealth, in cash, was waiting in Paris—as was Gloria.

His principal bogies had been the watchmen and the cleaning women. But both fears had vanished. The watchmen had proved friendly, and the cleaning women, a friendly trio who liked candy, readily agreed to visit his office while he was having a late dinner. His domestic arrangements were simple. He slept on a couch in his inner office, which also contained a vault to which he could retire in an emergency. To date there had been no emergency. . . .

Dr. Loxley pushed the mail aside impatiently. It was too early to expect a large response to the small rare-book advertisement he was running in a Sunday book-review supplement. But it was not too early for the coffee that Miss Marivole Boggs was willing to serve at all hours. What luck to have found so admirable a neighbor in the same corridor, and even, it might be said, in the same line! Rare books and antiques went very well together. Miss Boggs had been responsible for most of his infrequent customers. He glanced at his expensive wristwatch and left William Drayham's rare books without a pang.

The owner of *M. Boggs, Antiques,* as she described herself on the show window of her small shop at the end of the corridor, looked up at his entrance.

"Hello," she said. "I was hoping you'd come in."

"I couldn't resist," he said. His brown eyes took in the familiar room, resting for a moment on the suit of ancient armor that dominated one corner of the shop and the old Spanish chest that was Miss Boggs's pride and joy. "Well, I see nobody has bought either of them yet." It was one of their standing jokes that some day, when the rare-book business was better, he would buy them himself.

As Marivole Boggs poured his coffee she said, "The newspaper stories about that doctor are getting shorter every day. I'm beginning to believe he really *was* murdered."

They often discussed the missing Dr. Loxley, as indeed the

27

whole city was doing. At first it had been Miss Boggs's idea that the "society doctor" had murdered his wife in favor of a more glamorous patient who was now living in sin with him somewhere on the French or Italian Riviera.

Dr. Loxley had thought not. "Too romantic, Miss Boggs. I still think his body is in the river or floating on its way to the Gulf of Mexico. That scarf they found on the river bank looks like it."

"Anyway, the police seem to have stopped looking," said Miss Boggs.

"Anyway, this is good coffee, my dear. I hope you'll give me your special recipe. Do you still plan to leave this month?"

"At once," she said. "I'm flying to New York tomorrow, if I can get away. I want to be in London for the Exhibition; then on to Paris, Rome, and Zurich. I'm enormously relieved that you'll be here to keep an eye on things, Bill. Coffee at all hours, eh?"

"Morning, noon, and night," he agreed, rising to leave. Her change of plan had startled him for a moment; but he was quick to see a distinct advantage in it for himself. "Never fear, I'll be here waiting for you when you return."

Strolling back to his own shop, humming a jaunty air, he became aware of a man leaving the doorway of the office directly opposite his own. Something about the man's carriage seemed familiar. The man was heading toward the elevators and walking fast. In an instant they would meet.

And suddenly Dr. Loxley realized that the man was, indeed, familiar. He was his own brother-in-law, Lawrence Bridewell.

Loxley's first instinct was to turn and flee, his second to return to *M. Boggs, Antiques.* His final decision, made in a split second, was to see the encounter through. His disguise had fooled better men than Larry Bridewell, although none who knew him better. With his former neat beard and mustache now gone, and his blue eyes transformed by brown contact lenses, Dr. Loxley was, to all appearances, another man. After that first appalling moment of indecision he fumbled for a cigarette, realizing that after three weeks of growingly complacent safety, he was about to face the supreme test.

He tried and failed to light the cigarette. . . . Then the two men were face to face, glancing at each other as men do in passing—and suddenly the test was over.

Or was it? Bridewell continued on his way to the elevators,

still walking fast, and Loxley stumbled to his own door.

Did he dare look back? Had Bridewell turned to look back at *him?* Moving casually, Loxley stole a glance down the corridor. There was no doubt about it—Larry *was* looking back. Perhaps he had merely been troubled by an imagined resemblance. . . .

Dr. Loxley had some difficulty opening his own door, and just before he closed it, the thought occurred to him to look at the name on the door of the office from which his brother-in-law had emerged. Actually he knew very well what he would find there: *Jackson & Fortworth, Attorneys-at-Law;* and below, the significant words: *Private Investigations.*

He tried to take himself in hand and was annoyed to find that he was shaking. Experimentally he ventured a drink to see what it would do for him. It helped considerably. But the whole incident haunted him the rest of the day and gave him a bad night. In the morning, however, his fears had evaporated. He was his confident self again until, a few hours later, a second incident shook his nerve.

Returning from the cigar stand in the lobby, he passed the De Luxe Dog Salon in one of the street level corridors and, as he had often done before, paused to look into the windows at the fashionable dogs being barbered and prettified. It had always been an amusing spectacle, but this time, as he turned away, an appalling thing happened.

A well-dressed woman was approaching the salon with a haughty French poodle on a leash. The woman looked familiar. Good lord, she *was* familiar! She was Mrs. Montgomery Hyde, an old patient of his. Loxley's heart seemed to stop beating. Would she recognize him?

It was the dog that recognized him. With a refined little yelp the poodle jerked the leash from the woman's hand and flung himself against the doctor's legs.

With an effort Loxley recovered his balance and somehow managed to recover his poise. It was his worst moment since the murder. Automatically he disengaged himself from the poodle's attentions and pulled the black ears.

"There, there, fellow," he said to the excited animal in a voice that he hoped was not his own. "I beg your pardon, Madam. Your dog appears to have made a mistake."

To his intense relief Mrs. Montgomery Hyde agreed.

"Do forgive Toto's impulsiveness," she begged, snatching up the leash. "He loves everybody."

29

Dr. Loxley left the scene in almost a hurry. She had not recognized him! It seemed to him a miracle; but again he was annoyed to find himself shaking. And yet, wasn't it really a good omen? If Mrs. Hyde and his own brother-in-law had failed to recognize him, was there anything for him to fear?

Immediately he began to feel better. But when he had returned to his office, William Drayham again treated himself to a stiff drink.

In a moment of alert intelligence he realized that for three weeks he had permitted himself to become too complacent. His meeting with Mrs. Hyde had taught him something that was important for him to remember: he had almost spoken her name! In the first onslaught of panic he might well have betrayed himself. If it was important for him not to be recognized, it was equally important that *he* must not recognize anyone else.

It was clear to him now that this cat-and-mouse existence could not go on indefinitely. He must remain in hiding only until it was safe for him to emerge and get out of the country. Then William Drayham would ostentatiously pack his books and remove to New York. After that, the world was wide, with his immediate destination—Paris and Gloria.

For several days the chastened doctor lived cautiously, visiting *M. Boggs, Antiques* at intervals for coffee and to admire the suit of armor and the Spanish chest, which continued to fascinate him. He had promised Miss Boggs, now on her travels, not to cut the price on either if a buyer should turn up.

Twice, returning from the antique shop, he again caught a glimpse of his brother-in-law—both times entering the law office of Jackson & Fortworth, and had hurried to lock himself in his own office before Larry could emerge. What the devil did the fellow want with a firm of private investigators anyway?

The visit of Jackson, the senior lawyer of the firm, to the bookshop one morning took the doctor completely by surprise, or he might have locked the door.

"I've been intending to look in on you for some time, Mr. Drayham," said the lawyer cordially. "I'm Jackson, just across from you. Rare books have always interested me. Mind if I look around? I think that browse is the word."

Loxley rose from his chair abruptly, knocking a book from his desk to the floor. An icy fear had entered his heart. Was this the showdown at last, he wondered.

He shook hands effusively. "Glad to meet you, Mr. Jackson.

By all means, browse. Is there anything special I can show you?"

But Jackson was already browsing. When he had finished he strolled to the window. "Nice view of the river you have," he said appreciatively. "*My* windows all face an inner court." He walked to the door. "Just wanted to meet you, Mr. Drayham. I'll come in again when I have more time."

"Any time at all," said Loxley with warm courtesy.

Dr. Loxley sat down at his desk and reached for the lower drawer. Another little drink wouldn't hurt. What had the fellow really wanted? What had he hoped to learn? Or was he really one of those strange people who collected rare books?

One thing, however, was undeniably clear. Any day now he might have to leave the building and the city. If he was suspected, the blow would fall swiftly. At any minute the door might open again, and this time Jackson might not be alone. Why not get out of this trap immediately? What was there to stop him? His stock—three hundred-odd volumes of miscellaneous volumes bought at a storage house—could be left behind if necessary.

What stopped him was Gloria's cable from Paris: TROUBLE HERE. PHONING FRIDAY NIGHT.

This was Thursday. Whatever else happened, he must wait for Gloria's call. His hand moved toward the lower drawer, then withdrew. Coffee, not whiskey, was what he needed; and after luncheon he spent most of the afternoon with Miss Boggs's weird collection of antiques. There he had an unobstructed view of Jackson's door, and was not himself visible. If Larry Bridewell was among the lawyer's visitors, Loxley did not see him.

Exploring the antique shop he paused, as always, to admire its two star exhibits, the almost frightening suit of armor and the massive Spanish chest. In a pinch either would do as an emergency hiding place—if there was time enough to hide.

That evening he was startled to find his picture in the newspaper again—the face of Dr. B. Edward Loxley as he had looked, with the neat little beard and mustache, before he had murdered his wife. It seemed that he'd been arrested by an alert Seattle policeman, but had denied his identity.

Dr. Loxley drew a long breath of relief. After all, perhaps he was still safe in this city within a city. But what could Gloria have to say to him that required a call from Paris? Bad news of some kind. Bad for somebody.

31

A DOG IN THE DAYTIME

BY REX STOUT

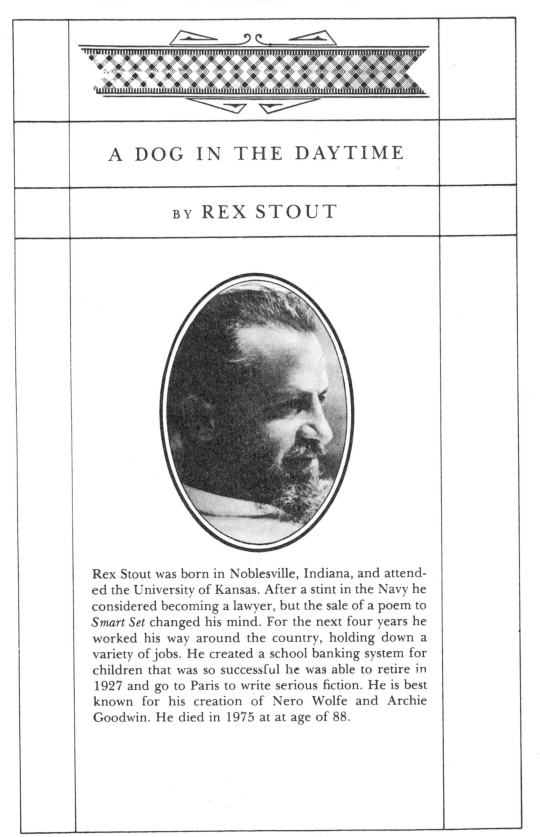

Rex Stout was born in Noblesville, Indiana, and attended the University of Kansas. After a stint in the Navy he
considered becoming a lawyer, but the sale of a poem to
Smart Set changed his mind. For the next four years he
worked his way around the country, holding down a
variety of jobs. He created a school banking system for
children that was so successful he was able to retire in
1927 and go to Paris to write serious fiction. He is best
known for his creation of Nero Wolfe and Archie
Goodwin. He died in 1975 at at age of 88.

I DO SOMETIMES TREAT MYSELF to a walk in the rain, though I prefer sunshine as a general rule. That rainy Wednesday, however, there was a special inducement: I wanted his raincoat to be good and wet when I delivered it. So with it on my back and my old brown felt on my head, I left Nero Wolfe's brownstone house on West 35th Street, Borough of Manhattan, and set out for Arbor Street, which is down in Greenwich Village.

Halfway there the rain stopped and my blood had pumped me warm, so I took the coat off, folded it wet side in, hung it on my arm, and proceeded. Arbor Street, narrow and only three blocks long, had on either side an assortment of old brick houses, mostly of four stories, which were neither spick nor span. Number 29 would be about the middle of the first block.

I reached it, but I didn't enter it. There was a party going on in the middle of the block. A police car was double-parked in front of one of the houses, and a uniformed cop was on the sidewalk in an attitude of authority toward a small gathering of citizens confronting him. As I approached I heard him demanding, "Whose dog is this?"

He was referring, evidently, to an animal with a wet black coat standing behind him. I heard no one claim the dog, but I wouldn't have, anyway, because my attention was diverted. Another police car rolled up and stopped behind the first one, and a man got out, nodded to the cop without halting, and went in the entrance of Number 29.

The trouble was, I knew the man, which is an understatement. I do not begin to tremble at the sight of Sergeant Purley Stebbins of Manhattan Homicide West, but his presence and manner made it a cinch that there was a corpse in that house, and if I demanded entry on the ground that I wanted to swap raincoats with a guy who had walked off with mine, there was no question what would happen. My prompt appearance at the scene of a homicide would arouse all Purley's worst instincts, and I might not get home in time for dinner, which was going to be featured by grilled squab with a brown sauce which Fritz calls *Venitienne* and is one of his best.

Purley had disappeared inside without spotting me. The cop was a complete stranger. As I slowed down to detour past him on the narrow sidewalk, he gave me an eye and demanded, "That your dog?"

The dog was nuzzling my knee, and I stooped to give him a pat on his wet black head. Then, telling the cop he wasn't mine, I went on by. At the next corner I turned right, heading back uptown. A wind had started in from the west, but everything was still damp from the rain.

I was well on my way before I saw the dog. Stopping for a light on Ninth Avenue in the Twenties, I felt something at my knee, and there he was. My hand started for his head in reflex, but I pulled it back. I was in a fix. Apparently he had picked me for a pal, and if I just went on he would follow, and you can't chase a dog on Ninth Avenue by throwing rocks. I could have ditched him by taking a taxi the rest of the way, but that would have been pretty rude after the appreciation he had shown of my charm. He had a collar on with a tag and could be identified, and the station house was only a few blocks away, so the simplest way was to convoy him there. I moved to the curb to reconnoiter, and as I did so a cyclone sailed around the corner and took my hat with it into the middle of the avenue.

I didn't dash out into the traffic, but you should have seen that dog. He sprang across the bow of a big truck, wiping its left front fender with his tail, braked landing to let a car by, sprang again and was under another car—or I thought he was—and then I saw him on the opposite sidewalk. He snatched the hat from under the feet of a pedestrian, turned on a dime, and started back. This time his crossing wasn't so spectacular, but he didn't dally. He came to me and stood, lifting his head and wagging his tail. I took the hat. It had skimmed a puddle of water on its trip, but I thought he would be disappointed if I didn't put it on, so I did. Naturally, that settled it. I flagged a cab, took the dog in with me, and gave the driver the address of Wolfe's house.

My idea was to take my hat hound upstairs to my room, give him some refreshment, and phone the ASPCA to send for him. But there was no sense in passing up such an opportunity for a little buzz at Wolfe, so, after leaving my hat and the raincoat on the rack in the hall, I proceeded to the office and entered.

"Where the deuce have you been?" Wolfe asked grumpily. "We were going over some lists at six o'clock, and it's a quarter to seven." He was in his oversized chair behind his desk with a book, and his eyes hadn't left the page to spare me a glance.

I answered him. "Returning that fool raincoat. Only, I didn't deliver it, because—"

"What's that?" he snapped. He was glaring at my companion.

"A dog."

"I see it is. I'm in no temper for buffoonery. Get it out of here."

"Yes, sir, right away. I can keep him in my room most of the time, but of course he'll have to come downstairs and through the hall when I take him out. He's a hat hound. There is a sort of problem. His name is Nero, which as you know means 'black,' and of course I'll have to change it. Ebony would do, or Jet, or Inky, or—"

"Bah. Flummery!"

"No, sir. I get pretty darned lonesome around here, especially during the four hours a day you're up in the plant rooms. You have your orchids, and Fritz has his turtle, and Theodore has his parakeets up in the potting room, so why shouldn't I have a dog? I admit I'll have to change his name, though he is registered as Champion Nero Charcoal of Bantyscoot."

It was a fizzle. I had expected to induce a major outburst, even possibly something as frantic as Wolfe leaving his chair to evict the beast himself, and there he was gazing at Nero with an expression I had never seen him aim at any human, including me.

"It's not a hound," he said. "It's a Labrador retriever."

That didn't faze me, from a bird who reads as many books as Wolfe does. "Yes, sir," I agreed. "I only said hound because it would be natural for a private detective to have a hound."

"Labradors," he said, "have a wider skull than any other dog, for brain room. A dog I had when I was a boy, in Montenegro, a small brown mongrel, had a rather narrow skull, but I did not regard it as a defect. I do not remember that I considered that dog to have a defect. Today I suppose I would be more critical. . . . When you smuggled that creature in here did you take into account the disruption it would cause in this household?"

It had backfired on me. I had learned something new about the big, fat genius: he would enjoy having a dog around, provided he could blame it on me and so be free to beef when he felt like it. As for me, when I retire to the country I'll have a dog, and maybe two, but not in town.

I snapped into reverse. "I guess I didn't," I confessed. "Okay, I'll get rid of him. After all, it's your house."

37

"I do not want to feel responsible," he said stiffly, "for your privation. I would almost rather put up with the dog than with your reproaches."

"Forget it." I waved a hand.

"Another thing," he persisted. "I refuse to interfere with any commitment you have made."

"I have made no commitment."

"Then where did you get it?"

"Well, I'll tell you."

I went and sat at my desk and did so. Nero—the four-legged one—came and lay at my feet with his nose just not touching the toe of my shoe. I reported the whole event, with as much detail as if I had been reporting a major case, and when I had finished Wolfe was, of course, quite aware that my presentation of Nero had been a gag. Ordinarily, he would have made his opinion of my performance clear, but this time he skipped it, and it was easy to see why. The idea of having a dog that he could blame on me had got in and stuck. When I came to the end there was a moment's silence; then he said:

"Jet would be an acceptable name for that dog."

"Yeah." I swiveled and reached for the phone. "I'll call the ASPCA to come for him."

"No." He was emphatic.

"Why not?"

"Because there is a better alternative. Call someone you know in the Police Department, anyone, give him the number on the dog's tag, and ask him to find out who the owner is. Then you can inform the owner directly."

He was playing for time. It could happen that the owner was dead or in jail or didn't want the dog back, and, if so, Wolfe could take the position that I had committed myself by bringing the dog home in a taxi and that it would be dishonorable to renege. However, I didn't want to argue, so I phoned a precinct sergeant I knew. He took Nero's number and said he would call me back. Then Fritz entered to announce dinner.

The squabs with the sauce were absolutely edible, as they always are, but other phenomena in the next couple of hours were not so pleasing. The table talk in the dining room was mostly one-sided and mostly about dogs. Wolfe kept it on a high level, no maudlin sentiment. He maintained that the Basenji was the oldest breed on earth, having originated in Central Africa around 5,000 B.C., whereas there was no trace of the Afghan hound earlier than around 4,000 B.C. To me, all it proved was that he had read a book.

Nero ate in the kitchen with Fritz and made a hit. Wolfe had told Fritz to call him Jet. When Fritz brought in the salad he announced that Jet had wonderful manners and was very smart.

"Nevertheless," Wolfe asked, "wouldn't you think him an insufferable nuisance as a member of the household?"

On the contrary, Fritz delcared, Jet would be most welcome.

After dinner, feeling that the newly formed Canine Canonizing League needed slowing down, I first took Nero out for a brief tour and then escorted him up the two flights to my room and left him there. I had to admit he was well-behaved. If I had wanted to take on a dog in town it could have been this one. In my room I told him to lie down, and he did, and when I went to the door to leave, his eyes, which were the color of caramel, made it plain that he would love to come along, but he didn't get up.

Down in the office Wolfe and I got at the lists. They were special offerings from orchid growers and collectors from all over the world, and it was quite a job to check the thousands of items and pick the few that Wolfe might want to give a try. I sat at his desk, across from him, with trays of cards from our files, and we were in the middle of it, around ten thirty, when the doorbell rang. I went to the hall and flipped a light switch and saw out on the stoop, through the one-way glass panel in the door, a familiar figure—Inspector Cramer of Homicide.

I went to the door, opened it six inches, and asked politely, "Now what?"

"I want to see Wolfe."

"It's pretty late. What about?"

"About a dog."

It is understood that no visitor, and especially no officer of the law, is to be conducted to the office until Wolfe has been consulted, but this seemed to rate an exception. I considered the matter for about two seconds, and then swung the door open and invited cordially:

"Step right in."

"Properly speaking," Cramer declared as one who wanted above all to be perfectly fair and square, "it's Goodwin I want information from."

He was in the red-leather chair at the end of Wolfe's desk, just about filling it. His big, round face was no redder than usual, his gray eyes no colder, his voice no gruffer. Merely normal.

Wolfe came at me: "Then why did you bring him in here without even asking?"

Cramer interfered for me: "I asked for you. Of course, you're in it. I want to know where the dog fits in. Where is it, Goodwin?"

I inquired innocently, "Dog?"

His lips tightened. "All right; I'll spell it. You phoned the precinct and gave them a tag number and wanted to know who owns the dog. When the sergeant learned that the owner was a man named Philip Kampf, who was murdered this afternoon in a house at Twenty-nine Arbor Street, he notified Homicide. The officer who had been on post in front of that house had told us that the dog went off with a man who had said it wasn't his dog. After we learned of your inquiry about the owner, the officer was shown a picture of you, and said it was you who enticed the dog. He's outside in my car. Do you want to bring him in?"

"No, thanks. I didn't entice."

"The dog followed you."

I gestured modestly. "Girls follow me, dogs follow me, sometimes even your own dicks follow me. I can't help—"

"Skip the comedy. The dog belonged to a murder victim, and you removed it from the scene of the murder. Where is the dog?"

Wolfe butted in. "You persist," he objected, "in imputing an action to Mr. Goodwin without warrant. He did not 'remove' the dog. I advise you to shift your ground if you expect us to listen."

His tone was firm but not hostile. I cocked an eye at him. He was probably being indulgent because he had learned that Jet's owner was dead.

"I've got another ground," Cramer asserted. "A man who lives in that house, named Richard Meegan, and who was in it at the time Kampf was murdered, has stated that he came here to see you this morning and asked you to do a job for him. He says you refused the job. That's what he says."

Cramer jutted his chin. "Now. A man at the scene of a murder admits he consulted you this morning. Goodwin shows up at the scene half an hour after the murder was committed, and he entices—okay, the dog goes away with him. The dog that belonged to the victim and had gone to that house with him. How does that look?" He pulled his chin in. "You know the last thing I want in a homicide is to find you or Goodwin anywhere within ten miles of it, because I know from experience what to expect. But when you're there, there you are, and I want to know how and why, and what, and I intend to. Where's the dog?"

Wolfe sighed and shook his head. "In this instance," he said, almost genially, "you're wasting your time. As for Mr. Meegan, he phoned this morning to make an appointment and came at eleven. Our conversation was brief. He wanted a man shadowed, but divulged no name or any other specific detail, because in his first breath he mentioned his wife—he was overwrought—and I gathered that his difficulty was marital. As you know, I don't touch that kind of work, and I stopped him. My bluntness enraged him and he dashed out. On his way he took his hat from the rack in the hall, and he took Mr. Goodwin's raincoat instead of his own. Now, Archie, proceed."

Cramer's eyes swiveled to me, and I obeyed: "I didn't find out about the switch in coats until the middle of the afternoon. His was the same color as mine, but mine's newer. When he phoned for an appointment this morning he gave me his name and address. I wanted to phone him to tell him to bring my coat back, but he wasn't listed, and Information said she didn't have him, so I decided to go get it. I walked, wearing Meegan's coat. There was a cop and a crowd and a PD car in front of Twenty-nine Arbor Street, and as I approached another PD car came, and Purley Stebbins got out and went in, so I decided to skip it, not wanting to go through the torture. There was a dog present, and it nuzzled me, and I patted it. Then I headed for home."

"Did you call the dog or signal it?"

"No. I was at Twenty-eighth Street and Ninth Avenue before I knew it was tailing me. I did not entice or remove. If I did—if there's some kind of a dodge about the dog—please tell me why I phoned the precinct to get the name of his owner."

"I don't know. With Wolfe and you I never know. Where is it?"

I blurted it out before Wolfe could stop me: "Upstairs in my room."

"Bring it down here."

I was up and going, but Wolfe called me sharply: "Archie!"

I turned. "Yes, sir."

"There's no frantic urgency." He said to Cramer, "The animal seems intelligent, but I doubt if it's up to answering questions. I don't want it capering around my office."

"Neither do I."

"Then why bring it down?"

"I'm taking it downtown. We want to try something with it."

Wolfe pursed his lips. "I doubt if that's feasible. Mr. Goodwin has assumed an obligation and will have to honor it. The creature has no master, and so presumably no home. It will have to be tolerated here until Mr. Goodwin gets satisfactory assurance of its future welfare. Archie?"

If we had been alone I would have made my position clear, but with Cramer there I was stuck. "Absolutely," I agreed, sitting down again.

"You see," Wolfe told Cramer, "I'm afraid we can't permit the dog's removal."

"Nuts. I'm taking it."

"Indeed? What writ have you? Replevin? Warrant for arrest as a material witness?"

Cramer opened his mouth, and shut it again. He put his elbows on the chair arms, interlaced his fingers, and leaned forward. "Look. You and Meegan check, either because you're telling it straight, or because you've framed it. But I'm taking the dog. Kampf, the man who was killed, lived on Perry Street, a few blocks away from Arbor Street. He arrived at Twenty-nine Arbor Street, with the dog on a leash, about five twenty this afternoon.

"The janitor of the house, named Olsen, lives in the basement, and he was sitting at his front window when he saw Kampf arrive with the dog and turn in at the entrance. About ten minutes later he saw the dog come out, with no leash, and right after the dog a man came out. The man was Victor Talento, a lawyer, the tenant of the ground-floor apartment. Talento's story is that he left his apartment to go to an appointment, saw the dog in the hall, thought it was a stray, and chased it out. Olsen says Talento walked off and the dog stayed there on the sidewalk."

Cramer unlaced his fingers and sat back. "About twenty minutes later, around ten minutes to six, Olsen heard someone yelling his name, and went to the rear and up one flight to the ground-floor hall. Two men were there—a live one and a dead one. The live one was Ross Chaffee, a painter, the tenant of the top-floor studio—that's the fourth floor. The dead one was the man that had arrived with the dog. He had been strangled with the dog's leash, and the body was at the bottom of the stairs. Chaffee says he found it when he came down to go to an appointment, and that's all he knows. He stayed there while Olsen went downstairs to phone. A squad car arrived at five fifty-eight. Sergeant Stebbins arrived at six ten. Goodwin arrived at six ten. Excellent timing."

Wolfe merely grunted.

Cramer continued: "You can have it all. The dog's leash was in the pocket of Kampf's raincoat, which was on him. The laboratory says it was used to strangle him. The routine is still in process. I'll answer questions within reason. The four tenants of the house were all there when Kampf arrived: Victor Talento, the lawyer, on the ground floor; Richard Meegan, whose job you say you wouldn't take, second floor; Jerome Aland, a nightclub comedian, third floor; and Ross Chaffee, the painter, with the top-floor studio. Aland says he was sound asleep until we banged on his door just before taking him down to look at the corpse. Meegan says he heard nothing and knows nothing."

Cramer sat forward again. "Okay, what happened? Kampf went there to see one of those four men, and had his dog with him. It's possible he took the leash off in the lower hall and left the dog there, but I doubt it. At least, it's just as possible that he took the dog along to the door of one of the apartments, and the dog was wet and the tenant wouldn't let it enter, so Kampf left it outside. Another possibility is that the dog was actually present when Kampf was killed, but we'll know more about that after we see and handle the dog. What we're going to do is take the dog in that house and see which door it goes to. We're going to do that now. There's a man out in my car who knows dogs." Cramer stood up.

Wolfe shook his head. "You must be hard put. You say Mr. Kampf lived on Perry Street. With a family?"

"No. Bachelor. Some kind of a writer. He didn't have to make a living; he had means."

"Then the beast is orphaned. He's in your room, Archie?"

"Yes, sir." I got up and started for the door.

Wolfe halted me. "One moment. Go in your room, lock the door, and stay there till I notify you. Go!"

I went. It was either that or quit my job on the spot, and I resign only when we haven't got company. Also assuming that there was a valid reason for refusing to surrender the dog to the cops, Wolfe was justified. Cramer, needing no warrant to enter the house because he was already in, wouldn't hesitate to mount to my room to do his own fetching, and stopping him physically would have raised some delicate points. Whereas breaking through a locked door would be another matter.

I didn't lock it, because it hadn't been locked for ten years and I didn't remember where the key was, so I left it open and stood on the sill to listen. If I heard Cramer coming I would shut the door and brace it with my foot. Nero, or Jet, depending on where you stand, came over to me, but I ordered him back, and he went without a murmur. From below came voices, not cordial, but not raised enough for me to get words. Before long there was the sound of Cramer's heavy steps tramping along the hall, then the slam of the front door.

I called down: "All clear?"

"No!" It was a bellow. "Wait till I bolt it!" And after a moment: "All right!"

I shut my door and descended the stairs. Wolfe was back in his chair behind his desk, sitting straight. As I entered he snapped at me: "A pretty mess. You sneak a dog in here to badger me, and what now?"

I crossed to my desk, sat, and spoke calmly: "We're 'way beyond that. You will never admit you bollixed it up yourself, so forget it. When you ask me what now, that's easy. I could say I'll take the dog down and deliver him at Homicide, but we're beyond that too. Not only have you learned that he is orphaned, as you put it, and therefore adopting him will probably be simple, but also you have taken a stand with Cramer, and of course you won't back up. If we sit tight, with the door bolted, I suppose I can take the dog out back for his outings, but what if the law shows up tomorrow with a writ?"

He leaned back and shut his eyes. I looked up at the wall clock: two minutes past eleven. I looked at my wrist watch: also two minutes past eleven. They both said six minutes past when Wolfe opened his eyes.

"From Mr. Cramer's information," he said, "I doubt if that case holds any formidable difficulties."

44

I had no comment.

"If it were speedily solved," he went on, "your commitment to the dog could be honored, at leisure. Clearly, the simplest way to settle this matter is to find out who killed Mr. Kampf. It may not be much of a job; if it proves otherwise, we can reconsider. An immediate exploration is the thing, and luckily we have a pretext for it. You can go to Arbor Street to get your raincoat, taking Mr. Meegan's with you, and proceed as the occasion offers. The best course would be to bring him here; but, as you know, I rely wholly on your discretion and enterprise in such a juncture."

"Thank you very much," I said bitterly. "You mean now?"

"Yes."

"They may still have Meegan downtown."

"I doubt if they'll keep him overnight. In the morning they'll probably have him again."

"I'll be hanged." I arose. "No client, no fee—no nothing except a dog with a wide skull for brain room." I went to the hall rack for my hat and Meegan's coat, and beat it.

The rain had ended and the wind was down. Dismissing the taxi at the end of Arbor Street, I walked to Number 29, with the raincoat hung over my arm. There was light behind the curtains of the windows on the ground floor, but none anywhere above, and none in the basement. Entering the vestibule, I inspected the labels in the slots between the mailboxes and the buttons. From the bottom up they read: Talento, Meegan, Aland, and Chaffee. I pushed Meegan's button, put my hand on the doorknob, and waited. No click. I twisted the knob and it wouldn't turn. Another long push on the button, and a longer wait. Nothing doing.

I considered pushing the button of Victor Talento, the lawyer who lived on the ground floor, where light was showing; instead, I voted to wait a while for Meegan, with whom I had an in. I moved to the sidewalk, propped myself against a fire hydrant, and waited.

I hadn't been there long enough to shift position more than a couple of times when the light disappeared on the ground floor of Number 29. A little later the vestibule door opened and a man came out. He turned toward me, gave me a glance as he passed, and kept going.

Thinking it unlikely that any occupant of that house was

being extended the freedom of the city that night, I cast my eyes around, and, sure enough when the subject had gone some thirty paces a figure emerged from an areaway across the street and started strolling after him. I shook my head in disapproval. I would have waited until the guy was ten paces farther. Saul Panzer would have made it ten more than that, but Saul is the best trailer alive.

As I stood deploring that faulty performance, an idea hit me. They might keep Meegan downtown another two hours, or all night, or he might even be up in his bed asleep. This was at least a chance to take a stab at something. I shoved off, in the direction taken by the subject, who was now a block away. Stepping along, I gained on him. A little beyond the corner I came abreast of the city employee, who was keeping to the other side of the street, but I wasn't interested in him. It seemed to me that the subject was upping the stroke a little, so I did, too, and as he reached the next intersection I was beside him.

I said: "Victor Talento?"

"No comment," he said, and kept going. So did I.

"Thanks for the compliment," I said, "but I'm not a reporter. My name's Archie Goodwin, and I work for Nero Wolfe. If you'll stop a second I'll show you my credentials."

"I'm not at all interested in your credentials."

"Okay. If you just came out for a breath of air you won't be interested in this, either. Otherwise, you may be. Please don't scream or look around, but you've got a homicide dick on your tail. He's across the street, ninety feet back."

"Yes," he conceded, without changing pace, "that's interesting. Is this your good deed for the day?"

"No. I'm out dowsing for Mr. Wolfe. He's investigating a murder just for practice, and I'm looking for a seam. I thought if I gave you a break you might feel like reciprocating. If you're just out for a walk, forget it, and sorry I interrupted. If you're headed for something you'd like to keep private, maybe you could use some expert advice. In this part of town at this time of night there are only two approved methods for shaking a tail, and I'd be glad to oblige."

He looked it over for half a block, with me keeping step, and then spoke: "You mentioned credentials."

"Right. We might as well stop under that light. The dick will, of course, keep his distance."

We stopped. I got out my wallet and let him have a look at my licenses, detective and driver's. He didn't skimp it, being a lawyer.

"Of course," he said, "I was aware that I might be followed."

"Sure."

"I intended to take precautions. But I suppose it's not always as simple as it seems. I have had no experience at this kind of maneuver. Who hired Wolfe to investigate?"

"I don't know. He says he needs practice."

He stood sizing me up by the street light. He was an inch shorter than I am, and some older, with his weight starting to collect around the middle. He was dark-skinned, with eyes to match.

"I have an appointment," he said.

I waited.

He went on: "A woman phoned me and I arranged to meet her. My wire could have been tapped."

"I doubt it. They're not that fast."

"I suppose not. The woman had nothing to do with the murder, and neither had I, but of course anything I do and anyone I see is suspect. I have no right to expose her to possible embarrassment. I can't be sure of shaking that man off."

I grinned at him. "And me, too."

"You mean you would follow me?"

"Certainly, for practice. And I'd like to see how you handle it."

He wasn't returning my grin. "I see you've earned your reputation, Goodwin. You'd be wasting your time, because this woman has no connection with this business, but I should have known better than to make this appointment. It's only three blocks from here. You might be willing to go and tell her I'm not coming. Yes?"

"Sure, if it's only three blocks. If you'll return the favor by calling on Nero Wolfe for a little talk. That's what I meant by reciprocating."

He considered it. "Not tonight. I'm all in."

"Tomorrow morning at eleven?"

"Yes, I can make it then."

"Okay." I gave him the address. "Now brief me."

He took a respectable roll of bills from his pocket and peeled off a twenty. "Since you're acting as my agent, you have a right to a fee."

I grinned again. "That's a neat idea, you being a lawyer, but

47

I'm not acting as your agent. I'm doing you a favor on request and expecting one in return. Where's the appointment?"

He put the roll back. "Have it your way. The woman's name is Jewel Jones, and she's at the southeast corner of Christopher and Grove Streets, or will be." He looked at his wrist. "We were to meet there at midnight. She's medium height, slender, dark hair and eyes, very good-looking. Tell her why I'm not coming, and say she'll hear from me tomorrow."

"Right. You'd better take a walk in the other direction to keep the dick occupied, and don't look back."

He wanted to shake hands to show his appreciation, but that would have been just as bad as taking the twenty, since before another midnight Wolfe might be tagging him for murder, so I pretended not to notice. He headed east and I, west, moving right along.

I had to make sure that the dick didn't switch subjects, but I let that wait until I got to Christopher Street. Reaching it, I turned the corner, went twenty feet to a stoop, slid behind it with only my head out, and counted a slow hundred. There were passers-by—a couple and a guy in a hurry—but no dick. I went on a block to Grove Street, passed the intersection, saw no loitering female, continued for a distance, then turned and back-tracked. I was on the fifth lap, and it was eight minutes past twelve, when a taxi stopped at the corner, a woman got out, and the taxi rolled off.

I approached. The light could have been better, but she seemed to meet the specifications. I stopped and asked, "Jones?" She drew herself up. I said, "From Victor."

She tilted her head back to see my face. "Who are you?" She seemed a little out of breath.

"Victor sent me with a message, but naturally I have to be sure it reaches the right party. I've anted half of your name and half of his, so it's your turn."

"Who are you?"

I shook my head. "You go first, or no message from Victor."

"Where is he?"

"No. I'll count ten and go. One, two, three, four—"

"My name is Jewel Jones. His is Victor Talento."

"That's the girl. I'll tell you." I did so, giving a complete version of my encounter with Talento, and including, of course, my name and status. By the time I finished she had developed a healthy frown.

48

She put a hand on my arm. "Come and put me in a taxi."

I stayed planted. "I'll be glad to, and it will be on me. We're going to Nero Wolfe's place."

"We?" She removed the hand. "You're crazy."

"One will get you ten I'm not. Look at it. You and Talento made an appointment at a street corner, so you had some good reason for not wanting to be seen together tonight. It must have been something fairly urgent. I admit the urgency didn't have to be connected with the murder of Philip Kampf, but it could be. I don't want to be arbitrary. I can take you to a homicide sergeant named Stebbins and you can discuss it with him, or I'll take you to Mr. Wolfe."

She had well-oiled gears. For a second, as I spoke, her eyes flashed like daggers, but then they went soft and appealing. She took my arm again, this time with both hands. "I'll discuss it with you," she said, in a voice she could have used to defrost her refrigerator. "I wouldn't mind that. We'll go somewhere."

I said come on, and we moved, with her hand hooked cozily on my arm. We hadn't gone far, toward Seventh Avenue, when a taxi came along and I flagged it and we got in. I told the driver, "Nine-sixteen West Thirty-fifth," and he started.

"What's that?" Miss Jones demanded.

I told her, Nero Wolfe's house. The poor girl didn't know what to do. If she called me a rat, that wouldn't help her any. If she kicked and screamed, I would merely tell the hackie, Headquarters. Her best bet was to try to thaw me, and if she had had time for a real campaign—say four or five hours—she might have made some progress, because she had a knack for it.

There just wasn't time enough. The taxi rolled to the curb and I had a bill ready for the driver. I got out, gave her a hand, and escorted her up the seven steps of the stoop. I pushed the button, and in a moment the stoop light shone on us, the chain bolt was released, and the door opened. I motioned her in and followed. Fritz was there.

"Mr. Wolfe up?" I asked.

"In the office." He was giving Miss Jones a look, the look he gives any strange female who enters that house. There is always in his mind the possibility, however remote, that she will bewitch Wolfe into a mania for a mate. I asked him to conduct her to the front room, put my hat and the raincoat on the rack, and went on down the hall to the office.

Wolfe was at his desk, reading; and curled up in the middle

49

of the room, on the best rug in the house, was the dog. The dog greeted me by lifting his head and tapping the rug with his tail. Wolfe greeted me by grunting.

"I brought company," I told him. "Before I introduce her I should—"

"Her? The tenants of the house are all men! I might have known you'd dig up a woman!"

"I can chase her if you don't want her. This is how I got her." I proceeded, not dragging it out, but including all the essentials. I ended up, "I could have grilled her myself, but it would have been risky. Just in a six-minute taxi ride she had me feeling—uh, brotherly. Do you want her or not?"

"Confound it." His eyes went to his book and stayed there long enough to finish a paragraph. "Very well, bring her."

I crossed to the connecting door to the front room, opened it, and requested, "Please come in, Miss Jones." She came, and as she passed through gave me a wistful smile that might have gone straight to my heart if there hadn't been a diversion. As she entered, the dog suddenly sprang to his feet and made for her, with sounds of unmistakable pleasure. He stopped in front of her, wagging his tail so fast it was only a blur.

"Indeed," Wolfe said. "How do you do, Miss Jones? I am Nero Wolfe. What's the dog's name?"

I claim she was good. The presence of the dog was a complete surprise to her. But without the slightest sign of fluster she put out a hand to give it a gentle pat, then went to the red-leather chair and sat down.

"That's a funny question right off," she said. "Asking me your dog's name."

"Pfui." Wolfe was digusted. "I don't know what position you were going to take, but from what Mr. Goodwin tells me I would guess you were going to say that the purpose of your appointment with Mr. Talento was a personal matter that had nothing to do with Mr. Kampf or his death, and that you knew Mr. Kampf either slightly or not at all. Now the dog has made that untenable. Obviously, he knows you well, and he belonged to Mr. Kampf. So you knew Mr. Kampf well. If you try to deny that, you'll have Mr. Goodwin and other trained men digging all around you, your past and your present, and that will be extremely disagreeable, no matter how innocent you may be of murder or any other wrongdoing. You won't like that. What's the dog's name?"

She looked at me and I looked back. In good light I would have qualified Talento's specification of "very good-looking." Not that she was unsightly, but she caught the eye more by what she looked than how she looked. It wasn't just something she turned on as needed; it was there even now, when she must have been pretty busy deciding how to handle the situation.

It took her only a few seconds to decide. "His name is Bootsy," she said. The dog, at her feet, lifted his head and wagged his tail.

"Good heavens," Wolfe muttered. "No other name?"

"Not that I know of."

"Your name is Jewel Jones?"

"Yes. I sing in a night club, but I'm not working right now." She made a little gesture, very appealing, but it was Wolfe who had to resist it, not me. "Believe me, Mr. Wolfe, I don't know anything about that murder. If I knew anything that could help I'd be perfectly willing to tell you, because I'm sure you're the kind of man who understands, and you wouldn't want to hurt me if you didn't have to."

"I try to understand," Wolfe said dryly. "You knew Mr. Kampf intimately?"

"Yes, I guess so." She smiled, as one understander to another. "For a while I did. Not lately—not for the past two months."

"You met the dog at his apartment on Perry Street?"

"That's right. For nearly a year I was there quite often."

"You and Mr. Kampf quarreled?"

"Oh, no, we didn't quarrel. I just didn't see him any more. I had other—I was very busy."

"When did you see him last?"

"About two weeks ago, at the club. He came to the club once or twice and spoke to me there."

"But no quarrel?"

"No, there was nothing to quarrel about."

"You have no idea who killed him, or why?"

"I certainly haven't."

Wolfe leaned back. "'Do you know Mr. Talento intimately?"

"No, not if you mean—of course, we're friends. I used to live there. I had the second-floor apartment."

"At Twenty-nine Arbor Street?"

"Yes."

"For how long? When?"

"For nearly a year. I left there—let's see—about three months ago. I have a little apartment on East Forty-ninth Street."

"Then you know the others, too? Mr. Meegan and Mr. Chaffee and Mr. Aland?"

"I know Ross Chaffee and Jerry Aland, but no Meegan. Who's he?"

"A tenant at Twenty-nine Arbor Street. Second floor."

She nodded. "Well, sure, that's the floor I had." She smiled. "I hope they fixed the rickety table for him. That was one reason I left. I hate furnished apartments, don't you?"

Wolfe made a face. "In principle, yes. I take it you now have your own furniture. Supplied by Mr. Kampf?"

She laughed—more of a chuckle—and her eyes danced. "I see you didn't know Phil Kampf."

"Not supplied by him, then?"

"A great big no."

"By Mr. Chaffee? Or Mr. Aland?"

"No and no." She went very earnest: "Look, Mr. Wolfe. A friend of mine was mighty nice about that furniture, and we'll just leave it. Mr. Goodwin told me what you're interested in is the murder, and I'm sure you wouldn't want to drag in a lot of stuff just to hurt me and a friend of mine, so we'll forget about the furniture."

Wolfe didn't press it. He took a hop. "Your appointment on a street corner with Mr. Talento. What was that about?"

She nodded. "I've been wondering about that—I mean, what I would say when you asked me—because I'd hate to have you think I'm a sap, and I guess it sounds like it. I phoned him when I heard on the radio that Phil was killed, there on Arbor Street. I knew Vic still lived there, and I simply wanted to ask him about it."

"You had him on the phone."

"He didn't seem to want to talk about it on the phone."

"But why a street corner?"

This time it was more like a laugh. "Now, Mr. Wolfe, *you're* not a sap. You asked about the furniture, didn't you? Well, a girl with furniture shouldn't be seen with Vic Talento."

"What is he like?"

She fluttered a hand. "Oh, he wants to get close."

Wolfe kept at her until after one o'clock, and I could report it all, but it wouldn't get you any farther than it did him. He couldn't trip her or back her into a corner. She hadn't been to Arbor Street for two months. She hadn't seen Chaffee or Aland or Talento for weeks, and of course not Meegan, since she had never heard of him before. She couldn't even try to guess who had killed Kampf.

The only thing remotely to be regarded as a return on Wolfe's investment of a full hour was her statement that, as far as she knew, there was no one who had both an attachment and a claim to Bootsy. If there were heirs, she had no idea who they were. When she left the chair to go, the dog got up, too. She patted him, and he went with us to the door. I took her to Tenth Avenue and put her in a taxi, and returned.

"Where's Bootsy?" I inquired.

"No," Wolfe said emphatically.

"Okay." I surrendered. "Where's Jet?"

"Down in Fritz's room. He'll sleep there. You don't like him."

"That's not true, but you can have it. It means you can't blame him on me. Anyhow, that will no longer be an issue after Homicide comes in the morning with a document and takes him away."

"They won't come."

"I offer twenty to one. Before noon."

He nodded. "That was, roughly, my own estimate of the probability, so while you were out I phoned Mr. Cramer. I suggested an arrangement, and I suppose he inferred that if he declined the arrangement the dog might be beyond his jurisdiction before tomorrow. I didn't say so, but I may have given him that impression."

"Yeah. You should be more careful."

"So the arrangement has been made. You are to be at Twenty-nine Arbor Street, with the dog, at nine o'clock in the morning. You are to be present throughout the fatuous performance the police have in mind, and keep the dog in view. The dog is to leave the premises with you, before noon, and you are to bring him back here. The police are to make no further effort to constrain the dog for twenty-four hours. While in that house you may find an opportunity to flush something or someone more contributive than Jewel Jones. . . ."

It was a fine, bright morning. I didn't take Meegan's raincoat, because I didn't need any pretext, and I doubted if the program would offer a likely occasion for the exchange.

The law was there in front waiting for me. The plainclothesman who knew dogs was a stocky, middle-aged guy who wore rimless glasses. Before he touched the dog he asked me its name, and I told him Bootsy.

"A heck of a name," he observed. "Also, that's some leash you've got."

"I agree. His was on the corpse, so I suppose it's in the lab." I handed him my end of the heavy cord. "If he bites you it's not on me."

"He won't bite me. Would you, Bootsy?" He squatted before the dog and started to get acquainted.

Sergeant Purley Stebbins growled a foot from my ear, "He should have bit you when you kidnapped him."

I turned. Purley was half an inch taller than I am and two inches broader. "You've got it twisted," I told him. "It's women that bite me. I've often wondered what would bite you."

We continued exchanging pleasantries, while the dog man, whose name was Larkin, made friends with Bootsy. It wasn't long before he announced that he was ready to proceed. He was frowning. "In a way," he said, "it would be better to keep him on leash after I go in, because Kampf probably did. . . . Or did he? How much do we actually know?"

"To swear to," Purley told him, "very little. But putting it all together from what we've collected, this is how it looks: When Kampf and the dog entered, it was raining and the dog was wet. Kampf removed the leash, either in the ground-floor hall or one of the halls above. He had the leash in his hand when he went to the door of one of the apartments. The tenant of the apartment let him in and they talked. The tenant socked him, probably from behind without warning, and used the leash to finish him. The murderer stuffed the leash in the pocket of the raincoat.

"It took nerve and muscle to carry the body out and down the stairs to the lower hall, but he had to get it out of his place and away from his door, and any of those four could have done it in a pinch. Of course, the dog was already outside, out on the sidewalk. While Kampf was in one of the apartments getting killed, Talento had come into the lower hall and seen the dog and chased it out."

"Then," Larkin objected, "Talento's clean."

"No. Nobody's clean. If it was Talento, after he killed Kampf he went out to the hall and put the dog in the vestibule, went back in his apartment and carried the body out and dumped it at the foot of the stairs, and then left the house, chasing the dog

54

on out to the sidewalk. You're the dog expert. Is there anything wrong with that?"

"Not necessarily. It depends on the dog and how close he was to Kampf. There wasn't any blood."

"Then that's how I'm buying it. If you want it filled in you can spend the rest of the day with the reports of the other experts and the statements made by the tenants."

"Some other day. That'll do for now. You're going in first?"

"Yeah. Come on, Goodwin." Purley started for the door, but I objected: "I'm staying with the dog."

Purley looked disgusted. "Then keep behind Larkin."

I changed my mind. From behind Larkin the view wouldn't be good. So I went into the vestibule with Purley. The inner door was opened by a homicide colleague, and we crossed to the far side of the small lobby. The colleague closed the door. In a minute he pulled it open again, and Larkin and the dog entered.

Two steps in, Larkin stopped, and so did the dog. No one spoke. The leash hung limp. Bootsy looked around at Larkin. Larkin bent over and untied the cord from the collar, and held it up to show Bootsy he was free. Bootsy came over to me and stood, his head up, wagging his tail.

"Nuts," Purley said, disgusted.

"You know what I really expected," Larkin said. "I never thought he'd show us where Kampf went when they entered yesterday, but I did think he'd go to the foot of the stairs, where the body was found, and I thought he might go on to where the body came from—Talento's door, or upstairs. Take him by the collar, Goodwin, and ease him over to the front of the stairs."

I obliged. He came without urging, but gave no sign that the spot held any special interest for him. We all stood and watched him. He opened his mouth wide to yawn.

"Fine," Purley rumbled. "Just fine. You might as well go on with it."

Larkin came and fastened the leash to the collar, led Bootsy across the lobby to a door, and knocked. In a moment the door opened, and there was Victor Talento, in a fancy rainbow dressing gown.

"Hello, Bootsy," he said, and reached down to pat.

Purley snapped, "I told you not to speak!"

Talento straightened up. "So you did." He was apologetic. "I'm sorry; I forgot. Do you want to try it again?"

"No. That's all."

Talento backed in and closed the door.

"You must realize," Larkin told Purley, "that a Labrador can't be expected to go for a man's throat. They're not that kind of dog. The most you could expect would be an attitude, or possibly a growl."

"You can have 'em," Purley said. "Is it worth going on?"

"By all means. You'd better go first."

Purley started up the stairs, and I followed him. The upper hall was narrow and not very light, with a door at the rear end and another toward the front. We backed up against the wall opposite the front door to leave enough space for Larkin and Bootsy. They came, Bootsy tagging, and Larkin knocked. Ten seconds passed before footsteps sounded; and then the door was opened by the specimen who had dashed out of Wolfe's place the day before and taken my coat with him. He was in his shirt sleeves and he hadn't combed his blond hair.

"This is Sergeant Larkin, Mr. Meegan," Purley said. "Take a look at the dog. Have you ever seen it before? Pat it."

Meegan snorted. "Pat it yourself."

"Have you ever seen it before?"

"No."

"Okay; thanks. Come on, Larkin."

As we started up the next flight the door slammed behind us, good and loud. Purley asked over his shoulder, "Well?"

"He didn't like him," Larkin replied from the rear, "but there are lots of people lots of dogs don't like."

The third-floor hall was a duplicate of the one below. Again Purley and I posted ourselves opposite the door, and Larkin came with Bootsy and knocked. Nothing happened. He knocked again, louder, and pretty soon the door opened to a two-inch crack and a squeaky voice came through:

"You've got the dog."

"Right here," Larkin told him.

"Are you there, Sergeant?"

"Right here," Purley answered.

"I told you that dog didn't like me. Once at a party at Phil Kampf's—I told you. I didn't mean to hurt it, but it thought I did. What are you trying to do—frame me?"

"Open the door. The dog's on a leash."

"I won't! I told you I wouldn't!"

Purley moved. His arm, out stiff, went over Larkin's shoulder, and his palm met the door and shoved hard. The door hesitated an instant, then swung open. Standing there, holding to its edge, was a skinny individual in red-and-green striped pajamas. The dog let out a low growl and backed up a little.

"We're making the rounds, Mr. Aland," Purley said, "and we couldn't leave you out. Now you can go back to sleep. As for trying to frame you—" He stopped because the door shut.

"You didn't tell me," Larkin complained, "that Aland had already fixed it for a reaction."

"No, I thought I'd wait and see. One to go." He headed for the stairs.

The top-floor hall had had someone's personal attention. It was no bigger than the others, but it had a nice, clean tan-colored runner, and the walls were painted the same shade and sported a few small pictures. Purley went to the rear door instead of the front, and we made room for Larkin and Bootsy. When Larkin knocked, footsteps responded at once, and the door swung wide open. This was the painter, Ross Chaffee, and he was dressed for it, in an old brown smock. He was by far the handsomest of the tenants—tall, erect, with features he must have enjoyed looking at in the mirror.

I had ample time to enjoy them, too, as he stood smiling at us, completely at ease, obeying Purley's prior instructions not to speak. Bootsy was also at ease. When it became quite clear that no blood was going to be shed, Purley asked, "You know the dog, don't you, Mr. Chaffee?"

"Certainly. He's a beautiful animal."

"Pat him."

"With pleasure." He bent gracefully. "Bootsy, do you know your master's gone?" He scratched behind the black ears. "Gone forever, Bootsy, and that's too bad." He straightened. "Anything else? I'm working. I like morning light."

"That's all, thanks." Purley turned to go, and I let Larkin and Bootsy by before following. On the way down the three flights no one had any remarks. As we hit the lower hall Victor Talento's door opened, and he emerged.

"The District Attorney's office telephoned," he said. "Are you through with me? They want me down there."

"We're through," Purley said. "We can run you down."

Talento said that would be fine and he would be ready in a minute. Purley told Larkin to give me Bootsy, and he handed me the leash.

I departed. Outside, the morning was still fine. The presence of two PD cars in front of the scene of a murder had attracted a small gathering, and Bootsy and I were objects of interest as we appeared and started off. We both ignored the stares. We moseyed along, in no hurry, stopping now and then to give Bootsy a chance to inspect something if he felt inclined. At the fourth or fifth stop, more than a block away, I saw the quartet leaving Number 29. Stebbins and Talento took one car, Larkin and the colleague the other, and they rolled off.

I shortened up on Bootsy a little, walked him west until an empty taxi appeared, stopped it, and got in. I took a five-dollar bill from my wallet and handed it to the hackie.

"Thanks," he said. "For what—down payment on the cab?"

"You'll earn it, brother," I assured him. "Is there somewhere within a block or so of Arbor and Court where you can park for anywhere from thirty minutes to three hours?"

"Not three hours for a finif."

"Of course not." I took out another five and gave it to him. "I doubt if it will be that long."

"There's a parking lot not too far. On the street without a passenger I'll be hailed."

"You'll have a passenger: the dog. I prefer the street. Let's see what we can find."

There are darned few legal parking spaces in all Manhattan at that time of day, and we cruised around several corners before we found one, on Court Street two blocks from Arbor. He backed into it and I got out, leaving the windows down three inches. I told him I'd be back when he saw me, and headed south, turning right at the second corner.

There was no police car at 29 Arbor, and no gathering. That was satisfactory. Entering the vestibule, I pushed the button under "Meegan" and put my hand on the knob. No click. Pushing twice more and still getting no response, I tried Aland's button and that worked. After a short wait the click came, and I entered, mounted two flights, and knocked with authority on Aland's door.

The squeaky voice came through: "Who is it?"

"Goodwin. I was just here with the others. I haven't got the dog."

The door swung slowly to a crack, and then wider. Jerome Aland was still in his gaudy pajamas. "What do you want now?" he asked. "I need some sleep!"

I didn't apologize. "I was going to ask you some questions when I was here before," I told him, "but the dog complicated it. It won't take long." Since he wasn't polite enough to move aside, I had to brush him, skinny as he was, as I went in.

He slid past me, and I followed him across the room to chairs. They were the kind of chairs that made Jewel Jones hate furnished apartments. He sat on the edge of one and demanded, "All right; what is it?"

It was a little tricky. Since he was assuming I was one of the homicide personnel, it wouldn't do for me to know either too much or too little. It would be risky to mention Jewel Jones, because the cops might not have got around to her at all.

"I'm checking some points," I told him. "How long has Richard Meegan occupied the apartment below you?"

"I've told you that a dozen times."

"Not me. I said I'm checking. How long?"

"Nine days. He took it a week ago Tuesday."

"Who was the previous tenant? Just before him."

"There wasn't any. It was empty."

"Empty since you've been here?"

"No, I've told you, a girl had it, but she moved out about three months ago. Her name is Jewel Jones, and she's a fine artist, and she got me my job at the night club where I work now." His mouth worked. "I know what you're doing. You're trying to make it nasty and you're trying to catch me getting my facts twisted. Bringing that dog here to growl at me—Can I help it if I don't like dogs?"

He ran his fingers, both hands, through his hair. When the hair was messed good he gestured like the night-club comedian he was. "Die like a dog," he said. "That's what Phil did—died like a dog."

"You said," I ventured, "that you and he were good friends." His head jerked up. "I did not!"

"Maybe not in those words. . . . Why? Weren't you?"

"We were not. I haven't got any good friends."

"You just said that the girl who used to live here got you a job. That sounds like a good friend. Or did she owe you something?"

"Of course not. Why do you keep bringing her up?"

"I didn't bring her up—you did. I only asked who was the former tenant in the apartment below you. Why? Would you rather keep her out of it?"

59

"I don't have to keep her out. She's not in it."

"Perhaps not. Did she know Philip Kampf?"

"I guess so. Sure, she did."

"How well did she know him?"

He shook his head. "If Phil was alive you could ask him, and he might tell you. Me, I don't know."

I smiled at him. "All that does, Mr. Aland, is make me curious. Somebody in this house murdered Kampf. So we ask you questions, and when we come to one you shy at, naturally we wonder why. If you don't like talking about Kampf and that girl, think what it could mean. For instance, it could mean that the girl was yours, and Kampf took her away from you, and that was why you killed him when he came here yesterday."

"She wasn't my girl!"

"Uh-huh. Or it could mean that although she wasn't yours, you were under a deep obligation to her, and Kampf had given her a dirty deal; or he was threatening her with something, and she wanted him disposed of, and you obliged. Or of course it could be merely that Kampf had something on you."

"You're in the wrong racket," he sneered. "You ought to be writing TV scripts."

I stuck with him only a few more minutes, having got all I could hope for under the circumstances. Since I was letting him assume that I was a city employee, I couldn't very well try to pry him loose for a trip to Wolfe's place. Also, I had two more calls to make, and there was no telling when I might be interrupted by a phone call or a courier to one of them from downtown. So I left.

I went down a flight to Meegan's door, and knocked and waited. Just as I was raising a fist to make it louder and better, there were footsteps inside, and the door opened. Meegan was still in his shirt sleeves and still uncombed.

"Well?" he demanded.

"Back again," I said, firmly but not offensively. "With a few questions. If you don't mind?"

"I certainly do mind."

"Naturally. Mr. Talento has been called down to the District Attorney's office. This might possibly save you another trip there."

He side-stepped and I went in. The room was the same size and shape as Aland's, above, and the furniture, though different, was no more desirable. The table against a wall was lopsided, probably the one that Jewel Jones hoped they had fixed for him. I took a chair beside it, and he took another and sat frowning at me.

"Haven't I seen you before?" he wanted to know.

"Sure, we were here with the dog."

"I mean before that. Wasn't it you in Nero Wolfe's office yesterday?"

"That's right."

"How come?"

I raised my brows. "Haven't you got the lines crossed, Mr. Meegan? I'm here to ask questions, not to answer them. I was in Wolfe's office on business. I often am. Now—"

"He's a fat, arrogant half-wit!"

"You may be right. He's certainly arrogant. Now I'm here on business." I got out my notebook and pencil. "You moved into this place nine days ago. Please tell me exactly how you came to take this apartment."

He glared. "I've told it at least three times."

"I know. This is the way it's done. I'm not trying to catch you in some little discrepancy, but you could have omitted something important. Just assume I haven't heard it before. Go ahead."

He groaned and dropped his head on his hands. Normally, he might not have been a bad-looking guy, with his blond hair and gray eyes and long, bony face; but now, having spent most of the night with Homicide and the D.A., he looked it, especially his eyes, which were red and puffy.

He lifted his head. "I'm a commercial photographer. In Pittsburgh. Two years ago I married a girl named Margaret Ryan. Seven months later she left me. I didn't know whether she went alone or with somebody. She just left. She left Pittsburgh, too—at least I couldn't find her there—and her family never saw her or heard from her. About five months later, about a year ago, a client of mine came back from a trip to New York and said he saw her in a theater here with a man. He spoke to her, but she claimed he was mistaken. He was sure it was her. I came to New York and spent a week looking around, but didn't find her. I didn't go to the police, because I didn't want to. You want a better reason, but that's mine."

"I'll skip that." I was writing in the notebook. "Go ahead."

"Two weeks ago I went to look at a show of pictures at the Fillmore Gallery in Pittsburgh. There was a painting there—an oil—a big one. It was called *Three Young Mares at Pasture,* and it was an interior, a room, with three women in it. One of them was on a couch, and two of them were on a rug on the floor. They were eating apples. The one on the couch was my wife. I was sure of it the minute I saw her, and after I stood and studied it I was surer than ever. There was absolutely no doubt of it."

"We're not challenging that," I assured him. "What did you do?"

"The artist's signature was Ross Chaffee. I went to the gallery office and asked about him. They thought he lived in New York. I had some work on hand I had to finish, and then I came to New York.

"I had no trouble finding Ross Chaffee; he was in the phone book. I went to see him at his studio, here in this house. First, I told him I was interested in that figure in his painting, that I thought she would be just right to model for some photographs I wanted to do, but he said that his opinion of photography as an art medium was such that he wouldn't care to supply models for it. He was bowing me out, so I told him how it was. I told him the whole thing. Then he was different. He sympathized with me and said he would be glad to help me if he could, but he had painted that picture more than a year ago, and he used so many different models for his pictures that it was impossible to remember which was which."

Meegan stopped, and I looked up from the notebook. He said aggressively, "I'm repeating that that sounded phony to me."

"Go right ahead. You're telling it."

"I say it was phony. A photographer might use hundreds of models in a year, and he might forget, but not a painter. Not a picture like that. I got a little tactless with him, and then I apologized. He said he might be able to refresh his memory and asked me to phone him the next day. Instead of phoning I went back the next day to see him, but he said he simply couldn't remember and doubted if he ever could. I didn't get tactless again. Coming in the house, I had noticed a sign that there was a furnished apartment to let, and when I left Chaffee I found the janitor and rented it, and moved in. I knew my wife had modeled for that picture, and I knew I could find her. I wanted to be as close as I could to Chaffee and the people who came to see him."

62

I wanted something, too. I wanted to say that he must have had a photograph of his wife along and I would like to see it, but of course I didn't dare; it was a cinch that he had already either given it to the cops, or refused to, or claimed he didn't have one. So I merely asked, "What kind of progress did you make?"

"Not much. I tried to get friendly with Chaffee, but I didn't get very far. I met the other two tenants, Talento and Aland, but that didn't get me anywhere. Finally I decided I would have to get some expert help, and that was why I went to see Nero Wolfe. You were there, so you know how that came out—that big blob!"

I nodded. "He has dropsy of the ego. What did you want him to do?"

"I've told you."

"Tell it again."

"I was going to have him tap Chaffee's phone."

"That's illegal," I said severely.

"All right; I didn't do it."

I flipped a page of the notebook. "Go back a little. During that week, besides the tenants here, how many of Chaffee's friends and acquaintances did you meet?"

"Just two, as I've told you. A young woman, a model, in his studio one day—I don't remember her name—and a man Chaffee said buys his pictures. His name was Braunstein."

"You're leaving out Philip Kampf."

Meegan leaned forward and put a fist on the table. "Yes, and I'm going on leaving him out. I never saw him or heard of him."

"What would you say if I said you were seen with him?"

"I'd say you were a dirty liar!" The red eyes looked redder. "As if I wasn't already having enough trouble, now you set on me about the murder of a man I never heard of! You bring a dog here and tell me to pat it!"

I nodded. "That's your hard luck, Mr. Meegan. You're not the first man who's had a murder for company without inviting it." I closed the notebook and put it in my pocket. I rose. "Stick around, please. You may be wanted downtown again."

I would have liked to get more details of his progress, or lack of progress, with Ross Chaffee, and his contacts with the other two tenants, but it seemed more important to have some words with Chaffee before I got interrupted. As I mounted the two flights to the top floor my wrist watch said twenty-eight minutes past ten.

"I know there's no use complaining," Ross Chaffee said, "about these interruptions to my work. Under the circumstances." He was being very gracious about it.

The top floor was quite different from the others. I don't know what his living quarters in front were like, but the studio in the rear was big and high and anything but crummy. There were pieces of sculpture around, big and little, and canvases of all sizes were stacked and propped against racks. The walls were covered with drapes, solid gray, with nothing on them. Each of two easels, one much larger than the other, held a canvas that had been worked on. There were several plain chairs and two upholstered ones, and an oversized divan.

I had been steered to one of the upholstered numbers, and Chaffee, still in his smock, had moved a plain one to sit facing me.

"Only don't prolong it unnecessarily," he requested.

I said I wouldn't. "There are a couple of points," I told him, "that we wonder about a little. Of course, it could be merely a coincidence that Richard Meegan came to town looking for his wife, and came to see you, and rented an apartment here, just nine days before Kampf was murdered, but a coincidence like that will have to stand some going over. Frankly, Mr. Chaffee, there are those—and I happen to be one of them—who find it hard to believe that you couldn't remember who modeled for an important figure in a picture you painted."

Chaffee was smiling. "Then you must think I'm lying."

"I didn't say so."

"But you do, of course." He shrugged. "To what end? What deep design am I cherishing?"

"I wouldn't know. You say you wanted to help Meegan find his wife."

"No, not that I wanted to. I was willing to. He is a horrible nuisance."

"It should be worth some effort to get rid of him. Have you made any?"

"I have explained what I did. In a statement, and signed it. I have nothing to add. I tried to refresh my memory. One of your colleagues suggested that I might have gone to Pittsburgh to look at the picture. I suppose he was being funny."

A flicker of annoyance in his fine dark eyes warned me that I was supposed to have read his statement.

I gave him an earnest eye. "Look, Mr. Chaffee. This thing is bad for all concerned. It will get worse instead of better until we find out who killed Kampf. You men in this house must know things about one another, and maybe some things connected with Kampf, that you're not telling. I don't expect a man like you to pass out dirt just for the fun of it, but any dirt that's connected with this murder is going to come out, and if you are keeping any to yourself you're a bigger fool than you look."

"Quite a speech." He was smiling again.

"Thanks. Now you make one."

"I'm not as eloquent as you are." He shook his head. "No, I don't believe I can help you any. I can't say I'm a total stranger to dirt—that would be smug; but what you're after—no. You have my opinion of Kampf, whom I knew quite well; he was in some respects admirable, but he had his full share of faults. I would say approximately the same of Talento. I have known Aland only casually. I know no more of Meegan than you do. I haven't the slightest notion why any of them might have wanted to kill Philip Kampf. If you expect—"

A phone rang. Chaffee crossed to a table at the end of the divan and answered it. He told it "Yes" a couple of times, and then: "But one of your men is here now. . . . I don't know his name; I didn't ask him. . . . He may be; I don't know. . . . Very well. The District Attorney's office. . . . Yes, I can leave in a few minutes."

He hung up and turned to me. I spoke first, on my feet: "So they want you at the D.A.'s office. Don't tell them I said so, but they'd rather keep a murder in the file till the cows come home than have the squad crack it. If they want my name they know where to ask."

I marched to the door, opened it, and was gone.

I was relieved to find the cab still waiting with its passenger perched on the seat looking out at the scenery. Jet seemed pleased to see me, and during the drive to 35th Street he sat with his rump braced against me for a buttress. The meter said only six dollars and something, but I didn't request any change from the ten I had given the driver. If Wolfe wanted to put me to work on a murder merely because he was infatuated with a dog, let it cost him something.

65

I noticed that when we entered the office Jet went over to Wolfe, behind his desk, without any sign of bashfulness or uncertainty, proving that the evening before, during my absence, Wolfe had made approaches; probably had fed him something, possibly had even patted him. Remarks occurred to me, but I saved them. I might be called on before long to spend some valuable time demonstrating that I had not been guilty of impersonating an officer, and that it wasn't my fault if the murder suspects mistook me for one.

Wolfe inquired, "Well?"

I reported. The situation called for a full and detailed account, and I supplied it, while Wolfe leaned back with his eyes closed. When I came to the end he asked no questions. Instead, he opened his eyes, and began, "Call the—"

I cut him off: "Wait a minute. After a hard morning's work I claim the satisfaction of suggesting it myself. I thought of it long ago. I'll call the gallery in Pittsburgh where Chaffee's picture was shown."

"Indeed. It's a shot at random."

"I know it is but I'm calling anyway."

I reached for the phone on my desk and got through to the Fillmore Gallery in no time, but it took a quarter of an hour, with relays to three different people, to get what I was after. I hung up and turned to Wolfe:

"The show ended a week ago yesterday. And I won't have to go to Pittsburgh. The picture was lent by Mr. Herman Braunstein of New York, who owns it. It was shipped back to him by express four days ago. They wouldn't give me Braunstein's address."

"The phone book."

I had it and was flipping the pages. "Here we are. Business on Broad Street, residence on Park Avenue. There's only one Herman."

"Get him."

"I don't think so. It might take all day. Why don't I go to the residence without phoning? The picture's probably there, and if I can't get in you can can fire me. I'm thinking of resigning anyhow."

He had his doubts, since it was my idea, but he bought it. After considering the problem a little, I went to the cabinet beneath the bookshelves, got out the Veblex camera, with accessories, and slung the strap of the case over my shoulder.

Before going I dialed Talento's number, to tell him not to bother to keep his appointment, but there was no answer. Either he was still engaged at the D.A.'s office or he was on his way to 35th Street, and if he came during my absence that was all right, since Jet was there to protect Wolfe.

A taxi took me to the end of a sidewalk canopy in front of one of the palace hives on Park Avenue in the Seventies, and I undertook to walk past the doorman without giving him a glance, but he stopped me. I said professionally, "Braunstein, taking pictures, I'm late," and kept going, and got away with it. I crossed the luxurious lobby to the elevator, which luckily was there with the door open, said, "Braunstein, please," and the operator shut the door and pulled the lever. We stopped at the twelfth floor, and I stepped out. There was a door to the right and another to the left. I turned right without asking, on a fifty-fifty chance, listening for a possible correction from the elevator man, who was standing by with his door open.

It was one of the simplest chores I have ever performed. In answer to my ring, the door was opened by a middle-aged female husky, in uniform with apron, and when I told her I had come to take a picture she let me in, asked me to wait, and disappeared. In a couple of minutes a tall and dignified dame with white hair came through an arch and asked what I wanted. I apologized for disturbing her and said I would deeply appreciate it if she would let me take a picture of a painting which had recently been shown at a Pittsburgh gallery, on loan by Mr. Braunstein. It was called *Three Young Mares at Pasture*. A Pittsburgh client of mine had admired it, and had intended to go back and photograph it for his collection, but the picture was gone before he had got around to it.

She wanted some information, such as my name and address and the name of my Pittsburgh client, which I supplied gladly without a script, and then she led me through the arch into a room not quite as big as Madison Square Garden. It would have been a pleasure, and also instructive, to do a little glomming at the rugs and furniture and especially the dozen or more pictures on the walls, but that would have to wait.

She went across to a picture near the far end, said, "That's it," and lowered herself onto a chair.

It was a nice picture. I had half expected the mares to be without clothes, but they were fully dressed. Remarking that I didn't wonder that my client wanted a photograph of it, I got busy with my equipment, including the flash bulbs. She sat and watched. I took four shots from slightly different angles, acting and looking professional, I hoped. Then I thanked her warmly on behalf of my client, promised to send her some prints, and left.

That was all there was to it.

Out on the sidewalk again, I walked west to Madison, turned downtown, and found a drug store. I went into the phone booth, and dialed a number.

Wolfe's voice came: "Yes? Whom do you want?"

I've told him a hundred times that's no way to answer the phone, but he's too pigheaded.

I spoke: "I want you. I've seen the picture, and it glows with color and life; the blood seems to pulsate under the warm skin. The shadows are transparent, with a harmonious blending—"

"Shut up! Yes or no?"

"Yes. You have met Mrs. Meegan. Would you like to meet her again?"

"I would. Get her."

I didn't have to look in the phone book for her address, having already done so.

I left the drug store and flagged a taxi.

There was no doorman problem at the number on East Forty-ninth Street. It was an old brick house that had been painted a bright yellow and modernized, but getting in was a little complicated. Pressing the button marked *Jewel Jones* in the vestibule was easy enough, but then it got more difficult.

A voice crackled from the grille: "Yes?"

"Miss Jones?"

"Yes. Who is it?"

"Archie Goodwin. I want to see you."

"What do you want?"

"Let me in and I'll tell you."

"No. What is it?"

"It's very personal. If you don't want to hear it from me I'll go and bring Richard Meegan, and maybe you'll tell him."

I heard the startled exclamation. After a pause: "Why do you say that? I told you I don't know any Meegan."

"You're 'way behind. I just saw a picture called *Three Young Mares at Pasture*. Let me in."

I turned and put my hand on the knob. There was a click,

and I pushed the door and entered. I crossed the little lobby to the self-service elevator, pushed the button marked 5, and ascended. When it stopped, I opened the door and emerged into a tiny foyer. A door was standing open, and on the sill was Miss Jones in a giddy négligée. She started to say something, but I rudely ignored it.

"Listen," I said, "there's no sense in prolonging this. Last night I gave you your pick between Mr. Wolfe and Sergeant Stebbins; now it's either Mr. Wolfe or Meegan. I should think you'd prefer Mr. Wolfe, because he's the kind of man who understands; you said so yourself. I'll wait here while you change, but don't try phoning anybody, because you won't know where you are until you've talked with Mr. Wolfe—and also because their wires are probably tapped."

She stepped to me and put a hand on my arm. "Archie, where did you see the picture?"

"I'll tell you on the way down. Let's go."

She gave the arm a gentle tug. "You don't have to wait out here. Come in and sit down."

I patted her fingers, not wishing to be boorish. "Sorry," I told her, "but I'm afraid of young mares. One kicked me once."

She turned and disappeared into the apartment, leaving the door open.

"Don't call me Mrs. Meegan!" Jewel Jones cried.

Wolfe was in as bad a humor as she was. True, she had been hopelessly cornered, with no weapons within reach, but he had been compelled to tell Fritz to postpone lunch until further notice.

"I was only," he said crustily, "stressing the fact that your identity is not a matter for discussion. Legally, you are Mrs. Richard Meegan. That understood, I'll call you anything you say. Miss Jones?"

"Yes." She was on the red-leather chair, but not in it. Perched on its edge, she looked as if she were set to spring up and scoot any second.

"Very well," Wolfe regarded her. "You realize, madam, that everything you say will be received skeptically. You are a competent liar. Your offhand denial of acquaintance with Mr. Meegan last night was better than competent. Now. When did Mr. Chaffee tell you that your husband was in town looking for you?"

"I didn't say Mr. Chaffee told me."

"Someone did. Who and when?"

She was hanging on. "How do you know someone did?"

He waggled a finger at her. "I beg you, Miss Jones, to realize the pickle you're in. It is not credible that Mr. Chaffee couldn't remember the name of the model for that figure in his picture. The police don't believe it, and they haven't the advantage of knowing, as I do, that it was you and that you lived in that house for a year, and that you still see Mr. Chaffee occasionally. When your husband came and asked Mr. Chaffee for the name of the model, and Mr. Chaffee pleaded a faulty memory, and your husband rented an apartment there and made it plain that he intended to persevere, it is preposterous to suppose that Mr. Chaffee didn't tell you. I don't envy you your tussles with the police after they learn about you."

"They don't have to learn about me, do they?"

"Pfui. I'm surprised they haven't got to you already, though it's been only eighteen hours. They soon will, even if not through me. I know this is no frolic for you, here with me, but they will almost make it seem so."

She was thinking. Her brow was wrinkled and her eyes stared straight at Wolfe. "Do you know," she asked, "what I think would be the best thing? I don't know why I didn't think of it before. You're a detective, you're an expert at helping people in trouble, and I'm certainly in trouble. I'll pay you to help me. I could pay you a little now."

"Not now or ever, Miss Jones." Wolfe was blunt. "When did Mr. Chaffee tell you that your husband was looking for you?"

"You won't even listen to me," she complained.

"Talk sense and I will. When?"

She edged back on the chair an inch. "You don't know my husband. He was jealous about me even before we married, and then he was worse. It got so bad I couldn't stand it, and that was why I left him. I knew if I stayed in Pittsburgh he would find me and kill me, so I came to New York. A friend of mine had come here—I mean just a friend. I got a job at a modeling agency and made enough to live on, and I met a lot of people. Ross Chaffee was one of them, and he wanted to use me in a picture and I let him. Of course, he paid me, but that wasn't so important, because soon after that I met Phil Kampf, and he got me a tryout at a night club and I made it. About then I had a scare, though. A man from Pittsburgh saw me at a theater and

70

spoke to me, but I told him he was wrong, that I had never been in Pittsburgh."

"That was a year ago," Wolfe muttered.

"Yes. I was a little leery about the night club, appearing in public like that, but months went by and nothing happened. And then all of a sudden Ross Chaffee phoned me that my husband had come and asked about the picture. I begged him not to tell him who it was, and he promised he wouldn't. You see, you don't know my husband. I knew he was trying to find me so he could kill me."

"You've said that twice. Has he ever killed anybody?"

"I didn't say anybody—I said me. I seem to have an effect on men." She gestured for understanding. "They just go for me. And Dick—well, I know him, that's all. I left him a year and a half ago, and he's still looking for me, and that's what he's like. When Ross told me he was here, I was scared stiff. I quit working at the club because he might happen to go there and see me, and I hardly left my apartment till last night."

Wolfe nodded. "To meet Mr. Talento. What for?"

"I told you."

"Yes, but then you were merely Miss Jones. Now you are also Mrs. Meegan. What for?"

"That doesn't change it any. I had heard on the radio about Phil being killed and I wanted to know about it. I rang Ross Chaffee and I rang Jerry Aland, but neither of them answered; so I rang Vic Talento. He wouldn't tell me anything on the phone, but he said he would meet me."

"Did Mr. Aland and Mr. Talento know you had sat for that picture?"

"Sure they did."

"And that Mr. Meegan had seen it and recognized you, and was here looking for you?"

"Yes, they knew all about it. Ross had to tell them, because he thought Dick might ask them if they knew who had modeled for the picture, and he had to warn them not to tell. They said they wouldn't, and they didn't. They're all good friends of mine."

She stopped to open her black leather bag, took out a purse, and fingered its contents. She raised her eyes to Wolfe. "I can pay you forty dollars now, to start. I'm not just in trouble; I'm in danger of my life, really I am. I don't see how you can refuse— You're not listening!"

71

Apparently he wasn't. With his lips pursed, he was watching the tip of his forefinger make little circles on his desk blotter. Her reproach didn't stop him, but after a moment he moved his eyes to me and said abruptly, "Get Mr. Chaffee."

"No!" she cried. "I don't want him to know—"

"Nonsense," he snapped at her. "Everybody will have to know everything, so why drag it out? . . . Get him, Archie, I'll speak to him."

I dialed Chaffee's number. I doubted if he would be back from his session with the D.A., but he was. I pitched my voice low so he wouldn't recognize it, and merely told him that Nero Wolfe wished to speak to him. Wolfe took it at his desk.

"Mr. Chaffee? This is Nero Wolfe. I've assumed interest in the murder of Philip Kampf and have done some investigating. . . . Just one moment, please; don't ring off. Sitting here in my office is Mrs. Richard Meegan, alias Miss Jewel Jones. . . . Please let me finish. I shall, of course, have to detain her and communicate with the police, since they will want her as a material witness in a murder case, but before I do that I would like to discuss the matter with you and the others who live in that house. Will you undertake to bring them here as soon as possible? . . . No, I'll say nothing further on the phone. I want you here, all of you. If Mr. Meegan is balky, you might as well tell him his wife is here—"

She was across to him in a leap that any young mare might have envied, grabbing for the phone and shrieking at it, "Don't tell him, Ross! Don't bring him! Don't—"

My own leap and dash around the end of the desk was fairly good, too. I yanked her back with enough enthusiasm so that I landed in the red-leather chair with her on my lap, and since she was by no means through, I wrapped my arms around her, pinning her arms to her sides, whereupon she started kicking my shins with her heels. She kept on kicking until Wolfe had finished with Chaffee. When he hung up she suddenly went limp against me.

Wolfe scowled at us. "An affecting sight," he snorted.

There were various aspects of the situation. One was lunch. For Wolfe it was unthinkable to have company in the house at mealtime, without feeding him or her, but he certainly wasn't going to sit at table with a female who had just pounced on him and clawed at him. The solution was simple: She and I were served in the dining room and Wolfe ate in the kitchen with Fritz. We were served, but she didn't eat much. She kept listening and looking toward the hall, though I assured her that care would be taken to see that her husband didn't kill her on these premises.

A second aspect was the reaction of three of the Arbor Street tenants to their discovery of my identity. I handled that myself. When the doorbell rang and I admitted them, at a quarter past two, I told them I would be glad to discuss my split personality with any or all of them later, if they still wanted to, but they would have to file it until Wolfe was through. Victor Talento had another beef that he wouldn't file—that I had double-crossed him on the message he had asked me to take to Jewel Jones. He wanted to get nasty about it and demanded a private talk with Wolfe, but I told him to go climb a rope.

I also had to handle the third aspect, which had two angles. There was Miss Jones's theory that her husband would kill her on sight, which might or might not be well-founded; and there was the fact that one of them had killed Kampf and might go to extremes if pushed. On that I took three precautions: I showed them the Marley .38 I had put in my pocket and told them it was loaded; I insisted on patting them from shoulders to ankles; and I kept Miss Jones in the dining room until I had them seated in the office, on a row of chairs facing Wolfe's desk. When he was in his chair behind his desk I went across the hall for her and brought her in.

Meegan jumped up and started for us. I stiff-armed him, and made it good. His wife got behind me, Talento and Aland left their chairs, presumably to help protect her. Meegan was shouting, and so were they. I detoured with her around back of them and got her to a chair at the end of my desk, and when I sat down I was in an ideal spot to trip anyone headed for her. Talento and Aland had pulled Meegan down onto a chair between them, and he sat staring at her.

"With that hubbub over," Wolfe said, "I want to be sure I have the names right." His eyes went from left to right. "Talento, Meegan, Aland, Chaffee. Is that correct?"

I told him yes.

"Then I'll proceed." He glanced up at the wall clock. "Twenty hours ago Philip Kampf was killed in the house where you gentlemen live. The circumstances indicate that one of you killed him. But I won't rehash the multifarious details which you have already discussed at length with the police; you are familiar with them. I have not been hired to work on this case; the only client I have is a dog, and he came to my office by chance. However—"

The doorbell rang. I asked myself if I had put the chain bolt on, and decided I had. Through the open door to the hall I saw Fritz passing to answer it. Wolfe started to go on, but was annoyed by the sound of voices, and stopped. He shut his eyes and compressed his lips, while the audience sat and looked at him.

Then Fritz appeared in the doorway and announced: "Inspector Cramer, sir."

Wolfe's eyes opened. "What does he want?"

"I told him you are engaged. He says he knows you are—that the four men were followed to your house and he was notified. He says he expected you to be trying some trick with the dog, and he knows that's what you are doing, and he intends to come in and see what it is. Sergeant Stebbins is with him."

Wolfe grunted. "Archie, tell— No. You'd better stay where you are. Fritz, tell him he may see and hear what I'm doing, provided he gives me thirty minutes without interruptions or demands. If he agrees to that, bring them in."

"Wait!" Ross Chaffee was on his feet. "You said you would discuss it with us before you communicated with the police."

"I haven't communicated with them. They're here."

"You told them to come!"

"No. I would have preferred to deal with you men first, and then call them, but here they are, and they might as well join us. Bring them, Fritz, on that condition."

"Yes, sir."

Fritz went. Chaffee thought he had something more to say, decided he hadn't, and sat down. Talento said something to him, and he shook his head. Jerry Aland, much more presentable now that he was combed and dressed, kept his eyes fastened on Wolfe. For Meegan, apparently, there was no one in the room but him and his wife.

Cramer and Stebbins marched in, halted three paces from the door, and took a survey.

"Be seated," Wolfe invited them. "Luckily, Mr. Cramer, your usual chair is unoccupied."

"Where's the dog?" Cramer demanded.

"In the kitchen. It's understood that you will be merely a spectator for thirty minutes?"

"That's what I said."

"Then sit down. But you should have one piece of information. You know the gentlemen, of course, but not the lady. Her current name is Miss Jewel Jones. Her legal name is Mrs. Richard Meegan."

"Meegan?" Cramer stared. "The one in the picture Chaffee painted?"

"That's right. Please be seated."

"Where did you get her?"

"That can wait. No interruptions and no demands. Confound it, sit down!"

Cramer went and lowered himself onto the red-leather chair. Purley Stebbins got one of the yellow ones and planted it behind Chaffee and Aland.

Wolfe regarded the quartet. "I was about to say, gentlemen, that it was something the dog did that pointed to the murderer for me. But before—"

"What did it do?" Cramer cut in.

"You know all about it," Wolfe told him coldly. "Mr. Goodwin related the events to you exactly as they happened. If you interrupt again, by heaven, you can take them all down to headquarters—not including the dog—and stew it out yourself!"

He went back to the four: "But before I come to the dog, another thing or two. I offer no comment on your guile with Mr. Meegan. You were all friends of Miss Jones's, and you refused to disclose her to a husband whom she had abandoned and professed to fear. I will even concede that there was a flavor of gallantry in your conduct. But when Mr. Kampf was murdered and the police swarmed in, it was idiotic to try to keep her out of it. They were sure to get to her. I got to her first, only because of Mr. Goodwin's admirable enterprise and characteristic luck."

He shook his head at them. "It was also idiotic of you to assume that Mr. Goodwin was a police officer, and admit him and answer his questions, merely because he had been present during the abortive experiment with the dog. You should have asked to see his credentials. None of you had any idea who he was. Even Mr. Meegan, who had seen him in this office in the morning, was bamboozled. I mention this to anticipate any possible official complaint that Mr. Goodwin impersonated an officer. You know he didn't. He merely took advantage of your unwarranted assumption."

75

He shifted in his chair. "Another thing: Yesterday morning Mr. Meegan called here by appointment to ask me to do a job for him. With his first words I gathered that it was something about his wife. I don't take that kind of work, and I was blunt with him. He was offended. He rushed out in a temper, grabbing a hat and raincoat from the rack in the hall, and he took Mr. Goodwin's coat instead of his own. Late in the afternoon Mr. Goodwin went to Arbor Street with the coat that had been left in error, to exchange it. He saw that in front of Number Twenty-nine there were collected two police cars, a policeman on duty, some people, and a dog. He decided to postpone his errand and went on by, after a brief halt during which he patted the dog. He walked home, and had gone nearly two miles when he discovered that the dog was following him. He brought the dog in a cab the rest of the way, to his house and this room."

He flattened a palm on his desk. "Now. Why did the dog follow Mr. Goodwin through the turmoil of the city? Mr. Cramer's notion that the dog was enticed is poppycock. Mr. Goodwin is willing to believe, as many men are, that he is irresistible both to dogs and to women, and doubtless his vanity impeded his intellect, or he would have reached the same conclusion I did. The dog didn't follow him; it followed the coat. You ask, as I did, how to account for Mr. Kampf's dog following Mr. Meegan's coat. I couldn't. I can't. Then, since it was unquestionably Mr. Kampf's dog, it couldn't have been Mr. Meegan's coat. It is better than a conjecture—it is next thing to a certainty—*that it was Mr. Kampf's coat!*"

His gaze leveled at the deserted husband. "Mr. Meegan. Some two hours ago I learned from Mr. Goodwin that you maintain that you had never seen or heard of Mr. Kampf. That was fairly conclusive, but before sending for you I had to verify my conjecture that the model who had sat for Mr. Chaffee's picture was your wife. I would like to hear it straight from you. Did you ever meet Philip Kampf alive?"

Meegan was meeting the gaze. "No."

"Don't you want to qualify that?"

"No."

"Then where did you get his raincoat?"

Meegan's jaw worked. He said, "I didn't have his raincoat, or if I did I didn't know it."

"That won't do. I warn you, you are in deadly peril. The

76

raincoat that you brought into this house and left here is in the hall now, there on the rack. It can easily be established that it belonged to Mr. Kampf and was worn by him. Where did you get it?"

Meegan's jaw worked some more. "I never had it, if it belonged to Kampf. This is a dirty frame. You can't prove that's the coat I left here."

Wolfe's voice sharpened: "One more chance. Have you any explanation of how Kampf's coat came into your possession?"

"No, and I don't need any."

He may not have been pure boob. If he hadn't noticed that he wore the wrong coat home—and he probably hadn't, in his state of mind—this had hit him from a clear sky and he had no time to study it.

"Then you're done for," Wolfe told him. "For your own coat must be somewhere, and I think I know where. In the police laboratory. Mr. Kampf was wearing one when you killed him and pushed his body down the stairs—and that explains why, when they were making that experiment this morning, the dog showed no interest in the spot where the body had lain. It had been enveloped, not in his coat but in yours. If you won't explain how you got Mr. Kampf's coat, then explain how he got yours. Is that also a frame?"

Wolfe pointed a finger at him. "I note that flash of hope in your eye, and I think I know what it means. But your brain is lagging. If, after killing Kampf, you took your raincoat off of him and put on him the one that you thought was his, that won't help you any. For in that case the coat that was on the body is Mr. Goodwin's, and certainly that can be established, and how would you explain that? It looks hopeless, and—"

Meegan was springing up, but before he even got well started Purley's big hands were on his shoulders, pulling him back and down.

And Jewel Jones was babbling, "I told you he would kill me! I knew he would! He killed Phil!"

Wolfe snapped at her, "How do you know he did?"

Judging by her eyes and the way she was shaking, she would be hysterical in another two minutes. Meanwhile, she poured it out:

"Because Phil told me—he told me he knew Dick was here looking for me, and he knew how afraid I was of him, and he said if I wouldn't come back to him he would tell Dick where I

77

was. I didn't think he really would—I didn't think Phil could be as mean as that—and I wouldn't promise.

"But yesterday morning he phoned me and told me he had seen Dick and told him he thought he knew who had posed for that picture. He said he was going to see him again in the afternoon and tell him about me if I didn't promise, and so I promised. I thought if I promised, it would give me time to decide what to do. But Phil must have gone to see Dick again, anyway."

"Where had they met in the morning?"

"At Phil's apartment, he said. And he said—that's why I know Dick killed him—he said Dick had gone off with his raincoat, and he laughed about it and said he was willing for Dick to have his raincoat if he could have Dick's wife." She was shaking harder now. "And I'll bet that's what he told Dick! I'll bet he said I was coming back and he thought that was a good trade—a raincoat for a wife! That was like Phil!"

She giggled. It started with a giggle, and then the valves burst open and here it came. When something happens in that office to smash a woman's nerves—as it has more than once—it usually falls to me to deal with it. But that time three other guys, led by Ross Chaffee, were on hand, and I was glad to leave Jewel Jones to them. As for Wolfe, he skedaddled. If there is one thing on earth he absolutely will not be in a room with, it's a woman in eruption. He got up and marched out. As for Meegan, Purley and Cramer had him.

When they left with him, they didn't take the dog. To relieve the minds of any of you who have the notion, which I understand is widespread, that it makes a dog neurotic to change its name, I might add that he responds to "Jet" now as if his mother had started calling him that before he had his eyes open.

As for the raincoat, Wolfe had been right about the flash in Meegan's eye. Kampf had been wearing Meegan's raincoat when he was killed, and of course that wouldn't do, so after strangling him Meegan had taken it off and put on the one he thought was Kampf's. Only, it was mine. As a part of the D.A.'s case I went down to headquarters and identified it. At the trial it helped the jury to decide that Meegan deserved the big one. After that was over I suppose I could have claimed it, but the idea didn't appeal to me. My new coat is a different color.

THE THREE WIDOWS

BY ELLERY QUEEN

Ellery Queen is the pseudonym of Manfred B. Lee and Frederic Dannay as well as the name of their fictional private detective. Born in 1905 in Brooklyn, New York, the cousins' first novel was *The Roman Hat Mystery* (1929). Together they produced 35 novels and 79 short stories and novelets before Lee's death in 1971. They won five Edgar awards from the Mystery Writers of America and received the Grand Master Award in 1960. Frederic Dannay is the editor of *Ellery Queen's Mystery Magazine*, now in its thirty-ninth year of publication.

TO THE NORMAL PALATE the taste of murder is unpleasant. But Ellery is an epicure in these matters and certain of his cases, he deposes, possess a flavor which lingers on the tongue. Among these dangerous delicacies he places high "The Case of the Three Widows."

Two of the widows were sisters: Penelope, to whom money was nothing and Lyra, to whom it was everything; consequently, each required large amounts of it. Both having buried thriftless husbands at an early age, they returned to the Murray Hill manse of their father with what everyone suspected was relief, for old Theodore Hood was generously provided with the coin of the Republic and he had always been indulgent with his daughters. Shortly after Penelope and Lyra repossessed their maiden beds, however, Theodore Hood took a second wife, a cathedral-like lady of great force of character. Alarmed, the sisters gave battle, which their stepmother grimly joined. Old Theodore, caught in their crossfire, yearned only for peace. Eventually he found it, leaving a household inhabited by widows exclusively.

One evening not long after their father's death Penelope the plump and Lyra the lean were summoned by a servant to the drawing-room of the Hood pile. They found waiting for them Mr. Strake, the family lawyer.

Mr. Strake's commonest utterance fell like a sentence from the lips of a judge; but tonight, when he pronounced, "Will you be seated, ladies?" his tone was so ominous that the crime was obviously a hanging one. The ladies exchanged glances and declined.

In a few moments the tall doors squealed into the Victorian walls and Sarah Hood came in feebly on the arm of Dr. Benedict, the family physician.

Mrs. Hood surveyed her stepdaughters with a sort of contempt, her head teetering a little. Then she said, "Dr. Benedict and Mr. Strake will speak their pieces, then I'll speak mine."

"Last week," began Dr. Benedict, "your stepmother came to my office for her semi-annual check-up. I gave her the usual thorough examination. Considering her age, I found her in extraordinarily good health. Yet the very next day she came down sick—for the first time, by the way, in eight years. I thought then that she'd picked up an intestinal virus, but Mrs. Hood made a rather different diagnosis. I considered it fantastic. However, she insisted that I make certain tests. I did, and she was right. She had been poisoned."

The plump cheeks of Penelope went slowly pink, and the lean cheeks of Lyra went slowly pale.

"I feel sure," Dr. Benedict went on, addressing a point precisely midway between the sisters, "that you'll understand why I must warn you that from now on I shall examine your stepmother every day."

"Mr. Strake," smiled old Mrs. Hood.

"Under your father's will," said Mr. Strake abruptly, also addressing the equidistant point, "each of you receives a small allowance from the income of the estate. The bulk of that income goes to your stepmother for as long as she shall live. But at Mrs. Hood's demise, you inherit the principal of some two million dollars, in equal shares. In other words, you two are the only persons in the world who will benefit from your stepmother's death. As I've informed both Mrs. Hood and Dr. Benedict, if there is a single repetition of this ghastly business I shall insist on calling in the police."

"Call them now!" cried Penelope.

Lyra said nothing.

"I could call them now, Penny," said Mrs. Hood with the same faint smile, "but you're both very clever and it might not settle anything. My strongest protection would be to throw the two of you out of this house; unfortunately, your father's will prevents me. Oh, I understand your impatience to be rid of me. You have luxurious tastes which aren't satisfied by my simple way of living. You'd both like to remarry, and with the money you could buy second husbands." The old lady leaned forward a little. "But I have bad news for you. My mother died at ninety-nine, my father at a hundred and three. Dr. Benedict tells me I can live another thirty years, and I have every intention of doing so." She struggled to her feet, still smiling. "In fact, I'm taking certain precautions to make sure of it," she said; and then she went out.

Exactly one week later Ellery was seated beside Mrs. Hood's

great mahogany four-poster, under the anxious eyes of Dr. Benedict and Mr. Strake.

She had been poisoned again. Fortunately, Dr. Benedict had caught it in time.

Ellery bent over the old lady's face, which looked more like plaster than flesh. "These precautions of yours, Mrs. Hood—"

"I tell you," she whispered, "it was impossible."

"Still," said Ellery, "it was done. So let's resume. You had your bedroom windows barred and a new lock installed on that door, the single key to which you've kept on your person at all times. You've bought your own food. You've done your own cooking in this room and you've eaten here alone. Clearly, then, the poison could not have been introduced into your food before, during, or after its preparation. Further, you tell me you purchased new dishes, have kept them here, and you and you alone have been handling them. Consequently, the poison couldn't have been put on or in the cooking utensils, china, glassware, or cutlery involved in your meals. How then was the poison administered?"

"That's the problem," cried Dr. Benedict.

"A problem, Mr. Queen," muttered Mr. Strake, "that I thought—and Dr. Benedict agreed—was more your sort of thing than the police's."

"Well, my sort of thing is always simple," replied Ellery, "provided you see it. Mrs. Hood, I'm going to ask you a great many questions. Is it all right, Doctor?"

Dr. Benedict felt the old lady's pulse, and he nodded. Ellery began. She replied in whispers, but with great positiveness. She had bought a new tooth brush and fresh tooth paste for her siege. Her teeth were still her own. She had an aversion to medication and took no drugs or palliatives of any kind. She drank nothing but water. She did not smoke, eat sweets, chew gum, use cosmetics . . . The questions went on and on. Ellery asked every one he could think of, and then he shook up his brain to think of more.

Finally, he thanked Mrs. Hood, patted her hand, and went out with Dr. Benedict and Mr. Strake.

"What's your diagnosis, Mr. Queen?" asked Dr. Benedict.

"Your verdict," said Mr. Strake.

"Gentlemen," said Ellery, "when I eliminated her drinking water by examining the pipes and faucets in her bathroom and finding they hadn't been tampered with, I'd ruled out the last possibility."

"And yet it's being administered orally," snapped Dr. Benedict. "That's my finding and I've been careful to get medical corroboration."

"If that is a fact, Doctor," said Ellery, "then there is only one possible remaining explanation."

"What's that?"

"Mrs. Hood is poisoning herself. If I were you I would call in a psychiatrist. Good day!"

Ten days later Ellery was back in Sarah Hood's bedroom. The old lady was dead. She had succumbed to a third poisoning attack.

On being notified, Ellery had promptly said to his father, Inspector Queen, "Suicide."

But it was not suicide. The most painstaking investigation by police experts, utilizing all the resources of criminological science, failed to turn up a trace of the poison, or of a poison container or other possible source, in Mrs. Hood's bedroom or bath. Scoffing, Ellery went over the premises himself. His smiled vanished. He found nothing to contradict either the old lady's previous testimony or the findings of the experts. He grilled the servants. He examined with remorseless efficiency Penelope, who kept weeping, and Lyra, who kept snarling. Finally, he left.

It was the kind of problem which Ellery's thinking apparatus, against all the protests of his body, cannot let alone. For forty-six hours he lived in his own head, fasting and sleepless, ceaselessly pacing the treadmill of the Queen apartment floor. In the forty-seventh hour Inspector Queen took him by the arm and put him to bed.

"I thought so," said the Inspector. "Over a hundred and one. What hurts, son?"

"My whole existence," mumbled Ellery; and he submitted to aspirins, an ice bag, and a rare steak broiled in butter.

In the middle of the steak he howled like a madman and clawed at the telephone.

"Mr. Strake? Ellery Queen! Meet me at the Hood house immediately!—yes, notify Dr. Benedict!—yes, now I know how Mrs. Hood was poisoned!"

CHALLENGE TO THE READER: *You now have all the facts. Pause and consider: How was Mrs. Hood poisoned?*

And when they were gathered in the cavern of the Hood drawing room Ellery peered at plump Penelope and lean Lyra and he croaked: "Which one of you is intending to marry Dr. Benedict?"

And then he said, "Oh, yes, it has to be that. Only Penelope and Lyra benefit from their stepmother's murder, yet the only person who could physically have committed the murder is Dr. Benedict . . . Did you ask how, Doctor?" asked Ellery. "Why, very simply. Mrs. Hood experienced her first poisoning attack the day after her semi-annual medical check-up—by you, Doctor. And thereafter, you announced, *you would examine Mrs. Hood every day*. There is a classic preliminary to every physician's examination of a patient. I submit, Dr. Benedict," said Ellery with a smile, "that you introduced the poison into Mrs. Hood's mouth on the very thermometer with which you took her temperature."

DANGER OUT OF THE PAST

BY ERLE STANLEY GARDNER

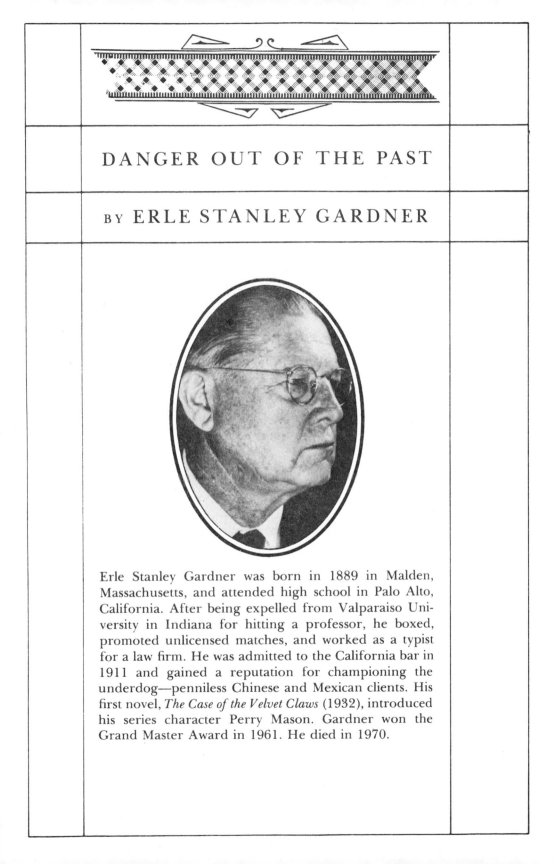

Erle Stanley Gardner was born in 1889 in Malden, Massachusetts, and attended high school in Palo Alto, California. After being expelled from Valparaiso University in Indiana for hitting a professor, he boxed, promoted unlicensed matches, and worked as a typist for a law firm. He was admitted to the California bar in 1911 and gained a reputation for championing the underdog—penniless Chinese and Mexican clients. His first novel, *The Case of the Velvet Claws* (1932), introduced his series character Perry Mason. Gardner won the Grand Master Award in 1961. He died in 1970.

THE ROADSIDE RESTAURANT OOZED an atmosphere of peaceful prosperity. It was a green-painted building set in a white graveled circle in the triangle where two highways joined.

Five miles beyond, a pall of hazy smog marked the location of the city; but out here at the restaurant the air was pure and crystal clear.

George Ollie slid down from the stool behind the cash register and walked over to look out of the window. His face held an expression which indicated physical well-being and mental contentment.

In the seven short years since he had started working as a cook over the big range in the rear he had done pretty well for himself—exceptionally well for a two-time loser—although no one here knew that, of course. Nor did *anyone* know of that last job where a confederate had lost his head and pulled the trigger. . . .

But all that was in the past. George Ollie, president of a luncheon club, member of the Chamber of Commerce, had no connection with the man who had been Prisoner Number 56289.

In a way, however, George owed something of his present prosperity to his criminal record. When he had started work in the restaurant, that bank job which had been "ranked" preyed on his mind. For three years he had been intent on keeping out of circulation. He had stayed in his room nights and had perforce saved all the money that he had made.

So, when the owner's heart had given out and it became necessary for him to sell almost on a moment's notice, George was able to make a down payment in cash. From then on, hard work, careful management, and the chance relocation of a main highway had spelled prosperity for the ex-con.

George turned away from the window, looked over the tables at the symmetrical figure of Stella, the head waitress, as she bent over the table taking the orders of the family that had just entered.

Just as the thrill of pride swept through George whenever he looked at the well-kept restaurant, the graveled parking place, and the constantly accelerating stream of traffic which poured by on the main highways—a traffic which furnished him with a

86

constantly increasing number of customers—so did George thrill with a sense of possessive pride whenever he looked at Stella's smoothly curved figure.

There was no question but what Stella knew how to wear clothes. Somewhere, George thought, there must in Stella's past have been a period of prosperity, a period when she had worn the latest Parisian models with distinction. Now she wore the light blue uniform, with the white starched cuffs above the elbow and the white collar, with that same air of distinction. She not only classed up the uniforms but she classed up the place.

When Stella walked, the lines of her figure rippled smoothly beneath the clothes. Customers looking at her invariably looked again. Yet Stella was always demure, never forward. She smiled at the right time and in the right manner. If the customer tried to get intimate, Stella always managed to create an atmosphere of urgency so that she gave the impression of an amiable, potentially willing young woman too busy for intimacies.

George could tell from the manner in which she put food down at a table and smilingly hurried back to the kitchen, as though on a matter of the greatest importance, just what was being said by the people at the table—whether it was an appreciative acknowledgment of skillful service, good-natured banter, or the attempt by predatory males to make a date.

But George had never inquired into Stella's past. Because of his own history, he had a horror of anything that even hinted of an attempt to inquire into one's past. The present was all that counted.

Stella herself avoided going to the city. She went on a shopping trip once or twice a month, attended an occasional movie, but for the rest stayed quietly at home in the little motel a couple of hundred yards down the roadway.

George was aroused from his reverie by a tapping sound. The man at the counter was tapping a coin on the mahogany. He had entered from the east door and George, contemplating the restaurant, hadn't noticed him.

During this period of slack time in the afternoon Stella was the only waitress on duty. Unexpectedly half a dozen tables had filled up and Stella was busy.

George departed from his customary post at the cash register to approach the man. He handed over a menu, filled a glass with water, arranged a napkin, spoon, knife, and fork, and stood waiting.

The man, his hat pulled well down on his forehead, tossed the menu to one side with a gesture almost of contempt.

"Curried shrimp."

"Sorry," George explained affably, "that's not on the menu today."

"Curried shrimp," the man repeated.

George raised his voice. Probably the other was hard of hearing. "We don't have them today, sir. We have—"

"You heard me," the man said. "Curried shrimp. Go get 'em."

There was something about the dominant voice, the set of the man's shoulders, the arrogance of manner, that tugged at George's memory. Now that he thought back on it, even the contemptuous gesture with which the man had tossed the menu to one side without reading it meant something.

George leaned a little closer.

"Larry!" he exclaimed in horror.

Larry Giffen looked up and grinned. "Georgie!" The way he said the name was contemptuously sarcastic.

"When . . . when did you . . . how did you get out?"

"It's okay, Georgie," Larry said. "*I* went out through the front door. Now go get me the curried shrimp."

"Look, Larry," George said, making a pretense of fighting the feeling of futility this man always inspired, "the cook is cranky. I'm having plenty of trouble with the help and—"

"You heard me," Larry interrupted. "Curried shrimp!"

George met Larry's eyes, hesitated, turned away toward the kitchen.

Stella paused beside the range as he was working over the special curry sauce.

"What's the idea?" she asked.

"A special."

Her eyes studied his face. "How special?"

"*Very* special."

She walked out.

Larry Giffen ate the curried shrimp. He looked around the place with an air of proprietorship.

"Think maybe I'll go in business with you, Georgie."

George Ollie knew from the dryness in his mouth, the feeling of his knees, that that was what he had been expecting.

Larry jerked his head toward Stella. "She goes with the joint."

Ollie, suddenly angry and belligerent, took a step forward. "She doesn't go with anything."

Giffen laughed, turned on his heel, started toward the door, swung back, said, "I'll see you after closing tonight," and walked out.

It wasn't until the period of dead slack that Stella moved close to George.

"Want to tell me?" she asked.

He tried to look surprised. "What?"

"Nothing."

"I'm sorry, Stella. I can't."

"Why not?"

"He's dangerous."

"To whom?"

"To you—to both of us."

She made a gesture with her shoulder. "You never gain anything by running."

He pleaded with her. "Don't get tangled in it, Stella. You remember last night the police were out here for coffee and doughnuts after running around like mad—those two big jobs, the one on the safe in the bank, the other on the theater safe?"

She nodded.

"I should have known then," he told her. "That's Larry's technique. He never leaves them anything to work on. Rubber gloves so there are no fingerprints. Burglar alarms disconnected. Everything like clockwork. No clues. No wonder the police were nuts. Larry Giffen never leaves them a clue."

She studied him. "What's he got on *you?*"

George turned away, then faced her, tried to speak, and couldn't.

"Okay," she said, "I withdraw the question."

Two customers came in, Stella escorted them to a table and went on with the regular routine. She seemed calmly competent, completely unworried. George Ollie, on the other hand, couldn't get his thoughts together. His world had collapsed. Rubber-glove Giffen must have found out about that bank job with the green accomplice, otherwise he wouldn't have dropped in.

News travels fast in the underworld. Despite carefully cultivated changes in his personal appearance, some smart ex-con while eating at the restaurant must have "made" George Ollie. He had said nothing to George, but had reserved the news as an

89

exclusive for the ears of Larry Giffen. The prison underworld knew Big Larry might have use for George—as a farmer might have use for a horse.

And now Larry had "dropped in."

Other customers arrived. The restaurant filled up. The rush-hour waitresses came on. For two and a half hours there was so much business that George had no chance to think. Then business began to slacken. By eleven o'clock it was down to a trickle. At midnight George closed up.

"Coming over?" Stella asked.

"Not tonight," George said. "I want to do a little figuring on a purchase list."

She said nothing and went out.

George locked the doors, put on the heavy double bolts, and yet, even as he turned out the lights and put the bars in place, he knew that bolts wouldn't protect him from what was coming.

Larry Giffen kicked on the door at 12:30.

George, in the shadows, pretended not to hear. He wondered what Larry would do if he found that George had ignored his threat, had gone away and left the place protected by locks and the law.

Larry Giffen knew better. He kicked violently on the door, then turned and banged it with his heel—banged it so hard that the glass rattled and threatened to break.

George hurried out of the shadows and opened the door.

"What's the idea of keeping me waiting, Georgie?" Larry asked with a solicitude that was overdone to the point of sarcasm. "Don't you want to be chummy with your old friend?"

George said, "Larry, I'm on the square. I'm on the legit. I'm staying that way."

Larry threw back his head and laughed. "You know what happens to rats, Georgie."

"I'm no rat, Larry. I'm going straight, that's all. I've paid my debts to the law and to you."

Larry showed big yellowed teeth as he grinned. "Ain't that nice, Georgie. *All* your debts paid! Now how about that National Bank job where Skinny got in a panic because the cashier didn't get 'em up fast enough?"

"I wasn't in on that, Larry."

Larry's grin was triumphant. "Says you! You were handling the getaway car. The cops got one fingerprint from the rear-view mirror. The F.B.I. couldn't classify that one print, but if

90

anyone ever started 'em checking it with *your* file, Georgie, your fanny would be jerked off that cushioned stool by the cash register and transferred to the electric chair—the hot seat, Georgie. . . . You never did like the hot seat, Georgie."

George Ollie licked dry lips. His forehead moistened with sweat. He wanted to say something but there was nothing he could say.

Larry went on talking. "I pulled a couple of jobs here. I'm going to pull just one more. Then I'm moving in with you, Georgie. I'm your new partner. You need a little protection. I'm giving it to you."

Larry swaggered over to the cash register, rang up No Sale, pulled the drawer open, raised the hood over the roll of paper to look at the day's receipts.

"Now, Georgie," he said, regarding the empty cash drawer, "you shouldn't have put away all that dough. Where is it?"

George Ollie gathered all the reserves of his self-respect. "Go to hell," he said. "I've been on the square and I'm going to stay on the square."

Larry strode across toward him. His open left hand slammed against the side of George's face with staggering impact.

"You're hot," Larry said, and his right hand swung up to the other side of George's face. "You're hot, Georgie," and his left hand came up from his hip.

George made a pretense at defending himself but Larry Giffen, quick as a cat, strong as a bear, came after him. "You're hot." . . . Wham . . . "You're hot." . . . Wham . . . "You're hot, Georgie."

At length Larry stepped back. "I'm taking a half interest. You'll run it for me when I'm not here, Georgie. You'll keep accurate books. You'll do all the work. Half of the profits are mine. I'll come in once in a while to look things over. Be damn certain that you don't try any cheating, Georgie.

"You wouldn't like the hot squat, Georgie. You're fat, Georgie. You're well fed. You've teamed up with that swivel-hipped babe, Georgie. I could see it in your eye. She's class, and she goes with the place, Georgie. Remember, I'm cutting myself in for a half interest. I'm leaving it to you to see there isn't any trouble."

George Ollie's head was in a whirl. His cheeks were stinging from the heavy-handed slaps of the big man. His soul felt crushed under a weight. Larry Giffen knew no law but the law of power, and Larry Giffen, his little malevolent eyes glittering with sadistic gloating, was on the move, coming toward him again, hoping for an opportunity to beat up on him.

George hadn't known when Stella had let herself in. Her key had opened the door smoothly.

"What's he got on you, George?" she asked.

Larry Giffen swung to the sound of her voice. "Well, well, little Miss Swivel-hips," he said. "Come here, Swivel-hips. I'm half owner in the place now. Meet your new boss."

She stood still, looking from him to George Ollie.

Larry turned to George.

"All right, Georgie, where's the safe? Give me the combination to the safe, Georgie. As your new partner I'll need to have it. I'll handle the day's take. Later on you can keep books, but right now I need money. I have a heavy date tonight."

George Ollie hesitated a moment, then moved back toward the kitchen.

"I said give *me* the combination to the safe," Larry Giffen said, his voice cracking like a whip.

Stella was looking at him. George had to make it a showdown. "The dough's back here," he said. He moved toward the rack where the big butcher knives were hanging.

Larry Giffen read his mind. Larry had always been able to read him like a book. Larry's hand moved swiftly. A snub-nosed gun nestled in Larry's big hand.

There was murder in the man's eye but his voice remained silky and taunting.

"Now, Georgie, you must be a good boy. Don't act rough. Remember, Georgie, I've done my last time. No one takes Big Larry alive. Give me the combination to the safe, Georgie. And I don't want any fooling!"

George Ollie reached a decision. It was better to die fighting than to be strapped into an electric chair. He ignored the gun, kept moving back toward the knife rack.

Big Larry Giffen was puzzled for a moment. George had always collapsed like a flat tire when Larry had given an order. This was a new George Ollie. Larry couldn't afford to shoot. He didn't want noise and he didn't want to kill.

"Hold it, Georgie! You don't need to get rough." Larry put away his gun. "You're hot on that bank job, Georgie. Remember I can send you to the hot squat. That's all the argument I'm going to use, Georgie. You don't need to go for a shiv.

Just tell me to walk out, Georgie, and I'll leave. Big Larry doesn't stay where he isn't welcome.

"But you'd better welcome me, Georgie boy. You'd better give me the combination to the safe. You'd better take me in as your new partner. Which is it going to be, Georgie?"

It was Stella who answered the question. Her voice was calm and clear. "Don't hurt him. You'll get the money."

Big Larry looked at her. His eyes changed expression. "Now that's the sort of a broad *I* like. Tell your new boss where the safe is. Start talking, babe, and remember you go with the place."

"There isn't any safe," George said hurriedly. "I banked the money."

Big Larry grinned. "You're a liar. You haven't left the place. I've been casing the joint. Go on, babe, tell me where the hell that safe is. Then Georgie here will give his new partner the combination."

"Concealed back of the sliding partition in the pie counter," Stella said.

"Well, well, well," Larry Giffen observed, "isn't *that* interesting?"

"Please don't hurt him," Stella pleaded. "The shelves lift out. . . ."

"Stella!" George Ollie said sharply, "Shut up!"

"The damage has been done now, Georgie boy," Giffen said.

He slid back the glass doors of the pie compartment, lifted out the shelves, put them on the top of the counter, then slid back the partition disclosing the safe door.

"Clever, Georgie boy, clever! You called on your experience, didn't you? And now the combination, Georgie."

Ollie said, "You can't get away with it, Larry. I won't . . . ."

"Now, Georgie boy, don't talk that way. I'm your partner. I'm in here fifty-fifty with you. You do the work and run the place and I'll take my half from time to time. But you've been holding out on me for a while, Georgie boy, so everything that's in the safe is part of my half. Come on with the combination. Of course, I could make a spindle job on it, but since I'm a half owner in the joint I hate to damage any of the property. Then you'd have to buy a new safe. The cost of that would have to come out of your half. You couldn't expect *me* to pay for a new safe."

Rubber-glove Giffen laughed at his little joke.

93

"I said to hell with you," George Ollie said.

Larry Giffen's fist clenched. "I guess you need a damn good working over, Georgie boy. You shouldn't be disrespectful. . . ."

Stella's voice cut in. "Leave him alone. I said you'd get the money. George doesn't want any electric chair."

Larry turned back to her. "I like 'em sensible, sweetheart. Later on, I'll tell you about it. Right now it's all business. Business before pleasure. Let's go."

"Ninety-seven four times to the right," Stella said.

"Well, well, well," Giffen observed. "She knows the combination. We both know what that means, Georgie boy, don't we?"

George, his face red and swollen from the impact of the slaps, stood helpless.

"It means she really is part of the place," Giffen said. "I've got a half interest in you too, girlie. I'm looking forward to collecting on that too. Now what's the rest of the combination?"

Giffen bent over the safe; then, suddenly thinking better of it, he straightened, slipped the snub-nosed revolver into his left hand, and said, "Just so you don't get ideas, Georgie boy—but you wouldn't, you know. You don't like the hot squat."

Stella, white-faced and tense, called out the numbers. Larry Giffen spun the dials on the safe, swung the door open, opened the cash box.

"Well, well, well," he said, sweeping the bills and money into his pocket. "It *was* a good day, wasn't it?"

Stella said, "There's a hundred-dollar bill in the ledger."

Big Larry pulled out the ledger. "So there is, so there is," he said, surveying the hundred-dollar bill with the slightly torn corner. "Girlie, you're a big help. I'm glad you go with the place. I think we're going to get along swell."

Larry straightened, backed away from the safe, stood looking at George Ollie.

"Don't look like that Georgie boy. It isn't so bad. I'll leave you enough profit to keep you in business and keep you interested in the work. I'll just take off most of the cream. I'll drop in to see you from time to time, and, of course, Georgie boy, you won't tell anybody that you've seen me. Even if you did it wouldn't do any good because I came out the front door, Georgie boy. I'm smart. I'm not like you. I don't have something hanging over me where someone can jerk the rug out from under me at any time.

"Well, Georgie boy, I've got to be toddling along. I've got a little job at the supermarket up the street. They put altogether too much confidence in that safe they have. But I'll be back in a couple of hours, Georgie boy. I've collected on part of my investment and now I want to collect on the rest of it. You wait up for me, girlie. You can go get some shut-eye, Georgie."

Big Larry looked at Stella, walked to the door, stood for a moment searching the shadows, then melted away into the darkness.

"You," Ollie said to Stella, his voice showing his heartsickness at her betrayal.

"What?" she asked.

"Telling him about the safe—about that hundred dollars, giving him the combination. . . ."

She said, "I couldn't stand to have him hurt you."

"You and the things you can't stand," Ollie said. "You don't know Rubber-glove Giffen. You don't know what you're in for now. You don't—"

"Shut up," she interrupted. "If you're going to insist on letting other people do your thinking for you, I'm taking on the job."

He looked at her in surprise.

She walked over to the closet, came out with a wrecking bar. Before he had the faintest idea of what she had in mind she walked over to the cash register, swung the bar over her head, and brought it down with crashing impact on the front of the register. Then she inserted the point of the bar, pried back the chrome steel, jerked the drawer open. She went to the back door, unlocked it, stood on the outside, inserted the end of the wrecking bar, pried at the door until she had crunched the wood of the door jamb.

George Ollie was watching her in motionless stupefaction. "What the devil are you doing?" he asked. "Don't you realize . . . ?"

"Shut up," she said. "What's this you once told me about a spindle job? Oh, yes, you knock off the knob and punch out the spindle—"

She walked over to the safe and swung the wrecking bar down on the knob of the combination, knocking it out of its socket, letting it roll crazily along the floor. Then she went to the kitchen, picked out a towel, polished the wrecking bar clean of fingerprints.

"Let's go," she said to George Ollie.

"Where?" he asked.

"To Yuma," she said. "We eloped an hour and a half ago—or hadn't you heard? We're getting married. There's no delay or red tape in Arizona. As soon as we cross the state line we're free to get spliced. You need someone to do your thinking for you. I'm taking the job.

"And," she went on, as George Ollie stood there, "in this state a husband can't testify against his wife, and a wife can't testify against her husband. In view of what I know now it might be just as well."

George stood looking at her, seeing something he had never seen before—a fierce, possessive something that frightened him at the same time it reassured him. She was like a panther protecting her young.

"But I don't get it," George said. "What's the idea of wrecking the place, Stella?"

"Wait until you see the papers," she told him.

"I still don't get it," he told her.

"You will," she said.

George stood for another moment. Then he walked toward her. Strangely enough he wasn't thinking of the trap but of the smooth contours under her pale blue uniform. He thought of Yuma, of marriage and of security, of a home.

It wasn't until two days later that the local newspapers were available in Yuma. There were headlines on an inside page:

RESTAURANT BURGLARIZED WHILE PROPRIETOR ON HONEYMOON

BIG LARRY GIFFEN KILLED IN GUN BATTLE WITH OFFICERS

The newspaper account went on to state that Mrs. George Ollie had telephoned the society editor from Yuma stating that George Ollie and she had left the night before and had been married in the Gretna Green across the state line. The society editor had asked her to hold the phone and had the call switched to the police.

Police asked to have George Ollie put on the line. They had a surprise for him. It seemed that when the merchant patrolman had made his regular nightly check of Ollie's restaurant at one

A.M., he found it had been broken into. Police had found a perfect set of fingerprints on the cash register and on the safe. Fast work had served to identify the fingerprints as those of Big Larry Giffen, known in the underworld as Rubber-glove Giffen because of his skill in wearing rubber gloves and never leaving fingerprints. This was one job that Big Larry had messed up. Evidently he had forgotten his gloves.

Police had mug shots of Big Larry and in no time at all they had out a general alarm.

Only that afternoon George Ollie's head waitress and part-time cashier had gone to the head of the police burglary detail. "In case we should ever be robbed," she had said, "I'd like to have it so you could get a conviction when you get the man who did the job. I left a hundred-dollar bill in the safe. I've torn off a corner. Here's the torn corner. You keep it. That will enable you to get a conviction if you get the thief."

Police thought it was a fine idea. It was such a clever idea they were sorry they couldn't have used it to pin a conviction on Larry Giffen.

But Larry had elected to shoot it out with the arresting officers. Knowing his record, officers had been prepared for this. After the sawed-off shotguns had blasted the life out of Big Larry the police had found the bloodstained hundred-dollar bill in his pocket when his body was stripped at the morgue.

Police also found the loot from three other local jobs on him, cash amounting to some $7000.

Police were still puzzled as to how it happened that Giffen, known to the underworld as the most artistic box man in the business, had done such an amateurish job at the restaurant. Giffen's reputation was that he had never left a fingerprint or a clue.

Upon being advised that his place had been broken into, George Ollie, popular restaurant owner, had responded in a way which was perfectly typical of honeymooners the world over.

"The hell with business," he had told the police. "I'm on my honeymoon."

THE OTHER HANGMAN

BY JOHN DICKSON CARR

John Dickson Carr was born on November 30, 1906, in
Uniontown, Pennsylvania. He was writing for a newspaper, covering sports and murder trials, by the age of
fourteen. His first novel, *It Walks By Night,* was published
in 1930. Two years later he married and moved to England. Carr wrote under his own name and the pseudonyms Carter Dickson and Carr Dickson. His specialty
was locked-room murders and other impossible crimes.
Many of his novels have historical settings. Carr received
the Grand Master Award in 1962. He died on February
27, 1977.

"WHY DO THEY ELECTROCUTE 'em instead of hanging 'em in Pennsylvania? What" (said my old friend, Judge Murchison, dexterously hooking the spittoon closer with his foot) "do they teach you youngsters in these newfangled law schools, anyway?

"That, son, *was* a murder case. It turned the Supreme Court's whiskers gray to find a final ruling, and for thirty years it's been argued about by lawyers in the back room of every saloon from here to the Pacific coast. It happened right here in this county—when they hanged Fred Joliffe for the murder of Randall Fraser.

"It was in '92 or '93; anyway, it was the year they put the first telephone in the courthouse, and you could talk as far as Pittsburgh except when the wires blew down. Considering it was the county seat, we were mighty proud of our town (population 3,500).

"The hustlers were always bragging about how thriving and growing our town was, and we had just got to the point of enthusiasm where every ten years we were certain the census taker must have forgotten half our population. Old Mark Sturgis, who owned the *Bugle Gazette* then, carried on something awful in an editorial when they printed in the almanac that we had a population of only 3,265. We were pretty riled about it.

"We were proud of plenty of other things, too. We had good reason to brag about the McClellan House, which was the finest hotel in the county; and I mind when you could get room and board, with apple pie for breakfast every morning, for two dollars a week. We were proud of our old county families that came over the mountains when Braddock's army was scalped by the Indians in 1755, and settled down in log huts to dry their wounds. But most of all we were proud of our legal batteries.

"Son, it was a grand assembly! Mind, I won't say that all of 'em were long on knowledge of the Statute Books; but they knew their *Blackstone* and their *Greenleaf on Evidence,* and they were powerful speakers. *And* there were some—the topnotchers—full of graces and book knowledge and dignity, who were hell on the exact letter of the law.

"Scotch-Irish Presbyterians, all of us, who loved a good debate and a bottle o' whiskey. There was Charley Connell, a

Harvard graduate and the District Attorney, who had fine white hands, and wore a fine high collar, and made such pathetic addresses to the jury that people flocked for miles around to hear him; though he generally lost his cases. There was Judge Hunt, who prided himself on his resemblance to Abe Lincoln, and so always wore a frock coat and an elegant plug hat.

"Why, there was your own grandfather, who had over two hundred books in his library, and people used to go up nights to borrow volumes of the encyclopedia.

"You know the big stone courthouse at the top of the street, with the flowers round it, and the jail adjoining? People went there as they'd go to a picture show nowadays; it was a lot better, too. Well, from there it was only two minutes walk across the meadow to Jim Riley's saloon. All the cronies gathered there—in the back room of course, where Jim had an elegant brass spittoon and a picture of George Washington on the wall to make it dignified. You could see the footpath worn across the grass until they built over that meadow.

"Besides the usual crowd, there was Bob Moran, the Sheriff, a fine strapping big fellow, but very nervous about doing his duty strictly. And there was poor old Nabors, a big, quiet, reddish-eyed fellow, who'd been a doctor before he took to drink. He was always broke, and he had two daughters—one of 'em consumptive—and Jim Riley pitied him so much that he gave him all he wanted to drink for nothing.

"Those were fine happy days, with a power of eloquence and theorizing and solving the problems of the nation in that back room, until our wives came to fetch us home.

"Then Randall Fraser was murdered, and there was hell to pay.

"Now if it had been anybody else but Fred Joliffe who killed him, naturally we wouldn't have convicted. You can't do it, son, not in a little community. It's all very well to talk about the power and grandeur of justice, and sounds fine in a speech. But here's somebody you've seen walking the streets about his business every day for years; and you know when his kids were born, and saw him crying when one of 'em died and you remember how he loaned you ten dollars when you needed it. . . .

"Well, you can't take that person out in the cold light of day and string him up by the neck until he's dead. You'd always be seeing the look on his face afterwards. And you'd find excuses for him no matter what he did.

"But with Fred Joliffe it was different. Fred Joliffe was the worst and nastiest customer we ever had, with the possible exception of Randall Fraser himself. Ever seen a copperhead curled up on a flat stone? And a copperhead's worse than a rattlesnake—that won't strike unless you step on it, and gives warning before it does.

"Fred Joliffe had the same brownish color and sliding movements. You always remembered his pale little eyes and his nasty grin. When he drove his cart through town—he had some sort of rag-and-bone business, you understand—you'd see him sitting up there, a skinny little man in a brown coat, peeping round the side of his nose to find something for gossip. And grinning.

"It wasn't merely the things he said about people behind their backs. Or to their faces, for that matter, because he relied on the fact that he was too small to be thrashed. He was a slick customer. It was believed that he wrote those anonymous letters that caused . . . but never mind that.

"Anyhow, I can tell you his little smirk *did* drive Will Farmer crazy one time, and Will *did* beat him within an inch of his life. Will's livery stable was burned down one night about a month later, with eleven horses inside, but nothing could ever be proved. He was too smart for us.

"That brings me to Fred Joliffe's only companion—I don't mean friend. Randall Fraser had a harness-and-saddle store in Market Street, a dusty place with a big dummy horse in the window. I reckon the only thing in the world Randall liked was that dummy horse, which was a dappled mare with vicious-looking glass eyes. He used to keep its mane combed.

"Randall was a big man with a fine mustache, a horseshoe pin in his tie, and sporty checked clothes. He was buttery polite, and mean as sin. He thought a dirty trick or a swindle was the funniest joke he ever heard. But the women liked him—a lot of them, it's no use denying, sneaked in at the back door of that harness store. Randall itched to tell it at the barber shop, to show what fools they were and how virile he was; but he had to be careful. He and Fred Joliffe did a lot of drinking together.

"Then the news came. It was in October, I think, and I heard it in the morning when I was putting on my hat to go down to the office. Old Withers was the Town Constable then. He got up early in the morning, although there was no need for it; and when he was going down Market Street in the mist about five

101

o'clock, he saw the gas still burning in the back room of Randall's store.

"The front door was wide open. Withers went in and found Randall lying on a pile of harness in his shirtsleeves, and his forehead and face bashed in with a wedging mallet. There wasn't much left of the face, but you could recognize him by his mustache and his horseshoe pin.

"I was in my office when somebody yelled up from the street that they had found Fred Joliffe drunk and asleep in the flour mill, with blood on his hands and an empty bottle of Randall Fraser's whiskey in his pocket. He was still in bad shape, and couldn't walk or understand what was going on, when the Sheriff—that was Bob Moran I told you about—came to take him to the lockup.

"Bob had to drive him in his own rag-and-bone cart. I saw them drive up Market Street in the rain, Fred lying in the back of the cart all white with flour, and rolling and cursing. People were very quiet. They were pleased, but they couldn't show it.

"That is, all except Will Farmer, who had owned the livery stable that was burned down.

" 'Now, by God, they'll hang him,' says Will.

"It's a funny thing, son: I didn't realize the force of that until I heard Judge Hunt pronounce sentence after the trial. They appointed me to defend him, because I was a young man without any particular practice, and somebody had to do it. The evidence was all over town before I got a chance to speak with Fred.

"You could see he was done for. A scissors grinder who lived across the street (I forget his name now) had seen Fred go into Randall's place about eleven o'clock. An old couple who lived up over the store had heard 'em drinking and yelling downstairs; at near on midnight they'd heard a noise like a fight and a fall; but they knew better than to interfere. Finally, a couple of farmers driving home from town at midnight had seen Fred stumble out of the front door, slapping his clothes and wiping his hands on his coat like a man with delirium tremens.

"I went to see Fred at the jail. He was sober, although he jerked a good deal. Those pale watery eyes of his were as poisonous as ever. I can still see him sitting on the bunk in his cell, sucking a brown-paper cigarette, wriggling his neck, and jeering at me. He wouldn't tell me anything, because he said I would go and tell the judge if he did.

" 'Hang *me*?' he says, and wrinkled his nose and jeered again. 'Hang *me*? Don't you worry about that, mister. Them so-and-so's will never hang me. They're too much afraid of me, them so-and-so's are. Eh, mister?'

"And the fool couldn't get it through his head right up until the sentence. He strutted in court, making smart remarks, and threatening to tell what he knew about people, and calling the judge by his first name. He wore a new dickey shirt-front he bought to look spruce in.

"I was surprised how quietly everybody took it. The people who came to the trial didn't whisper or shove; they just sat still as death and looked at him. All you could hear was a kind of breathing.

"It's funny about a courtroom, son: it has its own particular smell, which won't bother you unless you get to thinking about what it means; but you notice worn places and cracks in the walls more than you would anywhere else. You would hear Charley Connell's voice for the prosecution, a little thin sound in a big room, and Charley's footsteps creaking. You would hear a cough in the audience, or a woman's dress rustle, or the gas jets whistling. It was dark in the rainy season, so they lit the gas jets by two o'clock in the afternoon.

"The only defense I could make was that Fred had been too drunk to be responsible, and remembered nothing of that night (which he admitted was true). But, in addition to being no defense in law, it was a terrible frost besides. My own voice sounded wrong.

"I remember that six of the jury had whiskers, and six hadn't; and Judge Hunt, up on the bench with the flag draped on the wall behind his head, looked more like Abe Lincoln than ever. Even Fred Joliffe began to notice. He kept twitching round to look at the people, a little uneasy-like. Once he stuck out his neck at the jury and screeched, '*Say* something, can'tcha? Do something, can'tcha?'

"They did.

"When the foreman of the jury said, 'Guilty of murder in the first degree,' there was just a little noise from those people. Not a cheer, or anything like that. It hissed out all together, only once, like breath released, but it was terrible to hear. It didn't hit Fred until Judge Hunt was halfway through pronouncing sentence.

"Fred stood looking round with a wild, half-witted expression until he heard Judge Hunt say, '*And may God have mercy on your soul.*' Then he burst out, kind of pleading and kidding as though this was carrying the joke too far. He said, 'Listen, now, you don't *mean* that, do you? You can't fool me. You're only Jerry Hunt; I know who you are. You can't do that to me.' All of a sudden he began pounding the table and screaming, 'You ain't really a-goin' to hang me, are you?'

"But we were.

"The date of execution was fixed for the twelfth of November. The order was all signed. '. . . within the precincts of the said county jail, between the hours of eight and nine A.M., the said Frederick Joliffe shall be hanged by the neck until he is dead; an executioner to be commissioned by the Sheriff for this purpose, and the sentence to be carried out in the presence of a qualified medical practitioner; the body to be interred . . .' And the rest of it.

"Everybody was nervous. There hadn't been a hanging since any of that crowd had been in office, and nobody knew how to go about it exactly. Old Doc Macdonald, the Coroner, was to be there; and of course they got hold of Reverend Phelps, the preacher; and Bob Moran's wife was going to cook pancakes and sausage for the last breakfast.

"Maybe you think that's fool talk. But think for a minute of taking somebody you've known all your life, and binding his arms one cold morning, and walking him out in your own back yard to crack his neck on a rope—all religious and legal, with not a soul to interfere. Then you begin to get scared of the powers of life and death, and the thin partition between.

"Bob Moran was scared white for fear things wouldn't go off properly. He had appointed big, slow-moving, tipsy Ed Nabors as hangman. This was partly because Ed Nabors needed the fifty dollars that was the fee, and partly because Bob had a vague idea that an ex-medical man would be better able to manage an execution. Ed had sworn to keep sober; Bob Moran said he wouldn't get a dime unless he *was* sober; but you couldn't always tell.

"Nabors seemed in earnest. He had studied up the matter of scientific hanging in an old book he borrowed from your grandfather, and he and the carpenter had knocked together a big, shaky-looking contraption in the jail yard.

"It worked all right in practice, with sacks of meal; the trap went down with a boom that brought your heart up in your throat. But once they allowed for too much spring in the rope and it tore a sack apart. Then old Doc Macdonald chipped in about that fellow John Lee, in England—and it nearly finished Bob Moran.

"That was late on the night before the execution. We were sitting round the lamp in Bob's office, trying to play stud poker. There were tops and skipping ropes, all kinds of toys, all over that office. Bob let his kids play in there—which he shouldn't have done, because the door out of it led to a corridor of cells with Fred Joliffe in the last one.

"Of course, the few other prisoners, disorderlies and chicken thieves and the like, had been moved upstairs. Somebody had told Bob that the scent of an execution affects 'em like a cage of wild animals. Whoever it was, he was right. We could hear 'em shifting and stamping over our heads.

"Well, it was raining hard on the tin roof; maybe that was what put Doc Macdonald in mind of it. Doc was a cynical old devil. When he saw that Bob couldn't sit still, and would throw in his hand without even looking at the buried card, Doc says, 'Yes, I hope it'll go off all right. But you want to be careful about that rain. Did you read about that fellow they tried to hang in England?—and the rain had swelled the boards so's the trap wouldn't fall? They stuck him on it three times, but still it wouldn't work. . . .'

"Ed Nabors slammed his hand down on the table. I reckon he felt bad enough as it was, because one of his daughters had run away and left him, and the other was dying of consumption. But he was twitchy and reddish about the eyes; he hadn't had a drink for two days, although there was a bottle on the table.

"Nabors says, 'You shut up or I'll kill you. Damn you, Macdonald,' he says, and grabs the edge of the table. 'I tell you nothing *can* go wrong. I'll go out and test the thing again, if you'll let me put the rope round your neck.'

"And Bob Moran, says, 'What do you want to talk like that for anyway, Doc? Ain't it bad enough as it is?' he says. 'Now you've got me worrying about something else,' he says. 'I went down there a while ago to look at him, and he said the funniest thing, I ever heard Fred Joliffe say. He's crazy. He giggled and said God wouldn't let them so-and-so's hang him. It was terrible, hearing Fred Joliffe talk like that. What time is it, somebody?'

"It was cold that night. I dozed off in a chair, hearing the rain, and that animal cage snuffing upstairs. An old man was

105

singing that part of the hymn about while the nearer waters roll, while the tempest still is high.

"They woke me about half-past eight to say that Judge Hunt and all the witnesses were out in the jail yard, and they were ready to start the march. Then I realized that they were really going to hang him after all. I had to join behind the procession as I was sworn, but I didn't see Fred Joliffe's face and I didn't want to see it.

"They had given him a good wash, and a clean flannel shirt that they tucked under at the neck. He stumbled coming out of the cell and started to go in the wrong direction; but Bob Moran and the Constable each had him by one arm. It was a cold dark windy morning. His hands were tied behind.

"The preacher was saying something I couldn't catch. Everything went off smoothly enough until they got halfway across the jail yard. It's a pretty big yard. I didn't look at the contraption in the middle, but at the witnesses standing over against the wall with their hats off; and I smelled the clean air after the rain, and looked up at the mountains where the sky was getting pink.

"But Fred Joliffe did look at it, and went down flat on his knees. They hauled him up again. I heard them keep on walking, and go up the steps, which were creaky.

"I didn't look at the contraption until I heard a thumping sound, and we all knew something was wrong.

"Fred Joliffe was not standing on the trap, nor was the bag pulled over his head, although his legs were strapped. He stood with his eyes closed and his face towards the pink sky. Ed Nabors was clinging with both hands to the rope, twirling round a little and stamping on the trap. It didn't budge.

"Just then I heard Ed crying something about the rain having swelled the boards, and Judge Hunt ran past me to the foot of the contraption.

"Bob Moran started cursing. 'Put him on and try it, anyway,' he says, and grabs Fred's arm. 'Stick that bag over his head and give the thing a chance.'

" 'In His name,' says the preacher, 'you'll not do it if I can help it.'

"Bob ran over like a crazy man and jumped on the trap with both feet. It was stuck fast. Then Bob turned round and pulled an Ivor-Johnson forty-five out of his hip pocket. Judge Hunt got in front of Fred, whose lips were moving a little.

106

" 'He'll have the law, and nothing but the law,' says Judge Hunt. 'Put that gun away, you lunatic, and take him back to the cell until you can make the thing work. Easy with him, now.'

"To this day I don't think Fred Joliffe realized what had happened. I believe he only had his belief confirmed that they never meant to hang him after all. When he found himself going down the steps again, he opened his eyes. His face looked shrunken and dazed-like, but then it came to him in a blaze.

" 'I knew them so-and-so's would never hang me,' says he. His throat was so dry he couldn't spit at Judge Hunt, as he tried to do; but he marched straight and giggling across the yard. 'I knew them so-and-so's would never hang me,' he says.

"We all had to sit down a minute, and we had to give Ed Nabors a drink. Bob made him hurry up, although we didn't say much, and he was leaving to fix the trap again when the courthouse janitor came bustling into Bob's office.

" 'Call,' says he, 'on the new machine over there. Telephone.'

" 'Lemme out of here!' yells Bob. 'I can't listen to no telephone calls now. Come out and give us a hand.'

" 'But it's from Harrisburg,' says the janitor. 'It's from the Governor's office. You got to go.'

" 'Stay here, Bob.' says Judge Hunt. He beckons to me. 'Stay here, and I'll answer it,' he says.

"We looked at each other in a queer way when we went across the Bridge of Sighs. The courthouse clock was striking nine, and I could look down into the yard and see people hammering at the trap.

"After Judge Hunt had listened to that telephone call he had a hard time putting the receiver back on the hook.

" 'I always believed in Providence, in a way,' says he, 'but I never thought it was so personal-like. Fred Joliffe is innocent. We're to call off this business,' says he, 'and wait for a messenger from the Governor. He's got the evidence of a woman ... Anyway, we'll hear it later.'

"Now, I'm not much of a hand at describing mental states, so I can't tell you exactly what we felt then. Most of all was a fever and horror for fear they had already whisked Fred out and strung him up.

"But when we looked down into the yard from the Bridge of Sighs, we saw Ed Nabors and the carpenter arguing over a cross-cut saw on the trap itself; and the blessed morning light coming up in glory to show us we could knock that ugly con-

107

traption to pieces and burn it. The corridor downstairs was deserted. Judge Hunt had got his wind back, and being one of those stern elocutionists who like to make complimentary remarks about God, he was going on something powerful. He sobered up when he saw the door to Fred Joliffe's cell was open.

" 'Even Joliffe,' says the Judge, 'deserves to get this news first.'

"But Fred never did get that news, unless his ghost was listening. I told you he was very small and light. His heels were a good eighteen inches off the floor as he hung by the neck from an iron peg in the wall of the cell.

"He was hanging from a noose made in a child's skipping rope—black-faced dead already, with the whites of his eyes showing in slits, heels swinging over a kicked-away stool.

"No, son, we didn't think it was suicide for long. For a little while we were stunned, half crazy, naturally. It was like thinking about your troubles at three o'clock in the morning.

"But, you see, Fred's hands were still tied behind him. There was a bump on the back of his head, from a hammer that lay beside the stool. Somebody had walked in there with the hammer concealed behind his back, had stunned Fred when he wasn't looking, had run a slipknot in that skipping rope, and jerked him up a-flapping to strangle there.

"It was the creepiest part of the business, when we'd got that through our heads, and we all began loudly to tell each other where we'd been during the confusion. Nobody had noticed much and I was scared green.

"When we gathered round the table in Bob's office, Judge Hunt took hold of his nerve with both hands. He looked at Bob Moran, at Ed Nabors, at Doc Macdonald, and at me. One of us was the other hangman.

" 'This is a bad business, gentlemen,' says he, clearing his throat a couple of times like a nervous orator before he starts. 'What I want to know is, who under sanity would strangle a man when he thought we intended to do it anyway, on a gallows?'

"Then Doc Macdonald turned nasty. 'Well,' says he, 'if it comes to that, you might inquire where that skipping rope came from to begin with.'

" 'I don't get you,' says Bob Moran, bewildered-like.

" 'Oh, don't you?' says Doc, and sticks out his whiskers. 'Well, then, who was so dead set on this execution going through as

108

scheduled that he wanted to use a gun when the trap wouldn't drop?'

"Bob made a noise as though he'd been hit in the stomach. He stood looking at Doc for a minute, with his hands hanging down—and then he went for him. He had Doc back across the table, banging his head on the edge, when people began to crowd into the room at the yells. Funny, too; the first one in was the jail carpenter, who was pretty sore at not being told that the hanging had been called off.

" 'What do you want to start fighting for?' he says, fretful-like. He was bigger than Bob, and had him off Doc with a couple of heaves. 'Why didn't you tell me what was going on? They say there ain't going to be any hanging. Is that right?'

"Judge Hunt nodded, and the carpenter—Barney Hicks, that's who it was, I remember now—Barney Hicks looked pretty peevish, and says, 'All right, all right, but you hadn't ought to fight all over the joint like that.'

"Then he looks at Ed Nabors. 'What I want is my hammer. Where's my hammer, Ed? I been looking all over the place for it. What did you do with it?'

"Ed Nabors sits up, pours himself four fingers of rye, and swallows it.

" 'Beg pardon, Barney,' says he in the coolest voice I ever heard. 'I must have left it in the cell,' he says, 'when I killed Fred Joliffe.'

"Talk about silences! It was like one of those silences when the magician at the Opera House fires a gun and six doves fly out of an empty box. I just couldn't believe it.

"But I remember Ed Nabors sitting big in the corner by the barred window, in his shiny black coat and string tie. His hands were on his knees, and he was looking from one to the other of us, smiling a little. He looked as old as the prophets then; and he'd got enough liquor to keep the nerve from twitching beside his eye.

"He just sat there, very quietly, shifting the plug of tobacco around in his cheek, and smiling.

" 'Judge,' he says in a reflective way, 'you got a call from the Governor at Harrisburg, didn't you? Uh-huh. I knew what it would be. A woman had come forward, hadn't she, to confess Fred Joliffe was innocent and *she* had killed Randall Fraser? Uh-huh. The woman was my daughter. Jessie couldn't face telling it here, you see. That was why she went to the Governor.

109

She'd have kept quiet if you hadn't convicted Fred.'

" 'But why . . .' shouts the Judge. *Why?*'

" 'It was like this,' Ed goes on in that slow way of his. 'She'd been on pretty intimate terms with Randall Fraser, Jessie had. And both Randall and Fred were having a whooping lot of fun threatening to tell the whole town about it. She was pretty near crazy, I think. And on the night of the murder Fred Joliffe was too drunk to remember anything that happened. He thought he *had* killed Randall, I suppose, when he woke up and found Randall dead and blood on his hands.

" 'It's all got to come out now, I suppose,' says he, nodding. 'What did happen was that the three of 'em were in that back room, which Fred didn't remember. He and Randall had a fight while they were baiting Jessie. Fred whacked him hard enough with that mallet to lay him out, but all the blood he got was from a big splash over Randall's eye. Jessie . . . well, Jessie finished the job when Fred ran away, that's all.'

" 'But, you damned fool,' cries Bob Moran, and begins to pound the table, 'why did you have to go and kill Fred when Jessie had confessed?'

" 'You fellows wouldn't have convicted Jessie, would you?' says Ed, blinking round at us. 'No. But if Fred had lived after her confession, you'd have *had* to, boys. That was how I figured it out. Once Fred learned what did happen, that he wasn't guilty and she was, he'd never have let up until he'd carried that case to the Superior Court out of your hands.

" 'He'd have screamed all over the State until they either had to hang her or send her up for life. I couldn't stand that. As I say, that was how I figured it out, although my brain's not so clear these days. So,' says he, nodding and leaning over to take aim at the cuspidor, 'when I heard about that telephone call, I went into Fred's cell and finished *my* job.'

" 'But don't you understand,' says Judge Hunt, in the way you'd reason with a lunatic, 'that Bob Moran will have to arrest you for murder, and—'

It was the peacefulness of Ed's expression that scared us then. He got up from his chair, dusted his shiny black coat, and smiled at us.

" 'Oh, no,' says he very clearly. 'That's what you *don't* understand. You can't do a single damned thing to me. You can't even arrest me.'

" 'He's bughouse,' says Bob Moran.

" 'Am I?' says Ed affably. 'Listen to me. I've committed what you might call a perfect murder, because I've done it legally . . . Judge, what time did you talk to the Governor's office and get the order for the execution to be called off? Be careful now.'

"And I said, with the whole idea of the business suddenly hitting me, 'It was maybe five minutes past nine, wasn't it, Judge? I remember the courthouse clock striking when we were going over the Bridge of Sighs.'

" 'I remember it too,' says Ed Nabors. 'And Doc Macdonald will tell you that Fred Joliffe was dead before ever that clock struck nine. I have in my pocket,' says he, unbuttoning his coat, 'a court order which authorizes me to kill Fred Joliffe, by means of hanging by the neck—which I did—between the hours of eight and nine in the morning—which I also did. And I did it in full legal style before the order was countermanded. Well?'

"Judge Hunt took off his stovepipe hat and wiped his face with a bandana. We all looked at him.

" 'You can't get away with this,' says the Judge, and grabs the Sheriff's order off the table. 'You can't trifle with the law in that way. And you can't execute sentence alone. Look here! "In the presence of a qualified medical practitioner." What do you say to that?'

" 'Well, I can produce my medical diploma,' says Ed, nodding again. 'I may be a booze-hister, and mighty unreliable, but they haven't struck me off the register yet. . . . You lawyers are hell on the wording of the law,' says he admiringly, 'and it's the wording that's done for you this time. Until you get the law altered with some fancy words, there's nothing in that document to say that the doctor and the hangman can't be the same person.'

"After a while Bob Moran turned round to the Judge with a funny expression on his face. It might have been a grin.

" 'This ain't according to morals,' says he. 'A fine citizen like Fred shouldn't get murdered like that. It's awful. Something's got to be done about it. As you said yourself this morning, Judge, he ought to have the law and nothing but the law. Is Ed right, Judge?'

" 'Frankly, I don't know,' says Judge Hunt, wiping his face again. 'But so far as I know, he is. What are you doing, Robert?'

" 'I'm writing him out a check for fifty dollars,' says Bob Moran, surprised-like. 'We got to have it all nice and legal, haven't we?' "

DEATH CERTIFICATE

By GEORGE HARMON COXE

George Harmon Coxe was born on April 23, 1901, in Olean, New York, and spent a year each at Purdue and Cornell Universities. He worked in a lumber camp and an automobile factory before becoming a newspaper-man. In 1922 his stories appeared in *The American Boy* and *Detective Story*. He worked in advertising for three years and then returned to writing. His best known novel is *The Groom Lay Dead* (1944). Coxe wrote scripts for radio, television, and movies, and was a war correspondent during World War II. He received the Grand Master Award in 1963.

IN THE TWO YEARS that Dr. Paul Standish had acted as the city's medical examiner he had become acquainted with death in nearly all its violent forms, but not until the night Dr. Cheney was found dead had it ever occurred to him that the performance of his duty might some day become a personal matter.

The call from the telegraph bureau awakened him shortly after two thirty that morning. By the time he had dressed, a police car was waiting at the curb, and he rode along deserted pavements to the north side of town near the river. Here, in a street of grimy loft buildings and tenements, another police car had been backed around so that its headlights focused into an alleyway.

One of the officers gathered there spoke to Standish and he answered automatically, having no preparation for what came next, yet knowing in his first glance that the man who lay sprawled on the dusty cobblestones had been murdered. The back of the head was broken and bloody, and because he had become accustomed to approach each case as a diagnostician and view it with a clinical eye, he noticed the nondescript character of the worn suit and topcoat, and found them in keeping with the telegraph bureau's announcement. An unidentified man, the bureau had said, and that was what Paul Standish had expected until he turned the body over and realized that this man had once been his friend.

Recognition was swift and left him shaken and sick inside. The night air was suddenly cool and though he heard one of the officers speak, it was some seconds before he could recover from the shock and think reasonably.

"We went through his pockets as well as we could without moving him," the officer said. "Looks like he's clean. We figure some muggers slugged him on the walk and dragged him in here out of sight."

Standish forced himself to concentrate. He made sure about the pockets as he made his preliminary tests for *rigor mortis*. He knew then that there was nothing more to be done here; he knew that insofar as his job was concerned, his work, which was to determine the cause of death, was finished. Yet now, as his thoughts went back to the Dr. Cheney he had known ten years before when he was a young intern at City Hospital, he knew that it was not enough to write a report which said that this same Dr. Cheney had been murdered by a blunt instrument, and he turned to ask whose beat this was.

"Mine, sir," said a uniformed husky. "My flashlight picked him up when I turned in here at two fifteen on my way down the street."

"Did you turn it in here on your previous round? At what time?"

"One fifteen, sir. And there was no sign of him."

Standish straightened, a moderately tall man with good shoulders and a well-boned face that looked lean and angular in the glare of the headlights. For another moment he stared beyond the body, his eyes obscured and his normally easy mouth a tight grim line; then, speaking quietly, he asked if anyone was here from homicide.

"I am," a voice said. "Sergeant Wargo."

Standish recognized the man as an assistant of Lieutenant Ballard's. He had hoped Ballard would be here; he needed him now but he did not ask about the lieutenant who was his friend. He merely nodded as he heard the ambulance draw to a stop in the street, and asked the sergeant to wait.

Five minutes later, when the body had been removed, they stood on the sidewalk and Wargo, a young man of intelligence and ability who had not yet asked a question nor offered an opinion, said:

"We're pretty sure he was dragged into the alley, Doctor."

"Yes," Standish said. "But he wasn't killed on the sidewalk. He'd been dead at least three hours when I examined him."

Wargo whistled softly. Then, as though held by something in the doctor's manner that he did not understand, he said, "Do you know him?"

Standish nodded and took time to marshal his thoughts, knowing now that he would not be going back to bed and knowing also that he would need help.

"Ballard's not on call?"

"Not tonight," Wargo said. "The captain told him to get some rest because he's been going steadily ever since yesterday morning when Frankie Montanari jumped his bail. So has everybody in the department." Wargo grunted softly. "Even homicide, because I guess they figure when they find Frankie, it'll be a homicide job."

114

Dr. Standish had no interest in Montanari who had been about to be sentenced for bribery in a gambling case when he disappeared. The newspapers had intimated that the length of the sentence would depend on whether or not Montanari disclosed the real boss of the gambling syndicate that employed him, but Standish felt only annoyance that such a case should rob him of Lieutenant Ballard's help.

"I'm going to the morgue," he said, and then, standing beside the police car, he told Sergeant Wargo what he wanted him to do.

Dr. Cheney had as his office and living quarters the lower floor of a two-family house which stood on the east side of town in a neighborhood no more than a cut or two above the slums. There was a police car out front when Standish arrived and Sergeant Wargo was sitting on the steps waiting for him.

"The guy upstairs owns the place," Wargo said. "I got the key from him. This coupe"—he indicated a battered car in front of the police sedan—"is Doc Cheney's. There's no doctor's bag in it and I didn't find any in the office. You can have a look if you want."

Standish went into a poorly-furnished waiting room overlooking the porch. He inspected the adjoining private office and the living quarters beyond, finding no signs of prosperity and knowing finally that the bag, without which Cheney would never have made a professional call, was not here. Then, because he did not understand this any more than he understood the dead man's empty pockets, he examined the appointment book on the desk. "He made his last call at five."

"The guy upstairs saw him come in around six," Wargo said. "He thinks he went out around nine."

"What makes him think so?"

"He heard the doorbell ring, heard the doc answer it. He thinks he went out."

It was nearly six o'clock when Paul Standish reached his apartment and though he undressed, he did not go to bed but sat by the window and tried to find some reason for a murder that on the face of it seemed utterly senseless. That it was not his job to do so did not occur to him at all until Lieutenant Ballard put it into words at eight thirty that morning in his office at police headquarters, when Standish showed up there.

They had worked together often, these two, though it was generally Ballard who yelled for help and Dr. Standish who maintained it was not his job to do detective work. This time the shoe was on the other foot and though the lieutenant heard him out, he offered no encouragement, nor even agreement with the doctor's theory.

"Sergeant Wargo thinks it was a hold-up job," he said. "And I've got to go along. A couple of young punks jumped Cheney and maybe he gave them an argument and they sapped him— too hard."

"Three hours before he was found?"

"So what? Maybe it happened in their neighborhood and they got scared and went back and moved him. Hell, I can think of a dozen answers to that one."

Standish tried to be patient. "Someone called for Cheney at nine o'clock, otherwise he would have taken his car. He took his bag with him because it wasn't in his office. He's not found until three hours after he's killed and there's no bag, no identification on him. If I hadn't known him, he might have lain in the morgue for days before we knew who he was, and I say that doesn't shape up as a mugging job."

Ballard ran his fingers through his sandy hair and his shrewd gray eyes were troubled. He recognized sound reasoning when he heard it but he was a harried man just now, conscious of pressure from above that demanded he and every man on the force find a missing gambler named Frankie Montanari, an assignment which was a little out of his line.

"Look, Paul," he said, "right now I can't agree with you. I think a couple of thugs did the job and you know how we catch guys like that. We add some men to the district and keep our eyes open and the punks keep trying the same racket until we catch up with them. Before we get through, we'll know what jobs they've pulled. This Cheney thing will turn out to be one of 'em." He took a breath and said, "But even if I'm wrong, what do you want me to do?"

Paul Standish started to speak, then checked his reply when he realized it was inadequate. He took a moment to think, aware that if Ballard was right, there was nothing more to be done. But if Ballard was wrong, there could only be one answer: that Cheney had been killed deliberately and for a definite and clear-cut reason.

He wanted to know what that reason was. Like any good

diagnostician, he wanted to know why. Yet when he spoke of this, it sounded silly, even to him.

"I want to know why."

Ballard sighed heavily and threw up his hands. "Find Montanari and I'll put twenty men on it. Maybe they can answer you. I can't." He paused, gray eyes half-closed. "Who was this Cheney, a brother of yours or something?"

Mary Hayward asked Paul Standish a similar question at eleven thirty, after the last of his office patients had been taken care of. Mary, his nurse, secretary and Girl Friday, had medium-blonde hair and green eyes and a nicely-modeled figure. She was jealous of Standish's time and quite possibly of his affections. She believed he was wasting his talent as medical examiner, arguing that he would be much further ahead if he put this time into his own practice. And because she was young and forthright she spoke not too kindly about Dr. Cheney.

"I can't understand why you bother," she said. "I've heard you speak of him. I thought he was a bum."

Standish eyed her somberly, but because he was used to her ways and understood in some measure what was behind them, he took no offense at her words.

"He was no bum, Mary. He was resident physician at City Hospital when I was interning. He was a very nice guy."

"Ten years ago."

"He was a nice guy today. Weak, maybe. That's the worst you could say about him. You could call him a failure—a lot of people did—but he was a good doctor and I don't believe he ever consciously did a dishonest or unethical thing in his life."

He hesitated, no longer seeing Mary as his mind turned back. Speaking more to himself than to her, he told how Dr. Cheney had left the hospital to give all his time to his own practice and how, the following winter, a truck had skidded out of control and killed his wife and the two-year-old son she had been carrying across the street.

"Some people can take a thing like that and others can't. Cheney couldn't. It took the heart out of him and he closed his office. I don't know what was in his mind or what he wanted to do; I do know that it was the best thing that ever happened to those people in his neighborhood when he turned his back on the society he knew and opened that east side office. He collected enough to live on and if you wanted medical treatment you got it from Cheney no matter who you were."

117

The quiet sincerity of the young doctor's words impressed the girl and her eyes were soft and concerned. She said she was sorry, that she hadn't understood, and she remained that way until Standish glanced at his watch and stood up. When he said he was going to the morgue, and from there to the district attorney's office, Mary said:

"Don't forget your two o'clock appointment with Mr. Lane."

Standish frowned. "Cancel it. Call him up and—"

Mary interrupted him, her voice horrified and then indignant. She said that Mr. Lane was rich and that the thorough physical checkup that Standish was to give him would bring more of that kind of business to the office.

Standish was adamant. He said tomorrow or the next day would do just as well, that Mr. Lane would understand if Mary told him the doctor had been called out on an urgent matter.

"Urgent?" Mary was still indignant. She would have argued further if Standish had not opened the door and walked out.

One of the duties of the medical examiner's office was to see that a copy of all autopsy reports was sent to the district attorney and in the case of Dr. Cheney, Paul Standish delivered this report in person.

John Quinn, the district attorney, was in conference when Standish arrived and he had to wait a half-hour in the anteroom before the door finally opened and a thick-bodied, hard-jawed man with small, deep-set eyes and not much hair came out. His name was Mike Darrow and he was still talking.

"I'm getting a little fed up with this," he said to Quinn, who stood in the doorway. "If you want to see me again, you'd better subpoena me . . . Hi, Doc. How's it going?"

Standish stood up, making no reply, and started towards the private office. Quinn followed him in, his face flushed and his eyes angry behind the shell-rimmed glasses. He swore softly a moment before he glanced at the report Standish handed him, finally put his mind on it as the doctor told his story.

Standish knew the news was bad even before he finished. He could see it in Quinn's face and he had to listen while the other spoke of a budget that always kept him short-handed and made him dependent on police efforts.

"What exactly did you have in mind?" he said.

"I don't think Cheney was mugged," Standish said. "And if I'm right there has to be a reason. I thought you might know some things I don't know, that you might think of some reason."

Quinn said he was sorry. He could think of no reason for any deliberate attempt on Dr. Cheney, but maybe Standish could help him. "Where," he said, "would be a good place to hide a body?"

"Montanari's? How do you know he didn't run out on you?"

"I'll tell you," Quinn said, and he did, starting with Mike Darrow and going back to Prohibition days when Darrow had been a strong-arm man and hijacker. He enumerated a record of arrests that ranged from extortion to murder, commented profanely on the lack of convictions, and brought the record up to date by explaining the ramifications of Darrow's gambling syndicate, which had branched out into sporting events and made a mistake in trying to bribe certain college basketball players.

"When those kids told their story," Quinn said, "we dug back and found a couple of boxers who sang the same song. Montanari is the lad who offered the bribe and Darrow is his boss, though we can't prove it. And Montanari knew what the score was. I had his wife down. I told her he'd get only two years if he cooperated and gave us the goods on Darrow, and I promised to put in a word when he came up for parole. I told her he'd go away for ten long years if he refused to tell the truth. And then I got a break."

Quinn leaned across his desk. "His wife is going to have a baby in about six months. She hadn't told Frankie, but she did tell him after I talked to her, because yesterday when he turned up missing she came down here to see me. She said Frankie had promised her he would sing and I think he made the mistake of telling Darrow so." Quinn sat back and said, "That's why we're looking for a body. It's the sort of thing Darrow would do because he knows that Montanari's testimony would put him away for a long, long time."

Quinn stood up and shrugged. "I'm sorry, Doc. I don't know how I can help you. Until we find Frankie I won't even be able to think about anything else."

It was nearly five when Paul Standish returned to his office and Mary Hayward, who was checking records at her desk, took one look at his face and wisely made no comment when he went into his own office and closed the door.

119

It was, Standish realized as he shed his hat and coat, a mistake to have wasted any time on Quinn. And because he felt tired and beaten, it seemed now that it had been a mistake to concern himself with the Cheney death at all. He had spent hours accomplishing nothing and now he was through; in the future he would confine his efforts to those covered by the statutes governing his office.

At least, that is what he told himself. That is what he thought for a few minutes as he straightened his desk and busied himself with other matters. The trouble was, he was a stubborn man when confronted by a problem, medical or otherwise, and his mind kept going back, probing, testing, weighing the bits of information at hand. And finally, not realizing it, he was thinking of Old Doc Lathrop who had given him the job of assistant medical examiner at a time when Standish needed the work to pay his office rent.

It was Lathrop who had told him that through the experience gained by such work he would add to his knowledge as a diagnostician, and as he remembered some of the advice the grand old man had given him, one oft-repeated remark kept coming back. *The truth always rings true.* That was what Lathrop liked to say when faced with a difficult problem, and though it had sounded corny at times, Standish realized that this was all he needed now: the truth.

If Cheney had died at the hands of ordinary thugs, as Ballard maintained, he could be satisfied; if not, he had to know why—he had to know the truth.

He stood up, dark hair tousled and fatigue lining the angles of his eyes. He walked round the desk and sat down again, lighting a cigarette and then playing absently with his lighter. Just what made him think of Dr. Cheney's missing bag, he did not know but suddenly the idea was there and he reached for his own bag, wondering with new hope if the murder could be traced to something that Cheney had carried.

With his own bag open, he pawed through its familiar contents. He removed the stethoscope and saw the hypodermic kit, and though this gave way to further speculation he continued his search, taking out his pad of prescription blanks and then another, larger pad, his glance inspecting the printed form and then narrowing into a hot bright stare.

For another minute he sat quite motionless, his mind racing; then, not daring to hope that he had an answer, but desper-

120

ately, like a man grabbing at straws when all else has failed, he sat erect and reached for the telephone.

He got his number without delay, spoke briefly in quick, urgent accents. When he hung up there was new brightness in his eyes and that gleam was still there ten minutes later when he strode down a corridor in the City Hall and opened a door marked *Department of Health.*

The assistant he had spoken to was waiting behind a counter and as Standish thanked him for keeping the office open, he pushed a slip of paper across the counter which was a duplicate of the form Standish had seen in his bag. Across the top of the form were printed the words: Death Certificate. And this one had been filled out and signed by Dr. Edward Cheney.

"Is there anything wrong?" the assistant asked, held by the intentness of the doctor's inspection.

Standish said no, but he had a pencil out now as his glance took in the details and he wrote down the cause of death as stated by Dr. Cheney. Chronic gastric ulcer, hemorrhage into gastro-intestinal tract, spontaneous, is what Cheney had written, and Standish saw now that the deceased was one Charles Judson and that the certificate was dated the day before yesterday.

He had other questions to ask before he left and then he went out to his car and drove swiftly crosstown to Dr. Cheney's flat, the excitement riding him now in spite of his efforts to hold his hopes in check.

The two-family house looked even more depressing by daylight but Standish found the office unlocked, and the middle-aged woman who had been Cheney's secretary answered his question about Charles Judson and let him inspect Cheney's records. When he saw there was no card for Judson and was sure the secretary had no knowledge of the name, he again turned to the telephone, this time calling Lieutenant Ballard at police headquarters.

"I have a lead on the Cheney murder," he said. "I want to call on a fellow named Earle Jennings." He mentioned an address and said, "Can you meet me there in ten minutes?"

"No."

"Why not?" Standish said, surprised and a little annoyed at Ballard's curt reply.

"Because I'm up to my ears in this Montanari thing and I've got to go into a meeting with the captain and the commissioner

121

and I don't know how long I'll be. Call me back in an hour."

"An hour?" Standish said, outraged. "An hour?"

And then all the tension and the lack of sleep and the fatigue that he had been battling became too much for him and his normally even disposition dissolved abruptly, leaving his voice irascible and hard. He said he had been working on a murder that was really none of his business since two thirty that morning, and he finally had a lead, and if Ballard didn't want to know about it, it was all right with him. He had no intention of waiting an hour, or even fifteen minutes, and what did Ballard think of *that*.

Ballard finally interrupted him. He said wait a minute and to take it easy. "What makes this Jennings guy important?" he said. "Who is he, anyway?"

"He's an undertaker," Standish said, and hung up.

By the time he had parked his car and walked along the street to the colored, opaque window bearing the inscription, *Earle Jennings—Funeral Director*, Paul Standish was ashamed of his outburst and no longer so sure that his hunch was right. He stood for a moment looking at the narrow-front shop, sandwiched in between a stationery store and a bakery, aware that this was a run-down neighborhood, and tempted to go on by; that he did not was due not only to pride and native stubbornness but also to a well-entrenched and ever-present desire to know the truth.

Having come this far, he could not quit, and so he opened the door and stepped into a long, narrow room with somber walls, wicker furniture, and a threadbare rug. At the far end, near a curtained doorway, was a desk, but there was no one in the room so he walked on, past the desk, parting the curtains and finding himself in a short hall leading to a room in the back. As he stepped into this room, the man working over the casket heard him and wheeled.

A somberly-dressed shifty-eyed man, as tall as Standish but thinner, he had a heavy screwdriver in his hand and his glance was both startled and apprehensive.

"What's the idea?" he said.

"Are you Earle Jennings?"

"Yeah, why?"

"The Department of Health issued you a burial permit for a man named Charles Judson."

"Sure." There was defiance in the voice now but the eyes remained shifty. "We buried him this afternoon."

"Did you?" Standish glanced about, aware that the room was a sort of display room and noting the open doorway leading to the preparation room beyond. He moved slowly then, up to the table supporting the casket, then reaching for a handle and testing its weight. "I doubt it. Open this up and let's see."

Jennings swore viciously. He demanded to know who Standish was and when he found out, there was fear in his glance. He tried to bluster and when Standish started for him, he backed away, his manner changing.

"All right, Doc," he said. "You're off the beam but if you want to look, okay." He stepped up to the casket, unfastened the catches, and lifted the lid. As he moved aside, Standish took a quick look, then stopped to stare.

For there was a dead man inside the cheap, shallow box—a thin, almost undersized man. His name was Frankie Montanari and as Standish leaned forward he saw the bullet hole in the side of the head just above the hairline.

But even as he noticed this, he knew he had made a mistake. Sheer surprise had already robbed him of a vital second or two, and then it was too late. He tried to duck, sensing rather than hearing the sudden movement behind him, but even as he moved something smashed solidly in back of his head and pain exploded inside his brain.

The floor heaved and the room spun about him. He went down slowly, dizzily. He was on his knees. Then Jennings was tugging at him and he was helpless to resist the pressure that dragged him across the floor until vaguely, as from a great distance, he heard a door slam and blackness engulfed him.

Never quite losing consciousness, it took Paul Standish a while to find the strength to stand. By that time he knew he had been locked in some closet, and though he hurled himself at the door he had little room and could not get enough momentum in his charge to do any good.

Realizing finally that he could not break out alone, he began to think, and presently the pattern of Dr. Cheney's murder became clear. He knew now what had happened, and why. He also knew about what to expect and was ready for it when the door opened a few minutes later and he stepped out to find Mike Darrow standing there, a gun in his hand, Jennings beside him.

Darrow's blocky face was grim and uncompromising. "You had to stick your nose in, huh?" he said flatly.

Standish glanced about, weighing his chances and not liking the odds, knowing now that the district attorney's guess had been right when he said Montanari had made the mistake of going to Darrow.

"Frankie came to see you," Standish said. "To tell you he was going to talk."

"With a gun in his pocket," Darrow said. "This gun." He gestured with the automatic in his hand and laughed abruptly, an unpleasant sound. "I took it away from him."

"And after you'd shot him, you were stuck. It was a murder you hadn't planned. You had no alibi, and a body to get rid of, and you thought of a way." Standish hesitated, his bitterness at Darrow's cleverness erasing any immediate fear for himself. "You needed a death certificate and that meant a doctor, preferably a poor one, without a family. Someone crooked if possible—like Cheney."

He took a breath and said, "But Cheney was no crook. You found that out and you knew, once you'd tipped your hand, that you'd have to kill him. But that didn't matter to you because you'd already killed once and had no further penalty to pay. I guess Cheney knew, too."

He paused again, his bitterness festering as he realized what must have happened to the man who had once been his friend. Cheney had to sign or be killed, and even if he signed he must have known that his chance of survival was slim. But he had taken that chance because it was all he had, and in doing so had left behind one clue for whoever might be curious enough to make a search for it.

"The first certificate he made out," Darrow said, "he put down some funny words as the cause of death. I was afraid he was trying to tip off the health department. I made him write out another I could understand. What put you wise?"

"What difference does it make?"

"None." Darrow flattened his lips and his little eyes were implacable. "Tomorrow morning Frankie gets buried as Charles Judson and nobody's ever going to know what happened to him. Only now we need a deeper casket, Doc. To hold you too."

He spoke over his shoulder to Jennings but Standish did not hear him. His lean face was shiny with perspiration and his hands were damp. As he tried to think of some way out, he saw Jennings leave the room and come back lugging two saw-horses; then Darrow was prodding him with the gun, directing him through the preparation room to the storeroom in the back, forcing him to lift one end of a deeper casket while Jennings took the other.

Standish did not notice the weight of this burden; he was thinking about Ballard. He knew Darrow would not get away with his plan, since Ballard knew that Standish had come to see Jennings. When Standish turned up missing, Ballard would move in and eventually find out what had happened; but he could not expect Darrow to believe it.

Nevertheless, he tried. As they trudged back into the second room, he had his say and Darrow laughed at him, and now he knew that no matter what happened, he had to put up a fight, and quickly, before time ran out on him. Having nothing further to lose, the problem became simply a question of method, and he wasted no time feeling sorry for himself.

For they were putting the casket on the saw-horse now, he and Jennings, and Darrow was on the other side, and suddenly Standish's nerves were quiet and he knew what to do.

Feeling poised and ready now, not watching Darrow, he wedged his thigh under the edge of the casket as Jennings tried to adjust it and then, in one continuous movement, heaved mightily, tipping it towards Darrow.

What happened then took no more than a brief second, but to Paul Standish each detail was clear-cut and exact. He heard Jennings yell as the casket teetered and started to fall. He saw the gun flash and heard it hammer twice as Darrow fired wildly in his belated effort to jump clear; then the casket crashed and the floor shook, and above it all came Darrow's scream as his leg snapped under the casket.

After that, things were a little hazy for Paul Standish. He remembered seeing the automatic spin from Darrow's hand; he saw Jennings dive for it. He scrambled over the casket, aware that Jennings would reach it first but hoping he could get close. He watched the man scoop it up and straighten, knowing as it leveled that he would not be in time.

He saw the scared white face behind it and, still moving, watched the trigger finger tighten. Then the gun thundered and only when he saw Jennings' torso jerk did he realize that it was not this gun that had fired.

He stopped short then, hearing Darrow's moans, and he grabbed the gun from limp fingers as Jennings started to sag. Then he turned, unbelieving, and found Sergeant Wargo in the doorway to the hall, a short-barreled service revolver in his hand.

Jennings crumpled a joint at a time and fell over on his face. Darrow stopped groaning and the room was suddenly still. Wargo moved up, lowering his gun. He walked past Standish to glance at Darrow, who had fainted, and then at Montanari's casket.

Standish realized he was holding his breath and let it out, a little surprised that he could still move. He started to speak and had to clear his throat before any words came out. When he started to hand Wargo the automatic, he saw that his hands were trembling, and an odd weakness crept up the back of his legs as reaction hit him.

"Where," he said finally, "did you come from?"

"I was outside." Wargo motioned Standish to help him lift the casket from Darrow's leg. "This guy's going to the chair with one leg shorter than the other," he said and then, continuing with his answer, he added, "Ballard said the way you talked to him over the phone anything might happen and I'd better come out here and keep an eye on you. When I saw Mike come in, I thought I'd better have a look."

Lieutenant Ballard got the rest of the story a half-hour later, after Mike Darrow had been shipped to the hospital and Jennings had been removed. And because he was still shocked by what might have happened to his friend, his remarks were pointed and profane until he thought of something else; then he shrugged.

"What the hell," he said. "What am I crabbing about? We got Montanari and Darrow, and we know you were right about Doc Cheney. You got a good scare, and it served you right for not telling me the truth over the phone."

"I didn't know then," Standish said. "I didn't know I was going to find Montanari in the casket. All I knew was that Cheney would never have signed that death certificate of his own free will."

Ballard frowned, not understanding. He wanted to know why not. "Don't people die from ulcers and hemorrhages?"

"Certainly. There was nothing wrong with the wording."

"Then what tipped you off?"

Standish took his time because he wanted to make things clear. "Look," he said. "The law says that when a man dies suddenly, the death certificate must be signed by the medical examiner—unless there is a doctor in attendance who is familiar with the case. The law reads something like this: *Attending physicians will certify only to such deaths as those of persons to whom they have given bedside care during the last illness,* et cetera."

"I still don't get it," Ballard said.

"The death certificate said the hemorrhage was spontaneous. And due to chronic gastric ulcers. A physician *who had just been called in* could not know of that condition; he would have to be familiar with a case to make any such diagnosis."

"So—"

"So when I read that, I went to Doc Cheney's place and examined his records. He never had a patient named Judson, never called on one. If he *had* been called in and if there *had* been a man named Judson, and Cheney *had* found him dying, he would not have signed a death certificate. It would have been unethical and illegal."

Standish tipped one hand, let it fall. "And so I knew that the only way anyone could make Cheney sign such a certificate was by force. Because he was that kind of man. I don't believe he ever did a dishonest thing in his life, and he always did the best he could to make the truth ring true."

Ballard looked at Paul Standish and deep down in his eyes there was respect and approval. He seemed about to say something, checked himself. He took the doctor's arm and turned him towards the door.

"When you have faith in a guy," he said, under his breath, "you go all the way, don't you?"

Standish heard only part of Ballard's words and he was too tired to pay much attention to those. He wanted mostly a drink and something to eat. "What?" he said.

"Nothing," Ballard said. "Let's go see that good-looking secretary of yours that's always bawling you out. I've got an idea she's going to be sort of proud of you. Are you buying the drinks or am I?"

Standish said it did not matter. He said either way was all right so long as they drank first to Dr. Cheney.

STAN THE KILLER

BY GEORGES SIMENON

Georges Simenon was born Georges Sim in Liège, Belgium, on February 13, 1903. He left school at the age of sixteen and worked in a bakery, then in a bookstore, and finally on a newspaper, where he covered the police court. At seventeen he published his first novel, *Au Pont des Arches*. He wrote nearly two hundred popular novels under sixteen pseudonyms before his thirtieth birthday. His first novel about Maigret was *The Strange Case Of Peter the Lett* (1929). Altogether he wrote more than eighty novels about the popular detective. Simenon received the Grand Master Award in 1965.

MAIGRET PUFFED AT HIS PIPE as he walked along slowly, hands clasped behind his back. It was not a simple matter to push his heavy body through the morning mob in the Rue Saint-Antoine, where a bright sun poured down on carts and baskets of fruits and vegetables, blocking almost the entire width of the sidewalk.

It was marketing time—the time for feeling artichokes and tasting cherries, the time for scallops and chops to take turns in the scales.

"Fine asparagus, five francs a bundle!"

"Get your fresh whiting, just come in!"

Clerks in white aprons, butchers in fine checks; the smell of cheese from a dairy shop and farther off a whiff of roasting coffee; the ping of cash registers and the rumble of a bus; the distrustful glances of housewives—all the agitated business of alimentation . . . and in the midst of it the slow heavy progress of Maigret, on one of his most tormenting cases.

Across from the Rue de Birague there's a little café, with a scant three tables in front of it, called the Barrel of Burgundy. There Maigret settled himself, like any other weary passerby. He did not even look up at the tall thin waiter who came for his order. "Small white Mâcon," he muttered—and who was to guess that this occasionally inept new waiter at the Barrel of Burgundy was otherwise known as Detective Janvier?

The waiter returned with the wine precariously balanced on a tray. He wiped the table with a questionable cloth, and was even so clumsy as to drop a scrap of paper on the floor. Maigret picked it up as he left, and read:

> *The woman's gone out marketing. No sign of One-Eye. The Beard left early. The three others must be still in the hotel.*

At ten in the morning the crowd was getting even worse. Next to the Barrel, a grocery was having a sale and barkers kept entreating the passersby to sample cookies at two francs a box.

At the corner of the Rue de Birague you could see the sign of a dingy hotel, "Rooms by the month, the week or the day. Payment in advance." With doubtless intentional irony this rat-trap had chosen to call itself the Beauséjour.

129

Maigret sipped at his light dry white wine and stared apparently aimlessly at the teeming crowd in the spring sun. But his gaze soon settled on a window in the first floor of a house in the Rue de Birague opposite the hotel. At that window a little old man sat by a canary's cage and seemed to have no interest in life but to bask in the sun so long as the Lord should deign to leave him alive.

And this old gentleman, who took no notice of Maigret, was Sergeant Lucas, deftly aged some twenty years.

All this constituted a state of siege which is more vulgarly known to the police as a stakeout. It had lasted six days, and at least twice a day the Inspector came around for the latest news. At night his men were relieved by a patrolman, who was actually a detective from the Judiciary Police, and a wench who contrived to walk the streets without ever picking up a customer.

Maigret would have Lucas's report in a moment, by telephone; it would undoubtedly prove to be no more sensational than Janvier's.

The crowd shoved by so close to the tiny terrace of the Barrel of Burgundy that Maigret found himself constantly obliged to pull his legs back under his chair. And now, as he made one of these shifts, he suddenly realized that a man had sat down unnoticed at the same table. He was a little man, with red hair and sad eyes, whose mournful face had something of the clown about it.

"You again?" the Inspector grunted.

"I beg you to forgive me, Monsieur Maigrette, but I am certain that you will eventually come to understand me and to accept the proposition which I—" He broke off to say to the waiterly Janvier, "The same as my friend."

He had an extremely marked Polish accent. He presumably suffered from throat trouble; he constantly chewed at a "cigar" impregnated with creosote, which emphasized the clownishness of his appearance.

"You're getting on my nerves!" Maigret burst out. "Will you kindly tell me how you knew I'd come here this morning?"

"I did not know."

"Then why are you here? Are you going to try to convince me that this is an accidental meeting?"

"No."

130

The little man's reflexes were as leisurely as those of the slow-motion acrobats in vaudeville. His yellow eyes gazed around him, staring into emptiness. He spoke in a sad voice, unvarying in pitch, as though perpetually offering condolences.

"You are not nice to me, Monsieur Maigrette."

"That isn't answering my question. How do you happen to be here this morning?"

"I followed you."

"From Headquarters?"

"Long before that. From your home."

"So you admit you're spying on me?"

"I am not spying on you, Monsieur Maigrette. I have far too much respect and admiration for you! I have already stated to you that I shall one day be your collaborator . . ."

And he sighed nostalgically, contemplating the artificial ash of painted wood which tipped his creosote cigar.

There'd been nothing about it in any of the papers save one; and that one, which had got the tip the Lord knows where, uniquely complicated the Inspector's task.

The police have reason to believe that the Polish bandits, including Stan the Killer, are at this moment in Paris.

It was true enough, but silence would have been more helpful.

In four years a gang of unknown Poles had attacked five farms, always in the North of France, always with the same methods.

In each case it was an isolated farm, run by elderly people. The crime invariably took place the night of a market day; and the chosen victims were always those who had sold a good number of fowls and animals and had a large sum of cash on hand.

Nothing scientific about the procedure. Brutal attack, as in the days of the highway robbers. Absolute contempt for human life. These Poles were killers. They killed every human being they found on the farm, even down to the children; it was the one way of making sure they could never be identified.

Were there two of them? Or five, or eight?

In every case neighbors had noticed a small truck. One twelve-year old claimed he had seen a one-eyed man. Some asserted that the bandits wore black masks.

Whatever the facts, one thing was certain: Every inhabitant of each farm had had his throat sliced.

This was no business of the Paris police. This was up to the mobile units in the provinces, who worked on it for two years without remotely clarifying the mystery—a failure which did not reassure the countryside.

Then a report came in from Lille, where whole villages are Polish enclaves in French territory. The report was vague enough; it was impossible even to establish its ultimate source.

"The Poles say that this is Stan the Killer's gang . . ."

But when the police tried to question the coal miners one by one, the men had never heard of it, or muttered, "Well, they told me . . ."

"Who's 'they'?"

"I don't know. I forget. . . ."

Then came the crime near Rheims. There the gang over-looked a servant girl sleeping in the attic, who became the first survivor. She had heard the murderers talking in a language she thought was Polish. She had seen their masks through a hole in the boards; and had noticed that one of the men had only one eye and that another, a giant of a man, was extraordinarily hairy.

And so the police had come to refer to them as "Stan the Killer," "The Beard," and "One-Eye."

For months nothing more turned up, until a detective on the hotel squad made a discovery. His territory was on the Saint-Antoine district, which teems with Poles. And in a hotel in the Rue de Birague he observed a suspicious group which included a one-eyed man and a giant whose face was literally covered with hair.

They were seemingly poor people. The bearded giant and his wife rented a room by the week; but almost every night they gave shelter to several compatriots, sometimes two, sometimes as many as five, and often other Poles rented the adjoining room.

"You want to take this over, Maigret?" the director of the Judiciary Police suggested.

Everything was strictly hush-hush—and so the next day

one newspaper printed the story. The day after that Maigret found a letter in his mail—clumsily written in an almost childish hand, full of misspellings, on the cheap sort of paper sold in grocery stores:

You won't ever get Stan. Look out. Before you can take him, he'll have time to kill off plenty more.

The letter was no hoax, Maigret was certain; it *felt* right. It had the filthy aftertaste of the underworld.

"Be careful," the chief recommended. "Don't rush into an arrest. The man who's cut sixteen throats in four years won't hesitate to scatter a few bullets around him when he sees he's done for."

Which was why Janvier had become a waiter and Lucas a basking old man.

The noisy life of the quarter went on with no suspicion that a desperate man might at any moment start firing in all directions. . . .

And then Michael Ozep appeared.

His first meeting with Maigret had been four days ago. He had arrived at Headquarters and insisted on seeing the Inspector personally. Maigret had let him wait a good two hours; but the little man was undaunted. He entered the office, clicked his heels, bowed, and extended his hand:

"Michael Ozep, former officer in the Polish army, now professor of gymnastics in Paris—"

"Sit down. I'm listening."

The Pole spoke so volubly and with so pronounced an accent that it was sometimes impossible to follow him. He explained that he came of very good family, that he had been forced to leave Poland because of unmentionably intimate misfortunes (he allowed his listener to gather that he had been in love with his Colonel's wife), and that he had now sunk to worse depths of despair than ever because he could not accustom himself to leading a mediocre life.

"You understand, Monsieur Maigrette . . ." (it was impossible to wean him from that pronunciation) ". . . I am a gentleman. Here I am forced to give lessons to individuals of no culture and no education. I am a poor man . . . I have decided to commit suicide."

"A nut," Maigret thought to himself. An astonishing number

133

of the unbalanced feel the need of confiding their problems to the police; he was used to such visits.

"I tried it three weeks ago. I threw myself into the Seine from the Austerlitz bridge, but the river squad saw me and pulled me out."

Maigret invented a pretext to step into the next office and phone the river squad. The story was true.

"Six days later I tried to kill myself with illuminating gas, but the postman came with a letter and opened the door. . . ."

A phone call to the police station in Ozep's district. And again the story was true.

"I truly *want* to kill myself, do you understand? My existence has lost all value. A gentleman cannot consent to live in poverty and mediocrity. Therefore I thought that you might have need of a man like me. . . ."

"For what?"

"To help you to arrest Stan the Killer."

Maigret frowned. "You know him?"

"No. I have only heard talk about him. As a Pole, I am indignant that a man of my people should so violate the laws of hospitality. I should like to see Stan and his gang arrested. I know that he is resolved to sell his life dearly. Among those who go to arrest him, some will certainly be killed. Is it not better then that it should be I, since I already desire to die? Tell me where Stan is. I shall go and disarm him. If need be, I shall wound him so that he can do no more harm."

All Maigret found himself capable of saying was the traditional formula, "Leave your address. I'll write you a letter."

Michael Ozep had a furnished room in the Rue des Tournelles, not far from the Rue de Birague. The report of the investigating detective was in his favor. He had indeed been a second lieutenant in the Polish army when it was organized after Poland gained her independence. Then his trail vanished. In Paris he tried to teach gymnastics to the sons and daughters of small merchants. His suicide attempts were genuine.

Nevertheless Maigret sent him, with the chief's approval, an official letter ending:

> . . . *deeply regret that I cannot take advantage of your generous proposition for which my most sincere thanks. . . .*

Twice since then Ozep had appeared at the Quai des Orfèvres and insisted on seeing the Inspector. The second time he had even refused to leave, claiming that he could wait as long as he was obliged to, and thus almost forcibly occupying, hour after hour, one of the green plush armchairs in the waiting room.

And now Ozep sat there, at Maigret's table, in front of the Barrel of Burgundy.

"I wish to prove to you, Monsieur Maigrette, that I am of some use and that you can accept my services. It is now three days that I have been following you, and I am in a position to tell you everything that you have done during that time. I know too that the waiter who just brought my wine is one of your detectives and that there is another at the window across from us, near a canary cage."

Maigret clenched the bit of his pipe furiously between his teeth and kept his eyes turned away from the Pole, who kept on and on in his monotonous voice:

"I understand that when a strange man comes to you and says, 'I am a former officer of the Polish army and I wish to kill myself'—I understand why you would think, 'This may not be true.' But you have verified everything that I have told you. You have seen that I do not stoop to lies. . . ."

He was a mill grinding out words, rapidly, jerkily. It wore Maigret out merely to listen to him, especially since the accent so distorted each syllable that Maigret had to concentrate to follow the sense.

"You are not a Pole, Monsieur Maigrette. You do not speak the language; you do not comprehend the mentality. I earnestly desire to help you; for I cannot see the good name of my native land tarnished by . . ."

The Inspector was beginning to choke with anger. The former second lieutenant could hardly fail to observe the fact, but he continued nevertheless:

"If you try to capture Stan, what will he do? He has maybe two, maybe three revolvers in his pockets. He fires at everybody. Who knows how many ladies he wounds? How many little babies he kills? Then people will say that the police—"

"Will you shut up?"

"Now as for me, I am resolved to die. No one will weep for poor Ozep. You say to me, 'There is Stan!' And I follow him as I have followed you. I wait for the moment when there is no one near us and I say. 'You are Stan the Killer!' Then he fires at me and I shoot him in the leg. By the fact that he shoots me, you have your proof that he is Stan and you are not making a blunder. And since he is crippled by my shot . . ."

There was no stopping him. He would have gone on in spite of the entire universe.

"Supposing I have you arrested?" Maigret broke in crudely.

"Why?"

"To get a little peace!"

"What would you say? What has poor Ozep done in violation of the laws of France which instead he wishes only to defend and for which he is offering up his life?"

"Stuff it!"

"I beg your pardon? Are you agreeing?"

"Not in the least."

At that moment a woman went by, a woman with blonde hair and clear complexion, recognizably a foreigner. She was carrying a shopping bag and was headed for a butcher shop.

Maigret was following her with his eyes when he noticed that his companion had suddenly set to mopping his brow with an enormous handkerchief which all but swallowed up his small-featured face.

"That is the mistress of Stan, is it not?" Ozep asked.

"Will you leave me the blazes alone?"

"You have convinced yourself that this is the mistress of Stan, but you do not know which one is Stan. You think it is the one with the beard. Now the bearded one is called Boris. And the man with one eye is Sasha. He is not a Pole, but a Russian. If you should investigate them yourself you will learn nothing. In the hotel there are only Poles; they will refuse to answer or they will lie to you. Whereas I . . ."

No housewife shopping in the confusion of the Rue Saint-Antoine could suspect the subjects being discussed on the tiny terrace of the Barrel of Burgundy. The blonde foreigner was buying chops at a nearby butcher's stall; in her eyes there was something of that same lassitude that lay in the eyes of Michael Ozep.

"Perhaps you are angry with me because you fear that you may be called to account if I am killed? In the first place, I have no family. In the second place, I have written a letter in which I state that I alone, and purely of my own volition, have sought this death. . . ."

Poor Janvier stood on the threshold trying to figure out a way of telling Maigret that there was a telephone message for him. Maigret noticed the ambiguous pantomime, but went on watching the Pole and puffing forth little clouds of pipe smoke.

"Listen, Ozep."

"Yes Monsieur Maigrette?"

"If you're seen again anywhere around the Rue Saint-Antoine, I'll have you arrested!"

"But I live only—"

"You better move."

"You are refusing this offer which I—?"

"Get out!"

"But—"

"Get out, or I'll arrest you here and now!"

The little man rose, clicked his heels, bowed almost double, and executed a dignified retreat. Maigret had noticed one of his detectives nearby; now he signaled the man to follow the peculiar professor of gymnastics.

At last Janvier could deliver his message. "Lucas just phoned. He's spotted that they have guns in the room. Five Poles slept in the next room last night, leaving the door open between. Some of them had to sleep on the floor. Who the devil was that character you were talking to?"

"Nothing. . . . How much?"

Janvier slipped back into character, pointing at Ozep's glass. "You're paying monsieur's check? One franc twenty and one twenty makes two forty."

Maigret took a taxi to Headquarters. At the door of his office he found the detective who had set out after Ozep.

"You lost him?" he roared. "Aren't you ashamed of yourself? I give you the most childish job of shadowing and you—"

"I didn't lose him," the detective murmured humbly.

"Where is he?"

"Here."

"You pulled him in?"

"He pulled me."

For Ozep had, indeed, headed directly for Headquarters, where he had placidly installed himself and his sandwich in the waiting room, after announcing that he had an appointment with Inspector "Maigrette."

There're no kudos in paper work; but there may be the solution of a case.

137

Unwillingly, irritatedly, Maigret was adding up in one report in his own large handwriting the various information obtained in two weeks' siege of the Polish gang.

When he set down the facts in order he could see even more easily how very little they had learned. They did not even know precisely how many individuals belonged to the gang. The earlier reports, from the people who had seen or thought they had seen the bandits near the time of the attacks, stated that there were four of them, sometimes five. It was probable that they had other accomplices, who cased the farms and markets beforehand. That brought the number to six or seven, which seemed to correspond roughly with the number who hung around the nucleus in the Rue de Birague.

There were only three regular tenants, all of whom had filled out their cards according to regulations and displayed passports in perfect order: 1. Boris Saft, the one the police called The Beard, who seemed to live as man and wife with the pale blonde.

2. Olga Tzerewski, 28, born in Vilno.

3. Sasha Vorontsov, known as One-Eye.

Boris the Beard and Olga occupied one room, Sasha One-Eye the next; the door between was always left open.

The young woman did the shopping every morning and cooked the meals on an alcohol stove.

The Beard rarely went out, but spent most of his days stretched on the iron bedstead, reading Polish newspapers which he had one of the gang buy for him at the newspaper kiosk in the Place de la Bastille. Once the errand boy brought back an American fact-detective magazine in addition to the Polish periodicals. They all read that.

One-Eye went out often, always followed by one of Maigret's detectives. A fact of which he was probably aware, since he never did more than take long walks through Paris, stopping in many bars but never speaking to a soul.

As for the rest, they were what Lucas called "the floating population." People came and went, always the same lot, four or five of them. Olga fed them, and sometimes they slept on the floor overnight. There was nothing odd about this; it happens in all hotels with poor tenants—exiles who get together to rent a room and then put up any of their compatriots they come across.

On the floating population Maigret had a few notes:

1. The Chemist, so called because he had twice visited the Work Exchange to apply for a job in a chemical plant. His clothes were badly worn, but rather well cut. For hours he would wander around the streets of Paris like a man looking for any way to earn a little money; and once, for a whole day, he was employed as a sandwich-man.

2. Spinach, named after the implausible spinach-green hat which seemed even more unlikely in view of his faded pink shirt. Spinach went out particularly in the evenings, when he picked up tips opening car doors in front of the Montmartre bars.

3. Puffy, a fat, wheezy little man, better dressed than the others even if his shoes were not mates.

And there were two others who visited the hotel less regularly; it was hard to say if they belonged to the gang.

Maigret stared at the notes with the exasperated feeling that the most important detail was somehow eluding him. Finally he picked up his pen again and wrote: *These people give the impression of penniless foreigners, looking for any kind of work at all. But there's always vodka in the rooms, and sometimes impressive spreads of food. Maybe the gang knows it's being watched, and is putting on an act for the police. If one of them is Stan the Killer, it is probably either The Beard or One-Eye. But this is only guesswork.*

It was without the least enthusiasm that he brought his report to the chief.

"Nothing new?"

"Nothing specific. I'd swear the rascals have spotted one of our men and are simply amusing themselves seeing how often they can come in and go out on innocent errands. They know we can't keep a large section of the force mobilized on their account forever. Time's on their side; they have lots of it. . . ."

"You have a plan?"

"Look, chief. You know that ideas and I haven't been on speaking terms for a long time. I come and I go and I sniff around. You'll hear people say I'm waiting for inspiration; they're way off the track. What I'm waiting for is the one significant happening that never fails to turn up. The whole thing is being there when it does turn up so that I can take advantage of it."

"So you're waiting for a . . . happening?" The chief smiled. He knew his man.

"This much I'm convinced of: This *is* the Polish gang. Because of that fool of a reporter who keeps hanging around here picking up scraps of conversation, they're on their guard. Now what I want to know is, why did Stan write to me? Maybe because he knows the police always hesitate to make a forcible arrest? More probably out of sheer bravado. These killers have their pride—you might almost say, professional pride. But which of them is Stan? And why that nickname? It's more American than Polish.

"You know how I take my time before I reach any conclusions. Well, it's beginning to come. . . . The last two or three days I've begun to get the feel of the psychology of these boys. Very different from French murderers.

"They need money, not to retire to the country, or to have a fling in the night spots, or to clear out to foreign parts—but just simply to live their lives, which to them means doing nothing, eating, drinking, sleeping, spending your days stretched out on a bed, smoking cigarettes, and killing bottles of vodka. And they have this longing to be together—to dream together, gossip together, some nights sing together.

"The way I see it, after their first crime they lived like this until the money ran out; then they got ready for another job. Whenever the funds are low, they start in again, coldly, without remorse, without a trace of pity for the old people whose throats they cut—and whose life's savings they eat up in a few weeks or months. . . . And now that I've got the feel of it, I'm waiting—"

"I know. For the happening," the director smiled.

"Joke about it all you want. Just the same the happening may be here already."

"Where?"

"In the waiting room. The little man who calls me Maigrette and who wants at all costs to help in the arrest, even if it costs him his skin. He claims it's just another method of suicide."

"A crackpot?"

"Could be. Or an accomplice of Stan's who's using this method of keeping in touch with what we're doing. Any hypothesis fits; that's what makes my character with the creosote cigar so fascinating."

Maigret emptied his pipe by tapping it gently on the window ledge, so that the ashes fell somewhere on the Quai des Orfèvres, perhaps on the hat of a passerby.

"He bothers me, that little man," he added. "I've seen his face

140

somewhere. It's not in our files, but I've seen it. And I've seen the girl, too, the blonde; she's worth remembering. None of the others. Just those two."

The director of the Judiciary Police leaned forward. "We've been going on the assumption that the blonde is Stan's mistress. You associate her and the little man. You see the possible implication?"

"That my little man is Stan himself? Could be."

"Are you going to accept this man's offer?"

"I think so." The Inspector headed for the door. He felt he'd said enough. "You'll see, chief. I'll be amazed if we still need the stakeout by the end of this week."

And this was Thursday afternoon.

"Sit down! Doesn't it get on your nerves to suck at that filthy creosote cigar all day?"

"No, Monsieur Maigrette."

"That 'Maigrette' of yours is beginning to get me. . . . But anyway, let's get down to business. Are you still set on dying?"

"Yes, Monsieur Maigrette."

"And you still want to be entrusted with a perilous mission?"

"I wish to help you to arrest Stan the Killer."

"So if I told you to go up to One-Eye and fire a bullet into his leg, you'd do it?"

"Yes, Monsieur Maigrette. But you would first have to give me a revolver. I am a poor man and—"

"Now suppose I tell you to go to The Beard or One-Eye and say you have important information—that the police are coming to arrest them?"

"Gladly, Monsieur Maigrette. I shall wait until One-Eye passes by and then I shall perform my commission."

The lowering gaze of the Inspector had no effect on the little Pole. Rarely had Maigret seen a man who combined such self-assurance with such utter serenity. Michael Ozep spoke of killing himself or of visiting the Polish gang as simply, as naturally, as he might refer to brushing his teeth. He was as much at ease in police headquarters as in the Barrel of Burgundy.

"You've never met either of them?"

"No, Monsieur Maigrette."

"All right. I'm going to give you the job. And if there's any trouble, it's on your head." Maigret lowered his eyelids to conceal his too sharp interest in the other's reaction. "In a minute we'll go together to the Rue Saint-Antoine. I'll wait for you outside. You'll go up to the room, picking a time when the woman is there alone. You'll tell her you're a fellow Pole and you happened by chance to learn that the police are raiding the hotel tonight. . . ."

Ozep said nothing.

"You understand?"

"Yes."

"It's all set?"

"I must confess something to you, Monsieur Maigrette."

"You're turning yellow?"

"Yellow? I do not under—ah! yes. No, I am not turning yellow. But I should prefer to arrange the matter in a different way. You may think that I am taking much upon myself . . . is that how I say it? But I am a timid man with the ladies. And the ladies are intelligent, far more intelligent than we men. Therefore, she will see that I am lying. And because I know that she will see that I am lying, I shall blush. And when I blush . . ."

Maigret sat motionless, absorbing this unlikely explanation.

"I should prefer to talk to a man. To the one with the beard, if you like, or the one you call One-Eye, or anyone at all. . . ."

A ray of sunlight pierced slantwise through the office and lit full on Maigret's face. He seemed to be dozing, like a man whose injudiciously heavy lunch obliges him to take a siesta at his desk.

"It is exactly the same thing, Monsieur Maigrette."

But Monsieur Maigrette did not answer. The only sign that he was still alive was the slim blue spiral which rose from his pipe.

"I am desolated. You can ask of me what you wish; but you demand precisely the one thing which—"

"Stuff it!"

"I beg your pardon?"

"I say, 'Stuff it!' Which means, in French, to shut up. Where did you know the woman Olga Tzerewski?"

"I?"

"Answer me!"

"I do not understand what you mean. . . ."

"Answer me!"

"I do not know this woman. If I knew her, I would tell you so. I am a former officer of the Polish army and if I had not suffered misfortunes—"

"Where did you know her?"

"I swear to you, Monsieur Maigrette, by the head of my sainted mother and my poor father—"

"Where did you know her?"

"Why have you suddenly stopped being nice to me? You talk to me so brutally! To me who came here to place myself at your disposal, to prevent Frenchmen from being murdered by a compatriot—"

"Cut the pitch!"

"Pitch?"

"Sales talk, to you. You aren't selling me."

"Ask anything of me, no matter what—"

"That's what I'm doing!"

"Ask me anything else—to throw myself under a subway train—"

"I'm asking you to go see that woman and tell her that we'll make a raid tonight."

"You insist?"

"Take it or leave it."

"And if I refuse?"

"Then you'd better see to it that I never lay eyes on you again."

"Are you really going to arrest the gang tonight?"

"Probably."

"And you will allow me to help you?"

"Possibly. We'll see about that when you've finished your first job."

"At what time?"

"Your job?"

"No. At what time will you make the raid?"

"Let's say one in the morning."

"I am going."

"Where?"

"To find the woman."

"Just a minute! We're going together."

"It is better that I go alone. If one of them sees us, he will understand that I am assisting the police. . . ."

The Pole had hardly left the office, of course, before the Inspector had set a detective at his heels.

"Should I keep under cover?" the detective asked.

"No use. He's smarter than you are and he knows very well I'll have him followed."

And without losing a moment Maigret hurried downstairs and leaped into a taxi.

"Corner of Rue de Birague and Rue Saint-Antoine, as fast as you can make it!"

It was a radiant afternoon. Striped awnings lent a note of color to the shops. In their shadows dogs sprawled and napped, and all life seemed to run in slow motion. You felt that even the buses had a hard time making headway in the hot heavy air. Their wheels left tracks in the heated asphalt.

Maigret sprang out of the taxi into the house on the corner. On the second floor he opened a door without bothering to knock and found Lucas sitting at the window, still in the role of a quiet and curious elderly gentleman.

The room was shabby but clean. On the table lay the remains of a cold meal that Lucas had sent up from a delicatessen.

"Anything new, Inspector?"

"Anybody at home across the way?"

The room had been chosen for its strategic position; you could see straight into the two rooms of the Hotel Beauséjour which the Poles occupied.

In this heat all the windows stood wide open, including the window of another room which revealed a young girl asleep and scantily clad.

"Well, well, Lucas! Looks like you don't find your job too boring. . . ."

A pair of field glasses on a chair gave evidence that Lucas attended to his work conscientiously and missed no detail, however slight.

"At the moment," said the sergeant, "there are two of them in the rooms, but there'll be only one in a minute. The man's getting dressed. He stayed in bed all morning, as usual."

"That's The Beard?"

"Yes. There were three of them for lunch: The Beard, the woman, and One-Eye. One-Eye left as soon as he'd eaten. Then The Beard got up and began to dress. . . . Well! He's just put on a clean shirt. That doesn't happen very often."

Maigret came to the window to take his turn watching. The hairy giant was knotting his tie. The white shirt made an unexpected and therefore all the more dazzling splotch in the gray room.

You could see the man's lips move as he looked at himself in

144

the mirror. Behind him the blonde woman was cleaning up, gathering gray papers and rolling them into a ball, turning off the alcohol stove, dusting the frame of a bright-colored picture on the wall.

"If only we knew what they're saying!" Lucas sighed. "There are times when it drives me crazy. I watch them talking and talking and they never stop. They wave their arms around and I can't even guess what it's all about."

"The limitless resources of the police," said Maigret drily, "do not include a lip-reader who knows Polish."

"It gets on my nerves. I'm beginning to understand the torture it must be to be deaf. I'm beginning to see why people afflicted that way are generally so cranky."

"Don't talk so much! Do you think the woman will stay there?"

"This isn't the time she usually goes out. And if she meant to, she would have put on her gray suit."

Olga was wearing the same dark wool dress in which she had done her marketing that morning. While she cleaned up her bohemian establishment, she kept smoking a cigarette without ever taking it from her lips, in the fashion of the true smoker who needs tobacco from morning till night.

"She never talks," Maigret observed.

"This isn't the time she does that, either. It's in the evenings that she gets to talking, when they're all gathered around her. Or a few times when she's alone with the one I call Spinach—which doesn't happen very often. Either I'm badly mistaken or she has a weakness for Spinach. He's the best-looking of the lot."

It was a strange sensation to be in an unknown room like this, to look into the lives of people and come to know their smallest gestures.

"You're getting as snoopy as a concierge, Lucas."

"That's what I'm here for, isn't it? I can even tell you that the little girl over there—the one who's sleeping so soundly—was making love last night until three in the morning with a young man with an Ascot tie, who left at dawn, undoubtedly so he could get into his family's house unnoticed. . . . Hold on! Now the Beard's leaving."

"Look at that, will you! He's practically elegant!"

"You might say so. But he looks more like a foreign wrestler than a man of the world."

145

"Well, let's say a wrestler who's doing good business," Maigret conceded.

No goodbye kiss across the way. The man simply went—that is, he disappeared from the part of the room visible from the police observatory.

A little later he emerged onto the sidewalk and set off toward the Place de la Bastille.

"Derain will pick him up," Lucas announced, sitting there like a huge spider at the center of its web. "But he knows he's being followed. He won't do anything but walk around and maybe pick up a drink somewhere."

As for the woman, she had taken a road map out of a drawer and spread it on the table.

Ozep couldn't have taken a taxi, Maigret calculated; he must have come by subway, in which case he should arrive at any moment. "*If* he's coming," he corrected himself.

And he did come. They saw him arrive, hesitate, wander up and down the sidewalk, while the detective trailing him displayed great interest in a fish stall in the Rue Saint-Antoine.

Seen from above like this, the tiny Pole seemed even thinner, even more insignificant. Maigret experienced, for a moment, a pang of remorse. He could hear the poor devil's voice repeating a hundred times, in involved explanation, his famous "Monsieur Maigrette . . ."

He was hesitating, that was obvious. He seemed even to be afraid, to stare around him with a visible anguish.

"Do you know what he's looking for?" the Inspector asked Lucas.

"The little pale fellow? No. Maybe some money to get into the hotel?"

"He's looking for me. He's saying to himself that I must be somewhere around and if by some miracle I've changed my mind . . ."

Too late to change now; Michael Ozep had plunged into the dark hallway of the hotel. They could follow him in their minds. He would be climbing the stairs, reaching the second floor . . .

"He's still stalling," Maigret announced. The door should have opened before this. "He's on the landing. He's going to knock. He's knocked—look!"

The blonde girl trembled, shoved the map, with an instinctive movement, back in the dresser, and went toward the door. For a moment they could see nothing. The two were in the invisible part of the room. Then suddenly the woman appeared. Something about her had changed. Her steps were fast, decisive. She went straight to the window, closed it, then drew the dark curtains.

Lucas turned to the Inspector with a quizzical smile. "Think of that!" he laughed. But his smile faded as he noticed that Maigret was far more concerned than he had expected.

"What time is it, Lucas?"

"Three ten."

"In your opinion, what are the chances that one of the gang will come back to the hotel in the next hour?"

"I doubt it. Unless, as I was telling you, Spinach, if he knows The Beard is out of the way. You don't look very happy about things."

"I don't like the way she closed that window."

"Are you afraid for your little Pole?"

Maigret made no answer.

"Have you thought," Lucas went on, "that we haven't any real proof that he is in that room? It's true we saw him go into the hotel. But he might perfectly well have gone to some other room, while somebody else came—"

Maigret shrugged his shoulders and sighed.

"What time is it, Lucas?"

"Three twenty."

"Do you know what's going to happen?"

"Do you want to go over and see what's happening across the way?"

"Not yet. But I'm probably going to make a fool of myself. . . . Where can you telephone?"

"In the next room. He's a tailor who does piece work for one of the big houses, so he has to have a phone."

"Go to your tailor then. Try not to let him listen in. Telephone the chief, and tell him I want him to send me twenty armed men at once. They're to spread a cordon around the Hotel Beauséjour and wait for my signal."

Lucas's expression indicated the seriousness of this order, so out of character for Maigret, who usually laughed at police mobilization. "You think there'll be dirty work going on?"

"If it hasn't already gone on . . ."

His eyes remained fixed on the window, on the filthy glass

panes, on the crimson velvet curtains of the time of Louis-Phi-lippe.

When Lucas came back from the telephone, he found the Inspector still in the same place, still frowning thoughtfully.

"The boss says please be careful. There was a detective killed only last week, and now if there should be another accident—"

"Shut up, will you?"

"Do you think that Stan the Killer—"

"I don't think anything! I've thought so much about this case since this morning that I've got a headache. Now I'm satisfied just to have impressions; and if you want to know I have the impression that some disagreeable things are happening or are about to happen. What time is it?"

"Twenty-three after."

In the neighboring room the young girl was still asleep, her mouth open, her legs bent back. Higher up, on the fifth or sixth floor, somebody was trying to play an accordion, incessantly repeating, with the same false notes, the same fox-trot refrain.

"Do you want me to go over?" Lucas suggested.

Maigret gave him a harsh look, as if his subordinate had reproached him for lack of courage. "Just what do you mean by that?"

"Nothing. I can't help seeing you're worried about what may be going on over there, and I thought I could go and check—"

"And you think I'd hesitate to go myself? You're forgetting one thing: Once we're over there, it's too late. If we go and find nothing, we'll never pin anything on that gang. That's why I'm hesitating. . . . If only that wench hadn't closed the window!" He suddenly lifted his eyebrows. "Tell me: the other times, when she's been alone with a man, she's never closed the window, has she?"

"Never."

"Then she hadn't any suspicion of your presence here."

"She probably took me for just another foolish old man."

"So it isn't the girl who had the idea of closing the window, but the character who came in."

"Ozep?"

"Ozep or somebody else. It's the one who came in who told the girl to close the window before he showed himself."

He took his hat from the chair, emptied his pipe, scraped the bowl with his index finger.

"Where are you going, boss?"

"I'm waiting for our men to get here. . . . Look! There are two of them by the bus stop. And I recognize some others in that parked taxi. . . . If I stay inside five minutes without opening that window, you'll come in with our men."

"You have your gun?"

A few moments later Lucas could see Maigret crossing the street, could see Detective Janvier notice him and break off his task of wiping the tables on the terrace.

After what seemed a miraculously short interval, the window across the way opened. Maigret signaled to his sergeant to join him.

From across the street Lucas had gathered that the room was empty save for the Inspector. He stumbled up a dark staircase through the stench of bad cooking and worse plumbing and entered the room, only to start back as he found the body of a woman stretched out at his feet.

"Dead, of course," Maigret grunted.

It was as if the murderer had wished to leave his signature on his crime. The woman's throat had been cut, as with all the other victims of Stan. There was blood everywhere.

The bright picture on the wall turned out, on closer inspection, to be a portrait of Olga—even blonder, even more fresh-skinned than she had been in life. Lucas looked from the lushly alluring portrait to the unappetizing sight on the floor. He felt oddly like a drinking man who sees a bottle of fine brandy smashed.

"It was your Pole?"

Maigret shrugged his shoulders, still standing rooted in the middle of the room.

"Shall I give his description to our men so they can see that he doesn't leave the hotel?"

"If you wish."

"I'd like to put a man on the roof, just in case—"

"Go ahead."

"Shall I call the chief?"

"In a minute."

It was no easy job to talk with Maigret when he was like this. Lucas tried to put himself in his shoes. Maigret himself had said he'd make a fool of himself. But this was worse than looking foolish. He had mobilized a large body of police when it was too late, when the crime had already been committed under Maigret's very eyes—almost with his consent, since he'd been the one who had sent Ozep into the Hotel Beauséjour.

"And if any of the gang come back, shall I arrest them?"

An affirmative nod. Or rather a gesture of indifference. And at last Lucas went out.

"Where's Maigret?" the chief demanded of Lucas before he was halfway out of his car.

"In the room. Number nineteen on the second floor. The people in the hotel don't know about it yet."

A few moments later the director of the Judiciary Police found Maigret sitting in a chair in the middle of the room, two steps from the body.

"Well, my friend! It looks to me as though we were in a pretty fix!"

For answer he received a grunt.

"So the notorious killer was none other than the little man who offered you his services! You must admit, Maigret, you might have been somewhat less trustful; Ozep's attitude was, to say the least, suspicious. . . ."

A heavy vertical furrow seamed Maigret's brow and his jaws jutted out, giving his whole face a striking quality of power.

"You think he hasn't managed to slip out of the hotel yet?"

"I'm sure of it," the Inspector replied, as if he attached not the least importance to the matter.

"You haven't searched the hotel?"

"Not yet."

"You think he'll let himself be captured easily?"

Then Maigret's gaze detached himself slowly from the window, shifted toward the director.

"If I'm wrong, the man will try to kill as many people as he can before he's arrested. If I'm not wrong, things will take care of themselves."

"I don't understand, Maigret."

"I tell you again, chief: I can be wrong. Anybody can be wrong. In that case, I beg your pardon, because there's going to be trouble. The way this case seems to have solved itself doesn't satisfy me. There's something that doesn't fit, I can feel it. If Ozep was Stan, there was no reason why . . ." His voice trailed off.

"You're staying here, Maigret?"

"Pending further instructions, yes."

"Meanwhile, I'll go see what our men are doing outside."

150

They had arrested Spinach when, as Lucas had foreseen, he had come to pay his call on the young woman. When they told him that Olga had been killed, he turned pale; but he showed no reaction when they spoke of Ozep.

When this arrest was announced to Maigret, he merely mumbled, "What's it to me?" and resumed his strange tête-à-tête with the dead woman.

A half hour later it was One-Eye's turn to come home and be arrested on the threshold. He submitted impassively; but when they told him of the woman's death, he tried to break free from his handcuffs and leap upstairs.

"Who did it?" he shouted. "Who killed her? One of you, wasn't it?"

"It was Ozep, alias Stan the Killer."

The man quieted down as if by magic. He frowned as he repeated, "Ozep?"

"You aren't going to tell us you didn't know your boss's real name?"

It was the chief in person who conducted this hasty questioning in a corridor, and he had the impression that a faint smile crossed the prisoner's lips.

Then came another of the gang, the one they called the Chemist. He simply answered all questions with an air of absolute confusion, as if he had never heard of the woman nor of Ozep nor of Stan.

Maigret was still upstairs, mulling over the same problem, hunting for the key that would at last enable him to understand what had happened.

"All right . . ." he murmured when Lucas told him of the arrest of The Beard, who had begun by raging like a fiend and ended by bawling like a calf.

Suddenly he raised his head. "Do you notice something, Lucas? That's four that they've arrested, and not one of them's put up any real resistance. Whereas a man like Stan—"

"But since Stan is Ozep—"

"Have you found him?"

"Not yet. We had to let all the accomplices come home before we turned the hotel upside down. If they got a whiff of anything wrong, they'd never come into the mousetrap. Now that we have almost all of them, the big boss is laying siege to the establishment. Our men are downstairs and they're going to go through everything.

"Listen, Lucas . . ."

The sergeant had been about to leave. He paused, feeling for Maigret something akin to pity.

"One-Eye is not Stan. Spinach is not Stan. The Beard is not Stan. But I'm convinced that Stan lived in this hotel and was the focus around which the others gathered."

Lucas thought it better to say nothing. Let the Inspector have his monomania.

"If Ozep was Stan, he had no reason to come here to kill an accomplice. If he was not Stan . . ."

Suddenly Maigret rose, crossed to the wall and pulled down the brightly colored picture of Olga. He tore away the tape that framed it, revealing lines of lettering above and below the face. He handed it to Lucas.

The sergeant knew enough English to make out both the line above:

REAL LIFE DETECTIVE CASES

and the lines below:

THE PRETTY POLE AND THE

TERROR OF TERRE HAUTE

Maigret was smiling now. "Vanity," he said. "They can't ever resist it. They had to buy the magazine when they saw it on the stands, and she had to frame the picture.

"I knew I'd seen her face before. I do remember the case roughly. I kept some clippings on it. Very similar to ours. In the Middle West of America, four or five years ago. A gang attacking lonely farms, cutting throats . . . just like ours . . . and they had a woman leader. The American press took great pleasure in describing her atrocities."

"Then Stan . . .?"

". . . was Olga. Almost certainly. I'll be positive in an hour, now that I know what to look for in the office. Are you coming with me, Lucas?"

"But Ozep?" Lucas asked, as they settled back in the cab.

"It's Ozep I especially want to look up. That is, I'm hoping I'll find something about him. If he killed this woman, he must have had a motive. . . . Listen, Lucas: When I wanted to send him to the others, he agreed at once. But when I gave him an errand to the woman, he refused, and I was forced to use pressure, even to threaten him. In other words, the rest of the gang did not know him— *but the woman did.*"

152

It took a good half-hour to find the clippings in question. Order was not Maigret's dominant attribute.

"Read this! Always allowing for the exaggeration of the American press—they like to give the readers their money's worth. 'The Female Fiend . . .' 'The Deadly Pole . . .' 'Girl, twenty-three, Heads Murder Gang . . .'"

The press reveled in the exploits of the Polish girl and furnished many proofs of her photogenic qualities.

At eighteen Stephanie Polintskaja was already known to the Warsaw police. Around this time she met a man who married her and strove to curb her evil instincts. She had a child by him. One day the man came home from work to find that his wife had vanished with all the money and jewelry. The child's throat had been cut.

"You know who that man was?" Maigret asked.

"Ozep?"

"Here's his picture, and a good likeness. You understand now? Stephanie, nicknamed Stan, ran wild in America. How she escaped the American prisons I do not know. In any case she took refuge in France, surrounded herself with a fresh lot of brutes, and took up her old career.

"Her husband learns from the papers that she is in Paris, that the police are on her trail. Does he want to rescue her once more? I doubt it. I'm rather inclined to think that he wants to make sure that the detestable murderess of his child shall not escape punishment. That's why he offers me his services. He hasn't the guts to work alone. He's too much of a weakling. He needs the police to help him. And then, this afternoon, I force his hand. . . .

"Face to face with his former wife, what can he do? Kill or be killed! She certainly would not hesitate to destroy the only man outside the gang who could testify against her.

"So he killed . . . And do you want to know what I think? I'm betting that they'll find him somewhere in the hotel, more or less seriously wounded. After muffing two attempts at suicide, it would amaze me if he muffed the third. Now you can go back to the hotel and—"

"No use!" It was the chief's voice. "Stan the Killer hanged himself in a vacant room on the sixth floor. Good riddance!"

"He made it," Maigret sighed. "Poor devil!"

"You're sorry for him?"

"Indeed I am. Especially since I'm somewhat responsible for

his death. . . . I don't know if it means I'm getting old; but I certainly took long enough to find the solution—"

"What solution?" the director asked suspiciously.

"The solution to the whole problem!" Lucas intervened happily. "The Inspector has reconstructed the case in all its details."

"That so, Maigret?"

"It is. . . . You know, if you keep mulling over the same question . . . I don't think I've ever been so mad at myself in my life. I felt that the solution was there, within reach, that just one little touch. . . .And you all kept buzzing around me like horseflies, telling me about arrests that didn't mean a thing . . . And then I remembered the American detective magazine and the woman's face on the cover. . . ."

Maigret took a deep breath, loaded his pipe, and asked Lucas for matches. The afternoon vigil had used up all his own.

"What do you say, chief? It's seven o'clock. Suppose we three settle down to a nice glass of beer? Provided that Lucas gets rid of his wig and makes himself respectable again."

A CLUE FROM BING CROSBY

BY BAYNARD KENDRICK

Baynard Kendrick was born in Philadelphia, Pennsylvania, in 1894, and served in the Canadian Army during World War I. His blind detective, Captain Duncan Maclain, first appeared in *The Last Express* in 1937. Kendrick served during World War II preparing courses for the treatment of blinded veterans. His dramatic non-mystery novel, *Lights Out* (1945), drawn from this experience, became a highly successful film in 1951 as *Bright Victory*. Kendrick was a founding member of Mystery Writers of America, served as its first president, and received its Grand Master Award in 1966. He died on March 22, 1977.

ON FRIDAY, DECEMBER 20TH, a week to the day since six-year-old Ronnie Connaster had been kidnapped from Miss Murray's School, Arnold Cameron, Special Agent in Charge of the New York F.B.I., telephoned early in the morning to make an appointment with Captain Duncan Maclain. It was arranged for ten A.M. in Maclain's penthouse office twenty-six stories above 72nd Street and Riverside Drive.

Cameron arrived promptly, bringing with him Special Agent Hank Weeks and Alan Connaster, Ronnie's father. The men were silent, grim.

Captain Maclain, an ex-Intelligence Officer blinded in World War I, had carried on the work of a Private Investigator with the aid of his partner, Spud Savage, for nearly forty years. To him being a Licensed P.I. was a dedicated profession. He hoped by developing his remaining four senses, hearing, feeling, taste, and smell to the highest point of proficiency to prove to the world that a blind man with sufficient intelligence could be just as good as, if not a little bit better than, millions of people who had eyes with which to see.

Waiting for Cameron, the Captain had a gratified feeling that maybe after all these years he had at last succeeded. Duncan Maclain was no superman. He had certain peculiar talents that had proved most useful through the years to various law enforcement agencies, among them the New York Police Department, and on several occasions the F.B.I.

He had known Arnold Cameron for a long time, and worked with him before Cameron became S.A.C. of the New York office. The Captain was the first to admit that neither he nor any private operator could get to first base without the cooperation of the local police or the F.B.I.

Cameron hadn't said what this case was about, except that it concerned the kidnapping of Connaster's six-year-old son. The Captain had heard about Alan Connaster, President and Treasurer of Connaster Products, Inc., the big plant that sprawled over acres on the edge of Long Island City. It was one of those industrial mushrooms that had grown in importance since World War II, mainly through Connaster's personality and engineering genius. The company did a lot of top-security defense work, but the F.B.I. was quite capable of handling any violations of security on their own. Kidnapping, too, for that matter.

At 9:55 Rena, the Captain's secretary, showed the three men in. Maclain shook hands around. Cameron's grip was friendly as usual. Special Agent Hank Weeks was properly official, neither cold nor warm.

Alan Connaster wrung the Captain's hand with a grip that was full of despairing appeal. "Mr. Cameron thinks that you can help us, Captain Maclain. My son's been gone for a week now—more like a lifetime to Evelyn, my wife, and me. She has collapsed and is under a doctor's care. It isn't a question of money—I can pay a million and not be hurt. It's the life of my boy—our only child and we can never have another."

A strong man, Alan Connaster, the Captain judged. Six foot, slow spoken, powerful as flexible steel, and younger than one would imagine. From his voice—not yet forty. And right now he was on the verge of flying into little pieces.

Maclain went to the bar set in the paneled wall near the diamond-paned doors to the terrace. He sloshed a liberal portion of cognac into a bell goblet and took it to the red leather sofa where Connaster had slumped down.

"Slug it!" His face was grave with deep concern. "Your hand is as cold as a frozen fish. It won't help your boy if you crack now."

"Thanks. I guess you're right." Connaster downed the brandy in a gulp. "I'm afraid we're saddling you with a hopeless task."

"The world considers blindness hopeless. I haven't found it so." The Captain walked to his broad flat-top desk and sat down.

"He was kidnapped last Friday, December thirteenth, at ten past three," Arnold Cameron said. "He'd been to a Christmas party at his school—Miss Murray's at Sixty-sixth Street and Fifth Avenue. The Connasters live in a duplex at Eighty-second and Fifth—sixteen blocks away. Miss Murray saw Ronnie get into his father's Chrysler Imperial in front of the school at three ten. The car was driven by a substitute chauffeur, who called himself Jules Rosine.

"Rosine stuck up Leon Gerard, who has driven for the family for years, in Gerard's apartment on East Eighty-second Street—right across the street from the garage where the Chrysler is

157

kept. That was about eleven the night before. Rosine wore a stocking mask. He forced Leon to telephone at gunpoint. Leon talked to Mrs. Murchison, the Connasters' housekeeper, said he was ill, and would send a reliable man to take his place the next day. Nobody thought it suspicious since it had happened a few times before. Leon is getting along in years and his health isn't too good."

Cameron paused. The Captain said, "If you fellows believe his story, then I do too."

"We don't believe anything until we've convinced ourselves that it's true," Cameron went on. "Weeks found and released Leon in his apartment shortly after the kidnapping was reported to us on the evening of the thirteenth. The poor old guy was trussed up like a turkey with adhesive. Anyhow, nothing has been seen of Ronnie or this Jules Rosine since ten past three in the afternoon a week ago."

A hopeless task, Connaster had said. The Captain ran a hand through his dark graying hair. The details of Charles A. Lindbergh, Jr., Bobby Greenlease, Jr., and the tiny month-old Peter Weinberger, all coolly murdered by their kidnappers, were much too vivid in his mind not to realize that Connaster's fears were well grounded.

He kept his thoughts to himself and tried to speak reassuringly. "I've known Arnold Cameron for many years, Mr. Connaster. Neither he nor the F.B.I. considers this hopeless or he wouldn't have brought you here to talk with me." His dark sightless eyes, so perfect that many people thought he could see, turned from Connaster to fix themselves on the S.A.C. "You must have some very good reason for thinking Ronnie is still alive, Arnold."

"We happen, in this case, to know he was alive on Tuesday or Wednesday, and probably yesterday."

"What proof?"

"The sound of his voice, Captain, plus an answer to a couple of questions asked by Ronnie's mother—answers that only Ronnie would know."

"Then you must have made contact by phone." The Captain's eyebrows went up a fraction.

"No. They're the ones who have been in touch," Cameron said. "One-way touch, by Audograph records. Three of them. You've told me often that you live in a world of sound. I also know that you're the best man living on identification of voices.

Furthermore, you work with an Audograph all the time and are familiar with its sounds and foibles. Isn't that true?"

Maclain nodded. "I have one right here in my desk drawer." He referred to a compact efficient dictating machine used in thousands of business offices. Not more than nine inches square and five inches high, it records dictation on a flexible blue disc, and the dictation can be played back at the flip of a lever through its built-in loudspeaker, or through plugged-in headphones.

"Here's the first of the three—the first word from Ronnie's captors, for that matter, from Friday to Monday. Let the family suffer. Die a thousand deaths. It softens them up. I could—"

He broke off abruptly, leaned forward and put a brown manila envelope on the Captain's blotter. It was a standing mailing envelope for the feather-light discs. Seven inches square. Printed on the front was GRAY AUDOGRAM FOR—a space for the address—and below that the words PLEASE DO NOT FOLD. The envelopes, like the discs, could be obtained from any Audograph dealer in cities throughout the country.

For an instant the Captain stared at the envelope as though by sheer intentness, he might develop some superhuman power to penetrate its secret.

"That was mailed to Mrs. Connaster at her home," Cameron explained. "Air mail. It's postmarked: Miami, Florida, December fifteenth. That was last Sunday."

Maclain touched it gingerly with his forefinger. "I know what a working over you must have given these things. I was wondering about handwriting, or typing, on the address."

"Not this bird, Captain! He hasn't forgotten that we went through two million specimens of handwriting before we nailed LaMarca as kidnapper of the Weinberger baby. There's not even typewriting. No return address, of course. Mrs. Connaster's name and address has been stamped on with one of those kid's rubber stamps that has separate removable rubber letters. You can buy them in any toy store or five and ten."

The Captain took his Audograph machine from the deep bottom left-hand desk drawer. He put it on the desk, then brought up a hand microphone which he plugged into a six-slotted receptacle on the left-hand side of the machine. A switch in the handle of the mike controlled the playing of the record, turning it on when pressed in. For continuous playing, a flick of the thumb could lock the switch.

159

He took the record from the envelope, felt for the grooved side with his fingernail, and turning it upward put the record on the machine. Unlike a regular phonograph record, the Audograph recorded from the center to the edge.

The Captain slid it into place, turned on the machine, and pushed a lever over to LISTEN. A red indicator-light glowed. When recording, the light showed green. He locked the switch on the hand mike and set it down.

Out of nowhere the boyish treble of Ronnie Connaster's voice began to speak. Maclain reached out and turned the volume higher, as though that might help to bring the six-year-old closer to his home.

"Mommy, mommy, can you hear me? The man says to tell you that I'm all right and that if I talk in here you can hear me. He says that daddy can hear me, too, and that if you do what the man says he'll bring me home. Mommy, please tell daddy to do what the man says. I'm all right, but I'm scared, mommy. I don't want to spend Christmas here. I'm doing just what the man tells me to. Please hurry and do what the man says. I don't want to spend Christmas here. I don't like it and the man says he'll bring me home. So, please hurry."

Ronnie's voice quit abruptly. For an endless length of time— actually a few short seconds—the record revolved in mechanical silence. Cameron lit a cigarette. Smoke reached the Captain's nostrils. Leather squeaked as Connaster moved uneasily on the red sofa.

A man's voice took up where the child's voice had stopped; a harsh voice:

"Your son's been kidnapped, but he hasn't been harmed. It's to prove it that I'm letting him talk to you. You'll be better off if you keep the police out of this as well as the F.B.I. Press me too hard and you'll never hear his voice again, let alone see him. If you follow our instructions to the letter you'll have him back very shortly. In case you don't think that's your son who was speaking, I'm going to offer you further proof. Ask him any two questions you want—questions that only he can answer. Put it in a Personal in the New York Times of Tuesday, December the seventeenth. Sign it 'E.C.' You'll be answered by Ronnie on the next record we send to you. That's all for now. You'll never see me. Just call me: Junior."

"Is that all?" The Captain sat up straight in his chair.

"End of Record One," Cameron told him.

Maclain swiftly adjusted the disc to play the last few lines a second time.

160

Faintly, but clearly, through the man's last few words had come the sound of chimes pealing the opening bars of *Silent Night*. Then a singer had begun:

> *"Silent night,*
> *Holy night,*
> *All is—"*

The song had ended with the click of the mike as the man said, "Junior."

"The musical interlude," Cameron said glumly, "is the first song on Side One of Bing Crosby's Decca Recording DL-8128, entitled *Merry Christmas*. Sales to date about two million. On the last report from our bunion-ridden agents in Miami, they have found some two hundred radio, record, and music shops, supermarkets, drive-ins, and various other publicity-minded places of business, including second-hand-car lots that have P.A. systems working over-time. They have been deafening the public for a week or more to let them know the time of year. Number One on the Hit Parade is Bing's rendition of Christmas cheer.

"We don't think Ronnie's in Miami, anyhow. This Jules Rosine—who is trying hard to make us believe that that's his name by calling himself Junior—from the initials J.R.—just doesn't strike me as the type, Captain, who would mail a letter or anything from the same city where he has that boy. As a matter of fact, he jumps around the country like a twelve-legged flea. The second record is from Kansas City and the third one is from Cleveland."

The Captain sat pinching his upper lip and saying nothing.

Cameron put the second envelope on his desk. "Here's the one where Ronnie answers his mother's questions. Mailed Wednesday, December the eighteenth. Air mail from K.C."

There was a tremor in the Captain's sensitive fingers as he removed the first record and put the second on.

" *Mommy, the man says that you and daddy can hear me if I talk in here, but I don't see how you can hear me if I can't see you. He said I was to tell you what picture Ted Schuyler and I were going to see with Mrs. Murchison, and what I call my electric engine that pulls the train, and if I didn't tell you I wouldn't get back home. I thought you knew that Ted and I were going to see 'Snow White and the Seven Dwarfs'— except daddy wanted me to come to the plant to meet him and I drank the*

161

Pepsi-Cola the chauffeur got me and got so sleepy. And you know my engine is called the Camel because it has a humpback in its middle. I know you told me not to repeat things, but the man said unless I told you that and unless daddy did just what he says, I won't get home for Christmas. I don't want to stay here. There's nobody to play with and I want to come home."

The man's voice took it from there:

" That answers the questions you had in the Times and proves beyond doubt that your son's alive. Nobody is trying to torture you. You'll see when we write again that we're not after money. It's possible that we have even more of that than you. The next will tell you what we do want. We know what you want, but don't think we're fooling. Stay away from the police and the F.B.I. and do exactly what I tell you or your precious son is going to die. Cheerio! Junior."

"Junior seems to have split himself in two," the Captain said as he took off the record. "The *man* has become *we*. Do you think it's merely a coverup, Arnold, or is there really someone else involved beside the man?"

"Anywhere from two to two million. They're after something more precious to them than money." He put the third record on the desk. "Listen to this one and you'll see."

Agent Hank Weeks said, "I'm betting there's a woman. Purely because they've kept Ronnie harping on *the man*."

The Captain nursed his chin for a moment. "I'm inclined to agree." He put the final record on.

"Do you mind if I have another brandy?" Alan Connaster's voice was tight and dry.

"Drink up," the Captain said. "Ronnie isn't my son, but nevertheless these records are really getting me."

Connaster poured his drink and returned to his seat. "They're somehow worse than ransom notes to Evelyn and me. They're sadistic. Mean. I find myself wanting to answer Ronnie. Scream at him: 'Tell me where you are!'—as though he were hiding away in some ghostly world of his own. It's unbearable."

"I'd merely sound inane if I tried to express my sympathy." A cold fury was setting the Captain's skin to tingling. "This is the one from Cleveland?"

"Mailed air mail yesterday. Thursday the nineteenth. It arrived in New York this morning at seven. We have a tag out for them at the Post Office. They notified us right away."

The Captain flipped the lever to LISTEN and started the disc to play.

162

" *Mommy, did you hear what I told you about the picture show? The Seven Dwarfs? And my engine, the Camel, on the electric train? I wish that you and daddy would come for me, or answer me if you heard me, like the man said. He says he's telling daddy exactly what to do right now, and if daddy does it I'll come back home. Mommy, tell him to hurry, please. Hurry and do it because I miss you so much and I want to see the Macy's parade and get my Christmas presents.* "

More unbearable silence until the man cut in:

"*At six o'clock, P.M.—eighteen hours Service Time—you and your pilot, Steven Donegan, will take off from the air strip at your plant on Long Island, flying your Cessna Twin. You will file no flight plan with anyone. At your regular cruising speed of two hundred ten miles per hour, flying at eight thousand feet, you will follow the regular plane route from New York to Philadelphia, from Philadelphia to Baltimore, from Baltimore to Washington, from Washington to Richmond, from Richmond to Wilmington, North Carolina, from Wilmington to Charleston, South Carolina, from Charleston to Savannah, Georgia, from Savannah to Jacksonville, Florida, from Jacksonville to Daytona, from Daytona to Vero Beach, and from Vero Beach to Miami.*

"*Be on the alert. Somewhere between two of the places named you will be contacted by radio. When contact is made, if you broadcast an alarm your son will be killed. Remember we'll be tuned in on you. We want the complete plans of the SF800T Missile. Those plans consist of forty-four sheets of blueprints that were delivered to you by the Navy a month ago. You are the only one living who has immediate access to them all. Those forty-four blueprints are the price of your son. Particularly the details of the cone.*

"*Once they are received they will be checked immediately by engineers just as competent as you. If they are not approved, or any attempt at trickery is discovered, your boy will die. The clearer those specifications are, the quicker you get your son. Remember, it's his life that's at stake.*

"*Put the plans in a large portmanteau—not a dispatch case—and weight the portmanteau with a couple of sash weights. Paint the portmanteau with phosphorescent paint and be ready to drop it on a moment's notice. You will be contacted by the words: 'Cessna, come down!' and you will immediately start descending to a thousand feet, still holding your course. Watch the ground. One minute before the drop, you will be advised of that fact. Answer: 'Roger, Junior!' and look for a red flasher that will turn on on top of a car. When you spot it say: 'Condition red!' and drop the portmanteau as close as possible to the flasher.*

"*You will be directed if you have to make a second try. Follow the*

163

straightest compass course between points and there will be no trouble. Another record will tell you where to pick up your boy. If weather reports are generally bad don't attempt to start. That's your hard luck and you'll have to make another try. Happy landings! Junior."

"Sounds like something from out of the wild blue yonder," Maclain said as he stopped the record. "A modern Chekhov nightmare manufactured in Moscow. What are the chances of pulling off such a scheme?"

"My pilot, Steve, says there's a damn good chance," Connaster told him. "I'm a pilot, myself, and I agree. Junior knows that we'll break our necks to drop that luminous suitcase on his head, if possible. He also knows that the SF-800T is an ace we have in the hole. So I'm supposed to stake the life of my son against the safety of my country."

The Captain gnawed at his mustache. "At least the Soviets have one weakness that will never change: we know that it's impossible to fathom their way of thinking—but they fully believe that they know the thinking of every other country in the world. Now, it's the life of a child against the lives of untold millions. Tomorrow night! That's not much time to make up forty-four sheets of phony blueprints. What does the F.B.I. think, Arnold? What are you going to do?"

"Mr. Connaster is going to drop the plans as ordered," Cameron said promptly. "You're right about Soviet thinking. We've learned a lot since the days of Klaus Fuchs and Harry Gold. Today Naval Intelligence draws up two sets of plans— when the design is for anything as vital as the SF-800T. The second set is slightly different. To discover the bugs in it might take a corps of scientists half a year. That's the set we're feeding to Junior tomorrow night."

"Leaving three people only on the hot seat: Ronnie, my wife, and me!" Connaster's voice was low and deadly. "They're not going to keep Ronnie alive for six months. So they may find some bugs in a couple of days, and kill him then. Then there's always the chance when they get the plans that they'll consider it safer to murder him anyway."

"So we better get busy with what we have, Mr. Connaster: three records, the sound of a kidnapper's voice, and a snatch of song from a P.A. speaker." Maclain shook his head. "It's not very much, but somehow among us we've got to put it together. Before those plans are examined at all, we've got to find your boy. There is no other alternative."

164

"Knowing you as well as I do," Arnold Cameron said, "I have a vague uneasy feeling that you may be on to something that we've overlooked. I hope so."

"I have some questions." There were lines on Maclain's forehead and his mobile face was set in a look of concentration. "Why did this man pick Audograph records?"

"We have fifteen Audographs in our office at the plant," Connaster explained. "I also have one for dictation at home."

"Do you think he was an ex-employee, Arnold?"

"That's a possibility that we're checking. We're getting a run-down on everyone who has worked at Connaster Products since the war. It's a big job, but it's a top-security plant, so it shouldn't be impossible. But it is going to take time."

"Of which we have none," Connaster grunted. "Personally, I think it more likely that Junior called in as a salesman and saw the machines. Employees in our place are too closely checked for comfort."

"How would he know you had one home?"

"Maybe he didn't, but he knew I could always get one and take it home, since he's addressing his records to Evelyn there."

"Okay," Maclain said. "I'm going to start just as if I knew what I was talking about: the same voices made all those records—Ronnie's and Junior's. Let's take it for granted that it's the same man who picked up Ronnie, and drove you to work under the name of Jules Rosine. Would you know him again, Mr. Connaster, if you saw him?"

Connaster gave it a little thought. "I doubt it. He wore a chauffeur's livery. He was dark, I believe, seemed personable enough, slightly built—that is, he didn't impress me as being particularly big and strong. I didn't see him standing up. From the few words he spoke, I'd say he had a French accent. On the drive to Long Island, after dropping Ronnie at school in the morning, I was reading the paper and busy with some figures in the back seat of the car. Since I was occupied, I didn't give him too much thought, really."

"He is French, according to Leon Gerard," Hank Weeks stated positively. "He spoke fluent French to Leon when he held him up in his room and forced him to phone the housekeeper."

"So his speech on the records, while marking him as an educated man, has words in it that are as British as a dish of bubble-and-squeak," Maclain declared. " 'Phosphorescent paint'—'portmanteau'—'dispatch case.' We'd say brief case, or luminous suitcase. But his accent isn't really British—just the words he uses. Let's mark him as a French Canadian—Quebec or Montreal. Do you agree?"

"I think I'll buy that Canadian angle right now," Weeks said. "Since Igor Gouzenko skipped the Russian Embassy in Ottawa in 1946 and turned up Klaus Fuchs, they've had troubles aplenty with certain Reds in Canada."

"What would you guess his age to be?" the Captain asked.

"Between thirty and forty as a guess." Connaster sounded a little unsure.

"Well, later if nothing happens, it might pay you to run back through the Year Books of Graduates in Engineering at McGill—University of Toronto, too. A picture just might jog your memory enough to spot him. There's another point I'd like to get clear: Ronnie certainly wasn't kidnapped in your own car—that is, I don't think they'd chance driving him very far."

"Just across the Queensboro Bridge," Cameron said. "The police found Mr. Connaster's Imperial parked under the approach to the bridge on the Long Island side at six twenty. Ronnie was going to a movie with another boy, Ted Schuyler, at four. You heard that."

Maclain nodded. "I'm interested as to how this Rosine got him to come along without a fuss, and then transferred him to another car. That's not easy in New York City between three and four in the afternoon."

"You know as much as we do, Captain. From what Ronnie says on the records, the kidnapper gave him a line that Mr. Connaster wanted Ronnie to meet him at the plant. He bought Ronnie a bottle of Pepsi-Cola on the way. The police found the bottle still in the car and analyzed what was left. It showed Ronnie must have drunk three or four grains of Seconal. That would have put him out cold in fifteen minutes to half an hour, and he would have stayed out for eight to ten hours, maybe longer, according to the Medical Examiner. Of course they could have given him more on the trip, if they were driving far."

Maclain took a box of paper clips from his middle desk drawer and slowly began to chain them together.

"That's what I was trying to figure—how long would they drive Ronnie and how far. Let's say four hundred miles—ten hours driving. That would put them where they were going about four in the early morning. I think Junior lives there and owns a house most likely. It's not easy to rent a place to hide a child. It must be fairly large—the town, I mean, or the city. Far too dangerous to take him to a small town—"

"What about an isolated farm?" Agent Weeks broke in on the Captain's audible reverie.

"Not close enough to a post office and an airport." The Captain put his clips back in the drawer and closed it with a snap. "Let's consider these records: it's obvious that nobody is flying around the country with a kidnapped boy. So the boy's in one place—probably guarded by Junior's wife or some other woman. Women are better with children, anyhow. Now, listen to this."

He found the Miami record and put it on, keeping his hand held up for silence until it was through.

"That record was made by Ronnie and the man on the machine, and at the same time. The machine may be old, or defective, for there's a murmuring drone in the background that records itself all the way through. Junior didn't notice it, so it must be a noise that he's used to. He noticed the start of *Silent Night* quick enough and shut off the machine."

"The record was mailed from Miami, Captain," Cameron reminded him.

"That's my point, Arnold—nearness to an airport. I believe that record was made Saturday evening, giving Ronnie time to get instructions as to what he should say. Then Junior took it with him as soon as it was finished and caught a flight to Miami. In his suitcase he was carrying another Audograph machine. He mailed the record from Miami on Sunday. That would check as to time—ample time for him to stop off and make arrangements for the pickup with some deputy sheriff, or town constable confederate along the way."

"You're right there," Cameron said glumly. "Deputy sheriffs and constables are a dime a dozen, and a police car is made to order—two-way telephone, flasher and all. We can't police every point between here and Miami."

"So again the best bet is to find the woman and the boy," Maclain said. "She'll talk, I believe, if Junior has told her anything. We can be sure that if he'd made arrangements in Miami, the record wouldn't have been mailed from there, any more than if Ronnie was there. Anyhow, we know that after the record was mailed, he hopped the first flight for Kansas City."

167

"Typical Commie technique, that hopping about," Hank Weeks remarked. "The Boss, in his book 'Masters of Deceit,' says they call it 'dry cleaning'—driving three hundred miles to cover thirty so that no one will know where you've been or where you are."

"Go on, Captain." Cameron sounded impatient. "You've got this Commie Canuck with his Audograph in K.C. now. Where do we go from there—outside of Cleveland?"

Without replying, Maclain put on the second record and played it to the end. "I know that Ronnie made this record on the same machine that recorded record Number One. All the time that Ronnie is speaking you can hear that noise that runs through the first one. As soon as Junior starts to speak, the noise is gone. We must assume that the woman mailed this record to Junior in K.C., and he filled his part in on the Audograph he has with him. *The New York Times* is available in most cities the same, or the following day. The woman could have seen the personal and told Ronnie what to say, or Junior could have seen it and could have called her long-distance."

"Still more dry cleaning," Cameron said, "to help us Special Agents earn our pay, and put us through a wringer the way we're going through today. Let's hear Number Three."

The Cleveland record clinched the Captain's beliefs—a background noise when Ronnie was speaking, Junior's words clear.

"Could that noise come from a car or a plane?" Connaster asked. "I've used an Audograph in both, but I haven't been conscious of anything like that in the playbacks. Still, I might have overlooked it just as Junior has."

"It just won't hold water." The Captain's agile fingers beat a tattoo on the desk top. "I don't believe Ronnie and his captor made that first record while driving in a car. There's that *Silent Night* music, for one thing. Can you picture a man with a kidnapped boy in his car dictating a record and telling the boy what to say? Then a stop in front of a music store where there's a blaring P.A.?"

Hank Weeks said, "Hell, no! Nor can I picture the kid being flown around making records in a plane."

Maclain stood up abruptly. "Let's get what we can from the horse's mouth—the Sound Engineer at Gray Audograph. Let him hear these and see what he has to say."

In less than an hour they were in the Gray Audograph offices at 521 Fifth Avenue, talking to Carl Schantz, the com-

168

pany's Chief Sound Engineer. Schantz listened to Cameron, then played the three records through without comment.

Finished, he sat down in his desk chair and stared from one to another of his visitors through his gold-rimmed glasses. "The boy's voice and the man's—all of record One—was dictated to the same machine. The man's voice on records Two and Three was dictated to another machine. I'd say that both machines were old. Probably our Model Three, but there's nothing the matter with either of them."

"How do you know that?" Cameron asked. "The differences in the machines, I mean."

Schantz gave a slow smile. "You know from your work in the F.B.I. that there's a difference in every typewriter. Well, there's a difference in the needles of every dictating machine. They cut grooves of different depths on the records. The difference in those grooves is infinitesimal, but it shows up on a tape made by the electric micrometer on our testing machine—the one I just played those on." He handed the S.A.C. a wide piece of ruled paper marked in purple ink with three wavy parallel lines. "Look for yourself."

The lines made by record One, and the two lines made by Ronnie's voice on Two and Three were noticeably similar. There was a difference when Junior started to speak on the Kansas City and Cleveland records, but it still could be seen with the naked eye that those two lines were similar to each other.

"Does this mean that if we find those two machines and bring them in you can identify them for us?" Cameron's voice was eager.

"We'll give it a try."

"What about that noise in the background?"

Schantz shrugged. "I'm afraid I can't help you there."

"Could it come from a nearby power plant or high-tension lines, something like that?" the Captain asked him.

Schantz shook his head. "We have Audographs running in offices with air conditioners, calculators, and IBM sorting machines, sometimes right in the same room, and there's nothing but voice on the dictated record. Now and then, if you're not careful, you can get a loose connection in the six-hole receptacle where the mike plugs in. That will cause a nasty roar—but you can't dictate to the machine." He thought a moment. "The nearest thing to that noise I've heard was on a record dictated in an auto running at high speed with the windows open. The machine didn't pick up the motor, but it picked up the sound of the wind rushing by. That sound you have is steady like that, but deeper. It's almost like the lad was speaking through some distant hurricane." He sighed. "I'm really sorry I can't help you more."

"About those few lines of *Silent Night*—have you any ideas there?" the Captain asked as Schantz was showing them out.

"I thought of a radio in another room, but it's too muffled. It's probably outside the house, from a juiced-up P.A. system. If that's it, the place is right next door, or at the most across the street. Anyhow, it must be very near."

All afternoon the Captain sat in his penthouse office listening to the records that Cameron had left with him.

The background sound was all-enveloping. The longer he listened to it, the more it took possession of him, until he almost believed what Schantz had said about a distant hurricane.

He thought of the ocean. It could keep people awake the first night, and in a day or two the noise would be gone. But the ocean wouldn't record like that unless it were a wind-lashed sea.

Could they have the boy on a ship at sea? In a seven-day storm? And mailing records air mail to Junior in Kansas City? It showed how feeble the mind could get if you worked it on and on!

He kept coming back to that power plant. Why, when Schantz had said it wouldn't record? Could Schantz be wrong? Or could he, Maclain, whose ears had replaced his eyes, be clutching at straws and building into roaring volume some tiny wisp of sound? Was that noise, that suggested a thousand jet planes busy ripping the skies, merely the hum of a washing machine or an electric dryer? No, it had to be more.

Power, overwhelming power. It had to be. With the life of a six-year-old boy at stake, Maclain didn't dare to be wrong.

He would stick to his own obsessions, too: they'd taken the boy, maybe dressed as a girl, on a single trip of ten hours. Four hundred miles at least. Then why not into Canada? If Junior was a Canadian, his car would have Canadian tags. It would be easy to cross the International Bridge in the middle of the night with a sleeping little girl accompanied by her father and mother. . . .

The Captain jumped from the red sofa, shut off the Audograph, and took his Braille map of New York State from a flat cabinet drawer. Moving faster than the eye could follow, he traced a line from New York City to Buffalo. Just 375 miles!

Five minutes later he had Arnold Cameron on the phone. "I've got a fix, Arnold. Two points of sound—like hunting down a hidden radio. Now it's up to you to go get that boy!" For a minute more he talked on.

"Don't tell us how to run our business," Cameron cut in. "Get off the line so I can phone the Border Patrol of the Royal Canadian Mounted Police."

Just outside the city limits, running at right angles to the river between Stanley Avenue and the Parkway, is a short street with eight neat houses on it. Five on one side and three on the other. On the side with the three houses, and not quite forming a corner with the Parkway, stands the Maple Leaf Tavern, boasting ten spotless bedrooms on the second floor, and downstairs a very good restaurant and a bar.

At seven o'clock, on Friday, December 20th, Mr. Burns, who had owned and run the Maple Leaf for forty years, left his wife to superintend the cooking of dinner in the kitchen. He came into the bar to start his pickup with Bing Crosby's *Merry Christmas* record. The first few chimes introducing *Silent Night* had scarcely pealed forth from the loudspeaker over the Maple Leaf's front door, when Detective Sergeant McMurtrie of the Ontario Provincial Police walked into the bar.

He and Burns were old friends. McMurtrie, tall and cadaverous with sad black eyes, was a startling contrast to the sandy-haired Burns, a Scot grown fat with good living through the years.

They shook hands. McMurtrie ordered an ale and sat down at a table in the empty bar. Burns joined him a moment later carrying two bottles and glasses.

"I'll have an ale wi' ye, Mac."

"On me, if ye like. Looks to me like you've driven all your trade away wi' that racket over the front door."

"A racket ye call it! Don't be blasphemous, Mac. 'Tis one of God's songs, and there's others to come. I've been playing it every night now, except Sundays, for the past ten nights. 'Tis weather that's driven the trade away and not my offering passersby a bit of Christmas cheer."

"Hmph!" McMurtrie swallowed some ale, his Adam's apple

moving up and down. "And would ye have a permit, Burns, to play that thing? Seems to me the good folks on this street would be kicking with you disturbing their TV and their sleep."

" 'Tis you who know perfectly well I have a permit, McMurtrie. Even though I'm outside the city line, who but you has poked his long nose in here every chance he gets, checking every license and permit? And as for the folks on this street kicking, they're all good customers and friends of mine and glad of a little music."

"All?" McMurtrie narrowed his bushy brows. "Now there was one I recalled that you turned in for making subversive talk here during the war. What was his name?"

"Zwicker," Burns said. "Francois Zwicker. He owns the house right across the street. Number Three. God be praised, a year ago he lost his job at the Electric, where he was engineer, and moved away. The house stood vacant for a spell, then was rented for three months in the summer, to be vacant again until just this last Saturday."

"Rented, you say?"

"No, he and his missus are back, but it won't be for long, mark me. He'll hold a job nowhere with his anarchistic tongue. I've forbid him my place. His missus is no prize, either. Louise is her name, a Frenchie like him. Quebec or Three Rivers. She's there by herself right now. He's off again, hunting another job, I'd say."

A party of four came in. Burns finished his ale and got up to greet them. "The ale's on me, Mac. Drop in again, and a Merry Christmas to ye!"

Outside, the detective got in a big black car where four men were waiting for him. "Let's go and get the search warrant," he said. "Zwicker's the name. The house is Number Three." The car moved off.

An hour later, to the accompaniment of Bing's voice singing, *I'll Be Home for Christmas,* McMurtrie rang the doorbell of Number Three. The door was opened by a white-faced woman with burning black eyes and raven hair.

"Provincial Police, Mrs. Zwicker," McMurtrie said. "There are four men posted about the house, and we have a search warrant. Let me in, please. We've come to get the boy."

At six P.M., on Saturday, December 21st, Alan Connaster's Cessna Twin took off from the airstrip at Connaster Products,

172

on Long Island. With Steven Donegan and Connaster at the twin controls, it headed south as ordered. Instead of a phosphorescent-painted portmanteau, it was carrying Special Agent Hank Weeks, member of the F.B.I.

Ronnie, safe now with his mother, had come home in time for Macy's Christmas Parade.

Contact by radio was made at 8:20, and almost instantly a red flasher was turned on on the ground in a large open area about twenty miles north of New Bern, North Carolina. As the Cessna headed for a point directly over the flasher, Hank Weeks spoke into the microphone:

"Zwicker, this is a Special Agent of the F.B.I. speaking to you from the Cessna. Your wife has been arrested and we have the boy. She gave us the name of Walter Vollmer, the county official who is with you now in that patrol car. You were followed and we know exactly where you are—in between Vanceboro and Blount Creek. You are hopelessly trapped, for cars are posted all along U.S. Seventeen and along State Road Thirty-three, as well as the country road you came in on. They have heard this and are closing in right now. There's no use your trying to escape."

The Cessna began to climb. "There's just one thing that gripes me, Hank," Connaster said. "Think of all the trouble you'd have saved if you'd done what Steve and I wanted to—loaded that portmanteau with just one little bomb!"

'Way up north in the Maple Leaf Tavern, Mr. Burns turned over the *Merry Christmas* record for the third time and started *Silent Night* again. On guard in the empty house across the street—in the event that plans went wrong and Zwicker returned to his home—two members of the Ontario Provincial Police were playing gin rummy.

"It would be a silent night if Burns would shut that blasted thing off," one said to the other, slapping a card on the table.

"Aye," said the other.

They went on playing unaware of the noise that filled every room, every cranny and every house and every street for miles around. They had lived in the midst of its deep reverberation far too long to hear it—the stunning boom of the Horseshoe Falls of Niagara, dumping its endless deafening millions of gallons down a drop of 158 feet just a half block away.

GIDEON AND THE SHOPLIFTING RING

BY JOHN CREASEY (J. J. MARRIC)

John Creasey (J.J. Marric) was born in Southfields, Surrey, England, in 1908 and worked at various jobs before his first book was published in 1932 after he had accumulated 743 rejection slips. Creasey wrote more than six hundred books under twenty-eight pseudonyms. As J.J. Marric he wrote a 21-book series about George Gideon of Scotland Yard, starting with *Gideon's Day* (1955). Creasey, a remarkably prolific writer, created many other popular series characters, including the Baron, the Toff, Roger West, the Liberator, and Superintendent Folly. Creasey received the Grand Master Award in 1968. He died in 1973.

"BEATS ME HOW THEY DO it," complained Superintendent Lemaitre gloomily. There seemed no guile in the expression on his thin bony face, nor in the nasal twang of his voice. "I don't mind telling you, George, it's got me beat."

"So you said before," murmured George Gideon dryly. He was Commander of Scotland Yard's C.I.D., the Criminal Investigation Department, and so London's top detective. Lemaitre was his chief aide. Gideon placed a large hand on a folder on his desk, and a faint shadow from the flat-topped fingers showed from summer's bright light reflection off the Thames into this office. "Everybody who has handled the job says the same, sooner or later. How much do you think they've robbed the Oxford Street stores of this month?"

Lemaitre drew in a whistling breath, for deliberate emphasis.

"Thirty thousand quid's worth, they say."

"Who says?"

"The big store bosses say. I don't mind telling you, those bosses will make trouble before long. Shoplifting on this scale is something new in London. Why, they must use a whole blinkin' army!"

"Which 'they' this time?"

"Come off it, George! Someone's organizing the shoplifting, you know that as well as I do. Perfume, jewelry, stockings, fur coats, dresses, and what-have-you—they take 'em out by the ton. The hell of it is we can't catch anyone red-handed—with the stuff on them."

Gideon pursed his full lips, but made no comment. He was a much bigger and heavier man than Lemaitre, with slightly rounded, very thick shoulders, a big neck, rather heavy features, iron-gray hair.

He and Lemaitre had one thing above everything else in common—a love of London, and a knowledge of London and its people.

"Why the heck don't you say something, instead of sitting on your backside and looking at me as if I were a hippie?" Lemaitre demanded. When excited, the Cockney twang of his voice became almost shrill. "If this gets any worse we'll be in real trouble. You don't *want* the newspapers saying that the Yard's

175

slipping, or awkward questions being asked in the House of Commons, do you?"

"Might not be a bad thing," said Gideon. "Might make some of our chaps start thinking, instead of taking every known shoplifter found in Oxford Street off to the nick and then finding they haven't a thing on them. How many have been pulled in like that?"

"It's in the report."

"You tell me."

"Twenty-three!" shrilled Lemaitre. He leaned on the big desk in front of Gideon, arms widespread, knuckles white where he gripped the edge. "Well, what was wrong with that? A fortune's being lifted from those stores on Thursday nights, so we pull in all the known shoplifters. Go on, tell me. What's wrong with that? Go on, tell me, George."

"It didn't work."

"I'm asking you to tell me what will."

"The shoplifters all say they were after bargains on late-opening night, with their families," remarked Gideon. "They all had at least one member of their family with them. They—"

"Do you mean to tell me you think that half the shoplifters in London would go to Oxford Street on a Thursday night to *buy* stuff?" Lemaitre demanded, with withering sarcasm. "You're the one who's slipping, George."

"Wouldn't be surprised," said Gideon mildly. "Anyhow, each member of each shoplifter's family volunteered to be searched to make sure they weren't wearing stolen goods or carrying them out in shopping bags."

"They were searched all right. Why, last Thursday we had twenty policewomen and eighty plainclothes chaps in Oxford Street—and all being paid overtime."

Gideon chuckled.

"What's so funny?"

"A hundred of our people concentrating on the wrong crooks," said Gideon. "When you come to think of it, Lem, it *is* funny. Every shoplifter who was taken to the nick and every volunteer who was searched must have gone off home laughing his head off. We're likely to be guyed in *Punch* or the *Times* if this goes on. Any of these people you had to release been throwing money about lately? Especially in larger sums?"

"Can't say they have. They've all been doing all right, mind you, but they haven't been spending too free. Do you think

176

they've been paid to go along Oxford Street and draw our fire?"

"Of course."

"Had a nasty feeling it might be something like that. But who's doing the actual jobs? How do they get away? This is on such a big scale that it must take a lot of organizing. It's been going on for six weeks now, and getting worse every week," Lemaitre went on. "George, could you take a look yourself? You might spot something the rest of us keep missing."

"Tell you what I will do," said Gideon. "I'll catch a Number Fifteen bus at Regent Street and take a ride as far as Marble Arch."

"I daresay a bus is as good as any place for thinking," Lemaitre said. "Want me to come along with you?"

"I'd like you to follow and meet me when I get off the bus. Are our chaps out in strength tonight?"

"Couldn't spare so many—there's the big fight at Albert Hall. But we've got a dozen women and thirty men in Oxford Street."

"Have them stationed at the main street corner," Gideon ordered. "Then we can stop any cars or hold up traffic for ten minutes if we want to."

"That'll make you popular!" Lemaitre put on a knowing look. "You've been thinking about this, you old fox, haven't you?"

"I've been trying to."

He was driven in a Flying Squad car as far as Piccadilly Circus where he caught a bus at half-past six. The crowds were at their thickest. Regent Street was jammed outside the Galleries Lafayette and Dickens and Jones, if rather thinner at Liberty's.

When the bus crawled round Oxford Circus into Oxford Street, Gideon marveled at the seething mass of slow-moving people and cars.

On the warm evening the windows were open, the stink of gas fumes floated in, and the clatter and roar of engines and the occasional toot of a horn merged with the cackle of human voices. Every man, woman, and child seemed to be chattering at the same time. The canyon of Oxford Street made the voices echo, the big plate-glass windows acting as sounding boards.

Gideon sat and watched and thought, nursing a pair of binoculars.

Now and again the bus crawled to a traffic light and passed it. He glanced down and saw uniformed police and plainclothesmen carrying out his orders. He smiled faintly. If it were not for the big problem he would have been thoroughly enjoying himself. In a way he was. The Londoner in him loved the sight, the sounds, the families gathered together, the little knots of people talking, the sidewalk salesmen finding a tiny space to make their squeaking dogs or squealing dolls prance, or thrusting pairs of substandard or stolen stockings into the faces of pert young girls.

" 'Arf the price you'd pay inside, duckie. Wot about giving your young man a treat?"

Gideon thought, as he had so often done lately: *If I were organizing this shoplifting, how would I get the goods away on this vast scale?* Finding out who the organizer was would be comparatively easy once the police knew how it was done. *Well, how would I do it?* Shoplifters unknown to and unsuspected by us and by the store detectives must be used, but there can only be a limited number of them.

The volume of goods stolen on Thursday nights was too large for only a dozen or so clever crooks to handle in single raids. *There must be a ferry system*, Gideon thought. *The actual thief lifts the stuff, takes it outside, leaves it with an accomplice, then goes back for more.*

He had reached that point in his thinking last week, after Lemaitre and the Divisional men had brought the problem to him. The conclusion was the result of clear, rational thought, like all detective work. Assume that twenty thieves were busy; assume that each one stole £100 worth of goods on each raid—that would come to £2000. Thirty thousand might be an exaggeration by anxious and angry store owners, but even if £20,000 worth was stolen each night, that meant ten visits by each thief.

He looked at John Lewis', then along to D.H. Evans and Marshall & Snelgrove, and eventually to Selfridge's. Yes, it could be done. If a shoplifter started at Selfridge's, say, spent twenty minutes making a good haul, came out and handed the proceeds to the accomplice, he could go on to the next store and repeat the performance. Thus each big store could be raided in about an hour and a half, at the height of the rush hour period.

Gideon leaned forward in his seat.

How *would* he do it if he were organizing such a campaign? He did not have to think so hard now; the answer was obvious. He would use a taxi or an ordinary car—in fact, he would use three or four. Each would make a tour of the West End, driving along Oxford Street at normal or subnormal traffic speed.

They would keep close to the curb, so that the shoplifter could hand over the stolen goods easily.

Ah!

They would be private cars, not taxis. If a man or a woman were seen handing goods to a taxi driver or putting them into an empty taxi, it would be more noticeable than doing the same thing with a private car. What could be more natural than hubby driving along the curb and wifey coming along and popping the stuff into the back?

"I'll see you farther along the street, dear."

"Okay, darling."

It would all sound so normal.

Smiling broadly, Gideon used his binoculars and peered up and down the street. Most of the big stores being on the north side, it was easier to keep them all under survey.

He saw a woman in brown standing at the curb some distance from a corner, but not near a bus stop or outside a store entrance. A gray Morris 1000 pulled up. She gave a bright smile, handed a shopping bag to the driver, spoke briefly, then turned and hurried away. Gideon took the number of the car—one of the least noticeable kind in London—then followed the woman's progress along the street.

He saw her take a string shopping bag from her handbag as she turned into the entrance to Selfridge's.

"That looks like it," Gideon said with deep satisfaction. He sat back for as long as it took him to reach Marble Arch. Lemaitre was standing by a shoe-shop window, looking rather like a bookie when all the favorites had come in first. He moved forward, lips turned down.

"Waste of time, wasn't it?"

"Lem, have a dozen of our chaps on the tops of a dozen different buses," Gideon said. "Tell them to look out for—"

Lemaitre's eyes were already glistening.

"You mean you've got something?"

In fact, they caught eleven women shoplifters that night. Each of them had raided at least four shops. They also caught the drivers of three Morris 1000's, each loaded in the back and in the trunk compartment with "shopping." Five more women and one more driver were arrested from statements made. There was no school leader—it was a kind of cooperative caper.

"Now they can cooperate in jail," Lemaitre said, with deep satisfaction. "I always knew we'd get 'em, George."

DEAD MAN

BY JAMES M. CAIN

James M. Cain was born in Annapolis, Maryland, on
July 1, 1892, and graduated from Washington College.
He worked as a reporter for Baltimore newspapers, and
wrote for an Army newspaper during World War I.
After the war he taught journalism at St. John's College
and later wrote for H.L. Mencken's *American Mercury,*
which published his first short story. Cain's four major
novels are *The Postman Always Rings Twice* (1934), *Double
Indemnity* (1936), *Serenade* (1937), and *Mildred Pierce*
(1941). Cain received the Grand Master Award in 1969.
He died on October 27, 1977.

HE FELT THE TRAIN CHECK, knew what it meant. In a moment, from up toward the engine, came the chant of the railroad detective: "Rise and shine, boys, rise and shine." The hoboes began dropping off. He could hear them out there in the dark, cursing as the train went by. That was what they always did on these freights: let the hoboes climb on in the yards, making no effort to dislodge them there; for that would have meant a foolish game of hide-and-seek between two or three detectives and two or three hundred hoboes, with the hoboes swarming on as fast as the detectives put them off. What they did was let the hoboes alone until the train was several miles under way; then they pulled down to a speed slow enough for men to drop off, but too fast for them to climb back on. Then the detective went down the line, brushing them off, like caterpillars from a twig. In two minutes they would all be ditched, a crowd of bitter men in a lonely spot; but they always cursed, always seemed surprised.

He crouched in the coal gondola and waited. He hadn't boarded a flat or a refrigerator with the others, back in the Los Angeles yards, tempting though this comfort was. He wasn't long on the road, and he still didn't like to mix with the other hoboes, admit he was one of them. Also, he couldn't shake off a notion that he was sharper than they were, that playing a lone hand he might think of some magnificent trick that would defeat the detective, and thus, even at this ignoble trade, give him a sense of accomplishment, of being good at it. He had slipped into the gond not in spite of its harshness, but because of it; it was black, and would give him a chance to hide, and the detective, not expecting him there, might pass him by. He was nineteen years old, and was proud of the nickname they had given him in the pool room back home. They called him Lucky.

"Rise and shine, boys, rise and shine."

Three dropped off the tank car ahead, and the detective climbed into the gond. The flashlight shot around, and Lucky held his breath. He had curled into one of the three chutes for unloading coal. The trick worked. These chutes were dangerous, for if you stepped into one and the bottom dropped, it would dump you under the train. The detective took no chances. He first shot the flash, then held on to the side while he climbed over the chutes. When he came to the last one, where Lucky lay, he shot the flash, but carelessly, and not squarely into the hole, so that he saw nothing. Stepping over, he went on, climbed to the box car behind, and resumed his chant; there were more curses, more feet sliding on ballast on the roadbed outside. Soon the train picked up speed. That meant the detective had reached the caboose, that all the hoboes were cleared.

Lucky stood up, looked around. There was nothing to see, except hot-dog stands along the highway, but it was pleasant to poke your head up, let the wind whip your hair, and reflect how you had outwitted the detective. When the click of the rails slowed and station lights showed ahead, he squatted down again, dropped his feet into the chute. As soon as lights flashed alongside, he braced against the opposite side of the chute: that was one thing he had learned, the crazy way they shot the brakes on these freights. When the train jerked to a shrieking stop, he was ready, and didn't get slammed. The bell tolled, the engine pulled away, there was an interval of silence. That meant they had cut the train, and would be picking up more cars. Soon they would be going on.

"Ah-ha! Hiding out on me, hey?"

The flashlight shot down from the box car. Lucky jumped, seized the side of the gond, scrambled up, vaulted. When he hit the roadbed, his ankles stung from the impact, and he staggered for footing. The detective was on him, grappling. He broke away, ran down the track, past the caboose, into the dark. The detective followed, but he was a big man and began to lose ground. Lucky was clear, when all of a sudden his foot drove against a switch bar and he went flat on his face, panting from the hysteria of shock.

The detective didn't grapple this time. He let go with a barrage of kicks.

"Hide out on me, will you? Treat you right, give you a break, and you hide out on me. I'll learn you—"

Lucky tried to get up, couldn't. He was jerked to his feet, rushed up the track on the run. He pulled back, but couldn't get set. He sat down, dug in with his sliding heels. The detective kicked and jerked, in fury. Lucky clawed for something to hold on to, his hand caught the rail. The detective stamped on it. He pulled it back in pain, clawed again. This time his fingers closed on a spike, sticking an inch or two out of the tie. The detective

182

jerked, the spike pulled out of the hole, and Lucky resumed his unwilling run.

"Lemme go! Why don't you lemme go?"

"Come on! Hide out on me, will you? I'll learn you to hide out on Larry Nott!"

"Lemmo go! Lemme—"

Lucky pulled back, braced with his heels, got himself stopped. Then his whole body coiled like a spring and let go in one convulsive, passionate lunge. The spike, still in his hand, came down on the detective's head, and he felt it crush. He stood there, looking down at something dark and formless, lying across the rails. . . .

Hurrying down the track, he became aware of the spike, gave it a toss, heard it splash in the ditch. Soon he realized that his steps on the ties were being telegraphed by the listening rail, and he plunged across the ditch to the highway. There he resumed his rapid walk, trying not to run. But every time a car overtook him his heels lifted queerly, and his breath first stopped, then came in gasps as he listened for the car to stop. He came to a crossroads, turned quickly to his right. He let himself run here, for the road wasn't lighted as the main highway was, and there weren't many cars. The running tired him, but it eased the sick feeling in his stomach. He came to a sign that told him Los Angeles was seventeen miles, and to his left. He turned, walked, ran, stooped down sometimes, panting, to rest. After a while it came to him why he had to get to Los Angeles, and so soon. The soup kitchen opened at seven o'clock. He had to be there, in that same soup kitchen where he had had supper, so it would look as though he had never been away.

When the lights went off, and it came broad daylight with the suddenness of Southern California, he was in the city, and a clock told him it was ten minutes after five. He thought he had time. He pressed on, exhausted, but never relaxing his rapid, half-shuffling walk.

It was ten minutes to seven when he got to the soup kitchen, and he quickly walked past it. He wanted to be clear at the end of the line. so he could have a word with Shorty, the man who dished out the soup, without impatient shoves from behind, and growls to keep moving.

Shorty remembered him. "Still here, hey?"

"Still here."

"Three in a row for you. Holy smoke, they ought be collecting for you by the month."

"Thought you'd be off."

"Who, me?"

"Sunday, ain't it?"

"Sunday? Wake up. This is Saturday."

"Saturday? You're kidding."

"Kidding my eye, this is Saturday, and a big day in this town, too."

"One day looks like another to me."

"Not this one. Parade."

"Yeah?"

"Shriners. You get that free."

"Well, that's my name, Lucky."

"My name's Shorty, but I'm over six feet."

"Nothing like that with me. I really got luck."

"You sure?"

"Like, for instance, getting a hunk of meat."

"I didn't give you no meat."

"Ain't you going to?"

"Shove your plate over quick. Don't let nobody see you."

"Thanks."

"Okay, Lucky. Don't miss the parade."

"I won't."

He sat at the rough table with the others, dipped his bread in the soup, tried to eat, but his throat kept contracting from excitement and he made slow work of it. He had what he wanted from Shorty. He had fixed the day, and not only the day but the date, for it would be the same date as the big Shriners' parade. He had fixed his name, with a little gag. Shorty wouldn't forget him. His throat relaxed, and he wolfed the piece of meat.

Near the soup kitchen he saw signs: *Lincoln Park Pharmacy, Lincoln Park Cafeteria.*

"Which way is the park, buddy?" If it was a big park, he might find a thicket where he could lie down, rest his aching legs.

"Straight down, you'll see it."

There was a fence around it, but he found a gate, opened it, slipped in. Ahead of him was a thicket, but the ground was wet from a stream that ran through it. He crossed a small bridge, followed a path. He came to a stable, peeped in. It was empty, but the floor was thickly covered with new hay. He went in, made for a dark corner, burrowed under the hay, closed his eyes. For a few moments everything slipped away, except warmth, relaxation, ease. But then something began to drill into the back of his mind: Where did he spend last night? Where would he tell them he spent last night? He tried to think, but nothing would come to him. He would have said that he spent it where he spent the night before, but he hadn't spent it in Los Angeles. He had spent it in Santa Barbara, and come down in the morning on a truck. He had never spent a night in Los Angeles. He didn't know the places. He had no answers to the questions that were now pounding at him like sledge-hammers:

"What's that? Where you say you was?"

"In a flophouse."

"Which flophouse?"

"I didn't pay no attention which flophouse. It was just a flop-house."

"Where was this flophouse at?"

"I don't know where it was at. I never been to Los Angeles before. I don't know the names of no streets."

"What this flophouse look like?"

"Looked like a flophouse."

"Come on, don't give us no gags. What this flophouse look like? Ain't you got eyes, can't you say what this here place looked like? What's the matter, can't you talk?"

Something gripped his arm, and he felt himself being lifted. Something of terrible strength had hold of him, and he was going straight up in the air. He squirmed to get loose, then was plopped on his feet and released. He turned, terrified.

An elephant was standing there, exploring his clothes with its trunk. He knew then that he had been asleep. But when he backed away, he bumped into another elephant. He slipped between the two elephants, slithered past a third to the door, which was open about a foot. Out in the sunlight, he made his way back across the little bridge, saw what he hadn't noticed before: pens with deer in them, and ostriches, and mountain sheep, that told him he had stumbled into a zoo. It was after four o'clock, so he must have slept a long time in the hay. Back on the street, he felt a sobbing rise in his throat. *That* was where he had spent the night. "In the elephant house at Lincoln Park."

"What?"

185

"That's right. In the elephant house."

"What you giving us? A stall?"

"It ain't no stall. I was in the elephant house."

"With them elephants?"

"That's right."

"How you get in there?"

"Just went in. The door was open."

"Just went in there, seen the elephants, and bedded down with them?"

"I thought they was horses."

"You thought them elephants was horses?"

"It was dark. I dug in under the hay. I never knowed they was elephants till morning."

"How come you went in this place?"

"I left the soup kitchen, and in a couple of minutes I came to the park. I went in there, looking for some grass to lie down on. Then I come to this here place, looked to me like a stable, I peeped in, seen the hay, and hit it."

"And you wasn't scared of them elephants?"

"It was dark, I tell you, and I could hear them eating the hay, but I thought they was horses. I was tired, and I wanted some place to sleep."

"Then what?"

"Then when it got light, and I seen they was elephants, I run out of there, and beat it."

"Couldn't you tell them elephants by the smell?"

"I never noticed no smell."

"How many elephants was there?"

"Three."

He brushed wisps of hay off his denims. They had been fairly new, but now they were black with the grime of the coal gond. Suddenly his heart stopped, a suffocating feeling swept over him. The questions started again, hammered at him, beat into his brain.

"Where that coal dust come from?"

"I don't know. The freights, I guess."

"Don't you know it ain't no coal ever shipped into this part of the state? Don't you know that here all they burn is gas? Don't you know it ain't only been but one coal car shipped in here in six months, and that come in by a misread train order? Don't you know that car was part of that train this here detective was riding that got killed? *Don't you know that?* Come on, out

186

with it, *WHERE DID THAT COAL DUST COME FROM?"*

Getting rid of the denims instantly became an obsession. He felt that people were looking at him on the street, spying the coal dust, waiting till he got by, then running into drug stores to phone the police that he had just passed by. It was like those dreams he sometimes had, where he was walking through crowds naked, except that this was no dream, and he wasn't naked, he was wearing these denims, these tell-tale denims with coal dust all over them. He clenched his hands, had a moment of terrible concentration, headed into a filling station.

"Hello."

"Hello."

"What's the chances on a job?"

"No chances."

"Why not?"

"Don't need anybody."

"That's not the only reason."

"There's about forty-two other reasons, one of them is I can't even make a living myself, but it's all the reason that concerns you. Here's a dime, kid. Better luck somewhere else."

"I don't want your dime. I want a job. If the clothes were better, that might help, mightn't it?"

"If the clothes were good enough for Clark Gable in the swell gambling-house scene, that wouldn't help a bit. Not a bit. I just don't need anybody, that's all."

"Suppose I got better clothes. Would you talk to me?"

"Talk to you any time, but I don't need anybody."

"I'll be back when I get the clothes."

"Just taking a walk for nothing."

"What's your name?"

"Hook's my name. Oscar Hook."

"Thanks, Mr. Hook. But I'm coming back. I just got a idea I can talk myself into a job. I'm some talker."

"You're all of that, kid. But don't waste your time. I don't need anybody."

"Okay. Just the same, I'll be back."

He headed for the center of town, asked the way to the cheap clothing stores. At Los Angeles and Temple, after an hour's trudge, he came to a succession of small stores in a Mexican quarter that were what he wanted. He went into one. The storekeeper was a Mexican, and two or three other Mexicans were standing around, smoking.

"Mister, will you trust me for a pair of white pants and a shirt?"

"No trust. Hey, scram."

"Look. I can have a job Monday morning if I can show up in that outfit. White pants and a white shirt. That's all."

"No trust. What you think this is, anyway?"

"Well, I got to get that outfit somewhere. If I get that, they'll let me go to work Monday, I'll pay you soon as I get paid off Saturday night."

"No trust. Sell for cash."

He stood there. The Mexicans stood there, smoked, looked out at the street. Presently one of them looked at him. "What kind of job, hey? What you mean, got to have white pants a white shirt a hold a job?"

"Filling station. They got a rule you got to have white clothes before you can work there."

"Oh. Sure. Filling station."

After a while the storekeeper spoke. "Ha! Is a joke. Job in filling station, must have a white pants, white shirt. Ha! Is a joke."

"What else would I want them for? Holy smoke, these are better for the road, ain't they? Say, a guy don't want white pants to ride freights, does he?"

"What filling station? Tell me that?"

"Guy name of Hook, Oscar Hook, got a Acme station, Main near Twentieth. You don't believe me, call him up."

"You go to work there, hey?"

"I'm *supposed* to go to work. I *told* him I'd get the white pants and white shirt, somehow. Well—if I don't get them I don't go to work."

"Why you come to me, hey?"

"Where else would I go? If it's not you, it's another guy down the street. No place else I can dig up the stuff over Sunday, is there?"

He stood around. They all stood around. Then once again the storekeeper looked up. "What size you wear, hey?"

He had a wash at a tap in the back yard, then changed there, between piled-up boxes and crates. The storekeeper gave him a white shirt, white pants, necktie, a suit of thick underwear, and a pair of shoes to replace his badly-worn brogans. "Is pretty cold, night-time, now. A thick underwear feel better."

"Okay. Much obliged."

188

"Can roll this other stuff up."

"I don't want it. Can you throw it away for me?"

"Is pretty dirty."

"Plenty dirty."

"You no want?"

"No."

His heart leaped as the storekeeper dropped the whole pile into a rubbish brazier and touched a match to some papers at the bottom of it. In a few minutes, the denims and everything else he had worn were ashes.

He followed the storekeeper inside. "Okay, here is a bill, I put all a stuff on a bill, no charge you more than anybody else. Is six dollar ninety-eight cents, then is a service charge one dollar."

All of them laughed. He took the "service charge" to be a gyp overcharge to cover the trust. He nodded. "Okay on the service charge."

The storekeeper hesitated. "Well, six ninety-eight. We no make a service charge."

"Thanks."

"See you keep a white pants clean till Monday morning."

"I'll do that. See you Saturday night."

"*Adios.*"

Out in the street, he stuck his hand in his pocket, felt something, pulled it out. It was a dollar bill. Then he understood about the "service charge," and why the Mexicans had laughed. He went back, kissed the dollar bill, waved a cheery salute into the store. They all waved back.

He rode a street car down to Mr. Hook's, got turned down for the job, rode a street car back. In his mind, he tried to check over everything. He had an alibi, fantastic and plausible. So far as he could recall, nobody on the train had seen him, not even the other hoboes, for he had stood apart from them in the yards, and had done nothing to attract the attention of any of them. The denims were burned, and he had a story to account for the whites. It even looked pretty good, this thing with Mr. Hook, for anybody who had committed a murder would be most unlikely to make a serious effort to land a job.

But the questions lurked there, ready to spring at him, check and recheck as he would. He saw a sign: *5-Course Dinner, 35 Cents.* He still had ninety cents, and went in, ordered steak and fried potatoes, the hungry man's dream of heaven. He ate, put a ten-cent tip under the plate. He ordered cigarettes, lit one, inhaled. He got up to go. A newspaper was lying on the table. The headline read:

L.R. NOTT, R.R. MAN, KILLED

On the street, he bought a paper, tried to open it under a street light, couldn't, tucked it under his arm. He found Highway 101, caught a hay truck bound for San Francisco. Going out Sunset Boulevard, it unexpectedly pulled over to the curb and stopped. He looked warily around. Down a sidestreet, about a block away, were the two red lights of a police station. He was tightening to jump and run, but the driver wasn't looking at the lights. "I told them bums that air hose was leaking. They set you nuts. Supposed to keep the stuff in shape and all they ever do is sit around and play blackjack."

The driver fished a roll of black tape from his pocket and got out. Lucky sat where he was a few minutes, then climbed down, walked to the glare of the headlights, opened his paper. There it was:

L.R. NOTT, R.R. MAN, KILLED

The decapitated body of L.R. Nott, 1327 De Soto Street, a detective assigned to a northbound freight, was found early this morning on the track near San Fernando station. It is believed he lost his balance while the train was shunting cars at the San Fernando siding and fell beneath the wheels. Funeral services will be held tomorrow.

Mr. Nott is survived by a widow, formerly Miss Elsie Snowden of Mannerheim, and a son, L.R. Nott, Jr., 5.

He stared at it, refolded the paper, tucked it under his arm, walked back to where the driver was taping the air hose. He was clear, and he knew it. "Boy, do they call you Lucky? Is your name Lucky? I'll say it is."

He leaned against the trailer, let his eye wander down the street. He saw the two red lights of the police station—glowing. He looked away quickly. A queer feeling began to stir inside him. He wished the driver would hurry up.

Presently he went back to the headlights again, found the notice, re-read it. He recognized that feeling now; it was the old Sunday-night feeling that he used to have back home, when the bells would ring and he would have to stop playing hide in the twilight, go to church, and hear about the necessity for being saved. It shot through his mind, the time he had played hookey from church, and hid in the livery stable; and how lonely he had felt, because there was nobody to play hide with; and how he had sneaked into church, and stood in the rear to listen to the necessity for being saved.

His eyes twitched back to the red lights, and slowly, shakily, but unswervingly he found himself walking toward them.

"I want to give myself up."

"Yeah, I know, you're wanted for grand larceny in Hackensack, N.J."

"No, I—"

"We quit giving them rides when the New Deal come in. Beat it."

"I killed a man."

"You—? . . . When was it you done this?"

"Last night."

"Where?"

"Near here. San Fernando. It was like this—"

"Hey, wait till I get a card. . . . Okay, what's your name?"

"Ben Fuller."

"No middle name?"

"They call me Lucky."

"Lucky like in good luck?"

"Yes, sir. . . . Lucky like in good luck."

POSTICHE

BY MIGNON G. EBERHART

Mignon G. Eberhart was born Mignon Good on July 6, 1899, in Lincoln, Nebraska. She attended Wesleyan University for three years before marrying Alinson Eberhart, a civil engineer, whose work took them all over the world. She wrote her first novel, *The Patient in Room 18,* during one of those trips. It was published in 1929. Her second novel, *While the Patient Slept* (1930) won a $5,000 prize in a Doubleday, Doran contest. Her detectives include Susan Dare, Nurse Sarah Keate, and Lance O'Leary. A past president of Mystery Writers of America, Mrs. Eberhart received the Grand Master Award in 1970.

Postiche: A pretentious imitation, particularly used as an inartistic addition to an otherwise perfect work of art.—Encyclopaedia Britannica.

THE WIGGENHORN HOUSE could never have been a pleasant place: its slate roof was too heavy and dark; its turrets too many, its windows too high and too narrow. It was still less so on the cold, windy March afternoon when Susan Dare dismissed the taxi that had brought her from the train, and put her hand upon the gate.

Susan pressed the bell and thought of Jim's words to her over the telephone. "Go ahead, if you must, Susie," he'd said. "But if it looks like trouble, you get out. You take too many chances, my girl." He'd paused there, and then said in an offhand way: "Where'd you say the place is? Just outside Warrington? And what's the name of the people?" She'd told him, and had an impression that he'd written it.

The door opened. A plump little maid took Susan's bag and invited her to enter.

The interior of the house was exactly what one would expect. There was a great deal of heavy, darkly upholstered furniture; stiff curtains which looked dusty, and a musty smell tinged with camphor.

She had only a glimpse of the hall, however, for she was ushered at once into a hideous drawing room and from a jungle of armchairs a woman arose. She was a large woman, very fat, with a jolly smile, several chins, eyes that were almost hidden in folds of flesh and lightish, untidy hair. There was an open box of chocolates on the table beside her.

"Miss Dare, I suppose," she said in an asthmatic voice. "I was expecting you. I am Miss Wiggenhorn. Miriam Wiggenhorn. Do sit down. Will you have a tea?"

There was no tea in sight, so Susan said no, and thought Miss Wiggenhorn looked disappointed, "Now then, Miss Dare, I dare say you want to know exactly why I asked you to come here. I heard of you, you see, from John Van Dusen, our family lawyer. I believe he is acquainted with a woman for whom you did—er—something of the kind. A Mrs. Lasher." She picked up some embroidery hoops and then paused to glance quickly at Susan over them. Or at least so Susan thought.

"Yes."

"Yes. Well, at any rate, when things—owing to the confusion—to my own wish rather"—she floundered, threading a needle with care, and said: "So John said call in Miss Dare. Let her look around."

"Perhaps you'd better tell me just what it is about. I have only your note asking me to come. I ought to tell you that I'm not a detective, but a writer of mystery stories. And that I'm not at all sure of being able to help you."

"I think that's quite sufficient. I mean—Mrs. Lasher—Mr. Van Dusen—you see, Miss Dare, this is the trouble." She made a careful and intricate stitch, took a breath and said: "My uncle, Keller Wiggenhorn, died a few days ago. He was buried yesterday. And I want to make sure he—died a natural death."

"You mean you think he was murdered?"

"Oh, dear, no."

"Then what do you mean?"

Miriam Wiggenhorn ate a chocolate cream thoughtfully. Then she said: "I think I'd better tell you the whole story. I'll tell it briefly."

And denuded of Miss Wiggenhorn's panting breaths and hesitation it was certainly a brief enough story. Keller Wiggenhorn had been ailing for some time, owing to a serious heart weakness. Had been so ill in fact that for some three months he'd been obliged to have the care of a trained nurse. He had died suddenly, when alone. The doctor was not surprised; it was to be expected, he said. The nurse was not surprised although she regretted that she had not been with her patient when he was taken with the last and fatal attack. No one had known it even, although it had happened during the daytime. But the nurse had been out in the garden, taking her rightful air and exercise. Durrie had been in town ("Durrie?" said Susan. "My brother," said Miss Wiggenhorn. "Younger than I. We have lived with my uncle for many years.")—Durrie had been in town; the cook busy in the kitchen, and Miss Wiggenhorn herself had been in the kitchen. "Putting up pickled peaches—Uncle was very fond of them."

Only the maid might have known of his fatal attack, and she had not. For he had apparently merely felt faint at first and had called to the girl as she passed his door to hand him his bottle of smelling salts. The girl had done so, had asked if he wanted anything else, had been assured that he didn't. He was lying, she'd said, on a sort of couch, drawn up the windows so he could read. He had made no complaint, seemed no worse than usual. The girl had gone on about her work downstairs.

There were no sounds. He hadn't rung the bell on the table beside him.

It was perhaps an hour after that that the maid returned and found he was dead.

Miss Wiggenhorn paused again and Susan waited. There was nothing, certainly, in the recital so far to suggest the thing that Miss Wiggenhorn had implied and then denied.

"But you see," said Miriam Wiggenhorn. "He died in great pain and struggle."

"Struggle!" said Susan sharply.

"The pillows were tossed about, his clothing disheveled, there were—marks on his throat."

It was very still. In the stillness someone walked heavily across the floor above and stopped.

"The doctor said it was all right. That with that particular trouble he was likely to gasp for breath at the last. He signed a certificate at once. Mind you, Miss Dare, I'm not saying there was murder done."

"Whom do you suspect?" said Susan bluntly.

Miriam Wiggenhorn did not reply directly. Instead she put down her embroidery and turned to face Susan.

"I only want you to stay here for a few days. To consider the thing. I want him to have died naturally, of course. But I cannot forget the—look of things. The marks on his throat. The doctor says he made them himself—clutching—you see?—for air. I don't suspect anyone. There is no one to suspect. Durrie and I. A cook who has been with us for years. A maid who is—too stupid in the first place; and has no motive."

"The nurse?"

"The nurse was devoted to her patient. And he to her. She is a sweet, charming young woman. As you will see."

"Did anyone profit directly by your uncle's death?"

"You mean money and property? Yes, of course. He left his property and money—all his possessions, equally divided between Durrie and me. We were like children to him. He was only a moderately wealthy man. His will permits us to live on in exactly the same manner. There's no motive at all."

195

"But still you feel he was murdered?"

"I feel that I want to be sure he was not. That is all."

There were footsteps overhead again and then someone was running down the stairway in the hall beyond. Miss Wiggenhorn said:

"There's Durrie now."

"Do they—your family—know why I am here?" asked Susan.

"Oh, yes," said Miriam Wiggenhorn readily, and Durrie entered the room.

He was certainly much younger than his sister; young and slender with light-brown hair that had a crisp wave which any woman might have envied, light gray-blue eyes, and a handsome profile which just escaped being pretty. He looked Susan over from under thick blond eyelashes and said, "How do you do," shortly.

"Rosina's out for a walk," said Miriam. "Were you looking for her?"

"No," he said quickly. "Not at all. That is—have you seen the book I was reading?"

"What book?" asked Miriam. In the midst of the little distraction of explaining and searching Durrie looked up. "You write, don't you, Miss Dare?"

"Yes," said Susan, prepared to be modest. It wasn't necessary. He said, "Humph," with definite disfavor, took up a book from another table and went away.

"Dinner's at seven," said Miss Wiggenhorn. "I'll take you to your room."

Left to herself in an unaired guest room, Susan sat down and surveyed the worn red roses of a Brussels carpet blankly.

Marks on a dead man's throat. A doctor's certificate. No motives. No murder. Yet she was there.

She rose and went to the window. Nottingham lace curtains did not obscure the depressing view of a bare, cold March garden. As she looked, however, a woman came into view, walking with her head bent against the wind. She wore a dark cape which, when the wind blew, showed glimpses of a scarlet lining, and paused at a fountain as if waiting for something—paused and looked up suddenly at the house. Despite the gathering gloom Susan could see the outline of her face; a darkly beautiful face with a rich, full mouth. Rosina, that would be. The nurse. A sweet and charming young woman, Miriam had said.

196

Quite suddenly another figure was beside the nurse, coming swiftly from some shrub-masked path. It was Durrie, with no hat on and the collar of his coat turned up around his ears. He spoke to the woman briefly, they both turned to look directly upward at Susan's window and almost immediately moved away. They couldn't have seen her, of course; there was no light in her room. She pulled down the shade, and rang briskly for the maid.

Miss Wiggenhorn had said, leaving her, to question and explore as she liked.

And the little maid, Susan thought, had been prepared, for she answered her questions directly and fully and eyed her with a timorous look.

It was all exactly as Miss Wiggenhorn had already told her. The maid had heard Mr. Wiggenhorn call her, had entered the room and handed him his smelling salts.

"But didn't you think that perhaps he was having or about to have an attack?"

The maid hadn't. "He always liked to have things near him: his books, his spectacles; a glass of water; his smelling salts. I never thought anything about it."

"What did you do then?"

"I asked if there was anything else. The water glass was empty and he said to fill it and I did."

"Who found him? I mean after he was dead."

The girl's face paled a little but her eyes did not blink.

"I did. Dreadful, he looked. Everything was tossed about. Glass on the floor. Books—bottle with all the smelling salts spilled out of it. It looked as if he'd grabbed hold of the table cover and just jerked the whole thing off at once. He must have struggled—for a moment or two. I didn't hear anything at all. But then we'd shut the doors everywhere."

"Why? Was that customary?"

"I mean the doors to the back part of the house. Miss Miriam was making pickled peaches in the kitchen and the smell was all over the house. You know—vinegar and spices. So strong it was sort of sickening. The nurse said to shut the door of his bed-room."

"The nurse? What is her name?"

"Miss Hunt. Miss Rosina Hunt."

There was certainly something the girl wanted to tell—her plump face was bursting with it.

197

"I suppose Miss Hunt will be leaving soon?"

"She can't leave too soon," said the girl. "Not that she's not treated me well enough. But she's too bossy."

"Bossy?"

"Snappy—as if she owned the place. And stubborn! Even with Miss Miriam. After all, it's Miss Miriam's house. Hers and Mr. Durrie's."

"Mr. Durrie is not married?"

"No ma'am. Not him. Though he was engaged to be married once. But it didn't last long."

Susan said abruptly: "Will you show me the room in which Mr. Wiggenhorn died, please."

But at the end of a good half hour spent in that chilly huge bedroom Susan was little wiser than when she had entered it.

In the hall she met Miriam Wiggenhorn.

"Oh, you've been in his room?"

"Yes."

"That was right—John Van Dusen will be here to dinner. If there's anything—"

"There's nothing," said Susan, "yet."

Dinner. So she was to see the lawyer who had suggested sending for her. And the nurse would be there too. Rosina.

Miriam, now in cherry silk, was in the drawing-room when, half an hour later, Susan went down. With her was the lawyer, John Van Dusen, a spare, gray little man of fifty or so, who lifted his eyebrows, bowed to Susan and looked as if he were stuffed with sawdust.

And almost immediately Durrie came into the room, and then the nurse. And if the lawyer looked as if he were stuffed with sawdust, then the nurse looked as if she were charged with some high explosive. But she kept her beautiful dark eyes lowered and her red, rich mouth silent.

The dining room was dimly lighted. The food was very rich and very heavy and there was no conversation. The lawyer talked a little of politics and lifted his eyebrows a great deal; Durrie said nothing and looked at the nurse; the nurse looked at the tablecloth and Miriam looked at nobody and ate steadily.

After dinner Susan had vaguely expected a talk with the lawyer. Instead they played parcheesi. Played it till ten o'clock. There was somewhere in the house a clock which struck on a gasping, breathless note not unlike Miriam's panting voice. When it struck ten John Van Dusen rose, the par-

198

cheesi board disappeared, the nurse murmured and vanished.

"Good night, Miriam. Good night, Durrie. A pleasant evening. Good night, Miss Dare." The little lawyer paused and looked at Susan as if he had just become conscious of her presence. "Oh, yes," he said. "Miss Dare. So good of you to come. Not of course that there's any—er—reason for it. It really is absurd—the whole idea. Miriam is aware of my feeling, but she insisted—"

"Now, John," panted Miriam good-naturedly, "don't blame me for this. And don't trip on the step—it's likely to be slippery. Go with him to his car, Durrie."

Durrie obeyed.

Miriam looked at Susan.

"Well, my dear," she said expectantly. "How is it going? What did you think of John? He's a dear old fellow. But timid. Very timid. Wouldn't admit a murder if he saw it with his own eyes."

"Why is the nurse still here?" asked Susan.

"Rosina? Oh, I asked her to stay on for a little. During Uncle's long illness and her extreme devotion to him we became very fond of her."

The hall door opened and closed again and they could hear Durrie locking it.

"Well—how about some cake or sandwiches before you go to sleep. No? Very well. Just ring the bell if you do want anything."

Susan was still shuddering when she reached her room; her hostess's interest in food was, to say the least, inordinate.

And it was ubiquitous. Susan tossed and turned and between times dreamed of enormous boxes of chocolate creams pursuing her. Once, quite late, a sound of some kind in the hall roused her so thoroughly that she rose and opened her door cautiously and peered into the shadows of the night-lighted hall. There was, however, nothing there.

But she was still wide awake and tense when she heard it again. Or at least she heard a faint sound which was very like the creaking of the steps of a stairway. This time she reached the door softly and managed to open it without, she thought, being detected. And her care had its reward for she saw, coming very quietly from the landing of the stairs, the nurse, Rosina. She was wearing something long and dark and her face was hidden so that Susan saw only her thick, smooth black hair.

199

But as she passed under the light she turned suddenly and cast a sharp strange look at Miriam Wiggenhorn's door. A look so strange and pale and fiery, so full of malevolence, that Susan felt queer and shaken long after the nurse had glided away.

But there was no reason to suspect murder. She told Miriam Wiggenhorn that the next morning.

She did not add that there was something hidden, something secret and ugly, going on in the house. She said merely that she had thus far found no reason to suspect murder.

Miss Wiggenhorn took it with bland detachment and asked her, still blandly, to stay on a few days. She would welcome proof of Keller Wiggenhorn's death being natural; she wanted Susan to have plenty of time. Susan said in that case she would like to see both the lawyer and the doctor and forestalled an offer on Miriam's part to have them summoned. She would go to their offices, said Susan firmly, and Miriam embroidered a flower and then said Durrie would take her in his car.

It was then that Susan risked a direct question about the nurse. "I saw her last night coming very quietly up the stairway. What would she be doing on the first floor so late? Do you know?"

"How late?"

"I don't know exactly. I suppose only around midnight."

Miriam Wiggenhorn pondered very briefly and offered a—to her—sound explanation.

"I suppose she had gone down to the kitchen for a glass of milk," she said. "Or for something to eat. I hope you aren't going to involve little Rosina in this, Miss Dare."

"But there's only you and your brother and Rosina who had the opportunity," said Susan brutally. "That is, if you except the cook and housemaid."

"I suppose so," said Miriam Wiggenhorn. "Well—I'll ask Durrie to take you to see John. And the doctor."

She did so. Durrie looked sullen but consented, and said, during the six-mile drive into Warrington, not one word.

And neither the doctor nor the lawyer yielded anything to Susan's inquiries. Except that the lawyer again rather nervously put the responsibility for calling Susan upon Miriam's plump shoulders.

In the end Susan, still with a silent and sullen Durrie, returned to the Wiggenhorn house no wiser than when she had left. They approached it this time along an old drive leading to a porte-cochère at a side door. Through the shrubs Susan caught glimpses of the garden, and, once, of a kind of summer-house, except that it was much more substantial than most summer-houses are. Durrie caught her look and said: "My studio."

"Studio? Oh, you paint, then?"

"Well, yes and no. I sort of dabble around at this and that." He hesitated and then said suddenly: "Look here, Miss Dare, I don't know what on earth's got into Miriam. Uncle wasn't murdered. Why, there's no one who would want to murder Uncle. It's a perfectly senseless notion. I wish—I wish you'd tell her so and leave."

"And there were no outsiders in the house, anyway," said Susan. "Except the nurse and—"

"Rosina didn't do it! That's impossible. Why, she—she—I tell you she couldn't have done it. She thought the world of Uncle. And he of her."

"Will Rosina be leaving soon?"

"I suppose so. Just for a time. Until we can be married."

"Oh—"

"Yes."

"Did your uncle approve of your engagement?" asked Susan after a moment.

The reply was not what she expected.

"Yes," said Durrie. "He thought it was fine. Here you are, Miss Dare."

He opened the door for her. She lingered to watch as he walked around the car which he left standing in the drive and disappeared in the direction of the summer-house.

Susan went thoughtfully into the hideous drawing-room. Rosina, immaculate in her white uniform, was there reading, and she lifted her fine eyes to give Susan one long, smoldering look. She was not disposed to be communicative.

Yes, she had liked Mr. Wiggenhorn very much. Yes, it was too bad he died alone; she felt very badly about that.

"But it takes them that way. It can't be helped. But it wasn't murder," she added with sudden, vehement scorn. "If he was murdered, it was an absolutely perfect crime. So perfect that it fooled me and the doctor, and I'm not easily fooled."

Susan was very thoughtful during a dreary, silent lunch. But it was not until late afternoon that, during a solitary, slow walk up and down the damp garden paths, one small phrase out of all the things that had been said to her began to emphasize itself. Was dispelled and returned. Began to assume rather curious proportions. Under its insistency she finally let her fancy go and built up, with that as a premise, a curious fabric of murder. Or rather it built itself up, queerly, almost instantly, with the most terrifying logic.

It couldn't be. There were reasons why it couldn't be.

Yet—well, who would know? No one. Who could tell her what she must know? Come now, Susie, she could hear Jim saying: let's get down to brass tacks. How *could* it have been done?

The house was still quiet when at length she returned to it. She summoned the little housemaid to her own room again. "I want you to tell me again, exactly how you found Mr. Wiggenhorn."

The girl shut her eyes and twisted her white apron.

"Well, he was there on the couch. That's the first thing I saw, because he was all twisted—looked so queer, you know. Somehow I knew right away he was dead. I screamed and everybody—that is, Miss Wiggenhorn and cook and then the nurse—came running."

"And he had pulled off the cover of the table—"

"Oh, yes, and everything was spilled. Glass and water and—"

"Did you straighten the room?"

"Yes, ma'am. Right away. While Miss Wiggenhorn was telephoning for the doctor."

"What did you pick up?"

The girl's eyes opened widely. "Why, the—empty water glass. The bottle of smelling salts—"

"Was it open? I mean had Mr. Wiggenhorn used it?"

"Oh, yes, the stopper was out and it had fallen on its side."

"Then you gathered up the crystals of salts that had fallen out?"

"No, ma'am," said the girl. "The bottle must have been empty. There wasn't anything in it at all. Except a sort of mist—"

"Mist!" said Susan violently.

"Well—steam. As if it had had hot water in it—you know. Only the bottle was empty."

"I see," said Susan after a moment. "What did you do with it?"

"Why, I—I put it on the table. And straightened up the table

202

and wiped up the water that had spilled from the glass—"

"Wait. There was nothing in the glass?"

"No, ma'am. It had fallen on its side too. I took it and washed it and put it back on the table."

She waited for further questions. Finally Susan said: "Was there any unusual odor in the room?"

The girl thought and then shook her head decisively. "No, ma'am. I didn't notice anything. Not even smelling salts—but then, the bottle was empty. But we were all excited—everybody running around—putting up windows."

"Opening windows? Who?"

But she didn't know exactly. "Besides," she said, "the smell of the vinegar and spices was all over the house. Suffocating, it was."

"It must have been. Did you replace the stopper in the smelling-salts bottle?"

She was dubious. Then remembered: "Yes. When I cleaned the room the next day. It had rolled under the couch."

"Do you clean Mr. Durrie's studio?" asked Susan abruptly.

"Oh, no," said the girl. "He's got bottles and glass things in there. And he won't let me clean it. Miss Miriam does it. Only Miss Miriam and the nurse are allowed to go into the studio. And if you want smells," she added with vehemence, "that's the place to get them. He says it's chemical experiments. Me and the cook think it's dreadful."

"Oh," said Susan. I've got to go, thought Susan, blindly. I've got to leave. I've got to get out of here now. At once. Will they try to stop me? And I have no proof.

The girl was looking worried.

"What's the matter, miss? Have I done anything wrong?"

"No, no," said Susan sharply. "It's all right. Do your parents live near here?"

"Two miles away."

"You'd better go to them at once. Walk. Make some excuse. Don't tell anyone you have talked to me. But go."

"G-go," stammered the girl, looking frightened. "Now?"

Somehow, tersely, Susan convinced her and watched her scuttle anxiously downstairs. (Besides, she would be a valuable witness.) And still there was no proof. And no time to be lost.

The house was silent all around her. The hall empty, but shadowy and narrow. Which was Rosina's room?

She found it after opening doors to several cold, darkened

bedrooms. The nurse's red-lined cape was across a chair. Her books on a table: powder and creams and bottles quite evidently belonging to the nurse and not to Miriam, on the dressing table. In an adjoining bathroom were other things: a bathing cap, bath salts, sponge, toothpaste. She was exploring a large jar of bath powder with a cautious forefinger when there was a small rustle and Rosina herself stood in the doorway, eyes blazing.

"What are you doing in my things?"

"Searching," said Susan with false airiness.

"Searching! What for? I've nothing to conceal. I wish you'd get out of here."

"Nothing," said Susan, "would suit me better. Look here, when are you planning to be married?"

Rosina blinked.

"I don't know. Next summer. Why?"

"Why not immediately?"

"Why, I—we haven't—"

"Is there anything to prevent an immediate marriage?"

"Why—no! Certainly not!"

"Could you be married next week?"

"Y-Yes. Yes, of course."

"Tomorrow?"

"Yes."

Susan permitted herself to look incredulous. "Are you sure?" she said very softly.

For a long moment the nurse's fine black eyes blazed into Susan's. Then she said furiously:

"Certainly. It's no affair of yours, but you might like to know, since you are so officious, that that is exactly what I'm going to do. I shall be married, Miss Snoopy Dare, tomorrow."

They stepped out into the hall and Rosina banged her door and, furious, went downstairs. Susan waited and then returned once more to the same room.

She looked around it again. There were remarkably few places of concealment. None, indeed, except the old-fashioned mahogany wardrobe. She looked at it with disfavor, but finally opened one of the heavy mirrored doors and stepped up into it. The few dresses offered little concealment. And there was only one way out. And Jim had said something about danger. But she didn't think of all that until she had settled herself to wait.

Not an easy wait. For the space was narrow and cramped, the air not too good in spite of the small opening she had left to

204

enable her to see into the room, and a sense of danger, like a small red signal, became more and more marked. Danger in that muffled, orderly house. Danger—danger.

Minutes dragged on and Susan's muscles were numb and cramped. Suppose no one came. Suppose Rosina had decided on another course. But she wouldn't. And they knew, too, that Susan's own departure was imminent. Susan's eyes were blurred from staring too long and too fixedly at the crack of light. She closed them wearily.

And it was then that someone entered the room. Entered it so stealthily, so furtively that Susan felt only the faint jar of foot-steps on the old floor.

Her heart pounded in her throat and her eyes were glued again to that crack.

And too late she realized that the wardrobe itself might be the objective.

Suppose the door should suddenly, silently open—suppose the very torrent of her thoughts betrayed, telepathically, her hiding place. Suppose—something passed across Susan's range of vision and obscured for an instant that crack of light.

Obscured it. And then was gone as silently, as swiftly, as it had come. But not too swiftly for recognition.

It was a long ten minutes before Susan dared move and open the door and, cautiously, emerge from her hiding place.

It was not difficult to find what she sought. The pungent odor of bath salts guided her. The jar was closed again, but it had been opened and disturbed.

She was cautious, too, in returning to her own room.

Now then to get away. At once. Without fail.

Would they let her leave? She tossed her things in her bag and closed it: put on her coat. Knotted a yellow scarf with trembling hands and pulled her small brown hat at a jaunty angle over her light-brown hair. She looked pale and frightened. And was. But they had told her to go; at least Durrie had.

On the stairway she could hear their voices coming from the drawing-room.

Susan braced herself and entered.

And she need not have braced herself, for it was all very simple and easy. They agreed that if Miss Dare felt that she could do no more and wished to go, she must go. They were

205

very grateful to her. Her advice had relieved them greatly (this only from Miriam).

It was all very easy and very simple. Except that she didn't leave.

For something was wrong with the car.

"Wrong with the car?" panted Miriam. "Why, you were driving it only this morning."

"I know," said Durrie sulkily. "The thing won't start. I don't know what's wrong. You'll have to wait till morning, I guess, Miss Dare. There's only one night train in to Chicago. It leaves at six."

"A taxi," said Susan with stiff lips.

"Too late," said Durrie, looking at his watch. "It's five-thirty now and the roads are a fright. You can't possibly make it."

Miriam looked up from her embroidery hoops. "It looks as if you'll have to spend another night with us, Miss Dare. We are very happy, indeed, to have you."

Susan's bag dropped and her heart with it. She had a sudden, sharp pang of longing for Jim. "Very well," she said after a moment. "But—a theater engagement—I'll telephone—"

There was an instant of complete silence. Then Miriam said, panting: "Show her the telephone, Durrie. It's there in the hall, Miss Dare."

They were listening, all of them, while she called Chicago and then a familiar number. But Jim was not there. "Will you give him a message, please," Susan said. "Tell him Miss Dare can't keep her engagement for the theater tonight. That she's"—she hesitated and then made curious use of a conventional phrase. "Tell him," she said, "that she's unavoidably detained."

But if they thought the use curious they did not say so.

Jim would understand her message; they had had no theater engagement. But there was no way of knowing when he would return and find it.

Was there anything really wrong with the car? And what would they say when they discovered that the little housemaid had gone home?

They said nothing of it. Nothing at all. The cook, enormous in a white apron, served the meal. What did they know? Somehow Susan managed to get food past a stricture in her throat.

Later they played parcheesi again.

"Tired, Miss Dare?" said Rosina once when Susan had glanced surreptitiously at her watch. And Miriam, holding dice

206

in her fat, ringed hand, said: "Are you sure you have nothing to tell us, Miss Dare? Your view of Uncle's death, I mean? Does it coincide in every way with what we know of it?"

Susan had to speak without hesitation. "I'm afraid I've discovered nothing that wasn't already known. But I'll think it over carefully; sometimes it takes a little while for things to become clear in one's mind."

Miriam tossed the dice and Durrie took his turn. He said calmly: "Is that why you sent the girl away?"

The question fell into absolute silence. Long afterwards Susan was to remember the way Rosina's strong, wide, white hand closed upon the dice and held them rigidly. And her own swift, queer recollection of the empty room upstairs. The room where a kind old man had been cruelly murdered.

She couldn't have spoken. And Durrie, all at once white and strange, "You thought you'd fasten it on Rosina. But she didn't kill him. She—"

"*Durrie,*" said Miriam, "*Don't you know that only Rosina could have done it?*"

Durrie leaped to his feet. Rosina did not move and neither did Miriam.

And in the silence they all heard the sudden squealing of the brakes of an automobile at the side of the house.

"*Jim,*" thought Susan. "Oh, let it be Jim—"

It was. Durrie went to the door and let him in. He gave one look at Susan and said very pleasantly that he'd come to take her home.

There was a bad moment when Miriam Wiggenhorn raised an objection.

"But you have only begun the investigation, Miss Dare. This is most distressing—most inconclusive—"

Jim said crisply: "Miss Dare will put any evidence she has into your hands in due form—"

It puzzled them a little. And in the instant of perplexity Jim thrust Susan out the door and closed it smartly behind them.

The engine of his car was running. Thirty seconds later they had turned into the public road and the Wiggenhorn house was a dark, brooding bulk behind them. "J-Jim," said Susan shakily.

"Scared?"

"Terrified—"

His profile looked forbidding. He said grimly: "I got your message. Drove like hell. What have you been stirring up?"

"Oh," said Susan. "A man was murdered and I know who killed him. Can you remember chemistry?"

The car swerved, recovered, and Jim muttered. Susan went on:

"What was the name of that gas that's so dangerous? To breathe, I mean. It's heavier than air and if left open passes into the air. And when you transfer it from one container to another you have to be so careful not to breathe it—it burns the lungs or something."

"Wait a minute. Let me pull myself together." He lighted a cigarette and thought for a moment. "I know—you can see the fumes above the test tube. Otherwise you can't detect its presence except by smell. And if the tube is on its side all the gas escapes into the air. I'll remember it in a minute—hydrogen—"

"Hydrogen chloride," said Susan.

"Somebody die of it?"

"I think so," said Susan. "I'm sure—but somebody else can do the proving. I won't. They'll have to start with an autopsy."

Jim said: "Begin at the beginning."

Susan did. Jim said nothing till she had finished.

Then he said: "I begin to see the outline. Rich old man subject to heart attacks, likely to die of one, but doesn't. Somebody wants him to die at once. Hydrogen chloride is introduced into a smelling-salts bottle; bottle is green and thus no one is likely to perceive its apparent emptiness or its actual content. Maid hands man smelling salts, when he is alone. He gets a good big sniff of it before he can stop himself—that's bad, Susan. Think of the horrible pain—the shock—he dies really of the shock; his heart can't stand it. Ordinarily I think a person might live for some hours, or even days, and be conscious. But the murderer counted on that bad heart and won. It looks like a natural death. Anyway it is a successful murder. Durrie has a studio where he seems to do chemical experiments. The nurse would know something of chemistry. But the murder would have been perfect if Miriam hadn't suspected something. Which one did it?"

"It's funny," said Susan, "that you used the word a perfect murder. That very word is what started me thinking. Perfect. Too perfect!"

"Huh," said Jim with vehemence.

"Too perfect. No one suspected it was murder. And that was the motive, you see. Murder had to be suspected."

"Murder had to be—sorry, Susie, but I don't see."

"All right. Look at this. Durrie is in love with the nurse; wants to marry her. *His uncle didn't object.* And there was no motive at all, remember, for murder—no money motive. No question of thwarted love. No motive at all except—except that Rosina was a very wilful young woman—and Miriam, no less wilful, hated her."

"But Miriam approved the marriage."

"Oh, *did* she!" said Susan. "Then why were Rosina and Durrie obliged to steal meetings. In the garden at dusk. At midnight."

"How do you know Rosina had gone downstairs to see Durrie?"

"I didn't. But it's a good reason. Name a better one."

"Suppose she did," conceded Jim. "What then?"

"Miriam had ruled that house and Durrie in the smallest detail for years. She loved her rule—a previous engagement of Durrie's had been mysteriously broken off. The uncle was about to die anyway; here was a perfect plan to get rid of Rosina."

"Do you mean Miriam murdered the old man? But that doesn't make sense. She didn't gain by it."

"She did, Jim, if she could make Durrie think, in his heart, that it was murder. And that the newcomer, the nurse, was the only one who could have done it."

"You can't prove this, Susan, it's mere theory. How do you know it was Miriam?"

"You've said it yourself, Jim—there's a French term, postiche. It means a counterfeit, an inartistic addition to an otherwise perfect work of art. Well, the murder was perfect. *It was too perfect.* No one suspected it was murder. So Miriam had failed. Had failed unless she could get someone—someone without official standing—like me—to look into it; perhaps to discover some little thing, not too much (she was very sure of herself); but enough to make Durrie think *it might have been murder.* And that if it was murder, only Rosina could have done it. She didn't know exactly how much she could trust me to see or not to see. I think she meant to watch—to—to—gauge—me. If necessary to introduce a little evidence against the nurse, as she did. It's queer; her very words of praise for Rosina made me suspect the nurse. At first. She's very clever—Miriam Wiggenhorn."

"Then the housemaid was in danger from her—"

"The housemaid is a very valuable witness. And Miriam might have discovered that I had something of the true story from her. The real story. It wasn't just accident that Miriam was pickling peaches that afternoon, filling the house with a smell of vinegar that would mask any other smell. This isn't the season for putting up fruit. Besides there was the inartistic addition—"

"You mean her calling you and talking of murder when *nobody had suspected it was murder* shows that she thought of murder when, if she were innocent, she would have had no reason to suspect it. And that for some reason she was determined to suggest that it *was* murder."

"To suggest it anyway. The perfect murder, except for the inartistic addition. Postiche. And I," said Susan, "am it."

"But"—Jim paused and said in a helpless way: "All this is very nice. But angel, it's only theory. It isn't a bad idea, you know, to have proof."

"Oh, yes—proof. It's in my bag. Wrapped in a handkerchief and mixed with bath salts. But identifiable."

"What!"

"Smelling salts. When she emptied the bottle she kept the salts in case her investigation should need a little steering. Rosina, you see, has a fine temper. When I hinted there was something preventing their marriage as if I were suspicious about it, she flounced down to tell Durrie and Miriam that she wanted it to take place at once. Durrie agreed, of course. Rosina had much the stronger will. Miriam agreed, too—and came straight upstairs to plant the clue. Nobody in the house ever used smelling salts but Keller Wiggenhorn."

"Framing her."

"Exactly. I suppose she would have tried something more open, given time."

"How did you know it was Miriam?"

"Saw her."

"From where?" demanded Jim.

"N-never mind," said Susan in a small voice.

Jim stopped the car and looked at her intently. But when he spoke it was with an air of preoccupation. "There's guilt in your voice," he said absently. "But we'll skip it. Do you know, I have a queer sort of impulse. I'd like to—"

"To what?"

"To kiss you," said Jim unexpectedly, and did so.

THE HOMESICK BUICK

By JOHN D. MACDONALD

John D. MacDonald was born in 1916 in Sharon, Pennsylvania. He received a B.S. from Syracuse University and an M.B.A. from the Harvard Business School. His first mystery novel, *The Brass Cupcake,* was published in 1950. MacDonald has published more than sixty books, many of them mysteries about his Florida-based detective, Travis McGee. He is a former president of Mystery Writers of America and received the Grand Master Award in 1971. He is one of the few living writers whose admirers have organized a literary fan club, with a national membership of over 800.

To get to Leeman, Texas, you go southwest from Beaumont on Route 90 for approximately thirty miles and then turn right on a two-lane concrete farm road. Five minutes from the time you turn, you will reach Leeman. The main part of town is six lanes wide and five blocks long. If the hand of a careless giant should remove the six gas stations, the two theaters, Willow's Hardware Store, the Leeman National Bank, the two big air-conditioned five-and-dimes, the Sears store, four cafés, Rightsinger's dress shop, and The Leeman House, a twenty-room hotel, there would be very little left except the supermarket and four assorted drug stores.

On October 3rd, 1949, a Mr. Stanley Woods arrived by bus and carried his suitcase over to the Leeman House. In Leeman there is no social distinction of bus, train, or plane, since Leeman has neither airport facilities nor railroad station.

On all those who were questioned later, Mr. Stanley Woods seemed to have made very little impression. They all spoke of kind of a medium-size fella in his thirties, or it might be his forties. No, he wasn't fat, but he wasn't thin either. Blue eyes? Could be brown. Wore a gray suit, I think. Can't remember whether his glasses had rims or not. If they did have rims, they were probably gold.

But all were agreed that Mr. Stanley Woods radiated quiet confidence and the smell of money. According to the cards that were collected here and there, Mr. Woods represented the Groston Precision Tool Company of Atlanta, Georgia. He had deposited in the Leeman National a certified check for twelve hundred dollars and the bank had made the routine check of looking up the credit standing of Groston. It was Dun & Bradstreet double-A, but, of course, the company explained later that they had never heard of Mr. Stanley Woods. Nor could the fake calling cards be traced. They were of a type of paper and type face which could be duplicated sixty or a hundred times in every big city in the country.

Mr. Woods's story, which all agreed on, was that he was ". . . nosing around to find a good location for a small plant. Decentralization, you know. No, we don't want it right in town."

He rented Tod Bishner's car during the day. Tod works at

the Shell station on the corner of Beaumont and Lone Star Streets and doesn't have any use for his Plymouth sedan during the day. Mr. Woods drove around all the roads leading out of town and, of course, real estate prices were jacked to a considerable degree during his stay.

Mr. Stanley Woods left Leeman rather suddenly on the morning of October 17th under unusual circumstances.

The first person to note a certain oddness was Miss Trilla Price on the switchboard at the phone company. Her local calls were all right but she couldn't place Charley Anderson's call to Houston, nor, when she tried, could she raise Beaumont. Charley was upset because he wanted to wangle an invitation to go visit his sister over the coming weekend.

That was at five minutes of nine. It was probably at the same time that a car with two men in it parked on Beaumont Street, diagonally across from the bank, and one of the two men lifted the hood and began to fiddle with the electrical system.

Nobody agrees from what direction the Buick came into town. There was a man and a girl in it and they parked near the drug store. No one seems to know where the third car parked, or even what kind of car it was.

The girl and the man got out of the Buick slowly, just as Stanley Woods came down the street from the hotel.

In Leeman the bank is open on weekdays from nine until two. And so, at nine o'clock, C.F. Hethridge, who is, or was, the chief teller, raised the green shades on the inside of the bank doors and unlocked the doors. He greeted Mr. Woods, who went on over to the high counter at the east wall and began to ponder over his check book.

At this point, out on the street, a very peculiar thing happened. One of the two men in the first car strolled casually over and stood beside the Buick. The other man started the motor of the first car, drove down the street, and made a wide U-turn to swing in and park behind the Buick.

The girl and the man had gone over to Bob Kimball's window. Bob is second teller, and the only thing he can remember about the girl is that she was blonde and a little hard-looking around the mouth, and that she wore a great big alligator shoulder bag. The man with her made no impression on Bob at all, except maybe he was on the heavy side.

Old Rod Harrigan, the bank guard, was standing beside the front door, yawning, and picking his teeth with a broken match.

213

At this point C.F. Hethridge heard the buzzer on the big time-vault and went over and swung the door wide and went in to get the money for the cages. He was out almost immediately, carrying Bob's tray over to him. The girl was saying something about cashing a check and Bob had asked her for identification. She had opened the big shoulder bag as her escort strolled over to the guard. At the same moment the girl pulled out a small vicious-looking revolver and aimed it between Bob's eyes, her escort sapped Old Rod Harrigan with such gusto that it was four that same afternoon before he came out of it enough to talk. And then, of course, he knew nothing.

C.F. Hethridge bolted for the vault and Bob, wondering whether he should step on the alarm, looked over the girl's shoulder just in time to see Stanley Woods aim carefully and bring Hethridge down with a slug through the head, catching him on the fly, so to speak.

Bob says that things were pretty confusing and that the sight of Hethridge dying so suddenly sort of took the heart out of him. Anyway, there was a third car and it contained three men, two of them equipped with empty black-leather suitcases. They went into the vault, acting as though they had been all through the bank fifty times. They stepped over Hethridge on the way in, and on the way out again.

As they all broke for the door, Bob dropped and pressed the alarm button. He said later that he held his hands over his eyes, though what good that would do him, he couldn't say.

Henry Willows is the real hero. He was fuddying around in his hardware store when he heard the alarm. With a reaction-time remarkable in a man close to seventy, he took a little twenty-two rifle, slapped a clip into it, trotted to his store door, and quickly analyzed the situation. He saw Mr. Woods, whom he recognized, plus three strangers and a blonde woman coming out of the bank pretty fast. Three cars were lined up, each one with a driver. Two of the men coming out of the bank carried heavy suitcases. Henry leveled on the driver of the lead car, the Buick, and shot him in the left temple, killing him outright. The man slumped over the wheel, his body resting against the horn ring, which, of course, added its blare to the clanging of the bank alarm.

At that point a slug, later identified as having come from a Smith & Wesson Police Positive, smashed a neat hole in Henry's plate-glass store window, radiating cracks in all directions.

Henry ducked, and by the time he got ready to take a second shot, the two other cars were gone. The Buick was still there. He saw Bob run out of the bank, and later on he told his wife that he had his finger on the trigger and his sights lined up before it came to him that it was Bob Kimball.

It was agreed that the two cars headed out toward Route 90 and, within two minutes, Hod Abrams and Lefty Quinn had roared out of town in the same direction in the only police car. They were followed by belligerent amateurs to whom Henry Willows had doled out firearms. But on the edge of town all cars ran into an odd obstacle. The road was liberally sprinkled with metal objects shaped exactly like the jacks that little girls pick up when they bounce a ball, except they were four times normal size and all the points were sharpened. No matter how a tire hit one, it was certain to be punctured.

The police car swerved to a screaming stop, nearly tipping over. The Stein twins, boys of nineteen, managed to avoid the jacks in their souped-up heap until they were hitting eighty. When they finally hit one, the heap rolled over an estimated ten times, killing the twins outright.

So that made four dead. Hethridge, the Stein twins, and one unidentified bank robber.

Nobody wanted to touch the robber, and he stayed right where he was until the battery almost ran down and the horn squawked into silence. Hod Abrams commandeered a car, and he and Lefty rode back into town and took charge. They couldn't get word out by phone and within a very short time they found that some sharpshooter with a high-powered rifle had gone to work on the towers of local station WLEE and had put the station out of business.

Thus, by the time the Texas Rangers were alerted and ready to set up road blocks, indecision and confusion had permitted an entire hour to pass.

The Houston office of the FBI assigned a detail of men to the case and, from the Washington headquarters, two bank-robbery experts were dispatched by plane to Beaumont. Reporters came from Houston and Beaumont and the two national press services, and Leeman found itself on the front pages all over the country because the planning behind the job seemed to fascinate the average joe.

Mr. Woods left town on that particular Thursday morning. The FBI from Houston was there by noon, and the Washington contingent arrived late Friday. Everyone was very confident. There was a corpse and a car to work on. These would certainly provide the necessary clues to indicate which outfit had pulled the job, even though the method of the robbery did not point to any particular group whose habits were known.

Investigation headquarters were set up in the local police station and Hod and Lefty, very important in the beginning, had to stand around outside trying to look as though they knew what was going on.

Hethridge, who had been a cold, reserved, unpopular man, had, within twenty-four hours, fifty stories invented about his human kindness and generosity. The Stein twins, heretofore considered to be trash who would be better off in prison, suddenly became proper sons of old Texas.

Special Agent Randolph A. Sternweister who, fifteen years before, had found a law office to be a dull place, was in charge of the case, being the senior of the two experts who had flown down from Washington. He was forty-one years old, a chain smoker, a chubby man with incongruous hollow cheeks and gray hair which his wife, Claire, tells him is distinguished.

The corpse was the first clue. Age between thirty and thirty-two. Brown hair, thinning on top. Good teeth, with only four small cavities, two of them filled. Height, five foot eight and a quarter, weight a hundred and forty-eight. No distinguishing scars or tattoos. X-ray plates showed that the right arm had been fractured years before. His clothes were neither new nor old. The suit had been purchased in Chicago. The shirt, underwear, socks, and shoes were all national brands, in the medium-price range. In his pockets they found an almost full pack of cigarettes, a battered Zippo lighter, three fives and a one in a cheap trick billclip, eighty-five cents in change, a book of matches advertising a nationally known laxative, a white bone button, two wooden kitchen matches with blue and white heads, and a penciled map, on cheap notebook paper, of the main drag of Leeman—with no indication as to escape route. His fingerprint classification was teletyped to the Central Bureau files and the answer came back that there was no record of him. It was at this point that fellow workers noted that Mr. Sternweister became a shade irritable.

The next search of the corpse was more minute. No specific occupational callouses were found on his hands. The absence of laundry marks indicated that his linen, if it had been sent out, had been cleaned by a neighborhood laundress. Since Willows had used a .22 hollow-point, the hydraulic pressure on the brain fluids had caused the eyes of Mr. X to bulge in a disconcerting fashion. A local undertaker, experienced in the damage caused by the average Texas automobile accident, replaced the bulging eyeballs and smoothed out the expression for a series of pictures which were sent to many points. The Chicago office reported that the clothing store which had sold the suit was large and that the daily traffic was such that no clerk could identify the customer from the picture; nor was the youngish man known to the Chicago police.

Fingernail scrapings were put in a labeled glassine envelope, as well as the dust vacuumed from pants cuffs and other portions of the clothing likely to collect dust. The excellent lab in Houston reported back that the dust and scrapings were negative to the extent that the man could not be tied down to any particular locality.

In the meantime the Buick had been the object of equal scrutiny. The outside was a mass of prints from the citizens of Leeman who had peered morbidly in at the man leaning against the horn ring. The plates were Mississippi license plates and, in checking with the Bureau of Motor Vehicle Registration, it was found that the plates had been issued for a 1949 Mercury convertible which had been almost totally destroyed in a head-on collision in June, 1949. The motor number and serial number of the Buick were checked against central records and it was discovered that the Buick was one which had disappeared from Chapel Hill, North Carolina, on the 5th of July, 1949. The insurance company, having already replaced the vehicle, was anxious to take possession of the stolen car.

Pictures of Mr. X, relayed to Chapel Hill, North Carolina, and to myriad points in Mississippi, drew a large blank. In the meantime a careful dusting of the car had brought out six prints, all different. Two of them turned out to be on record. The first was on record through the cross-classification of Army prints. The man in question was found working in a gas station in Lake Charles, Louisiana. He had a very difficult two hours until a bright police officer had him demonstrate his procedure for brushing out the front of a car. Ex-Sergeant Golden braced his left hand against the dashboard in almost the precise place where the print had been found. He was given a picture of Mr. X to study. By that time he was so thoroughly annoyed at the forces of law and order that it was impossible to ascertain whether or not he had ever seen the man in question. But due to the apparent freshness of the print it was established—a reasonable assumption—that the gangsters had driven into Texas from the East.

The second print on record was an old print, visible when dust was carefully blown off the braces under the dismantled front seat. It belonged to a garage mechanic in Chapel Hill who once had a small misunderstanding with the forces of law and order and who was able to prove, through the garage work orders, that he had repaired the front seat mechanism when it had jammed in April, 1949.

Butts in the ashtray of the car showed that either two women, or one woman with two brands of lipstick, had ridden recently as a passenger. Both brands of lipstick were of shades which would go with a fair-complexioned blonde, and both brands were available in Woolworths, Kress, Kresge, Walgreens—in fact, in every chain outfit of any importance.

One large crumb of stale whole-wheat bread was found on the floor mat, and even Sternweister could make little of that, despite the fact that the lab was able to report that the bread had been eaten in conjunction with liverwurst.

Attention was given to the oversized jacks which had so neatly punctured the tires. An ex-OSS officer reported that similar items had been scattered on enemy roads in Burma during the late war and, after examining the samples, he stated confidently that the OSS merchandise had been better made. A competent machinist looked them over and stated with assurance that they had been made by cutting eight-inch rod into short lengths, grinding them on a wheel, putting them in a jig, and spot-welding them. He said that the maker did not do much of a job on either the grinding or the welding, and that the jig itself was a little out of line. An analysis of the steel showed that it was a Jones & Laughlin product that could be bought in quantity at any wholesaler and in a great many hardware stores.

The auditors, after a careful examination of the situation at the bank, reported that the sum of exactly $94,725 had disappeared. They recommended that the balance remaining in Stanley Woods' account of $982.80 be considered as forfeited, thus reducing the loss to $93,742.20. The good citizens of Leeman preferred to think that Stanley had withdrawn his account.

Every person who had a glimpse of the gang was cross-examined. Sternweister was appalled at the difficulty involved in even establishing how many there had been. Woods, the blonde, and the stocky citizen were definite. And then there were two with suitcases—generally agreed upon. Total, so far—five. The big question was whether each car had a driver waiting. Some said no—that the last car in line had been empty. Willows insisted angrily that there had been a driver behind each wheel. Sternweister at last settled for a total of eight, seven of whom escaped.

No one had taken down a single license number. But it was positively established that the other two cars had been either two- or four-door sedans in dark blue, black, green, or maroon, and that they had been either Buicks, Nashes, Oldsmobiles, Chryslers, Pontiacs, or Packards— or maybe Hudsons. And one lone woman held out for convertible Cadillacs. For each person that insisted that they had Mississippi registration, there was one equally insistent on Louisiana, Texas, Alabama, New Mexico, and Oklahoma. And one old lady said that she guessed she knew a California plate when she saw one.

On Saturday morning, nine days after the sudden blow to the FDIC, Randolph Sternweister paced back and forth in his suite at the hotel, which he shared with the number two man from the Washington end, one Buckley Weed. Weed was reading through the transcripts of the testimony of the witnesses, in the vain hope of finding something to which insufficient importance had been given. Weed, though lean, a bit stooped, and only thirty-one, had, through osmosis, acquired most of the personal mannerisms of his superior. Sternweister had noticed this and for the past year had been on the verge of mentioning it. As Weed had acquired Sternweister's habit of lighting one cigarette off the last half-inch of the preceding one, any room in which the two of them remained for more than an hour took on the look and smell of any hotel room after a Legion convention.

"Nothing," Sternweister said. "Not one censored, unmentionable, unprintable, unspeakable thing! My God, if I ever want to kill anybody, I'll do it in the Pennsy Station at five fifteen.

"The Bureau has cracked cases when the only thing it had to go on was a human hair or a milligram of dust. My God, we've got a whole automobile that weighs nearly two tons, and a

219

whole corpse! They'll think we're down here learning to rope calves. You know what?"

"What, Ran?"

"I think this was done by a bunch of amateurs. There ought to be a law restricting the practice of crime to professionals. A bunch of wise amateurs. And you can bet your loudest argyles, my boy, that they established identity, hideout, the works, before they knocked off that vault. Right now, blast their souls, they're being seven average citizens in some average community, making no splash with that ninety-four grand. People didn't use to move around so much. Since the war they've been migrating all over the place. Strangers don't stick out like sore thumbs any more. See anything in those transcripts?"

"Nothing."

"Then stop rattling paper. I can't think. Since a week ago Thursday fifty-one stolen cars have been recovered in the South and Southwest. And we don't know which two, if any, belonged to this mob. We don't even know which route they took away from here. Believe it or not—nobody saw 'em!"

As the two specialists stared bleakly at each other, a young man of fourteen named Pink Dee was sidling inconspicuously through the shadows in the rear of Louie's Garage. (Tow car service—open 24 hrs.) Pink was considered to have been the least beautiful baby, the most unprepossessing child, in Leeman, and he gave frank promise of growing up to be a rather coarse joke on the entire human race. Born with a milk-blue skin, dead white hair, little reddish weak eyes, pipe-cleaner bones, narrow forehead, no chin, beaver teeth, a voice like an unoiled hinge, nature had made the usual compensation. His reaction-time was exceptional. Plenty of more rugged and more normal children had found out that Pink Dee could hit you by the time you had the word out of your mouth. The blow came from an outsize, knobbly fist at the end of a long thin arm, and he swung it with all the abandon of a bag of rocks on the end of a rope. The second important item about Pink Dee came to light when the Leeman School System started giving IQs. Pink's was higher than they were willing to admit the first time, as it did not seem proper that the only genius in Leeman should be old Homer Dee's only son. Pink caught on, and the second time he was rated he got it down into the cretin class. The third rating was ninety-nine and everybody seemed happy with that.

At fourteen Pink was six foot tall and weighed a hundred and twenty pounds. He peered at the world through heavy lenses and maintained, in the back room of his home on Fountain Street, myriad items of apparatus, some made, some purchased. There he investigated certain electrical and magnetic phenomena, having tired of building radios, and carried on a fairly virulent correspondence on the quantum theory with a Cal Tech professor who was under the impression that he was arguing with someone of more mature years.

Dressed in his khakis, the uniform of Texas, Pink moved through the shadows, inserted the key he had filched into the Buick door, and then into the ignition lock. He turned it on in order to activate the electrical gimmicks, and then turned on the car radio. As soon as it warmed up he pushed the selective buttons, carefully noting the dial. When he had the readings he turned it to WLEE to check the accuracy of the dial. When WLEE roared into a farm report, Louie appeared and dragged Pink out by the thin scruff of his neck.

"What the hell?" Louie said.

Being unable to think of any adequate explanation, Pink wriggled away and loped out.

Pink's next stop was WLEE, where he was well known. He found the manual he wanted and spent the next twenty minutes with it.

Having been subjected to a certain amount of sarcasm from both Sternweister and Weed, Hod Abrams and Lefty Quinn were in no mood for the approach Pink Dee used.

"I demand to see the FBI," Pink said firmly, the effect spoiled a bit by the fact that his voice change was so recent that the final syllable was a reversion to his childhood squeaky-hinge voice.

"He demands," Hod said to Lefty.

"Go away, Pink," Lefty growled, "before I stomp on your glasses."

"I am a citizen who wishes to speak to a member of a Federal agency," Pink said with dignity.

"A citizen, maybe. A taxpayer, no. You give me trouble, kid, and I'm going to warm your pants right here in this lobby."

Maybe the potential indignity did it. Pink darted for the stairs leading up from the lobby. Hod went roaring up the stairs after him and Lefty grabbed the elevator. They both snared him outside Sternweister's suite and found that they had a job on their hands. Pink bucked and contorted like a picnic on which a

221

well-populated hornet's nest has just fallen.

The door to the suite opened and both Sternweister and Weed glared out, their mouths open.

"Just . . . just a fresh . . . kid," Hod Abrams panted.

"I know where the crooks are!" Pink screamed.

"He's nuts," Lefty yelled.

"Wait a minute," Randolph Sternweister ordered sharply. They stopped dragging Pink but still clung to him. "I admit he doesn't look as though he knew his way home, but you can't tell. You two wait outside. Come in here, young man."

Pink marched erectly into the suite, selected the most comfortable chair, and sank into it, looking smug.

"Where are they?"

"Well, I don't know exactly . . ."

"Outside!" Weed said with a thumb motion.

". . . but I know how to find out."

"Oh, you know how to find out, eh? Keep talking. I haven't laughed in nine days," Sternweister said.

"Oh, I had to do a little checking first," Pink said in a lofty manner. "I stole the key to the Buick and got into it to test something."

"Kid, experts have been over that car, half-inch by half-inch."

"Please don't interrupt me, sir. And don't take that attitude. Because, if it turns out I have something, and I know I have, you're going to look as silly as anything."

Sternweister flushed and then turned pale. He held hard to the edge of a table. "Go ahead," he said thickly.

"I am making an assumption that the people who robbed our bank started out from some hideout and then went back to the same one. I am further assuming that they were in their hideout some time, while they were planning the robbery."

Weed and Sternweister exchanged glances. "Go on."

"So my plan has certain possible flaws based on these assumptions, but at least it uncovers one possible pattern of investigation. I know that the car was stolen from Chapel Hill. That was in the paper. And I know the dead man was in Chicago. So I checked Chicago and Chapel Hill a little while ago."

"Checked them?"

"At the radio station, of course. Modern car radios are easy to set to new stations by altering the push buttons. The current settings of the push buttons do not conform either to the

Chicago or the Chapel Hill areas. There are six stations that the radio in the Buick is set for and . . ."

Sternweister sat down on the couch as though somebody had clubbed him behind the knees. "Agh!" he said.

"So all you have to do," Pink said calmly, "is to check areas against the push-button settings until you find an area *where all six frequencies are represented by radio stations in the immediate geographical vicinity.* It will take a bit of statistical work, of course, and a map of the country, and a supply of push pins should simplify things, I would imagine. Then, after the area is located, I would take the Buick there and, due to variations in indiVidual sets and receiving conditions, you might be able to narrow it down to within a mile or two. Then, by showing the photograph of the dead gangster around at bars and such places . . ."

And that was why, on the following Wednesday, a repainted Buick with new plates and containing two agents of the Bureau roamed through the small towns near Tampa on the West Florida Coast, and how they found that the car radio in the repainted Buick brought in Tampa, Clearwater, St. Pete, Orlando, Winter Haven, and Dunedin on the push buttons with remarkable clarity the closer they came to a little resort town called Tarpon Springs. On Thursday morning at four, the portable floodlights bathed three beach cottages in a white glare, and the metallic voice of the P.A. system said, "You are surrounded. Come out with your hands high. You are surrounded."

The shots, a few moments later, cracked with a thin bitterness against the heavier sighing of the Gulf of Mexico. Mr. Stanley Woods, or, as the blonde later stated, Mr. Grebbs Fainstock, was shot, with poetic justice, through the head, and that was the end of resistance.

On Pink Dee Day in Leeman, the president of the Leeman National Bank turned over the envelope containing the reward. It came to a bit less than six percent of the recovered funds, and it is ample to guarantee, at some later date, a Cal Tech degree.

In December the Sternweisters bought a new car. When Claire demanded to know why Randolph insisted on delivery *sans* car radio, his only answer was a hollow laugh.

She feels that he has probably been working too hard.

THE CONTRADICTORY CASE

BY HUGH PENTECOST

Hugh Pentecost was born Judson Pentecost Philips in
Massachusetts on August 10, 1903. His first short story,
"Room Number Twenty-three," was published in 1925
while he was a sophomore at Columbia University. Pentecost is founding member of the Mystery Writers of
America, served as the organization's third president,
and received its Grand Master Award in 1972. He has
created many series detectives, including artist John
Jericho, public-relations man Julian Quist, hotel man-
ager Pierre Chambrun, and magazine columnist Peter
Styles. Pentecost founded the Sharon, Connecticut,
Playhouse. He lives in Canaan, Connecticut, with his
wife, actress Norma Burton.

LIEUTENANT PASCAL OF THE Homicide Squad threw his cigarette out the window of the hotel room and into the alley below—a violation of a city ordinance. Then he turned.

"All right, sonny," he said, gently. "Let's have it."

"Don't call me sonny!"

Pascal regarded the witness, crouched in the worn, upholstered armchair opposite him, with a speculative eye. He was about five feet tall with reddish-blond hair and a turned-up nose. The bellboy's uniform made him look like a fifteen-year-old kid out of military school.

Actually, from preliminary questioning, Pascal knew that Eddie Connors was twenty-eight.

"Sorry, Eddie," Pascal said. "That was just my clumsy way of trying to sound friendly."

"Cops aren't anybody's friends," Eddie said. His eyes were red-rimmed and hunted-looking.

Pascal was a square, swarthy man with thick, curly, black hair and a prematurely lined face—lines that came from good humor. He was puzzled by Eddie Connors. You don't ordinarily find someone admitting to a particularly brutal murder so readily.

"Let's go back to the beginning," Pascal said. "When did Mr. Sam Lorrimer check into the hotel?"

"Two weeks ago," Eddie said. "Two weeks ago yesterday."

"How do you happen to remember so well, Eddie?"

"You couldn't forget him once you saw him," Eddie said. "Six feet five, cowboy boots, big Stetson hat. You might not remember some people, but you'd remember him. I carried his bags up here for him."

"To this room?"

"Yes," Eddie said. He kept staring down at the threadbare carpet as if he could still see the big body lying there.

"And you saw more of him after that?"

"Yes."

"But you'd never seen him before that?"

"No."

Pascal lit a fresh cigarette. He looked idly around, at the Gideon Bible on the bedside table, at the top of the dresser, at the shabby mahogany writing desk in the corner. No ashtray.

He dropped the match on the carpet and then put his foot on it.

"Eddie, isn't it true you took bets here at the hotel for a Times Square bookmaker?"

"Yes."

"His name is Mike Braxton?" Pascal asked.

"So you found out," Eddie said.

"Sure I found out, Eddie. That's my job—finding out. There was a betting slip in Lorrimer's hand, clenched tight in it, when he was found. You gave him that slip, didn't you?"

"Yes."

"He had bet a thousand dollars on a horse called Samovar."

"That's right."

"Samovar came in at twenty-to-one."

Eddie Connors moistened his lips. "That's why I killed him."

"*Non sequitur,*" Pascal said.

"What?"

"It doesn't follow, Eddie. The horse won, but it was no skin off your back. Mike Braxton was the one who had to worry. He had to pay off."

"No," Eddie said.

"Explain, please," Pascal said.

"I didn't place the bet." Eddie still stared at the rug. "I figured a twenty-to-one shot wouldn't come in. I just hung onto the thousand bucks. I figured the horse would lose and I'd have the money and no one would be the wiser. But when the horse won—"

"You killed Lorrimer?"

Eddie nodded.

"Why?"

"Because when he asked Braxton for his money he wouldn't get it. Then I'd be in a jam."

"What could he do to you? He couldn't have you arrested. It isn't legal to place bets. All you had to do was give him back his thousand dollars and say you couldn't get the bet down."

"He would have been sore."

"So you killed him so he wouldn't get sore at you?"

Eddie squirmed around in his chair. "I didn't figure all the angles, I guess. I just did the first thing that came into my head."

"So tell me what came into your head, Eddie—in sequence."

"I took the money and gave him the receipt slip. Then I went out and I got thinking how this was an easy thousand bucks for me. So I didn't take it to Braxton. I went down in the basement—to a room I've got there. I listened to the race on the radio. When the horse won I knew I was in a hell of a hole."

"So you came up here and killed him?"

"Yes."

"You looped that gold chain around his neck and choked him until he was dead?"

"Yes."

"Where did you get the chain? It's gold."

"I had it."

"Where did you get it, Eddie?"

"It—it was a gift. A fellow who stayed here once. I—I did a favor for him. He gave it to me."

"So you took the chain and came up here to Lorrimer's room, put the chain around his neck, and choked him to death."

"Yes." It was a whisper.

The ash dribbled off the end of Pascal's cigarette and down his shirt front. He brushed it away, absently. "I want to get a clear picture of this. Lorrimer was six feet five. He was a cattleman from Texas, all muscle and rawhide, the whole two hundred and ten pounds of him. You're five feet."

"Five feet one and a half."

"Five feet one and a half. You weigh about a hundred and ten pounds, soaking wet. But you overpowered Lorrimer, looped a chain around his neck, and strangled him. Eddie, he could have broken you over his knee like a piece of kindling."

"Maybe I—I took him by surprise," Eddie said.

"Maybe," Pascal said. "After you killed him why didn't you take the betting slip out of his hand? That gave you away."

"I didn't think of it," Eddie said. "I guess I was rattled."

Pascal sighed. "Medical science isn't always accurate, Eddie. For instance, it's a myth that a doctor can tell just exactly how long a man has been dead. But he can make a rough guess. The medical examiner says Lorrimer had been dead *at least* one hour when he was found. Maybe more—but *at least* one hour."

"So what?" Eddie said, lifting his eyes to Pascal for the first time.

"So Lorrimer was killed *before* Samovar came in at twenty-to-one. You said you killed him because you were in a jam *after* the horse won. I may not be very efficient, Eddie, but whatever I

227

may not do, you can bet on it I always check details like that."

"Oh," Eddie said, in a hollow voice.

"So you had no motive, Eddie, and I just can't swallow the idea of your overpowering Lorrimer. That's out of a comic strip. It's been fun, Eddie. But it won't do. Do you want to think up another one?"

Eddie sat motionless in the chair, chewing on his stubby fingers. Pascal walked over to the window and stood staring down at the street twelve floors below. Finally he dropped his cigarette out the window and watched it float downward. He still found it difficult to forget the picture of the giant Sam Lorrimer, lying on the faded rug, the gold chain eating into the flesh of his neck. The Merrilton Hotel was no kind of a place for Sam Lorrimer to die. Once it may have been a class-A hotel, but down through the years it had degenerated into a cheap theatrical hangout. Lorrimer should have died outdoors, with prairie grass in his face. "Hell, I should be writing soap operas!" Pascal muttered, and turned away from the window.

"Well, Eddie?"

Eddie drew a deep breath. "I didn't kill him," he said.

"Fine," Pascal said, cheerfully. "Let's hear how this version goes."

"Part of what I told you is true," Eddie said. "Every day for two weeks this Lorrimer called me up here and placed a bet on the horses. Not much, you understand. About fifty bucks. Every day he lost. Braxton had taken seven, eight hundred dollars off him. Then today he comes up with a thousand bucks on a twenty-to-one shot. I—I figured, like I told you, it was easy money for me. So I—I didn't pass it on to Braxton and I went down in the basement and listened to the race. When Samovar won I knew I was in a jam."

"Go ahead, Eddie."

"Well—I came upstairs and in the lobby I see a guy I know is a hood for Braxton—a killer, you understand."

"What's his name?"

"I don't know."

"Did you ever see him before?"

"No! That is—sure I saw him before, or how would I know he was Braxton's hood?"

"Miracles do happen," Pascal said, dryly. "So you saw this killer."

"I knew right away they'd sent him to get me," Eddie said.

"Why?"

"Because I didn't place the bet."

"Oh, Eddie!" Pascal sounded tired.

"What's the matter?"

"Braxton should have pinned a medal on you. You saved him twenty thousand bucks by not placing it."

"But I held out on him. I knew he wouldn't stand for that. That's why I told you I killed Lorrimer."

"Brother!" Pascal said.

"I figured I'd better run the risk of getting off with that. I'd be safer in jail with Braxton's killer looking for me."

"We will now have a short interlude of organ music," Pascal said. "Eddie, Eddie! I admit I am no Sherlock Holmes, but give me credit for some brains. I told you I may overlook a lot of things, but I always check."

"What do you mean?" Eddie looked up, deep anxiety in his red eyes.

"Well, there's a girl at the switchboard," Pascal said. "Lorrimer called you to his room at five minutes to one. You went there. About ten minutes later you came downstairs in the elevator. There'd been another call for you from the occupant of Room Twelve-fourteen. This occupant of Room Twelve-fourteen wanted to see you at once. You went up there, stayed another ten or fifteen minutes. Then you came down, told one of the boys to take over for you because you had to go to Gorton's. There you bought some pancake make-up—telling the clerk you needed it for someone who wanted to cover up a black eye. You were back in the hotel in about fifteen minutes and went upstairs again, presumably to take the package to Room Twelve-fourteen. No one saw you again for about an hour—*after* Lorrimer's body was discovered by the floor maid. Now, Eddie, would you like to fit all those facts into your story of listening to the race in the basement, seeing a killer wandering around the lobby, being afraid Braxton would have you murdered for doing him a big favor?"

"No," Eddie said sharply. "I wouldn't."

"I suppose I can get it out of the girl in Room Twelve-fourteen," Pascal said.

"*No!*" Eddie twisted from side to side in the chair. "Damn you!"

"I know, Eddie. Nobody ever likes us. But would you like to take one more try at this story?"

Eddie sat hunched in the chair, looking shriveled and much older. Pascal lit another cigarette, hesitated, and dropped the match on the top of the bureau.

"You know, Eddie," he said gently, "a cop looks like a blank wall—sort of a one-dimensional character—to most people. He's a blank wall with a gun and a tough approach and a tin badge, and nothing behind him. But that isn't true, Eddie. I'm a man, just like you. I've got a girl I'm crazy about. I eat food, just like you. I feel warm and cold, just like you; I even get scared, just like you. So it might be, if you told me the truth, I'd understand."

Eddie covered his face with his hands. "I'd rather of died than mix her up in this," he said.

"Who, Eddie?"

"Miss Russell."

"The girl in Room Twelve-fourteen?"

Eddie nodded. "She's the only woman ever treated me like a—like a man."

Pascal's eyes narrowed to keep out the smoke from his cigarette. "Tell me about it, Eddie."

"She checked in two weeks ago."

"Same time as Lorrimer?"

"That was a coincidence," Eddie said, quickly. "They had no connection with each other."

"I see."

"She's beautiful," Eddie said. "Taller than me—but warm, and kind, and beautiful. She's a dancer. Part of a team called Russell and Sebastian. I guess they do hotel work and night clubs. It's—it's just a professional association. This Sebastian is an s.o.b."

"In what way, Eddie?"

"He's tall," Eddie said, "and dark—with sideburns! He's always been nasty to me. And—well, there's more to it."

"Take your time," Pascal said.

"Sebastian doesn't stay here in the hotel," Eddie said. "He'd just come here to call for her when they had a job."

"They didn't work regularly?"

"No. Maybe two-three times a week. I guess they did fill-ins and parties and stuff like that. The first day Linda was here I—"

"Linda?"

"Linda Russell. Her first name is Linda. The first day she was here she sent for a bellhop and I happened to take the call." A slow red color began to creep up into Eddie's cheeks. "Maybe, like you said, Lieutenant, you're human. Maybe you eat and sleep and got a girl and get scared. *But you're not five foot one and a half!*" It was bitterness, dredged up from a deep, dark well. "People don't pat you on the head, and call you 'sonny' and offer you candy instead of tips. People don't try to hold you on their lap and treat you like you were in the sixth grade, when you're a *man*, and you feel like a *man* feels, and you want the things a *man* wants. You want to make love, and you want to be a big shot, and stand on your own feet, and be *respected*. You don't want to be called *cute!*" The breath came out of him in a long sigh. "That's something that isn't behind your blank wall, Lieutenant, something you don't know about."

"No, Eddie," Pascal said, "but I can see it would be rough. Really rough."

"You're telling me! Well, Linda didn't treat me that way. She never made one crack about my being small. She talked to me like I was anyone else. It got so when she wanted something she'd ask for me specially. She had a radio record-player in her room and a collection of good hot records. She'd ask me to sit down and listen, and she'd offer me a cigarette, and sometimes a drink. She talked about herself when she was a kid, and about the dancing racket, and what a mean s.o.b. this Sebastian is—but he's a good dancer and he has the in with the booking agents. Then—twice she let me take her out to dinner when I was off. And she danced with me, and she—she treated me like anyone."

"Go on, Eddie."

"I guess I opened my yap plenty to her, too. I told her how tough it was when I was a kid, being so small—and how I couldn't ever get a decent job for the same reason. Then, the last time we were out, she let me kiss her good night. And it wasn't like she was doing me a favor. It was like she *wanted* to! Blast it, Lieutenant, don't you see I'd rather go to the chair than have you bother her with five minutes of your third degree on my account?"

"It wouldn't be on your account, Eddie. It's on Lorrimer's account."

"But I've accidentally got her into it," Eddie said. "By just being there when—when—"

"When Lorrimer was killed?"

"I don't know when he was killed, but I was with Linda when the commotion started out in the hall—when the maid found him."

Pascal glanced at the window, sighed, dropped his cigarette on the rug and heeled it out. "Who gave her the black eye, Eddie?"

"You've seen her!" Eddie's voice shook.

"No. But she sent you out to buy stuff to cover a black eye, didn't she?"

"Okay," Eddie said. "I'll tell you. Only let her alone, will you, Lieutenant, let her alone!"

"If I can," Pascal said. "I promise you I will, if I can, Eddie."

"You had it fairly straight," Eddie said. "Lorrimer sent for me just before one."

"How are you so sure of the time?"

"Because while I was talking to him the maid from room service knocked on his door and said his lunch was there. He had his lunch served every day at one o'clock. Same thing always—a scotch sour, a turkey sandwich on toast, and iced coffee. The maid always knocks on his door and leaves the wagon with his lunch on it out in the hall. He gets it when he's ready."

"I see."

"He had just got a phone call and he was talking when the maid knocked. He told me to tell the maid to leave it as usual."

"Who was he talking to on the phone?"

"I don't know," Eddie said. "From the way he talked I figured it was a babe. You know—he made his voice sound kind of sweet and laughing."

"Go ahead, Eddie."

"Well, Lorrimer was stretched out on the bed and he'd been figuring something out with a pencil and paper from the racing form. He handed me the thousand dollars—two five-hundred-dollar bills—and told me to get it down on Samovar. I wrote him out a slip and beat it out of there. I figured I'd better get to Braxton quick. There was something fishy about that bet."

"Fishy?"

"Look, a guy bets fifty bucks every day for a couple of weeks and loses every dime of it. Suddenly he lays a thousand bucks on a rank outsider. *It figures he knows something!* Braxton couldn't refuse the bet on account of he'd taken Lorrimer's

232

money for two weeks and there'd be a stink if he refused. But he'd want to spread as much of that grand around as he could—maybe lay a covering bet on the horse himself. I knew I'd better get to him quick.

"I was on my way when Fay, on the switchboard, told me Linda had called and wanted to see me as quick as I could get there. I figured I had just time to go up and tell her why I didn't have any time at the moment, and then get over to Braxton.

"I went up to her room and knocked. She usually opened the door for me, but this time she called out to me to come in. Her voice sounded kind of muffled, like she was on the far side of the room. She was sitting in a chair with her back to me. The shades were drawn and the room was kind of dark. She had a handkerchief up to her face and she was crying.

" 'Don't come any closer, Eddie,' she said. 'I don't want you to see me!'

" 'What's the matter?' I asked her.

" 'I—I had a little trouble,' she said. 'I've got a—a black eye.'

" 'Did somebody hit you?' I asked her.

"She started to cry. Lieutenant, it was like red clouds rolling up in front of me. I was shaking all over.

" 'Who was it?' I asked her.

"She just shook her head back and forth. Then she started laughing and crying at the same time. 'It's so embarrassing,' " she said.

" 'You got to tell me who it was!' I said. I told myself whoever it was I'd kill him for this. I had a pretty good idea, too. Sebastian, her dancing partner. As far as I knew she didn't see any other guys in the hotel. I swore I'd get him if it was the last thing I ever did. But she tried to calm me down. She said all she wanted was some special kind of make-up they have in some drug stores that you can cover up a black eye with. She said Gorton's, down a couple of blocks from here, had it and would I go get some. She had written down on a piece of paper what she wanted."

"Did she admit it was Sebastian who'd given her the black eye?" Pascal asked.

"No. She saw how churned up I was and she just kept trying to calm me down. But it had to be him."

"Okay, Eddie. Go ahead."

"She was lying down with a wet cloth over her eye when I got back. I put the package on the bureau and she asked me to turn on the radio. There's a small station that does classical music.

" 'Don't go, Eddie,' she said. 'Stay and talk to me.'

"So I sat down beside the bed, still burning up with ideas of what I'd do to Sebastian. Then suddenly the music stopped on the radio and the announcer said they were going to bring us the feature race from Belmont. I guess I nearly fainted. In the excitement I'd forgot about Lorrimer's dough in my pocket. I'd forgot everything except helping Linda. I just sat there, frozen, waiting to hear the race. If Samovar won I was in the soup but good." Eddie drew a deep breath. "Samovar won."

"You told Linda about it?" Pascal asked.

"No. It was *my* headache, Lieutenant. I just sat there, trying to think what to do. It seemed like the only thing was to take it over the fence. Then I heard a commotion in the hall. It was the maid. She'd come to get the lunch dishes in Lorrimer's room and she'd found him. I was stuck. I left Linda, but I couldn't leave the hotel. By the time I got downstairs the prowl-car cops had the place sealed up."

"Go on, Eddie."

"That's all," Eddie said. "The first cop to look over the crime sees the slip in Lorrimer's hand. He finds out I'm the guy who takes the bets in the hotel and he holds me. Then—then you came along."

Pascal was silent for a long time. He seemed to be debating something with himself. Finally he walked over toward the door.

"We'd better get you tidied up, Eddie," he said. "The girl gives you an alibi, if your stories check. You're going to need it when the D.A. begins hunting around for a suspect."

"Do you have to drag Linda into it?" Eddie asked.

" 'Fraid so," Pascal said. "Come on."

Pascal knocked on the door of Room 1214. There was considerable delay before it was opened by Linda Russell. She wasn't tall, except in relation to Eddie. Pascal understood at once what Eddie had seen in her. She was beautiful, and her voice was soft and husky and a little anxious. Her wide brown eyes moved from Pascal to Eddie.

"Eddie, what's happened?"

Pascal introduced himself. "Eddie needs an alibi, Miss Russell, and from what he's told me you may be able to give it to him."

"I tried to keep you out of it, Linda," Eddie said.

"Yes, he even confessed to the murder to keep you out of it," Pascal said.

"But Eddie! Didn't you know I'd be only too happy to tell the lieutenant you were here?" It was a loving reproach.

"I didn't want you mixed up in it," Eddie said.

"Foolish! Won't you both come in?"

"Thanks, Miss Russell," Pascal said.

The shades in the room were raised now and the late afternoon sun made a bright pattern on the faded beige rug. Pascal moved over and stood by the bureau, glancing down at the odds and ends on its surface—a lipstick, a little box of powder, a hand mirror, nail scissors and an orange wood stick, a small package wrapped in green paper, a handbag with the gold initials "L.R." on the clasp.

"Can you tell me just exactly what your connection was with Eddie this afternoon?" Pascal asked.

"Of course," Linda Russell said. "I called downstairs and asked for him about one o'clock. I—I was in trouble."

"The black eye?" Pascal asked.

"Yes. I wanted some special makeup from the drug store. I couldn't get it myself, looking the way I did. You can see what a wonderful job it does." She raised her fingers to her eye.

"You'd never know," Pascal admitted.

"Eddie went and got it and brought it back for me. I was pretty upset. Eddie and I have become good friends and he stayed here talking to me for quite a while."

"How long did he stay, Miss Russell?"

"I should think it must have been an hour," she said.

"Was there any special reason for his leaving when he did?" Pascal asked.

"The commotion in the hall," Linda said. "It—the maid had discovered the murder."

Pascal hesitated, rubbing his jaw thoughtfully. "Well, I guess that does it for you, Eddie. We know you did go to the drug store and that you couldn't have run the errand in much less than fifteen minutes. Miss Russell accounts for the rest of your time."

"You were foolish not to come to me right away, Eddie," Linda said.

"Yes, wasn't he," Pascal said. He looked down at the dresser top, his eyes on the green paper package.

"Have you any leads, Lieutenant?" Linda asked. "Any idea who might have killed the man?"

"It's a puzzling case," Pascal said. "It begins with a bet that wasn't a bet. A coincidence that wasn't a coincidence. Then we had a murderer who didn't kill anybody. Then we have an alibi that isn't an alibi. It's very confusing."

Linda frowned slightly. "I don't follow you, Lieutenant. Coincidence?"

"That you, Miss Russell, and Sam Lorrimer registered here at the Merrilton at the same time."

Linda drew in her breath, sharply. "But what has that got to do with—?"

"You didn't know Sam Lorrimer?"

"Of course not. I never even laid eyes on him. I don't know what he looked like even now."

"No, you wouldn't know what he looks like now. The face swollen and black, the tongue protruding, the spine bent backwards in the last terrible effort to draw breath. No, you wouldn't know what he looks like now."

"Lieutenant!" Eddie shouted. "Cut that out! What the hell kind of a way is that to talk in front of a—"

"—a lady, Eddie? I'm sorry, but as I told you, I may be less than brilliant, but I always check. I talked to the chief of police in Lorrimer's hometown in Texas. Lorrimer once owned a ranch there, but he lost the whole thing, kit and caboodle, in a card game with some sharper. And Lorrimer's wife ran off with the sharper. Lorrimer, the chief said, always swore he'd get revenge. He worked and made some money and about three weeks ago he headed north to find the sharper and his wife."

Linda stood very still, her hands at her side. "Why are you telling us this, Lieutenant?"

"Lorrimer's wife's name was Linda," Pascal said.

"So there are a million girls named Linda!" Eddie cried. "What are you trying to do?"

"Look here, Lieutenant," Linda said. "The fact that my name is Linda may be a coincidence, but I'm not the Linda you're looking for. If I were, it must be clear to you that I didn't kill this man. I provided Eddie with an alibi, but it so happens the same set of facts alibis me."

"No," Pascal said, in a flat voice.

"But of course they do," Eddie said. "She was here. She couldn't leave the room on account of her eye. I stayed with her for an hour or more—just the time when Lorrimer got knocked off."

"No," Pascal said. He sighed. "I spoke of an alibi that isn't an alibi, Eddie. It could work for you. The fifteen minutes in which you and Linda *weren't* together could be accounted for in your case by your trip to the drug store. But where was Linda during those fifteen minutes?"

"Right here in my room!" Linda said. "Putting cold compresses on my eye."

"The black eye that isn't a black eye," Pascal said. He reached out, suddenly, picked up the package on the bureau, and ripped off the green-paper wrapping. "Isn't this the stuff you bought at the drugstore, Eddie?"

Eddie stared at it, his eyes slowly widening.

"A black eye," Pascal said, in the voice of a platform lecturer, "is caused by a hemorrhaging under the skin as a result of a blow. The hemorrhage extends to the eyeball, making it blurred and bloodshot. Your eyes, both of them, are clear as a winter day, Miss Russell. No black eye—not recently."

Linda said nothing. She stood there, her face draining of color, her teeth clamped down over her lower lip.

"Eddie, while you were getting the make up for the black eye that isn't a black eye, Miss Russell—or Mrs. Lorrimer—was visiting her husband down the hall."

"Prove it!" Linda said. She didn't sound husky and sympathetic any longer.

"She *couldn't* have killed him!" Eddie cried out in a kind of despair. "You said so yourself, Pascal. You said *I* couldn't, because I was too small, because I wasn't strong enough to overpower Lorrimer. Well, *she isn't strong enough either!*"

Pascal nodded. "Nice point, Eddie. She didn't kill him. She only helped."

"Are you crazy, Lieutenant?" Linda said.

"It has been suggested before," Pascal said. His hand moved quickly again and he picked up Linda's handbag. "This is an odd type bag, Miss Russell. Nothing to carry it by. No handle. No strap. But there are some gold loops here to which something was fastened. A gold chain, perhaps?"

"Yes," she said, readily. "It broke. I'm having it fixed. But what has that to do with—"

"Lorrimer was strangled to death with that gold chain, Miss Russell."

"*Strangled!*" There was a look of total disbelief in her eyes.

"Does that surprise you?" Pascal asked, softly. "Didn't anyone tell you he'd been strangled with a gold chain, Miss Russell?"

"No!" Her eyes were suddenly very bright. "I assumed—"

"You assumed what?"

"Nothing," she said, quickly. "I just thought that—"

"—that he'd been poisoned?" Pascal's voice was deadly quiet. Suddenly he overturned the handbag and dumped its contents on the bureau top. Linda took a quick step toward him and then stopped. The contents of the bag spilled out—lipstick, compact, money, pencil, lists, keys, and a small medicine bottle. Pascal picked up the bottle. He unscrewed the top and held the bottle to his nose.

"Listen to me, Lieutenant," Linda said. "I wanted to protect Eddie as best I could. He's a nice kid. But I'm not going to the chair on his account."

"No," Pascal said, thoughtfully, "you're not."

"You're right about Sam Lorrimer. He was my husband. It wasn't a coincidence my coming here to the Merrilton the same time he did. I was warned by a friend back in Texas that he was on his way north to find me and Mike."

"Mike Braxton was the sharper who cleaned your husband, wasn't he, Linda?" Pascal said. "Don't tell me—I checked. Mike Braxton is the man you ran away with and with whom you've been living. There is no dance team of Russell and Sebastian. No booking agent in town ever heard of them. Sebastian is a strong-arm boy for Braxton. I—"

"You checked," Linda said bitterly. "I came here to try to talk Sam out of his idea for revenge. Naturally I tried to keep my relationship to him hidden from everybody else in the hotel, because if I wasn't successful, then Mike and I were going to have to get rid of him. In self-defense, you understand!"

"Sure," Pascal said. "In self-defense."

"This crazy Eddie fell for me," Linda said. She ignored the groan that came from Eddie. "He saw me talking to Sam out here in the hall once. Sam was acting fresh. Today, when I told Eddie I had a black eye, he thought it was Sam. *I told him it was Sam!*"

"No!" Eddie cried out. "You didn't. You never said who it was. You—"

"She just let you *think* it," Pascal said.

"Eddie had the gold chain," Linda said. "I gave it to him

238

yesterday to have it fixed for me. How could I guess he would use it to kill a man?"

"He couldn't have—without your help," Pascal said. "He couldn't have handled Lorrimer, even if he took him by surprise. He isn't big enough."

"Then you mean Eddie didn't kill him?"

"Oh, he killed him," Pascal said. He looked down at the boy hunched in the chair. "I'm sorry, Eddie. I'm sorry as hell. But you did kill him. But you couldn't have done it without Linda's help. Will you tell me about it, Eddie, or shall I tell you?"

Eddie didn't speak. He sat in the chair, his face covered by his trembling hands.

"I had nothing to do with it!" Linda cried. "I never left this room. I—"

"Please," Pascal said, wearily. "Let's get it over with. You meant to use Eddie as an alibi. You told him about your black eye—faking it. You sent him out for the make-up. He went, all right, but all the time he thought Lorrimer was responsible. He was burning. When he came back from the drug store he was at the explosion point. Instead of coming straight here he went to Lorrimer's room. I don't think he had a plan. He knocked, and when Lorrimer didn't answer, he went in. Lorrimer was lying on the floor. He was unconscious, but alive. Eddie had that gold chain in his pocket. He hadn't got around to having it repaired. He was crazy with anger, and he looped the chain around Lorrimer's neck and choked him till he was dead. But he couldn't have done it unless Lorrimer had been helpless. The pity of it is, if he'd waited a little longer Lorrimer would have been dead when he found him—dead from the poison you put in his whiskey sour while the tray stood outside his door."

"You haven't a shred of proof—"

"Please," Pascal said. "I checked. I knew the drink had been poisoned. I know now that the poison came from this bottle and a laboratory test will prove it. You were surprised when you heard Lorrimer'd been strangled, Linda. It looked like an out. Well—it isn't. Because Eddie couldn't have managed it without your help—which makes you his accomplice." He shook his head. "A contradictory case," he said. "The bet that wasn't a bet. The coincidence that wasn't a coincidence. The black eye that wasn't a black eye. And a passionate love for a fine girl—who wasn't a fine girl at all. . . . Come on, both of you."

THE MISSING SISTER CASE

By ROSS MACDONALD

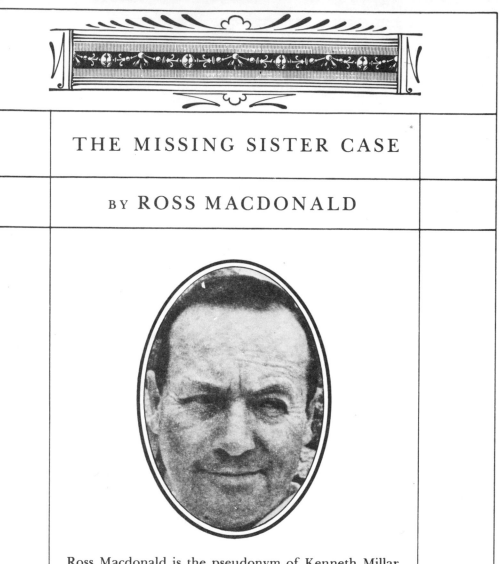

Ross Macdonald is the pseudonym of Kenneth Millar, who was born in California on December 13, 1915, and raised in Ontario, Canada. He served in the Navy in World War II and received his doctorate from the University of Michigan in 1951. His first mystery novel, *The Dark Tunnel,* was published in 1944. His famous private detective Lew Archer first appeared in *The Moving Target (1949).* Ross Macdonald lives in Santa Barbara, California, with his wife, Margaret Millar, who also writes mysteries. He received the Grand Master Award in 1973.

I PICKED HER UP on the Daylight. Or maybe she picked me up. With some of the nicest girls, you never know.

She seemed to be very nice, and very young. She had a flippant nose and wide blue eyes, the kind that men like to call innocent. Her hair bubbled like boiling gold around her small blue hat. When she turned from the window to hear my deathless comments on the landscape and the weather, she wafted spring odors toward me.

She laughed in the right places, a little hectically. But in between, when the coversation lagged, I could see a certain somberness in her eyes, a pinched look around her mouth like the effects of an early frost. When I asked her to join me in the buffet car for a drink, she said, "Oh, no. Thank you. I couldn't possibly."

"Why not?"

"I'm not quite twenty-one, for one thing. You wouldn't want to contribute to the delinquency of a minor?"

"It sounds like a pleasant enterprise."

She veiled her eyes and turned away. The green hills plunged backward past the train window like giant dolphins against the flat blue background of the sea. The afternoon sun was bright on her hair. I hoped I hadn't offended her.

I hadn't. After a while she leaned toward me and touched my arm with hesitant fingertips.

"Since you're so kind, I'll tell you what I would like." She wrinkled her nose in an anxious way. "A sandwich? Would it cost so very much more than a drink?"

"A sandwich it is."

On the way to the diner she caught the eye of every man on the train who wasn't asleep. Even some of the sleeping ones stirred, as if her passing had induced a dream. I censored my personal dream. She was too young for me, too innocent. I told myself that my interest was strictly paternal.

She asked me to order her a turkey sandwich, all white meat, and drummed on the tablecloth until it arrived. It disappeared in no time. She was ravenous. "Have another," I said.

She gave me a look which wasn't exactly calculating, just questioning. "Do you really think I should?"

"Why not? You're pretty hungry."

"Yes, I am. But—" She blushed. "I hate to ask a stranger—"

"No personal obligation. I like to see hungry people eat."

"You're awfully generous. And I am awfully hungry. Are you sure you can afford it?"

"Money is no object. I just collected a thousand-dollar fee in San Francisco. If you can use a full-course dinner, say so."

"Oh, no, I couldn't accept that. But I will confess that I could eat another sandwich."

I signaled to the waiter. The second sandwich went the way of the first while I drank coffee. She ate the olives and slices of pickle, too.

"Feeling better now? You were looking a little peaked."

"Much better, thank you. I'm ashamed to admit it, but I hadn't eaten all day. And I've been on short rations for a week."

I looked her over deliberately. Her dark blue suit was new, and expensively cut. Her bag was fine calfskin. Tiny diamonds winked in the white-gold case of her wrist watch.

"I know what you're thinking," she said. "I could have pawned something. Only I couldn't *bear* to. I spent my last cent on my ticket—I waited till the very last minute, when I had just enough to pay my fare."

"What were you waiting for?"

"To hear from Ethel. But we won't go into that." Her eyes shuttered themselves, and her pretty mouth became less pretty. "It's my worry."

"All right."

"I don't mean to be rude, or ungrateful. I thought I could hold out until I got to Los Angeles. I would have, too, if you hadn't broken me down with kindness."

"Forget about my kindness. I hope there's a job waiting for you in Los Angeles. Or maybe a husband?"

"No." The idea of a husband, or possibly a job, appealed to her sense of humor. She giggled like a schoolgirl. "You have one more guess."

"Okay. You flunked out of school and couldn't face the family."

"You're half right. But I'm still enrolled at Berkeley, and I have no intention of flunking out. I'm doing very well in my courses."

"What are you taking?"

"Psychology and sociology, mostly. I plan to be a psychiatric social worker."

242

"You don't look the type."

"I am, though." The sign of early frost showed on her face again. I couldn't keep up with her moods. She was suddenly very serious. "I'm interested in helping people in trouble. I've seen a great deal of trouble. And so many people need help in the modern world."

"You can say that again."

Her clear gaze came up to my face. "You're interested in people, too, aren't you? Are you a doctor, or a lawyer?"

"What gave you that idea?"

"You mentioned a fee you earned, a thousand-dollar fee. It sounded as if you were a professional man."

"I don't know if you'd call my job a profession. I'm a private detective. My name is Archer."

Her reaction was disconcerting. She gripped the edge of the table with her hands and pushed herself away from it. She said in a whisper as thin and sharp as a razor, "Did Edward hire you? To spy on me?"

"Of course. Naturally. It's why I mentioned the fact that I'm a detective. I'm very cunning. And who in hell is Edward?"

"Edward Illman." She was breathing fast. "Are you sure he didn't employ you to contact me? Cross your heart?"

The waiter edged toward our table, drawn by the urgent note in her voice. "Anything the matter, lady?"

"No. It's all right, thank you. The sandwiches were fine."

She gave him a strained smile, and he went away.

"I'll make a clean breast of everything," I said. "Edward employed me to feed you drugged sandwiches. The kitchen staff is in my pay, and you'll soon begin to feel the effects of the drug. After that comes the abduction, by helicopter."

"Please. You mustn't joke about such things. I wouldn't put it past him, after what he did to Ethel."

"Ethel?"

"My sister, my older sister. Ethel's a darling. But Edward doesn't think so. He hates her—he hates us both. I wouldn't be surprised if he's responsible for all this."

"All what?" I said. "We seem to be getting nowhere. Obviously you're in some sort of a bind. You want to tell me about it, I want to hear about it. Now, take a deep breath and start over, from the beginning. Bear in mind that I don't know these people from Adam. I don't even know your name."

"I'm sorry, my name is Clare Larrabee." Dutifully, she in-

243

haled. "I've been talking like a silly fool, haven't I? It's because I'm so anxious about Ethel. I haven't heard from her for several weeks. I have no idea where she is or what's happened to her. Last week, when my allowance didn't come, I began to get really worried. I phoned her house in West Hollywood and got no answer. Since then I've been phoning at least once a day, with never an answer.

"So finally I swallowed my pride and got in touch with Edward. He said he hasn't seen her since she went to Nevada. Not that I believe him, necessarily. He'd just as soon lie as tell the truth. He perjured himself right and left when they arranged the settlement."

"Let's get Edward straight," I said. "Is he your sister's husband?"

"He was. Ethel divorced him last month. And she's well rid of him, even if he did cheat her out of her fair share of the property. He claimed to be a pauper, practically, but I know better. He's a very successful real estate operator—you must have heard of the Illman Tracts."

"This is the same Illman?"

"Yes. Do you know him?"

"Not personally. I used to see his name in the columns. Quite a Casanova, isn't he?"

"Edward is a dreadful man. Why Ethel ever married him . . . Of course she wanted security, to be able to send me to college, and everything. But I'd have gone to work, gladly, if I could have stopped the marriage. I could see what kind of a husband he'd make. He even had the nerve to make a—make advances to me at the wedding reception."

"And now you're thinking he had something to do with your sister's disappearance?"

"Either that, or she did away with—No, I'm sure it's Edward. He sounded so smug on the long-distance telephone yesterday, as if he'd just swallowed the canary. I tell you, that man is capable of anything. If something's happened to Ethel, I know who's responsible."

"Probably nothing has. She could have gone off on a little trip by herself."

"You don't know Ethel. We've always kept in close touch, and she's been so punctual with my allowance. She'd never dream of going away and leaving me stranded at school without any money. I held out as long as I could, expecting to hear from her. When I got down below twenty dollars, I decided to take the train home."

"To Ethel's house in West Hollywood?"

"Yes. It's the only home I have since Daddy passed away. Ethel's the only family I have. I couldn't bear to lose Ethel."

"Do you have taxi fare?"

She shook her head, shame-faced.

"I'll drive you out. I don't live far from there myself. My car's stashed in a garage near Union Station."

"You're being good to me." Her hand crept out across the tablecloth and pressed the back of mine. "Forgive me for saying those silly things, about Edward hiring you."

I told her that would be easy.

We drove out Sunset and up into the hills. Afternoon was changing into evening. The late sunlight flashed like intermittent searchlights from the western windows of the hillside apartment buildings. Clare huddled anxiously in the far corner of the seat. She didn't speak, except to direct me to her sister's house.

It was a flat-roofed building set high on a sloping lot. The walls were redwood and glass, and the redwood had not yet weathered gray. I parked on the slanting blacktop drive and got out. Both stalls of the carport under the house were empty. The draperies were pulled over the picture windows that overlooked the valley.

I knocked on the front door. The noise resounded emptily through the building. I tried it. It was locked. So was the service door at the side.

I turned to the girl at my elbow. She was clutching the handle of her overnight bag with both hands, and looking pinched again. I thought that it was a cold homecoming for her.

"Nobody home," I said.

"It's what I was afraid of. What shall I do now?"

"You share this house with your sister?"

"When I'm home from school."

"And it belongs to her?"

"Since the divorce it does."

"Then you can give me permission to break in."

"All right. But please don't damage anything if you can help it. Ethel is very proud of her house."

The side door had a spring-type lock. I took a rectangle of

245

plastic out of my wallet and slipped it into the crack between the door and the frame. The lock slid back easily.

"You're quite a burglar," she said in a dismal attempt at humor.

I stepped inside without answering her. The kitchen was bright and clean, but it had a slightly musty, disused odor. The bread in the breadbox was stale. The refrigerator needed defrosting. There was a piece of ham moldering on one shelf, and on another a half-empty bottle of milk which had gone sour.

"She's been gone for some time," I said. "At least a week. We should check her clothes."

"Why?"

"She'd take some along if she took a trip on her own."

She led me through the living room, which was simply and expensively furnished in black iron and net, into the master bedroom. The huge square bed was neatly made and covered with a pink quilted silk spread. Clare avoided looking at it, as though the conjunction of a man and a bed gave her a guilty feeling. While she went through the closet I searched the vanity and the chest of drawers.

They were barer than they should have been. Cosmetics were conspicuous by their absence. I found one thing of interest in the top drawer of the vanity, hidden under a tangle of stockings: a bankbook issued by the Las Vegas branch of the Bank of Southern California. Ethel Illman had deposited $30,000 on March 14 of this year. On March 17 she had withdrawn $5,000. On March 20 she had withdrawn $6,000. On March 22 she had withdrawn $18,995. There was a balance in her account, after service charges, of $3.65.

Clare said from the closet in a muffled voice, "A lot of her things are gone. Her mink stole, her good suits and shoes, a lot of her best summer clothes."

"Then she's probably on a vacation." I tried to keep the doubt out of my voice. A woman wandering around with $30,000 in cash was taking a big chance. I decided not to worry Clare with that, and put the little bankbook in my pocket.

"Without telling me? Ethel wouldn't do that." She came out of the closet, pushing her fine light hair back from her forehead. "You don't understand how close we are to each other, closer than sisters usually are. Ever since Father died—"

"Does she drive her own car?"

"Of course. It's a last year's Buick convertible, blue."

246

"If you're badly worried, go to Missing Persons."

"No. Ethel wouldn't like that. She's a very proud person, and shy. Anyway, I have a better idea." She gave me that questioning-calculating look of hers.

"Involving me?"

"Please." Her eyes in the darkening room were like great soft centerless pansies, purple or black. "You're a detective and evidently a good one. And you're a man. You can stand up to Edward and make him answer questions. He just laughs at me. Of course I can't pay you in advance—"

"Forget the money for now. What makes you so certain that Illman is in on this?"

"I just know he is. He threatened her in the lawyer's office the day they made the settlement. She told me so herself. Edward said that he was going to get that money back if he had to take it out of her hide. He wasn't fooling, either. He's beaten her more than once."

"How much was the settlement?"

"Thirty thousand dollars and the house and the car. She could have collected much more, hundreds of thousands, if she'd stayed in California and fought it through the courts. But she was too anxious to get free from him. So she let him cheat her and got a Nevada divorce instead. And even then he wasn't satisfied."

She looked around the abandoned bedroom, fighting back tears. Her skin was so pale that it seemed to be phosphorescent in the gloom. With a little cry she flung herself face down on the bed and gave herself over to grief.

I said to her shaking back, "You win. Where do I find him?"

He lived in a cottage hotel on the outskirts of Bel Air. The gates of the walled pueblo were standing open, and I went in. A few couples were strolling on the gravel paths among the palm-shaded cottages, walking off the effects of the cocktail hour or working up an appetite for dinner. The women were blonde and had money on their backs. The men were noticeably older than the women, except for one, who was noticeably younger.

I passed an oval swimming pool and found Edward Illman's cottage, number twelve. Light streamed from its open French windows onto a flagstone terrace. A young woman in a narrow-waisted, billowing black gown lay on a chrome chaise at the edge of the light. With her arms hanging loose from her naked shoulders she looked like an expensive French doll which somebody had accidentally dropped there. Her face was polished and plucked and painted, expressionless as a doll's. But her eyes snapped open at the sound of my footsteps.

"Who goes there?" she said with a slight Martini accent. "Halt and give the password or I'll shoot you dead with my atomic wonder-weapon." She pointed a wavering finger at me and said, "Bing. Am I supposed to know you? I have a terrible memory for faces."

"I have a terrible face for memories. Is Mr. Illman home?"

"Uh-huh. He's in the shower. He's always taking showers. I told him he's got a scour-and-scrub neurosis, his mother was frightened by a washing machine." Her laughter rang like cracked bells. "If it's about business you can tell me."

"Are you his confidential secretary?"

"I was." She sat up on the chaise, looked pleased with herself. "I'm his fiancée, at the moment."

"Congratulations."

"Uh-huh. He's loaded." Smiling to herself, she got to her feet. "Are you loaded?"

"Not so it gets in my way."

She pointed her finger at me and said bing again and laughed, teetering on her four-inch heels. She started to fall forward. I caught her under the armpits.

"Too bad," she said to my chest. "I don't think you have a terrible face for memories at all. You're much prettier than old Teddy-bear."

"Thanks. I'll treasure the compliment."

I set her down on the chaise, but her arms twined round my neck like smooth white snakes and her body arched against me. She clung to me like a drowning child. I had to use force to detach myself.

"What's the matter?" she said with an up-and-under look.

A man appeared in the French windows, blotting out most of the light. In a white terry-cloth bathrobe he had the shape and bulk of a Kodiak bear. The top of his head was as bald as an ostrich egg. He carried a chip on each shoulder, like epaulets.

"What goes on?"

"Your fiancee swooned, slightly."

"Fiancée, hell. I saw what happened." Moving very quickly and lightly for a man of his age and weight, he pounced on

248

the girl on the chaise and began to shake her. "Can't you keep your hands off anything in pants?"

Her head bobbed back and forth. Her teeth clicked like castanets.

I put a rough hand on his shoulder. "Leave her be."

He turned on me. "Who do you think you're talking to?"

"Edward Illman, I presume."

"And who are you?"

"The name is Archer. I'm looking into the matter of your wife's disappearance."

"I'm not married. And I have no intention of getting married. I've been burned once." He looked down sideways at the girl. She peered up at him in silence, hugging her shoulders.

"Your ex-wife, then," I said.

"Has something happened to Ethel?"

"I thought you might be able to tell me."

"Where did you get that idea? Have you been talking to Clare?"

I nodded.

"Don't believe her. She's got a down on me, just like her sister. Because I had the misfortune to marry Ethel, they both think I'm fair game for anything they want to pull. I wouldn't touch either one of them with an insulated pole. They're a couple of hustlers, if you want the truth. They took me for sixty grand, and what did I get out of it but headaches?"

"I thought it was thirty."

"Sixty," he said, with the money light in his eyes. "Thirty in cash, and the house is worth another thirty easily."

I looked around the place, which must have cost him a hundred dollars a day. Above the palms, the first few stars sparkled like solitaire diamonds.

"You seem to have some left."

"Sure I have. But I work for my money. Ethel was strictly from nothing when I met her. She owned the clothes on her back and what was under them and that was all. So she gives me a bad time for three years and I pay off at the rate of twenty grand a year. I ask you, is that fair?"

"I hear you threatened to get it back from her."

"You have been talking to Clare, eh? All right, so I threatened her. It didn't mean a thing. I talk too much sometimes and I have a bad temper."

"I'd never have guessed."

The girl said, "You hurt me, Teddy. I need another drink. Get me another drink, Teddy."

"Get it yourself."

She called him several bad names and wandered into the cottage, walking awkwardly like an animated doll.

He grasped my arm. "What's the trouble about Ethel? You said she disappeared. You think something's happened to her?"

I removed his hand. "She's missing. Thirty thousand in cash is also missing. There are creeps in Vegas who would knock her off for one big bill, or less."

"Didn't she bank the money? She wouldn't cash a draft for that amount and carry it around. She's crazy, but not that way."

"She banked it all right, on March fourteenth. Then she drew it all out again in the course of the following week. When did you send her the draft?"

"The twelfth or the thirteenth. That was the agreement. She got her final divorce on March eleventh."

"And you haven't seen her since?"

"I have not. Frieda has, though."

"Frieda?"

"My secretary." He jerked a thumb toward the cottage. "Frieda went over to the house last week to pick up some of my clothes I'd left behind. Ethel was there, and she was all right then. Apparently she's taken up with another man."

"Do you know his name?"

"No, and I couldn't care less."

"Do you have a picture of Ethel?"

"I did have some. I tore them up. She's a well-stacked blonde, natural blonde. She looks very much like Clare, same coloring, but three or four years older. You should be able to get a picture from Clare. And while you're at it, tell her for me she's got a lot of gall setting the police on me. I'm a respectable businessman in this town."

He puffed out his chest under the bathrobe. It was thickly matted with brown hair, which was beginning to grizzle.

"No doubt," I said. "Incidentally, I'm not the police. I run a private agency. My name is Archer."

"So that's how it is, eh?" The planes of his broad face gleamed angrily in the light. He cocked a fat red fist. "You come here pumping me. Get out, by God, or I'll throw you out!"

"Calm down. I could break you in half."

His face swelled with blood and his eyes popped. He swung a

250

roundhouse right at my head. I stepped inside of it and tied him up. "I said calm down, old man. You'll break a vein."

I pushed him off balance and released him. He sat down very suddenly on the chaise. Frieda was watching us from the edge of the terrace. She laughed so heartily that she spilled her drink.

Illman looked old and tired and he was breathing raucously through his mouth. He didn't try to get up. Frieda came over to me and leaned her weight on my arm.

"Why didn't you hit him," she whispered, "when you had the chance? He's always hitting other people." Her voice rose. "Teddy-bear thinks he can get away with murder."

"Shut your yap," he said, "or I'll shut it for you."

"Button yours, muscle-man. You'll lay a hand on me once too often."

"You're fired."

"I already quit."

They were a charming couple. I was on the point of tearing myself away when a bellboy popped out of the darkness.

"A gentleman to see you, Mr. Illman."

The gentleman was a brown-faced young Highway Patrolman, who stepped forward rather diffidently into the light. "Sorry to trouble you, sir. Our San Diego office asked me to contact you as soon as possible."

Frieda looked from me to him and began to gravitate in his direction. Illman got up heavily and stepped between them.

"What is it?"

The patrolman unfolded a teletype flimsy and held it up to the light. "Are you the owner of a blue Buick convertible, last year's model?" He read off the license number.

"It was mine," Illman said. "It belongs to my ex-wife now. Did she forget to change the registration?"

"Evidently she did, Mr. Illman. In fact, she seems to've forgotten the car entirely. She left it in a parking space above the public beach in La Jolla. It's been sitting there for the last week, until we hauled it in. Where can I get in touch with her?"

"I don't know. I haven't seen her for some time."

The patrolman's face lengthened and turned grim. "You mean she's dropped out of sight?"

"Out of my sight, at least. Why?"

"I hate to have to say this, Mr. Illman. There's a considerable quantity of blood on the front seat of the Buick, according to this report. They haven't determined yet if it's human blood, but it raises the suspicion of foul play."

"Good heavens! It's what we've been afraid of, isn't it, Archer?" His voice was as thick as corn syrup with phony emotion. "You and Clare were right after all."

"Right about what, Mr. Illman?" The patrolman looked slightly puzzled.

"About poor Ethel," he said. "I've been discussing her disappearance with Mr. Archer here. Mr. Archer is a private detective and I was just about to engage his services to make a search for Ethel." He turned to me with a painful smile pulling his mouth to one side. "How much did you say you wanted in advance? Five hundred?"

"Make it two. That will buy my services for four days. It doesn't buy anything else, though."

"I understand that, Mr. Archer. I'm sincerely interested in finding Ethel for a variety of reasons, as you know."

He was a suave old fox. I almost laughed in his face. But I played along with him. I liked the idea of using his money to hang him, if possible.

"Yeah. This is a tragic occurrence for you."

He took a silver money clip shaped like a dollar sign out of his bathrobe pocket. I wondered if he didn't trust his roommate. Two bills changed hands. After a further exchange of information, the patrolman went away.

"Well," Illman said. "It looks like a pretty serious business. If you think I had anything to do with it, you're off your rocker."

"Speaking of rockers, you said your wife was crazy. What kind of crazy?" .

"I was her husband, not her analyst. I wouldn't know."

. "Did she need an analyst?"

"Sometimes I thought so. One week she'd be flying, full of big plans to make money. Then she'd go into a black mood and talk about killing herself." He shrugged. "It ran in her family."

"This could be an afterthought on your part."

His face reddened.

I turned to Frieda, who looked as if the news had sobered her. "Who was this fellow you saw at Ethel's house last week?"

"I dunno. She called him Owen, I think. Maybe it was his first name, maybe it was his last name. She didn't introduce us." She said it as if she felt cheated.

"Describe him?"

"Sure. A big guy, over six feet, wide in the shoulders, narrow in the beam. A smooth hunk of male. And young," with a malicious glance at Illman. "Black hair, and he had all of it, dreamy dark eyes, a cute little hairline mustache. I tabbed him for a gin-mill cowboy from Vegas, but he could be a movie star if I was a producer."

"What made you think she'd taken up with him?"

"The way he moved around the house, like he owned it. He poured himself a drink while I was there. And he was in his shirtsleeves. A real sharp dresser. Custom-made stuff."

"You have a good eye."

"For men, she has," Illman said.

"Lay off me," she said in a hard voice, with no trace of the Martini drawl. "Or I'll really walk out on you and then where will you be?"

"Right where I am now. Sitting pretty."

"That's what you think."

I interrupted their communion. "Do you know anything about this Owen character, Illman?"

"Not a thing. He's probably some jerk she picked up in Nevada while she was sweating out the divorce."

"Have you been to San Diego recently?"

"Not for months."

"That's true," Frieda said. "I've been keeping close track of Teddy. I have to. Incidentally, it's getting late and I'm hungry. Go and put on some clothes, darling. You're prettier with clothes on."

"More than I'd say for you," he leered.

I left them and drove back to West Hollywood. The night-blooming girls and their escorts had begun to appear on the Strip. Gusts of music came from the doors that opened for them. But when I turned off Sunset, the streets were deserted.

All the lights were on in the redwood house on the hillside. I parked in the driveway and knocked on the front door. The draperies over the window beside it were pulled to one side, then fell back into place. A thin voice drifted out to me.

"Is that you, Mr. Archer?"

I said that it was. Clare opened the door inch by inch. Her face was almost haggard.

"I'm so relieved to see you."

"What's the trouble?"

"A man was watching the house. He was sitting there at the

curb in a long black car. It looked like an undertaker's car. And it had a Nevada license."

"Are you sure?"

"Yes. It lighted up when he drove away. I saw it through the window. He only left a couple of minutes ago."

"Did you get a look at his face?"

"I'm afraid not. I didn't dare go out. I was petrified. He shined a searchlight on the window."

"Take it easy. There are plenty of big black cars in town, and quite a few Nevada licenses. He was probably looking for some other address."

"No. I had a—a kind of a fatal feeling when I saw him. I just *know* that he's connected in some way with Ethel's disappearance. I'm scared."

She leaned against the door, breathing quickly. She looked very young and vulnerable. I said, "What am I going to do with you, kid? I can't leave you here alone."

"Are you going away?"

"I have to. I saw Edward. While I was there, he had a visitor from the HP. They found your sister's car abandoned near San Diego." I didn't mention the blood.

"Edward killed her!" she cried. "I knew it."

"That I doubt. She may not even be dead. I'm going to San Diego to find out."

"Take me along, won't you?"

"It wouldn't be good for your reputation. Besides, you'd be in the way."

"No, I wouldn't. I promise. I have friends in San Diego. Just let me drive down there with you and I can stay with them."

"You wouldn't be making this up?"

"Honest, I have friends there. Gretchen Falk and her husband, they're good friends of Ethel's and mine. We lived in San Diego for a while, before she married Edward. The Falks will be glad to let me stay with them."

"Hadn't you better phone them first?"

"I can't. The phone's disconnected. I tried it."

"Are you sure these people exist?"

"Of course!" she said.

I gave in. I turned out the lights, locked the door, and put her bag in my car. Clare stayed very close to me.

As I was backing out, a car pulled in behind me, blocking the entrance to the driveway. I opened the door and got out. It was a black Lincoln with a searchlight mounted over the windshield.

Clare said, "He's come back."

The searchlight flashed on. Its bright beam swiveled toward me. I reached for the gun in my should holster and got a firm grip on nothing. Holster and gun were packed in the suitcase in the trunk of my car. The searchlight blinded me.

A black gun emerged from the dazzle, towing a hand and an arm. They belonged to a quick-stepping cube-shaped man in a double-breasted flannel suit. A snap-brim hat was pulled down over his eyes. His mouth was as full of teeth as a barracuda's. It said, "Where's Dewar?"

"Never heard of him."

"Owen Dewar. You've heard of him."

The gun dragged him forward another step and collided with my breastbone. His free hand palmed my flanks. All I could see was his unchanging smile, framed in brilliant light. I felt a keen desire to do some orthodontic work on it. But the gun was an inhibiting factor.

"You must be thinking of two other parties," I said.

"No dice. This is the house and that's the broad. Out of the car, lady."

"I will not," she said in a tiny voice behind me.

"Out, or I'll blow a hole in your boy friend here."

Reluctantly she clambered out. The teeth looked down at her ankles as if they wanted to chew them. I made a move for the gun. It dived into my solar plexus, doubling me over. Its muzzle flicked the side of my head. It pushed me back against the fender of my car. I felt a worm of blood crawling past my ear.

"You coward! Leave him alone." Clare flung herself at him. He sidestepped neatly, moving on the steady pivot of the gun against my chest. She went to her knees on the blacktop.

"Get up, lady, but keep your voice down. How many boy friends you keep on the string, anyway?"

She got to her feet. "He isn't my boy friend. Who are you? Where is Ethel?"

"That's a hot one." The smile intensified. "You're Ethel. The question is, where's Dewar?"

"I don't know any Dewar."

"Sure you do, Ethel. You know him well enough to marry him. Now tell me where he is and nobody gets theirselves hurt." The flat voice dropped, and added huskily, "Only I haven't got much time to waste."

"You're wrong," she said. "You're completely mistaken. I'm not Ethel. I'm Clare. Ethel's my older sister."

He stepped back and swung the gun in a quarter circle, covering us both. "Turn your face to the light. Let's have a good look at you."

She did as she was told, striking a rigid pose. He shifted the gun to his left hand and brought a photograph out of his inside pocket. Looking from it to her face, he shook his head doubtfully.

"I guess you're leveling at that. You're younger than this one, and thinner." He handed her the photograph. "She your sister?"

"Yes. It's Ethel."

I caught a glimpse of the picture over her shoulder. It was a blown-up candid shot of two people. One was a pretty blonde who looked like Clare five years from now. She was leaning on the arm of a tall dark man with a hairline mustache. They were smirking at each other and there was a flower-decked altar in the background.

"Who's the man?" I said.

"Dewar. Who else?" said the teeth behind the gun. "They got married in Vegas last month. I got this picture from the Chaparral Chapel. It goes with the twenty-five-dollar wedding." He snatched it out of Clare's hands and put it back in his pocket. "It took me a couple of weeks to run her down. She used her maiden name, see."

"Where did you catch up with her? San Diego?"

"I didn't catch up with her. Would I be here if I did?"

"What do you want her for?"

"I don't want her. I got nothing against the broad, except that she tied up with Dewar. He's the boy I want."

"What for?"

"You wouldn't be interested. He worked for me at one time." The gun swiveled brightly toward Clare. "You know where your sister is?"

"No, I don't. I wouldn't tell you if I did."

"That's no way to talk now, lady. My motto's cooperation. From other people."

I said, "Her sister's been missing for a week. The HP found her car in San Diego. It had bloodstains on the front seat. Are you sure you didn't catch up with her?"

"I'm asking you the questions, punk." But there was a trace of uncertainty in his voice. "What happened to Dewar if the blonde is missing?"

"I think he ran out with her money."

Clare turned to me. "You didn't tell me all this."

"I'm telling you now."

The teeth said, "She had money?"

"Plenty."

"The bum! The bum took us both, eh?"

"Dewar took you for money?"

"You ask too many questions, punk. You'll talk yourself to death one of these days. Now stay where you are for ten minutes, both of you. Don't move, don't yell, don't telephone. I might decide to drive around the block and come back and make sure."

He backed down the brilliant alley of the searchlight beam. The door of his car slammed. All its lights went off together. It rolled away into darkness and didn't come back.

It was past midnight when we got to San Diego, but there was still a light in the Falks' house. It was a stucco cottage on a street of identical cottages in Pacific Beach.

"We lived here once," Clare said. "When I was going to high school. That house, second from the corner." Her voice was nostalgic and she looked around the jerry-built tract as if it represented something precious to her. The pre-Illman era in her young life.

I knocked on the front door. A big henna-head in a housecoat opened it on a chain. But when she saw Clare beside me, she flung the door wide.

"Clare honey, where you been? I've been trying to phone you in Berkeley, and here you are. How are you, honey?"

She opened her arms and Clare walked into them.

"Oh, Gretchen," she said with her face on the redhead's breast. "Something's happened to Ethel, something terrible."

"I know it, honey, but it could be worse."

"Worse than murder?"

"She isn't murdered. Put that out of your mind. She's pretty badly hurt, but she isn't murdered."

Clare stood back to look at her face. "You've seen her? Is she here?"

The redhead put a finger to her mouth, which was big and generous-looking, like the rest of her. "Hush, Clare. Jake's asleep, he has to get up early, go to work. Yeah, I've seen her, but she isn't here. She's in a nursing home over on the other side of town."

"You said she's badly hurt?"

"Pretty badly beaten, yeah, poor dear. But the doctor told me she's pulling out of it fine. A little plastic surgery and she'll be as good as new."

"Plastic surgery?"

"Yeah, I'm afraid she'll need it. I got a look at her face tonight, when they changed the bandages. Now take it easy, honey. It could be worse."

"Who did it to her?"

"That lousy husband of hers."

"Edward?"

"Heck, no. The other one, that calls himself Dewar."

I said, "Have you seen Dewar?"

"I saw him a week ago, the night he beat her up, the dirty rotten bully." Her deep contralto growled in her throat. "I'd like to get my hands on him just for five minutes."

"So would a lot of people, Mrs. Falk."

She glanced inquiringly at Clare. "Who's your friend? You haven't introduced us."

"I'm sorry. Mr. Archer, Mrs. Falk. Mr. Archer is a detective, Gretchen."

"I was wondering. Ethel didn't want me to call the police. I told her she ought to, but she said no. The poor darling's so ashamed of herself, getting mixed up with that kind of a louse. She didn't even get in touch with *me* until tonight. Then she saw in the paper about her car being picked up, and she thought maybe I could get it back for her without any publicity. Publicity is what she doesn't want most. I guess it's a tragic thing for a beautiful girl like Ethel to lose her looks."

I said, "There won't be any publicity if I can help it. Did you go to see the police about her car?"

"Jake advised me not to. He said it would blow the whole thing wide open. And the doctor told me he was kind of breaking the law by not reporting the beating she took. So I dropped it."

"How did this thing happen?"

"I'll tell you all I know about it. Come on into the living room, kids, let me fix you something to drink."

Clare said, "You're awfully kind, Gretchen, but I must go to Ethel. Where is she?"

"The Mission Rest Home. Only don't you think you better wait till morning? It's a private hospital, but it's awful late for visitors."

"I've got to see her," Clare said. "I couldn't sleep a wink if I didn't. I've been so worried about her."

Gretchen heaved a sigh. "Whatever you say, honey. We can try, anyway. Give me a second to put on a dress and I'll show you where the place is."

She led us into the darkened living room, turned the television set off and the lights on. A quart of beer, nearly full, stood on a coffee table beside the scuffed sofa. She offered me a glass, which I accepted gratefully. Clare refused. She was so tense she couldn't even sit down.

We stood and looked at each other for a minute. Then Gretchen came back, struggling with a zipper on one hip.

"All set, kids. You better drive, Mr. Archer. I had a couple of quarts to settle my nerves. You wouldn't believe it, but I've gained five pounds since Ethel came down here. I always gain weight when I'm anxious."

We went out to my car, and turned toward the banked lights of San Diego. The women rode in the front seat. Gretchen's opulent flesh was warm against me.

"Was Ethel here before it happened?" I said.

"Sure she was, for a day. Ethel turned up here eight or nine days ago, Tuesday of last week it was. I hadn't heard from her for several months, since she wrote me that she was going to Nevada for a divorce. It was early in the morning when she drove up—in fact, she got me out of bed. The minute I saw her, I knew that something was wrong. The poor kid was scared, really scared. She was as cold as a corpse and her teeth were chattering. So I fed her some coffee and put her in a hot tub, and after that she told me what it was that'd got her down."

"Dewar?"

"You said it, mister. Ethel never was much of a picker. When she was hostessing at the Grant coffee shop back in the old days, she was always falling for the world's worst phonies. Speaking of phonies, this Dewar takes the cake. She met him in Las Vegas when she was waiting for her divorce from Illman. He was a big promoter, to hear him tell it. She fell for the story, and she fell for him. A few days after she got her final decree, she married him. Big romance. Big deal.

"They were going to be business partners, too. He said he

had some money to invest, twenty-five thousand or so, and he knew of a swell little hotel in Acapulco that they could buy at a steal for fifty thousand. The idea was that they should each put up half, and go and live in Mexico in the lap of luxury for the rest of their lives. He didn't show her any of his money, but she believed him. She drew her settlement money out of the bank and came to L.A. with him to close up her house and get set for the Mexican deal."

"He must have hypnotized her," Clare said. "Ethel's a smart business woman."

"Not with something tall, dark, and handsome, honey. I give him that much. He's got the looks. Well, they lived in L.A. for a couple of weeks, on Ethel's money of course, and he kept putting off the Mexican trip. He didn't want to go anywhere, in fact—just sit around the house and drink her liquor and eat her good cooking."

"He was hiding out," I said.

"From what? The police?"

"Worse than that. Some gangster pal from Nevada was gunning for him, still is. Ethel wasn't the only one he fleeced."

"Nice guy, eh? Anyway, Ethel started to get restless. She didn't like sitting around with all that money in the house, waiting for nothing. Last Monday night—a week ago Monday, that is—she had a showdown with him. Then it all came out. He didn't have any money or anything else. He wasn't a promoter, he didn't know of any hotel in Acapulco. His whole buildup was as queer as a three-dollar bill. Apparently he made his living gambling, but he was even all washed up with that. Nothing. But she was married to him now, he said, and she was going to sit still and like it or he'd knock her block off.

"He meant it, too, Ethel said. She's got the proof of it now. She waited until he drank himself to sleep that night, then she threw some things in a bag, including her twenty-five thousand, and came down here. She was on her way to get a quickie divorce in Mexico, but Jake and me talked her into staying for a while and thinking it over. Jake said she could probably get an annulment right in California, and that would be more legal."

"He was probably right."

"Yeah? Maybe it wasn't such a bright idea after all. We kept her here just long enough for Dewar to catch her. Apparently she left some letters behind and he ran down the list of her friends until he found her at our place. He talked her into

260

going for a drive to talk it over. I didn't hear what was said—they were in her room—but he must have used some powerful persuasion. She went out of the house with him as meek as a lamb and they drove away in her car.

"That was the last I saw of her until she got in touch with me tonight. When she didn't come back I wanted to call the police, but Jake wouldn't let me. He said I had no business coming between a man and his wife and all that guff. I gave Jake a piece of my mind tonight on that score. I ought to've called the cops as soon as Dewar showed his sneaking face on our front porch."

"What exactly did he do to her?"

"He gave her a bad clobbering, that's obvious. Ethel didn't want to talk about it much tonight. The subject was painful to her in more ways than one."

"Did he take her money?"

"He must have. It's gone. So is he."

We were on the freeway which curved past the hills of Balboa Park. The trees of its man-made jungle were restless against the sky. Below us on the other side, the city sloped like a frozen cascade of lights down to the black concavity of the bay.

The Mission Rest Home was in the eastern suburbs, an old stucco mansion which had been converted into a private hospital. The windows in its thick stucco walls were small and barred and there were lights in some of them.

I rang the doorbell. Clare was so close to my back I could feel her breath. A woman in a purple flannelette wrapper opened the door. Her hair hung in two gray braids, which were ruler-straight. Her hard black eyes surveyed the three of us, and stayed on Gretchen.

"What is it now, Mrs. Falk?" she said brusquely.

"This is Mrs.—Miss Larrabee's sister Clare."

"Miss Larrabee is probably sleeping. She shouldn't be disturbed."

"I know it's late," Clare said in a tremulous voice. "But I've come all the way from San Francisco to see her."

"She's doing well, I assure you of that. She's out of danger."

"Can't I just go in for a teensy visit? Ethel will want to see me, and Mr. Archer has some questions to ask her. Mr. Archer is a private detective."

"This is very irregular." Reluctantly she opened the door. "Wait here and I'll see if she is awake. Please keep your voices down. We have other patients."

We waited in a dim, high-ceilinged room which had once been the reception room of the mansion. The odors of mustiness and medication blended depressingly in the stagnant air.

"I wonder what brought her here," I said.

"She knew old lady Lestina," Gretchen said. "She stayed with her at one time, when Mrs. Lestina was running a boarding-house."

"Of course," Clare said. "I remember the name. That was when Ethel was going to San Diego State. Then Daddy got killed and she had to drop out of school and go to work." Tears glimmered in her eyes. "Poor Ethel. She's always tried so hard, and been so good to me."

Gretchen patted her shoulder. "You bet she has, honey. Now you have a chance to be good to her."

"Oh, I will. I'll do everything I can."

Mrs. Lestina appeared in the arched doorway. "She's not asleep. I guess you can talk to her for a very few minutes."

We followed her to a room at the end of one wing of the house. A white-uniformed nurse was waiting at the door. "Don't say anything to upset her, will you? She's always fighting sedation as it is."

The room was large but poorly furnished, with a mirrorless bureau, a couple of rickety chairs, a brown-enameled hospital bed. The head on the raised pillow was swathed in bandages through which tufts of blonde hair were visible. The woman sat up and spread her arms. The whites of her eyes were red, suffused with blood from broken vessels. Her swollen lips opened and said, "Clare!" in a tone of incredulous joy.

The sisters hugged each other, with tears and laughter. "It's wonderful to see you," the older one said through broken teeth. "How did you get here so fast?"

"I came to stay with Gretchen. Why didn't you call me, Ethel? I've been worried sick about you."

"I'm dreadfully sorry, darling. I should have, shouldn't I? I didn't want you to see me like this. And I've been so ashamed of myself. I've been such a terrible fool. I've lost our money."

The nurse was standing against the door, torn between her duty and her feelings. "Now you promised not to get excited, Miss Larrabee."

"She's right," Clare said. "Don't give it a second thought. I'm going to leave school and get a job and look after you. You need some looking after for a change."

"Nuts. I'll be fine in a couple of weeks." The brave voice issuing from the mask was deep and vibrant. "Don't make any rash decisions, kiddo. The head is bloody but unbowed." The sisters looked at each other in the silence of deep affection.

I stepped forward to the bedside and introduced myself. "How did this happen to you, Miss Larrabee?"

"It's a long story," she lisped, "and a sordid one."

"Mrs. Falk has told me most of it up to the point when Dewar made you drive away with him. Where did he take you?"

"To the beach—I think it was in La Jolla. It was late and there was nobody there and the tide was coming in. And Owen had a gun. I was terrified. I didn't know what more he wanted from me. He already had my twenty-five thousand."

"He had the money?"

"Yes. It was in my room at Gretchen's house. He made me give it to him before we left there. But it didn't satisfy him. He said I hurt his pride by leaving him. He said he had to satisfy his pride." Contempt ran through her voice like a thin steel thread.

"By beating you up?"

"Apparently. He hit me again and again. I think he left me for dead. When I came to, the waves were splashing on me. I managed somehow to get up to the car. It wasn't any good to me, though, because Owen had the keys. It's funny he didn't take it."

"Too easily traced," I said. "What did you do then?"

"I hardly know. I think I sat in the car for a while wondering what to do. Then a taxi went by and I stopped him and told him to bring me here."

"You weren't very wise not to call the police. They might have got your money back. Now it's a cold trail."

"Did you come here to lecture me?"

"I'm sorry. I didn't mean—"

"I was half crazy with pain," she said. "I hardly knew what I was doing. I couldn't bear to have anybody see me."

Her fingers were active among the folds of the sheets. Clare reached out and stroked her hands into quietness. "Now, now, darling," she crooned. "Nobody's criticizing you. You take things nice and easy for a while, and Clare will look after you."

The masked head rolled on the pillow. The nurse came forward, her face solicitous. "I think Miss Larrabee has had enough, don't you?"

She showed us out. Clare lingered with her sister for a

moment, then followed us to the car. She sat between us in brooding silence all the way to Pacific Beach. Before I dropped them off at Gretchen's house, I asked for her permission to go to the police. She wouldn't give it to me, and nothing I could say would change her mind.

I spent the rest of the night in a motor court, trying to crawl over the threshold of sleep. Shortly after dawn I disentangled myself from the twisted sheets and drove out to La Jolla.

La Jolla is a semi-detached suburb of San Diego, a small resort town half surrounded by sea. It was a gray morning. The slanting streets were scoured with the sea's cold breath, and the sea itself looked like hammered pewter.

I warmed myself with a short-order breakfast and went the rounds of the hotels and motels. No one resembling Dewar had registered in the past week. I tried the bus and taxi companies. Dewar must have slipped out of town unnoticed. But I did get a lead on the taxi driver who had taken Ethel to the Mission Rest Home. He had mentioned the injured woman to his dispatcher, and the dispatcher gave me his name and address. Stanley Simpson, 38 Calle Laureles.

Simpson was a paunchy, defeated-looking man who hadn't shaved for a couple of days. He came to the door of his tiny bungalow in his underwear, rubbing sleep out of his eyes. "What's the pitch, bub? If you got me up to try and sell me something, you're in for a disappointment."

I told him who I was and why I was there. "Do you remember the woman?"

"I hope to tell you I do. She was bleeding like a stuck pig, all over the back seat. It took me a couple of hours to clean it off. Somebody pistol-whipped her, if you ask me. I wanted to take her to the hospital, but she said no. Hell, I couldn't argue with her in that condition. Did I do wrong?"

"If you did, it doesn't matter. She's being taken good care of. I thought you might have got a glimpse of the man that did it to her."

"Not me, mister. She was all by herself, nobody else in sight. She got out of a parked car and staggered out into the road. I couldn't just leave her there, could I?"

"Of course not. You're a Good Samaritan, Simpson. Exactly where did you pick her up?"

"Down by the Cove. She was sitting in this Buick. I dropped a party off at the beach club and I was on my way back—"

"What time?"

"Around ten o'clock, I guess it was. I can check my schedule."

"It isn't important. Incidentally, did she pay you for the ride?"

"Yeah, she had a buck and some change in her purse. She had a hard time making it. No tip," he added gloomily.

"Tough cheese."

His fogged eyes brightened. "You're a friend of hers, aren't you? Wouldn't you say I rate a tip on a run like that? I always say, better late than never."

"Is that what you always say?" I handed him a dollar.

The Cove was a roughly semicircular inlet at the foot of a steep hill surmounted by a couple of hotels. Its narrow curving beach and the street above it were both deserted. An offshore wind had swept away the early morning mist, but the sky was still cloudy, and the sea grim. The long swells slammed the beach like stone walls falling, and broke in foam on the rocks that framed the entrance to the Cove.

I sat in my car and watched them. I was at a dead end. This seaswept place, under this iron sky, was like the world's dead end. Far out at sea a carrier floated like a chip on the horizon. A Navy jet took off from it and scrawled tremendous nothings on the distance.

Something bright caught my eye. It was in the trough of a wave a couple of hundred yards outside the Cove. Then it was on a crest: the aluminum air-bottle of an Aqualung strapped to a naked brown back. Its wearer was prone on a surfboard, kicking with black-finned feet toward the shore.

He was kicking hard, and paddling with one arm, but he was making slow progress. His other arm dragged in the opaque water. He seemed to be towing something, something heavy. I wondered if he had speared a shark or a porpoise. His face was inscrutable behind his glass mask.

I left my car and climbed down to the beach. The man on the surfboard came toward me with his tiring one-armed stroke, climbing the walled waves and sliding down them. A final surge picked him up and set him on the sand, almost at my feet. I dragged his board out of the backwash and helped him to pull in the line that he was holding in one hand. His catch was nothing native to the sea. It was a man.

The end of the line was looped around his body under the armpits. He lay face down like an exhausted runner, a big man,

265

fully clothed in soggy tweeds. I turned him over and saw the aquiline profile, the hairline mustache over the blue mouth, the dark eyes clogged with sand. Owen Dewar had made his escape by water.

The skindiver took off his mask and sat down heavily, his chest working like a great furred bellows. "I go down for abalone," he said between breaths. "I find this. Caught between two rocks at thirty-forty feet."

"How long has he been in the water?"

"It's hard to tell. I'd say a couple of days, anyway. Look at his color. Poor stiff. But I wish they wouldn't drown themselves in my hunting grounds."

"Do you know him?"

"Nope. Do you?"

"Never saw him before," I said, with truth.

"How about you phoning the police, Mac? I'm pooped. And unless I make a catch I don't eat today. There's no pay in fishing for corpses."

"In a minute."

I went through the dead man's pockets. There was a set of car keys in his jacket pocket and an alligator wallet on his hip. It contained no money, but the driver's license was decipherable: Owen Dewar, Mesa Court, Las Vegas. I put the wallet back, and let go of the body. The head rolled sideways. I saw the small hole in his neck, washed clean by the sea.

"Holy Mother!" the diver said. "He was shot."

I got back to the Falk house around midmorning. The sun had burned off the clouds and the day was turning hot. By daylight the long treeless street of identical houses looked cheap and rundown. It was part of the miles of suburban slums that the building boom after the war had scattered all over Southern California.

Gretchen was sprinkling the brown front lawn with a desultory hose. She looked too big for the pocket-handkerchief yard. The sunsuit that barely covered her various bulges made her look even bigger. She turned off the water when I got out of my car.

"What gives? You've got trouble on your face if I ever saw trouble."

"Dewar is dead. Murdered. A skindiver found him in the sea off La Jolla."

She took it calmly. "That's not such bad news, is it? He had it coming. Who killed him?"

"I told you a gunman from Nevada was on his trail. Maybe he caught him. Anyway, Dewar was shot and bled to death from a neck wound. Then he was dumped in the ocean. I had to lay the whole thing on the line for the police, since there's murder in it."

"You told them what happened to Ethel?"

"I had to. They're at the rest home talking to her now."

"What about Ethel's money? Was the money on him?"

"Not a trace of it. And he didn't live to spend it. The police pathologist thinks he's been dead for a week. Whoever got Dewar got the money at the same time."

"Will she ever get it back, do you think?"

"If we can catch the murderer and he still has it with him. That's a big if. Where's Clare, by the way? With her sister?"

"Clare went back to L.A."

"What for?"

"Don't ask me." She shrugged her rosy shoulders. "She got Jake to drive her down to the station before he went to work. I wasn't up. She didn't even tell me she was going." Gretchen seemed peeved.

"Did she get a telegram or a phone call?"

"Nothing. All I know is what Jake told me. She talked him into lending her ten bucks. I wouldn't mind so much, but it was all the ready cash we had, until payday. Oh, well, I guess we'll get it back, if Ethel recovers her money."

"You'll get it back," I said. "Clare seems to be a straight kid."

"That's what I always used to think. When they lived here, before Ethel met Illman and got into the chips, Clare was just about the nicest kid on the block. In spite of all the trouble in her family."

"What trouble was that?"

"Her father shot himself. Didn't you know? They said it was an accident, but the people on the street—we knew different. Mr. Larrabee was never the same after his wife left him. He spent his time brooding, drinking and brooding. Clare reminded me of him, the way she behaved last night after you left. She wouldn't talk to me or look at me. She shut herself up in her room and acted real cold. If you want the honest truth, I don't like her using my home as if it was a motel and Jake was a taxi service. The least she could of done was say goodbye to me."

"It sounds as if she had something on her mind."

All the way back to Los Angeles I wondered what it was. It took me a little over two hours to drive from San Diego to West Hollywood. The black Lincoln with the searchlight and the Nevada license plates was standing at the curb below the redwood house. The front door of the house was standing open.

I transferred my automatic from the suitcase to my jacket pocket, making sure that it was ready to fire. I climbed the terraced lawn beside the driveway. My feet made no sound in the grass. When I reached the porch I heard voices from inside. One was the gunman's hoarse and deathly monotone.

"I'm taking it, sister. It belongs to me."

"You're a liar."

"Sure, but not about this. The money is mine."

"It's my sister's money. What right have you got to it?"

"This. Dewar stole it from me. He ran a poker game for me in Vegas, a high-stakes game in various hotels around town. He was a good dealer and I trusted him with the house take. I let it pile up for a week, that was my mistake. I should've kept a closer watch on him. He ran out on me with twenty-five grand or more. That's the money you're holding, lady."

"I don't believe it. You can't prove that story. It's fantastic."

"I don't have to prove it. Gelt talks, but iron talks louder. So hand it over, eh?"

"I'll die first."

"Maybe you will at that."

I edged along the wall to the open door. Clare was standing flat against the opposite wall of the hallway. She was clutching a sheaf of bills to her breast. The gunman's broad flannel back was to me, and he was advancing on her.

"Stay away from me, you." Her cry was thin and desperate. She was trying to merge with the wall, pressed by terror.

"I don't like taking candy from a baby," he said in a very reasonable tone. "Only I'm going to have that money back."

"You can't have it. It's Ethel's. It's all she has."

He raised his armed right hand and slapped the side of her face with the gun barrel, lightly. Fingering the welt it left, she said in a kind of despairing stupor, "You're the one that hurt Ethel, aren't you? Now you're hurting me. You like hurting people, don't you?"

"Listen to reason, lady. It ain't just the money, it's a matter of business. I let it happen once, it'll happen again. I can't afford to let anybody get away with nothing. I got a reputation to live up to."

I said from the doorway, "Is that why you killed Dewar?"

He let out an animal sound and whirled in my direction. I shot before he did, twice. The first slug rocked him back on his heels. His bullet went wild, plowed the ceiling. My second slug took him off balance and slammed him against the wall. His blood spattered Clare and the money in her hands. She screamed once, very loudly.

The man from Las Vegas dropped his gun. It clattered on the parquetry. His hands clasped his perforated chest, trying to hold the blood in. He slid down the wall slowly, his face a mask of smiling pain, and sat with a bump on the floor. He blew red bubbles and said, "You got me wrong. I didn't kill Dewar. I didn't know he was dead. The money belongs to me. You made a big mistake, punk."

"So did you."

He went on smiling, as if in fierce appreciation of the joke. Then his red grin changed to a rictus, and he slumped.

Clare looked from him to me, her eyes wide and dark with the sight of death. "I don't know how to thank you. He was going to kill me."

"I doubt that. He was just combining a little pleasure with business."

"But he shot at you."

"It's just as well he did. It leaves no doubt that it was self-defense."

"Is it true what you said? That Dewar's dead? He killed him?"

"You tell me."

"What do you mean?"

"You've got the money that Dewar took from your sister. Where did you get it?"

"It was here, in the house. I found it in the kitchen."

"That's kind of hard to swallow, Clare."

"It's true." She looked down at the blood-spattered money in her hands. The outside bill was a hundred. Unconsciously she tried to wipe it clean on the front of her dress. "He had it hidden here. He must have come back and hid it."

"Show me where."

"You're not being very nice to me. And I'm not feeling well."

"Neither is Dewar. You didn't shoot him yourself, by any chance?"

269

"How could I? I was in Berkeley when it happened. I wish I was back there now."

"You know when it happened, do you?"

"No." She bit her lip. "I don't mean that. I mean I was in Berkeley all along. You're a witness, you were with me on the train coming down."

"Trains run both ways."

She regarded me with loathing. "You're not nice at all. To think that yesterday I thought you were nice."

"You're wasting time, Clare. I have to call the police. But first I want to see where you found the money. Or where you say you did."

"In the kitchen. You've got to believe me. It took me a long time to get here from the station on the bus. I'd only just found it when he walked in on me."

"I'll believe the physical evidence, if any."

To my surprise the physical evidence was there. A red-enameled flour canister was standing open on the board beside the kitchen sink. There were fingerprints on the flour and a floury piece of oilskin wrapping in the sink.

"He hid the money under the flour," Clare said. "I guess he thought it would be safer here than if he carried it around with him."

It wasn't a likely story. On the other hand, the criminal mind is capable of strange things. Whose criminal mind, I wondered: Clare's or Owen Dewar's or somebody else's?

"Where did you get the bright idea of coming back here and looking for it?"

"Ethel suggested it last night, just before I left her. She told me this was his favorite hiding place while she was living with him. She discovered it by accident one day."

"Hiding place for what?"

"Some kind of drug he took. He was a drug addict. Do you still think I'm lying?"

"Somebody is. But I suppose I've got to take your word until I get something better. What are you going to do with the money?"

"Ethel said if I found it, that I was to put it in the bank."

"There's no time for that now. You better let me hold it for you. I have a safe in my office."

"No. You don't trust me. Why should I trust you?"

"Because you can trust me, and you know it. If the cops

impound it you'll have to prove ownership to get it back."

She was too spent to argue. She let me take it out of her hands. I riffled through the bills and got a rough idea of their sum. There was easily twenty-five thousand there. I gave her a receipt for that amount and put the sheaf of bills in my inside pocket.

It was after dark when the cops got through with me. By that time I was equipped to do a comparative study on the San Diego and Los Angeles P.D.'s. With the help of a friend in the D.A.'s office, Clare's eyewitness account, and the bullet in the ceiling, I got away from them without being booked.

The dead man's record also helped. He had been widely suspected of shooting Bugsy Siegel, and had fallen heir to some of Siegel's holdings. His name was Jack Fidelis. R.I.P.

I drove out Sunset to my office. The Strip was lighting up for business again. The stars looked down on its neon conflagration like hard bright knowing eyes. I pulled the Venetian blinds and locked the doors and counted the money: $26,380.

I wrapped it up in brown paper, sealed it with wax, and tucked it away in the safe. I would have preferred to tear it in little pieces and flush the green confetti down the drain. Two men had died for it. I wasn't eager to become the third.

I had a steak in the restaurant at International Airport, then hopped a shuttle plane to Las Vegas. There I spent a rough night in various gambling joints, watching the suckers blow their vacation money, pinching my own pennies, and talking to some of the guys and girls that raked the money in. The rest of Illman's two hundred dollars bought me the facts I needed.

I flew back to Los Angeles in the morning, picked up my car, and headed for San Diego. I was tired enough to sleep standing up, like a horse. But something heavier than sleep or tiredness sat on the back of my neck and pressed the gas pedal down to the floorboards. It was the thought of Clare.

Clare was with her sister in the Mission Rest Home. She was waiting outside the closed door of Ethel's room when Mrs. Lestina took me down the hall. She looked as if she had passed a rougher night than mine. Her grooming was careless, hair uncombed, mouth unpainted. The welt from Fidelis' gun had turned blue and spread to one puffed eye. And I thought how very little it took to break a young girl down into a tramp, if she was vulnerable, or twist her into something worse than a tramp.

271

"Did you bring it with you?" she said as soon as Mrs. Lestina was out of earshot. "Ethel's angry with me for turning it over to you."

"I'm not surprised."

"Give it to me. Please." Her hand clawed at my sleeve. "Isn't that what you came for, to give it back to me?"

"It's in the safe in my office in Los Angeles. That is, if you're talking about the money."

"What else would I be talking about? You'll simply have to go back there and get it. Ethel can't leave here without it. She needs to pay her bill."

"Is Ethel planning to go someplace?"

"I persuaded her to come back to Berkeley with me. She'll have better care in the hospital there, and I know of a good plastic surgeon—"

"It'll take more than that to put Ethel back together again."

"What do you mean?"

"You should be able to guess. You're not a stupid girl, or are you? Has she got you fooled the way she had me fooled?"

"I don't know what you're talking about. But I don't like it. Every time I see you, you seem to get nastier."

"This is a nasty business. It's rubbing off on all of us, isn't it, kid?"

She looked at me vaguely through a fog of doubt. "Don't you dare call me kid. I thought you were a real friend for a while, but you don't even like me. You've said some dreadful things. You probably think you can scare me into letting you keep our money. Well, you can't."

"That's my problem," I said. "What to do with the money."

"You'll give it back to Ethel and me, that's what you'll do. There are laws to deal with people like you—"

"And people like Ethel. I want to talk to her."

"I won't let you. My sister's suffered enough already."

She spread her arms across the width of the door. I was tempted to go away and send her the money and forget the whole thing. But the need to finish it pushed me, imperative as a gun at my back.

I lifted her by the waist and tried to set her aside. Her entire body was rigid and jerking galvanically. Her hands slid under my arms and around my neck and held on. Her head rolled on my shoulder and was still.

Suddenly, like delayed rain after lightning, her tears came. I stood and held her vibrating body, trying to quench the dangerous heat that was rising in my veins, and wondering what the hell I was going to do.

"Ethel did it for me," she sobbed. "She wanted me to have a good start in life."

"Some start she's giving you. Did she tell you that?"

"She didn't have to. I knew. I tried to pretend to myself, but I knew. When she told me where to look for the money last night—the night before last."

"You knew Ethel took it from Dewar and hid it in her house?"

"Yes. The thought went through my mind and I couldn't get rid of it. Ethel's always taken terrible chances, and money means so much to her. Not for herself. For me."

"She wasn't thinking of you when she gambled away the money she got from Illman. She went through it in a week."

"Is that what happened to it?"

"That's it. I flew to Las Vegas last night and talked to some of the people that got her money, dealers and stickmen. They remembered her. She had a bad case of gambling fever that week. It didn't leave her until the money was gone. Then maybe she thought of you."

"Poor Ethel. I've seen her before when she had a gambling streak."

"Poor Dewar," I said.

The door beside us creaked open. The muzzle of a blue revolver looked out. Above it Ethel's eyes glared red from her bandaged face.

"Come in here, both of you."

Clare stretched out her hands towards her sister. "No, Ethel. Darling, you mustn't. Give me that gun."

"I have a use for it. I know what I'm doing."

She backed away, supporting herself on the doorknob.

I said to Clare, "We better do as she says. She won't hurt you."

"Nor you unless you make me. Don't reach for your gun, and don't try anything funny. You know what happened to Dewar."

"Not as well as you do."

"Don't waste any tears on that one. Save them for yourself. Now get in here." The gun wagged peremptorily.

I edged past her with Clare at my back. Ethel shut the door and moved to the bed, her eyes never leaving mine. She sat on its edge and supported the elbow of her gun arm on her knee, hunched far over like an aged wreck of a woman.

It was strange to see the fine naked legs dangling below her hospital gown, the red polish flaking off her toenails. Her voice was low and resonant.

"I don't like to do this. But how am I going to make you see it my way if I don't? I want Clare to see it, too. It was self-defense, understand. I didn't intend to kill him. I never expected to see him again. Fidelis was after him and it was only a matter of time until he caught up with Owen. Owen knew that. He told me himself he wouldn't live out the year. He was so sure of it he was paralyzed. He got so he wouldn't even go out of the house.

"Somebody had to make a move, and I decided it might as well be me. Why should I sit and wait for Fidelis to come and take the money back and blow Owen's head off for him? It was really my money, anyway, mine and Clare's."

"Leave me out of this," Clare said.

"But you don't understand, honey," the damaged mouth insisted. "It really was my money. We were legally married, so what was his was mine. I talked him into taking it in the first place. He'd never have had the guts to do it alone. He thought Fidelis was God himself. I didn't. But I didn't want to be there when Jack Fidelis found him. So I left him.

"I took the money out of his pillow when he was asleep and hid it where he'd never look for it. Then I drove down here. I guess you know the rest. He found a letter from Gretchen in the house and traced me through it. He thought I was carrying the money. When it turned out that I wasn't, he took me out to the beach and beat me up. I wouldn't tell him where it was. He threatened to shoot me then. I fought him for the gun and it went off. It was a clear case of self-defense."

"Maybe it was. You'll never get a jury to believe it, though. Innocent people don't dump their shooting victims in the drink."

"But I didn't. The tide was coming in. I didn't even touch him after he died. He just lay there and the water took him."

"While you stood and watched?"

"I couldn't get away. I was so weak I couldn't move for a long time. Then when I finally could, it was too late. He was gone, and he had the keys to the car."

"He drove you out to La Jolla, did he?"

"Yes."

274

"And held a gun on you at the same time. That's quite a trick."

"He did, though," she said. "That is the way it happened."

"I hear you telling me, Mrs. Dewar."

She winced behind her mask at the sound of her name. "I'm not Mrs. Dewar," she said. "I've taken back my maiden name. I'm Ethel Larrabee."

"We won't argue about the name. You'll be trading it in for a number anyway."

"I don't think I will. The shooting was self-defense, and once he was dead the money belonged to me. There's no way of proving he stole it, now that Fidelis is gone. I guess I owe you a little thanks for that."

"Put down your gun, then."

"I'm not that grateful," she said.

Clare moved across the room toward her. "Let me look at the gun, Ethel. It's father's revolver, isn't it?"

"Be quiet, you little fool."

"I won't be quiet. These things have to be said. You're way off by yourself, Ethel, I'm not with you. I want no part of this, or the money. You don't understand how strange and dreadful—"

Her voice broke. She stood a few feet from her sister, held back by the gun's menace, yet strongly drawn toward it. "That's father's revolver, isn't it? The one he shot himself with?"

"What if it is?"

"I'll tell you, Ethel Larrabee," I said. "Dewar didn't pull a gun on you. You were the one that had the gun. You forced him to drive you out to the beach and shot him in cold blood. But he didn't die right away. He lived long enough to leave his marks on you. Isn't that how it happened?"

The bandaged face was silent. I looked into the terrible eyes for assent. They were lost and wild, like an animal's.

"Is that true, Ethel? Did you murder him?" Clare looked down at her sister with pity and terror.

"I did it for you," the masked face said. "I always tried to do what was best for you. Don't you believe me? Don't you know I love you? Ever since father killed himself I've tried—"

Clare turned and walked to the wall and stood with her forehead against it. Ethel put the muzzle of the gun in her mouth. Her broken teeth clenched on it the way a smoker bites on a pipestem. The bone and flesh of her head muffled its roar.

I laid her body out on the bed and pulled a sheet up over it.

THE CASE OF THE
PINCHBECK LOCKET

BY ERIC AMBLER

Eric Ambler was born in London in 1909. He studied
engineering at the University of London but abandoned
that career to write songs and sketches for vaudeville,
then worked as an advertising copywriter before starting
to write suspense fiction. His first novel, *The Dark Fron-
tier,* was published in 1936, and his most famous is *A
Coffin for Dimitrios,* published in England under the title
Mask of Dimitrios (1939). Others include *Background to
Danger, Cause for Alarm,* and *Journey into Fear.* Ambler
received the Grand Master Award in 1975. He has written a number of films, including the screenplay of
Nicholas Monsarrat's *The Cruel Sea.*

THE WINTER AFTERNOON on which Dr. Jan Czissar chose to introduce his peculiar personality into the life of Assistant Commissioner Mercer of Scotland Yard was cold and depressing. And Mercer, besides having a cold and being depressed, was also busy. Had Dr. Czissar not been in the possession of a letter of introduction from, as Sergeant Flecker put it, "one of the 'Ome Office brass hats," he would not have seen the assistant commissioner at all.

The letter was brief. Having presented his compliments, the writer said that Dr. Jan Czissar had been, until September, 1938, a distinguished member of the Czech police organization, that he was a welcome guest in Britain, and that any courtesy extended to him would be very much appreciated.

Mercer had dealt with distinguished visitors to Scotland Yard before. There would be the preliminary exchange of courtesies, then a tour of the buildings conducted by Inspector Denton, who would appear, as if by accident, a few moments after the visitor had entered Mercer's room and, finally, the farewell handshake and a safe conduct to a taxi.

Dr. Czissar was a plump middle-aged man of rather more than medium height, with a round pale face and a pair of sad brown eyes magnified to cowlike proportions by a pair of thick glasses. He wore a long gray raincoat which reached nearly to his ankles and carried an unfurled umbrella. As he entered the room, he stopped, clicked his heels, clapped the umbrella to his side as if it were a rifle, bowed, and said distinctly: "Dr. Jan Czissar. Late Prague police. At your service."

"Delighted, doctor. Take a seat."

"It is good of you," said the doctor suddenly, "to see me so promptly. It is an honor to be received at Scotland Yard. In common with my late colleagues of the Czech police, I have always admired your institution."

Mercer was used to dealing with this sort of thing. He smiled deprecatingly. "We do our best. Ours is a law-abiding country." And then his ears caught the sound they had been waiting for—the sound of Inspector Denton's footsteps approaching. He rose. "Well, doctor, now that you're here, I expect you'd like to see something of our organization, eh?"

Time had given the question a purely rhetorical significance for Mercer. For him, Dr. Czissar was already safely under the wings of the approaching Inspector Denton. And then the unbelievable happened.

Dr. Czissar said: "Oh, no, thank you. I will not trouble you."

For a moment Mercer thought he had misunderstood.

"Well, doctor. What can we do for you?"

"Pardon. It is I who can do something for you. I think," he added slowly, "that I can help you to discover a crime. Clever criminals are so stupid, are they not?"

"Very good of you. Now, if you'll just put the whole thing in writing and mail it to me, we'll look into it."

Dr. Czissar's thin smile vanished. The cowlike eyes flashed. "It is unnecessary. The matter is in writing and here." He put a newspaper clipping under Mercer's nose. "Please," he said firmly, "to read."

Again Mercer sat down. His eyes met those of Dr. Czissar. He read.

The clipping, from a Wessex weekly newspaper dated a fortnight previously, was the report of an inquest.

The body of a woman of sixty had been washed up in Shingles Bay and had been identified as that of Mrs. Sarah Fallon, of Seahurst, a village five miles from the seaside resort of Seabourne. Her husband had died fifteen years earlier, leaving her a large fortune and Seahurst Grange with its twenty-acre park. Soon after his death she had assumed the guardianship of his niece, Helen Fallon, who had married, eleven years later, Arthur Barrington, a Seabourne coal and builders' merchant. Since their marriage the Barringtons had lived with Mrs. Fallon at the Grange.

On the evening of November 4 Barrington had reported to the police that Mrs. Fallon had disappeared. That afternoon Mrs. Barrington had, at her aunt's request, driven her into Seabourne to do some shopping. As Mrs. Fallon had said that she might call on a friend for tea, her niece had left her at South Square at a quarter to three, put the car in the municipal car park, and spent the afternoon in a movie. They had arranged to meet at South Square at six o'clock. Mrs. Fallon had not kept the appointment, and later, when attempts to trace her movements through her friends had failed, the police had been informed.

Eight days later her body was found by a coastguard.

The post-mortem had revealed the cause of death as being

shock following a fracture of the skull. The fracture could have been caused by violent contact with any blunt hard surface. It would have been consistent with a fall from a high cliff. She had not entered the water until several hours after death. The state of decomposition suggested that she had probably died on the date of her disappearance. Her doctor added that she had suffered from a cardiac disturbance and was liable to dizziness.

A child, Annie Smith, had given evidence of the finding, on the seventh of the month (three days after the disappearance), of a heart-shaped pinchbeck locket at the foot of Sea Head cliff, a local beauty spot within a few minutes' walk of South Square.

Mrs. Barrington had identified the locket as having belonged to her aunt. Her aunt, who had attached great sentimental value to the locket, had always worn it. Her aunt had been in the habit of sitting on the seat on the cliff during the afternoon. She had not, however, done so for several days prior to her disappearance as she had had a cold.

The coroner, summing up, had said there seemed very little doubt that the deceased had, after she had left her niece on the afternoon of the fourth, changed her mind about visiting her friends and walked up the hill to the cliff. Then, fatigued by the walk after her recent illness, she had had an attack of giddiness and fallen to her death on the beach below. High tide had been at six o'clock. Her body must have lain on the beach until ultimately carried out to sea.

A verdict of accidental death had been returned.

Mercer looked up. "Well, doctor?"

"Mrs. Fallon," said Dr. Czissar decisively, "was murdered."

"Impossible!" said Mercer.

"And what of the furnace?" asked the doctor.

"The furnace?" Mercer looked blank.

"Yes, the furnace. It went out, you know. The furnace at Seahurst Grange went out on the day Mrs. Fallon disappeared."

Mercer sighed and leaned back.

"Sergeant," he said, "get out the file on the Fallon case. Ah, thank you, sergeant. Here we are. All open and aboveboard. The niece first.

"She spent the afternoon just as she says she did. Car park and movie attendants both confirm that she spent the afternoon at Seabourne. She arrived home at seven o'clock, having waited for half an hour in South Square and spent ten minutes telephoning her aunt's friends. Barrington returned home

279

soon afterwards. He had left at two-thirty to keep a business appointment in Haywick—that's fourteen miles farther west along the coast—at three. He kept the appointment and several others that he had made in the Haywick district for that afternoon. Anyway, no murderer in his senses would try to push anybody off the cliff. There's a coast-guard station a quarter of a mile away. He would be too scared of being seen. Satisfied?"

Dr. Czissar smiled serenely. "Attention, please," he said. "I will present the case to you."

He raised one finger. "First," he said. "The thing that attracts my attention is this matter of the locket. So curious, I think. It is found at the bottom of the cliff. Therefore, Mrs. Fallon was killed by falling from the cliff. So simple. Perhaps a little too simple, do you think? It is found three days after the accident. Therefore it must have fallen on a place *not covered by the tide*. Six tides would certainly have buried it or swept it away, don't you think? Yesterday I went to Seabourne. I looked at the cliff. The cliff overhangs a little. I tried a little experiment. It is quite impossible to drop an object from the top of the cliff so that it lands on the beach above the high tide mark."

Mercer shrugged. "The clasp was broken. She probably clutched at it as she fell. She had heart trouble. It would be a natural gesture. It might fall anywhere."

"Mrs. Fallon," continued Dr. Czissar, "was murdered for her money by Arthur and Helen Barrington who, because they did not want to be found out, arranged alibis for themselves. They were not very useful alibis because nobody knew exactly when Mrs. Fallon was killed. In my opinion she was killed between half-past two and twenty-five minutes to three on the afternoon of her disappearance. She was placed in the sea after six that evening.

"At half-past two Barrington left to keep his appointment at Haywick. But instead of driving straight there, he stopped his car a little way down the road and walked back to the drive. Five minutes later his wife left to motor Mrs. Fallon into Seabourne. As soon as she was out of sight of the house, but in the drive, she stopped. Her husband then killed Mrs. Fallon with the weapon he had ready. He then went back to his car and drove to his appointment at Haywick. Mrs. Barrington drove on to Seabourne."

"And where, pray, was the body?" inquired Mercer acidly.

"On the floor at the back of Mrs. Barrington's car, with a rug covering it. They could not leave it among the trees in case it should by chance be discovered. Barrington could not take it in his car. In the large municipal car park, Mrs. Barrington's car would be safe from inspection. There is only one attendant and he is at the gate. At half-past five, I think, Mrs. Barrington left the cinema, returned to her car and drove to the Haywick dunes, where she had arranged to meet her husband. High tide was at six. It would be dusk then, too. And that place is very lonely and deserted. The chances of Barrington's being seen as he carried the body to the water were small. Mrs. Barrington then drove back to Seabourne to make the inquiries of her aunt's friends. That is all, I think."

"I don't see where the furnace comes into it," the inspector remarked.

"The rug and the car mats would be soaked with blood, inspector. Mrs. Barrington would no doubt put them into the furnace. Even such thick materials would be destroyed, but they would put the fire out unless the dampers were also opened. The niece of a rich aunt would not know much about furnaces—and the furnace at the Grange went out, inspector, the day Mrs. Fallon was killed."

"You have yet to explain, Dr. Czissar," said Mercer, "the presence of the locket on the beach."

"Ah, yes. The locket." Dr. Czissar smiled. "It was," said Dr. Czissar, "something I saw the other day in a second-hand jeweler's window that reminded me of the Barringtons."

He put his hand in his pocket. It reappeared holding something swinging from a thin chain. It was a pinchbeck locket in the shape of a heart.

"The jeweler said," went on Dr. Czissar, "that these things are quite common. One can buy such a locket almost anywhere if one tries."

He looked at his watch. "I suggest also that you find out if Barrington purchased the new car mats and rug before or after the murder and if anyone saw his wife driving towards Haywick on the fourth. And a detailed account of Barrington's movements after five thirty would, no doubt, provide you with more of the evidence you need for a conviction."

He got suddenly to his feet. "But I must really be going. So kind of you. Enchanted. Enchanted."

Then Dr. Czissar was gone.

Mercer drew a deep breath and picked up the telephone.

"I want," he said, "to speak to the chief constable of Wessex."

THE DESTRUCTORS

BY GRAHAM GREENE

Graham Greene was born in 1904 in Hertfordshire, England, and educated at Oxford. He worked for four years as a subeditor on *The Times* (London) and published his first novel, *The Man Within,* in 1929. Greene served with the Foreign Office in West Africa during World War II. He calls his espionage thrillers his "entertainments," and separates them from his more serious novels with their somber religious overtones. His works include *The End of the Affair, The Quiet American, Our Man in Havana,* and *The Comedians.* He received the Grand Master Award in 1976.

IT WAS ON THE EVE OF AUGUST Bank Holiday that the latest recruit became the leader of the Wormsley Common Gang. No one was surprised except Mike, but Mike at the age of nine was surprised by everything. "If you don't shut your mouth," somebody once said to him, "you'll get a frog down it." After that Mike had kept his teeth tightly clamped except when the surprise was too great.

The new recruit had been with the gang since the beginning of the summer holidays, and there were possibilities about his brooding silence that all recognized. He never wasted a word even to tell his name until that was required of him by the rules. When he said "Trevor" it was a statement of fact, not as it would have been with the others a statement of shame or defiance. Nor did anyone laugh except Mike, who finding himself without support and meeting the dark gaze of the newcomer, opened his mouth and was quiet again. There was every reason why T., as he was afterwards referred to, should have been an object of mockery—there was his name (and they substituted the initial because otherwise they had no excuse not to laugh at it), the fact that his father, a former architect and present clerk, had "come down in the world" and that his mother considered herself better than the neighbors. What but an odd quality of danger, of the unpredictable, established him in the gang without any ignoble ceremony of initiation?

The gang met every morning in an impromptu car park, the site of the last bomb of the first blitz. The leader, who was known as Blackie, claimed to have heard it fall, and no one was precise enough in his dates to point out that he would have been one year old and fast asleep on the down platform of Wormsley Common Underground Station. On one side of the car park leaned the first occupied house, No. 3, of the shattered Northwood Terrace—literally leaned, for it had suffered from the blast of the bomb and the sidewalls were supported on wooden struts. A small bomb and some incendiaries had fallen beyond, so that the house stuck up like a jagged tooth and carried on the further wall relics of its neighbor, a dado and the remains of a fireplace. T., whose words were almost confined to voting "Yes" or "No" to the plan of operations proposed each day by Blackie, once startled the whole gang by saying broodingly, "Wren built that house, father says."

"Who's Wren?"

"The man who built St. Paul's."

"Who cares?" Blackie said. "It's only old Misery's."

Old Misery—whose real name was Thomas—had once been a builder and decorator. He lived alone in the crippled house, doing for himself: Once a week you could see him coming back across the common with bread and vegetables, and once, as the boys played in the car park, he put his head over the smashed wall of his garden and looked at them.

"Been to the loo," one of the boys said, for it was common knowledge that since the bombs fell something had gone wrong with the pipes of the house and Old Misery was too mean to spend money on the property. He could do the redecorating himself at cost price, but he had never learned plumbing. The loo was a wooden shed at the bottom of the narrow garden with a star-shaped hole in the door; it had escaped the blast which had smashed the house next door and sucked out the window frames of No. 3.

The next time the gang became aware of Mr. Thomas was more surprising. Blackie, Mike, and a thin yellow boy, who for some reason was called by his surname Summers, met him on the common coming back from the market. Mr. Thomas stopped them. He said glumly, "You belong to the gang that play in the car park?"

Mike was about to answer when Blackie stopped him. As the leader he had responsibilities. "Suppose we are?" he said.

"I got some chocolates," Mr. Thomas said. "Don't like 'em myself. Here you are. Not enough to go 'round, I don't suppose. There never is," he added with somber conviction. He handed over three packets of Smarties.

The gang were puzzled and perturbed by this action and tried to explain it away. "Bet someone dropped them and he picked 'em up," somebody suggested.

"Pinched 'em, then got in a funk," another added.

"It's a bribe," Summers said. "He wants us to stop bouncing balls on his wall."

"We'll show him we don't take bribes," Blackie said, and they sacrificed the whole morning to the game of bouncing that only Mike was young enough to enjoy. There was no sign from Mr. Thomas.

Next day T. astonished them all. He was late at the rendezvous, and the voting for that day's exploit took place without him. At Blackie's suggestion the gang was to disperse in pairs, take buses at random, and see how many free rides could be snatched from unwary conductors (the operation was to be carried out in pairs to avoid cheating). They were drawing lots for their companions when T. arrived.

"Where you been, T.?" Blackie asked. "You can't vote now. You know the rules."

"I've been *there*," T. said. He looked at the ground, as though he had thoughts to hide.

"Where?"

"At Old Misery's."

Mike's mouth opened and then hurriedly closed again with a click. He had remembered the frog.

"At Old Misery's?" Blackie said. There was nothing in the rules against it, but he had a sensation that T. was treading on dangerous ground. He asked hopefully, "Did you break in?"

"No. I rang the bell."

"And what did you say?"

"I said I wanted to see his house."

"What did he do?"

"He showed it to me."

"Pinch anything?"

"No."

"What did you do it for then?"

The gang had gathered round: It was as though an impromptu court were about to form and to try some case of deviation. T. said, "It's a beautiful house," and still watching the ground, meeting no one's eyes, he licked his lips first one way, then the other.

"What do you mean, a beautiful house?" Blackie asked with scorn.

"It's got a staircase two hundred years old like a corkscrew. Nothing holds it up."

"What do you mean, nothing holds it up. Does it float?"

"It's to do with opposite forces, Old Misery said."

"What else?"

"There's paneling."

"Like in the Blue Boar?"

"Two hundred years old."

"Is Old Misery two hundred years old?"

Mike laughed suddenly and then was quiet again. The meeting was in a serious mood. For the first time since T. had strolled into the car park on the first day of the holidays his position was in danger. It only needed a single use of his real name and the gang would be at his heels.

"What did you do it for?" Blackie asked. He was just—he had no jealousy—and he was anxious to retain T. in the gang if he could. It was the word "beautiful" that worried him—that belonged to a class world that you could still see parodied at the Wormsley Common Empire by a man wearing a top hat and a monocle, with a haw-haw accent. He was tempted to say, "My dear Trevor, old chap," and unleash his hell hounds. "If you'd broken in," he said sadly—that indeed would have been an exploit worthy of the gang.

"This was better," T. said. "I found out things." He continued to stare at his feet, not meeting anybody's eye, as though he were absorbed in some dream he was unwilling—or ashamed—to share.

"What things?"

"Old Misery's going to be away all tomorrow and Bank Holiday."

Blackie said with relief, "You mean we could break in?"

"And pinch things?" somebody asked.

Blackie said, "Nobody's going to pinch things. Breaking in—that's good enough, isn't it? We don't want any court stuff."

"I don't want to pinch anything," T. said. "I've got a better idea."

"What is it?"

T. raised eyes as gray and disturbed as the drab August day. "We'll pull it down," he said. "We'll destroy it."

Blackie gave a single hoot of laughter and then, like Mike, fell quiet, daunted by the serious implacable gaze. "What'd the police be doing all the time?" he said.

"They'd never know. We'd do it from inside. I've found a way in." He said with a sort of intensity, "We'd be like worms, don't you see, in an apple. When we came out again there'd be nothing there—no staircase, no panels, nothing but just walls—and then we'd make the walls fall down—somehow."

"We'd go to jug," Blackie said.

"Who's to prove? And anyway we wouldn't have pinched anything." He added without the smallest flicker of glee, "There wouldn't be anything to pinch after we'd finished."

"I've never heard of going to prison for breaking things," Summers said.

"There wouldn't be time," Blackie said. "I've seen house-breakers at work."

"There are twelve of us," T. said. "We'd organize."

"None of us know how. . . ."

"I know," T. said. He looked across at Blackie, "Have you got a better plan?"

"Today," Mike said tactlessly, "we're pinching free rides. . . ."

"Free rides," T. said. "You can stand down, Blackie, if you'd rather. . . ."

"The gang's got to vote."

"Put it up then."

Blackie said uneasily, "It's proposed that tomorrow and Monday we destroy Old Misery's house."

"Hear, hear," said a fat boy called Joe.

"Who's in favor?"

T. said, "It's carried."

"How do we start?" Summers asked.

"He'll tell you," Blackie said. It was the end of his leadership. He went away to the back of the car park and began to kick a stone, dribbling it this way and that. There was only one old Morris in the park, for few cars were left there except lorries: without an attendant there was no safety. He took a flying kick at the car and scraped a little paint off the rear mudguard. Beyond, paying no more attention to him than to a stranger, the gang had gathered round T.; Blackie was dimly aware of the fickleness of favor. He thought of going home, of never returning, of letting them all discover the hollowness of T.'s leadership, but suppose after all what T. proposed was possible—nothing like it had ever been done before. The fame of the Wormsley Common Gang would reach around London.

There would be headlines in the papers. Even the grown-up gangs who ran the betting at the all-in wrestling and the barrow boys would hear with respect of how Old Misery's house had been destroyed. Driven by the pure, simple, and altruistic ambition of fame for the gang, Blackie came back to where T. stood in the shadow of Misery's wall.

T. was giving his orders with decision: it was as though this plan had been with him all his life, pondered through the seasons, now in his fifteenth year crystallized with the pain of puberty. "You," he said to Mike, "bring some big nails, the biggest you can find, and a hammer. Anyone else who can, better bring a hammer and a screwdriver. We'll need plenty of them. Chisels too. Can anybody bring a saw?"

"I can," Mike said.

"Not a child's saw," T. said. "A real saw."

Blackie realized he had raised his hand like any member of the gang.

"Right, you bring one, Blackie. But now there's a difficulty. We want a hacksaw."

"What's a hacksaw?" someone asked.

"You can get 'em at Woolworth's," Summers said.

The fat boy called Joe said gloomily, "I knew it would end in a collection."

"I'll get one myself," T. said. "I don't want your money. But I can't buy a sledge hammer."

Blackie said, "They are working on Number Fifteen. I know where they'll leave their stuff for Bank Holiday."

"Then that's all," T. said. "We meet here at nine sharp."

"I've got to go to church," Mike said.

"Come over the wall and whistle. We'll let you in."

On Sunday morning all were punctual except Blackie, even Mike. Mike had a stroke of luck. His mother felt ill, his father was tired after Saturday night, and he was told to go to church alone with many warnings of what would happen if he strayed.

Blackie had had difficulty in smuggling out the saw, and then in finding the sledge hammer at the back of No. 15. He now approached the house from a lane at the rear of the garden, for fear of the policeman's beat along the main road. The tired evergreens kept off a stormy sun: another wet Bank Holiday was being prepared over the Atlantic, beginning in swirls of dust under the trees. Blackie climbed the wall into Misery's garden.

There was no sign of anybody anywhere. The loo stood like a tomb in a neglected graveyard. The curtains were drawn. The house slept. Blackie lumbered nearer with the saw and the sledge hammer. Perhaps after all nobody had turned up: the plan had been a wild invention. But when he came close to the back door he could hear a confusion of sound, hardly louder than a hive in swarm: a clickety-clack, a bang bang bang, a scraping, a creaking, a sudden painful crack. He thought: it's true, and whistled.

They opened the back door to him and he came in. He had at once the impression of organization, very different from the old happy-go-lucky ways under his leadership. For a while he wandered up and down the stairs looking for T. Nobody addressed him: he had a sense of great urgency and already he could begin to see the plan. The interior of the house was being carefully demolished without touching the outer walls. Summers with hammer and chisel was ripping out the skirting boards in the ground-floor dining room; he had already smashed the panels of the door. In the same room Joe was heaving up the parquet blocks, exposing the soft-wood floorboards over the cellar. Coils of wire came out of the damaged skirting and Mike sat happily on the floor, clipping the wires.

On the curved stairs two of the gang were working hard with an inadequate child's saw on the banisters—when they saw Blackie's big saw they signaled for it wordlessly. The time he next saw them, a quarter of the banisters had been dropped into the hall. He found T. at last in the bathroom—he sat moodily in the least-cared-for room in the house, listening to the sounds coming up from below.

"You've really done it," Blackie said with awe. "What's going to happen?"

"We've only just begun," T. said. He looked at the sledge hammer and gave his instructions. "You stay here and break the bath and the wash basin. Don't bother about the pipes. They come later."

Mike appeared at the door. "I've finished the wire, T."

"Good. You've just got to go wandering round now. The kitchen's in the basement. Smash all the china and glass and bottles you can lay hold of. Don't turn on the taps—we don't want a flood—yet. Then go into all the rooms and turn out drawers. If they are locked get one of the others to break them open. Tear up any papers you find and smash all the ornaments. Better take a carving knife with you from the kitchen. The bedroom's opposite here. Open the pillows and tear up the sheets. That's enough for the moment. And you, Blackie, when you've finished in here crack the plaster in the passage with your sledge hammer."

"What are you going to do?" Blackie asked.

"I'm looking for something special," T. said.

It was nearly lunchtime before Blackie had finished and went in search of T. Chaos had advanced. The kitchen was a shambles of broken glass and china. The dining room was stripped of parquet, the skirting was up, the door had been taken off its hinges, and the destroyers had moved up a floor. Streaks of light came in through the closed shutters where they worked with the seriousness of creators—and destruction is a form of creation. A kind of imagination had seen this house as it had now become.

Mike said, "I've got to go home for dinner."

"Who else?" T. asked, but all the others on one excuse or another had brought provisions with them.

They squatted in the ruins of the room and swapped unwanted sandwiches. Half an hour for lunch and they were at work again. By the time Mike returned, they were on the top floor, and by six the superficial damage was completed. The doors were all off, all the skirtings raised, the furniture pillaged and ripped and smashed—no one could have slept in the house except on a bed of broken plaster. T. gave his orders—eight o'clock next morning, and to escape notice they climbed singly over the garden wall into the car park. Only Blackie and T. were left; the light had nearly gone and when they touched a switch, nothing worked—Mike had done his job thoroughly.

"Did you find anything special?" Blackie asked.

T. nodded. "Come over here," he said, "and look." Out of both pockets he drew bundles of pound notes. "Old Misery's savings," he said. "Mike ripped out the mattress, but he missed them."

"What are you going to do? Share them?"

"We aren't thieves," T. said. "Nobody's going to steal anything from this house. I kept these for you and me—a celebration." He knelt down on the floor and counted them out— there were seventy in all. "We'll burn them," he said, "one by one," and taking it in turns they held a note upwards and lit the top corner, so that the flame burned slowly towards their fingers. The gray ash floated above them and fell on their heads like age. "I'd like to see Old Misery's face when we are through," T. said.

"You hate him a lot?" Blackie asked.

"Of course I don't hate him," T. said. "There'd be no fun if I hated him." The last burning note illuminated his brooding face. "All this hate and love," he said, "it's soft, it's hooey. There's only things, Blackie," and he looked round the room

290

crowded with the unfamiliar shadows of half things, broken things, former things. "I'll race you home, Blackie."

Next morning the serious destruction started. There were two casualties—Mike and another boy whose parents were off to Southend and Brighton in spite of the slow warm drops that had begun to fall and the rumble of thunder in the estuary like the first guns of the old blitz. "We've got to hurry," T. said.

Summers was restive. "Haven't we done enough?" he said. "I've been given a bob for slot machines. This is like work."

"We've hardly started," T. said. "Why, there's all the floors left, and the stairs. We haven't taken out a single window. You voted like the others. We are going to *destroy* this house. There won't be anything left when we've finished."

They began again on the first floor picking up the top floorboards next the outer wall, leaving the joists exposed. Then they sawed through the joists and retreated into the hall as what was left of the floor heeled and sank. They had learned with practice and the second floor collapsed more easily. By the evening an odd exhilaration seized them as they looked down the great hollow of the house. They ran risks and made mistakes; when they thought of the windows it was too late to reach them. "Cor," Joe said and dropped a penny down into the dry rubble-filled well. It cracked and spun among the broken glass.

"Why did we start this?" Summers asked with astonishment.

T. was already on the ground, digging at the rubble, clearing a space along the outer wall. "Turn on the taps," he said. "It's too dark for anyone to see now and in the morning it won't matter."

The water overtook them on the stairs and fell through the floorless rooms.

It was then they heard Mike's whistle at the back. "Something's wrong," Blackie said. They could hear his urgent breathing as they unlocked the door.

"The bogies?" Summers asked.

"Old Misery," Mike said. "He's on his way." He put his head between his knees and retched. "I ran all the way," he said with pride.

"But why?" T. said. "He told me . . ." He protested with the fury of the child he had never been, "It isn't fair."

"He was down at Southend," Mike said, "and he was on the train coming back. Said it was too cold and wet." He paused and gazed at the water. "My, you've had a storm here. Is the roof leaking?"

"How long will he be?"

"Five minutes. I gave Ma the slip and ran."

"We better clear," Summers said. "We've done enough anyway."

"Oh, no, we haven't. Anybody could do this—"

"This" was the shattered hollowed house with nothing left but the walls. Yet walls could be preserved. Façades were valuable. They could build inside again more beautifully than before. This could again be a home. T. said angrily, "We've got to finish. Don't move. Let me think."

"There's no time," a boy said.

"There's got to be a way," T. said. "We couldn't have got this far . . ."

"We've done a lot," Blackie said.

"No. No, we haven't. Somebody watch the front."

"He may come in at the back."

"Watch the back too." T. began to plead, "Just give me a minute and I'll fix it. I swear I'll fix it." But his authority had gone with his ambiguity. He was only one of the gang. "Please," he said.

"Please," Summers mimicked him and then suddenly struck home with the fatal name. "Run along home, Trevor."

T. stood with his back to the rubble like a boxer knocked groggy against the ropes. He had no words as his dreams shook and slid. Then Blackie acted before the gang had time to laugh, pushing Summers backward. "I'll watch the front, T.," he said, and cautiously he opened the shutters of the hall. The gray, wet common stretched ahead, and the lamps gleamed in the puddles. "Someone's coming, T. No, it's not him. What's your plan, T.?"

"Tell Mike to go out to the loo and hide close beside it. When he hears me whistle, he's to count ten, then start to shout."

"Shout what?"

"Oh, 'Help'—anything."

"You hear, Mike," Blackie said. He was the leader again. He took a quick look between the shutters. "He's coming, T."

"Quick, Mike. The loo. Stay here, Blackie, all of you."

"Where are you going, T.?"

"Don't worry. I'll see to this. I said I would, didn't I?"

Old Misery came limping off the common. He had mud on

292

his shoes and he stopped to scrape them on the pavement's edge. He didn't want to soil his house, which stood jagged and dark between the bomb sites, saved so narrowly, as he believed, from destruction. Even the fanlight had been left unbroken by the bomb's blast.

Somewhere somebody whistled. Old Misery looked sharply round. He didn't trust whistles. A child was shouting; it seemed to come from his own garden. Then a boy ran into the road from the car park. "Mr. Thomas," he called, "Mr. Thomas."

"What is it?"

"I'm terribly sorry, Mr. Thomas. One of us got taken short and we thought you wouldn't mind and now he can't get out."

"What do you mean, boy?"

"He's got stuck in your loo."

"He'd no business . . . Haven't I seen you before?"

"You showed me your house."

"So I did. So I did. That doesn't give you the right to . . ."

"Do hurry, Mr. Thomas. He'll suffocate."

"Nonsense. He can't suffocate. Wait till I put my bag in."

"I'll carry your bag."

"Oh, no, you don't. I carry my own."

"This way, Mr. Thomas."

"I can't get in the garden that way. I've got to go through the house."

"But you *can* get in the garden this way, Mr. Thomas. We often do."

"You often do?" He followed the boy with a scandalized fascination. "When? What right . . .?"

"Do you see? The wall's low."

"I'm not going to climb walls into my own garden. It's absurd."

"This is how we do it. One foot here, one foot there, and over." The boy's face peered down, an arm shot out, and Mr. Thomas found his bag taken and deposited on the other side of the wall.

"Give me back my bag," Mr. Thomas said. From the loo a boy yelled and yelled. "I'll call the police."

"Your bag's all right, Mr. Thomas. Look. One foot there. On your right. Now just above. To your left." Mr. Thomas climbed over his own garden wall. "Here's your bag, Mr. Thomas."

"I'll have the wall built up," Mr. Thomas said, "I'll not have you boys coming over here, using my loo." He stumbled on the path, but the boy caught his elbow and supported him. "Thank you, thank you, my boy," he murmured automatically.

Somebody shouted again through the dark. "I'm coming, I'm coming," Mr. Thomas called. He said to the boy beside him, "I'm not unreasonable. Been a boy myself. As long as things are done regular; I don't mind you playing round the place Saturday mornings. Sometimes I like company. Only it's got to be regular. One of you asks leave and I say Yes. Sometimes I'll say No. Won't feel like it. And you come in at the front door and out at the back. No garden walls."

"Do get him out, Mr. Thomas."

"He won't come to any harm in my loo," Mr. Thomas said, stumbling slowly down the garden. "Oh, my rheumatics," he said. "Always get 'em on Bank Holiday. I've got to go careful. There's loose stones here. Give me your hand. Do you know what my horoscope said yesterday? 'Abstain from any dealings in first half of week. Danger of serious crash.' That might be on this path," Mr. Thomas said. "They speak in parables and double meanings." He paused at the door of the loo. "What's the matter in there?" he called. There was no reply.

"Perhaps he's fainted," the boy said.

"Not in my loo. Here, you, come out," Mr. Thomas said, and giving a great jerk at the door, he nearly fell on his back when it swung easily open. A hand first supported him and then pushed him hard. His head hit the opposite wall and he sat heavily down. His bag hit his feet. A hand whipped the key out of the lock and the door slammed. "Let me out," he called and heard the key turn in the lock. "A serious crash," he thought and felt dithery and confused and old.

A voice spoke to him softly through the star-shaped hole in the door. "Don't worry, Mr. Thomas," it said, "we won't hurt you, not if you stay quiet."

Mr. Thomas put his head between his hands and pondered. He had noticed that there was only one lorry in the car park, and he felt certain that the driver would not come for it before the morning. Nobody could hear him from the road in front, and the lane at the back was seldom used. Anyone who passed there would be hurrying home and would not pause for what they would certainly take to be drunken cries. And if he did call "Help," who on a lonely Bank Holiday evening, would have the courage to investigate? Mr. Thomas sat on the loo and pondered with the wisdom of age.

After a while it seemed to him that there were sounds in the silence—they were faint and came from the direction of his house. He stood up and peered through the ventilation hole. Between the cracks in one of the shutters he saw a light—not the light of a lamp but the wavering light that a candle might give. Then he thought he heard the sound of hammering and scraping and chipping. He thought of burglars—perhaps they had employed the boy as a scout; but why should burglars engage in what sounded more and more like a stealthy form of carpentry? Mr. Thomas let out an experimental yell, but nobody answered. The noise could not even have reached his enemies.

Mike had gone home to bed, but the rest stayed. The question of leadership no longer concerned the gang. With nails, chisels, screwdrivers—anything that was sharp and penetrating—they moved around the inner walls worrying at the mortar between the bricks. They started too high, and it was Blackie who hit on the damp course and realized the work could be halved if they weakened the joints immediately above. It was a long, tiring, unamusing job, but at last it was finished. The gutted house stood there balanced on a few inches of mortar between the damp course and the bricks.

There remained the most dangerous task of all, out in the open at the edge of the bomb site. Summers was sent to watch the road for passers-by, and Mr. Thomas sitting on the loo heard clearly now the sound of sawing. It no longer came from his house and that a little reassured him. He felt less concerned. Perhaps the other noises too had no significance.

A voice spoke to him through the hole, "Mr. Thomas."

"Let me out," Mr. Thomas said.

"Here's a blanket," the voice said, and a long gray sausage was worked through the hole and fell on Mr. Thomas's head.

"There's nothing personal," the voice said. "We want you to be comfortable tonight."

"Tonight," Mr. Thomas repeated incredulously.

"Catch," the voice said. "Penny buns—we've buttered them—and sausage rolls. We don't want you to starve, Mr. Thomas."

Mr. Thomas pleaded desperately. "A joke's a joke, boy. Let me out and I won't say a thing. I've got rheumatics. I got to sleep comfortable."

"You wouldn't be comfortable—not in your house, you wouldn't. Not now."

"What do you mean, boy?" but the footsteps receded. There was only the silence of night: no sound of sawing. Mr. Thomas tried one more yell, but he was daunted and rebuked by the silence—a long way off an owl hooted and made off again on its muffled flight through the soundless world.

At seven the next morning the driver came to fetch his lorry. He climbed into the seat and tried to start the engine. He was vaguely aware of a voice shouting, but it didn't concern him. At last the engine responded and he backed the lorry until it touched the great wooden shore that supported Mr. Thomas's house. That way he could drive right out and down the street without reversing. The lorry moved forward, was momentarily checked as though something were pulling it from behind, and then went on to the sound of a long rumbling crash. The driver was astonished to see bricks bouncing ahead of him while stones hit the roof of his cab. He put on his brakes. When he climbed out the whole landscape had suddenly altered. There was no house beside the car park, only a hill of rubble. He went round and examined the back of his car for damage and found a rope tied there that was still twisted at the other end round part of a wooden strut.

The driver again became aware of somebody shouting. It came from the wooden structure which was the nearest thing to a house in that desolation of broken brick. The driver climbed the smashed wall and unlocked the door. Mr. Thomas came out of the loo. He was wearing a gray blanket to which flakes of pastry adhered. He gave a sobbing cry. "My house," he said. "Where's my house?"

"Search me," the driver said. His eye lit on the remains of a bath and what had once been a dresser and he began to laugh. There wasn't anything left anywhere.

"How dare you laugh," Mr. Thomas said. "It was my house."

"I'm sorry," the driver said, making heroic efforts, but when he remembered the sudden check to his lorry, the crash of bricks falling, he became convulsed again. One moment the house had stood there with such dignity between the bomb sites like a man in a top hat, and then, bang, crash, there wasn't anything left—not anything. He said, "I'm sorry. I can't help it. There's nothing personal, but you got to admit it's funny."

DANGER AT DEERFAWN

BY DOROTHY B. HUGHES

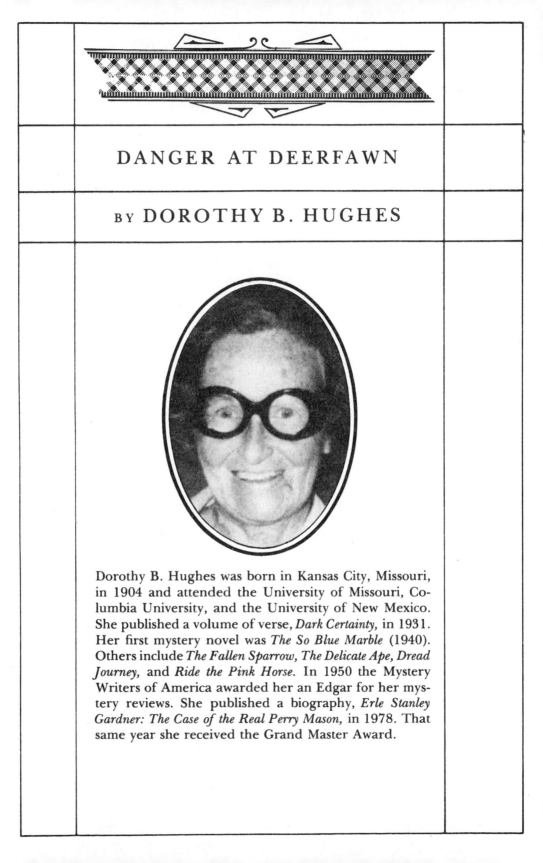

Dorothy B. Hughes was born in Kansas City, Missouri, in 1904 and attended the University of Missouri, Columbia University, and the University of New Mexico. She published a volume of verse, *Dark Certainty,* in 1931. Her first mystery novel was *The So Blue Marble* (1940). Others include *The Fallen Sparrow, The Delicate Ape, Dread Journey,* and *Ride the Pink Horse.* In 1950 the Mystery Writers of America awarded her an Edgar for her mystery reviews. She published a biography, *Erle Stanley Gardner: The Case of the Real Perry Mason,* in 1978. That same year she received the Grand Master Award.

DORIAN SAID, "TOMORROW WE GO to Deerfawn Manor."

"Not me," said Jix. Inelegantly when you figure we were in Stratford-upon-Avon, Shakespeare's hometown. But then Shakespeare was a great one for the vernacular himself.

"Not me," I echoed also ungrammatically, thankful that Jix at last had taken a stand against his sister's youthful vigor. When I, an assistant-assistant professor of drama from the unsuccessful side of the family, had greedily clutched at the gift horse of a summer in England keeping an eye on my young Hunter cousins, I hadn't considered that Twenty-seven doesn't have the bottomless pit of vitality of Nineteen and Twenty-two.

"And may I ask why not?" Dorian set her elbows on the table, almost but not quite bowling over our mugs of ale. The oaken tables at the Mace and Swan, an old Tudor black-and-white, timber-and-brick pub on Sheep Street, slanted in a Cotswolds downhill.

If Dorian had her way we wouldn't miss one Roman clump of stones, one Saxon antic column, one eroded Norman tympanum, nor one field or hall where the Edwards and Henrys and Charleses might have stopped to rest their horses and yeomen in that order. She'd been mesmerized last term by a fair-haired Briton who was giving a course in English history at Miss Waverly's Finishing School for Young Ladies—now called, in reverse snobbery, Waverly Junior College.

"I'm tired," I said. "My feet hurt. Tomorrow I plan to do nothing more strenuous than recline by the banks of the Avon and commune with the swans."

"And you?" Dorian's gray eyes stoned her brother.

"I'm up to here with manor houses," murmured Jix, his eyes on the touring South Carolina girl several tables away—the one who looked like a strawberry ice-cream cone, not the one who looked like a flute.

"Then I'll go alone." It was all of eight miles to Deerfawn. But Dorian was of an age where for status a girl must have males in tow, if only a big brother and an aging cousin. "And you can forget about the Triumph."

Jix had hire-purchased a snazzy red Triumph convertible in London. The deal was one of those with the privilege of applying the payments on full purchase later. Jix wanted it for keeps. Dorian had a way with their father. But Jix had to toe the line for her support; this tour was Dorian's party, her graduation gift.

Without removing his eyes from South Carolina, Jix agreed, "Okay, okay, I'll go." If he hadn't been wearing that particularly noxious brown-and-mustard hound's-tooth jacket he'd bought in Cambridge, he'd probably have been invited South before now.

Dorian's eyes traveled thoughtfully to Brummel Coombe, two tables away. In the Mace and Swan, two tables removed was close enough for me, in an absent-minded gesture, to have hoisted the young English squire's mug as easily as my own. Ignoring the intervening table, Dorian addressed Brummel, more or less publicly, "Why don't you join us tomorrow?"

He couldn't come out with a final, "No, thank you"—he was too well-bred for that. Brummel was Upper-U, from the crown of his smooth flaxen head to his well-rubbed handmade London shoes.

What he said was, in that inimitable, gentle British way, "Thank you very much, but I'm afraid you'd be a bit crowded." We had given him a lift from the theater last night; we were all stopping at the Oak and Swan, an old Tudor black-and-white timber-and-brick inn, likewise on Sheep Street.

"There'll be plenty of room." Dorian tried to keep her voice as quiet and unimpassioned as his but I could detect the victory in it. "Kell isn't going."

"That's right," I said to his questioning expression. "I'm going to take it easy tomorrow."

Brummel smiled on Dorian. You'd think from that smile he'd be as enchanted to go touring with her as vice versa. "If there's room—" He broke off with something like alarm. "Where's Clara?"

The flute answered him. "She said she was going down to the Sweetpotato." Because of the size of the Mace and Swan, anybody's business was everybody's.

Before her words were half piped, Brummel pushed away from his chair, and mumbling something like, "Excuse me one moment," was away.

That Brummel should be smitten with Clara was beyond comprehension. Yet never willingly did he let her out of his sight. Touring German girls we'd previously encountered were scrubbed and polished as by laundry soap and whetstone. Not Clara. Her streaky blonde hair hung unwashed and uncombed now over one shoulder, now another, and her yellow pallor was heightened by smudges of green eye-shadow and a smear of pink lipstick. The only outfit she'd ever been seen wearing was a man's black sweater which hung to her knees, and slacks which might have once been rose-colored but were now a gritty red. Even Jix, who had not reached the age of discrimination if a female was under thirty, couldn't stomach careless Clara. While Brummel, the tweed-and-flannels, best-public-school lamb, followed her as if she were Mary of the children's nursery rhyme.

"Well," Dorian breathed, as the door closed behind him.

I said callously, "Give up, Dorian, it's no good."

"And let her take over?" Sometimes in Dorian, there was resemblance to Medea. "Come on."

"Not me," Jix echoed himself. Strawberry Ice Cream was gazing at him drippingly, I thought, Tom Swiftly.

Dorian didn't wait for more palaver. I caught up with her halfway down the block. "Do you think you're being quite smart?" I asked. "You'll never get anywhere chasing after him. Men don't like it." This hadn't been true since Victorian times but we men kept saying it.

"I am not chasing after him," Dorian retorted loftily. "I merely want to tell him what time we're leaving in the morning. I don't intend to sit up swilling ale all night like you and Jix."

By then we'd reached the Sweetpotato caff, a British version of an American juke-box joint, complete with blaring Elvis Presley records. Definitely non-Tudor, it was enormously popular with Stratford's younger set and with haversack tourists. The size of the Sweetpotato made the Mace and Swan seem spacious, and the saturation point had been reached before our arrival.

Clara's tour was there in numbers, including the bearded wonder she hung on when she could escape Brummel's attention. This was a dour character whose eyeglasses were usually focused on the pen scratches he made in a small black notebook. Neither Clara nor Brummel was present.

We started back to the pub. Halfway along the block, Dorian let out a muted pang. "Look!"

Across the street, just emerging from the close of the Oak and Swan, were the elusive two. Dorian dug her talons into my arm, indicating we were to give the appearance of having saun-

300

tered out for a breath of chill, damp night air, but we were counter-observed.

"I say there, Dorian." Brummel didn't yell—English gentlemen don't yell. However, in the hush, his words were quite clear. He came slanting over, leaving Clara in the shadows of the gateway. As he fell in with us, he said, "I'm sorry I had to run out like that. I'd be delighted to go with you tomorrow." Any knucklehead not bemused by Anglophilia would know that he'd checked with Clara.

Because I was annoyed with the way he brushed off either girl at will, I spoke up. "Is Clara going to Deerfawn tomorrow too?"

"No, she's going to Leamington—" He caught his breath. "Did you say Deerfawn?" His face was a study in anxiety, apprehension, and any and all other synonyms for almost fright.

Dorian didn't notice. She was ahead, opening the door—she hadn't learned to wait for men to do the amenities. "Yes, we're doing Deerfawn Manor House in the morning. Is ten o'clock all right? We want to go on to the ruins of St. Orlgwulf's Abbey in the afternoon." Prattling, she led Brummel inside.

I don't know why I looked back toward the close. But I did. The deserted Clara was still there, an incongruously sad little ghost, clutching the shadows. Her dirt was erased by the darkness; only her pale face and hair were visible.

She wasn't my problem; Dorian was. I followed the others into the pub, shutting Clara away in the night. Jix had moved to the southern exposure in our absence. Brummel now had Jix's place and Dorian seemed to have given up the idea of retiring for the night. This made me the happy old fifth wheel. I could now go back to the inn and get a decent night's sleep.

I was as bright at breakfast next morning as Jix was bleary. Dorian was her normal effervescent self; she didn't need sleep. We'd finished our canned fruit juice and corn flakes, our fried eggs and scarcely cooked bacon with warm tomato, our cold toast and pot of orange marmalade—the traditional English breakfast—and we were dallying over our milk-and-sugar tea when Brummel appeared in the dining room.

We exchanged good mornings and the inevitable weather data before he said shamefacedly, "I'm afraid I can't go with you today after all. Something has come up."

Dorian, after one unbelievably stricken blink, should have

301

been recruited for the Stratford players—her consoling smile was that convincing. "I'm terribly sorry, Brummel. But if you can't, you can't. Maybe some other day."

You could tell he thought it was terribly decent of her to take it so well, and after a few more apologies, he backed away.

"Evidently Clara isn't going to the Spa today." I was sorry as soon as I'd said it. "Long as there's room, I think I'll go Deerfawning with you. I've recovered my youth."

"You can drive," Jix said morosely. He was stuck with the trip because he'd talked Strawberry Ice Cream into meeting him there. Even his cherished jacket failed to uplift him.

It was a blue-sky day, one of the few when we could let down the top of the convertible without bailing. Eight miles is longer in England than in the United States. Who wants to speed through lanes dappled darkly with tall woods, and greened with smooth meadows where the sheep graze in motionless pattern, wearing red badges on their haunches to distinguish them from the pale saffron stones? To augment our leisurely pace, whenever a crumbling rock pile appeared on the horizon we had to stop at the nearest lay-by while Dorian loped back to investigate its import.

It was, therefore, close to eleven when we reached the gatehouse of Deerfawn Manor. The gatekeeper was on hand to collect our two-and-sixes and to present us with pink admission tickets from a wheel such as we used to have in movie houses before automation. We drove on up the cobbled half mile to the courtyard in the rear of the great Georgian house.

Deerfawn was not a National Trust—it wasn't that ancient. But the handbills at the desk of the Oak and Swan had built up a pretty picture of its fine carved staircase, its priceless library, its art masterpieces, and of the marble Folly in its woods, the only remnant of the original manor not destroyed in the Civil War. The English had a Civil War too. There were also peacocks—there were always peacocks—and formal gardens. Although the information had surely been compiled by the Marquis of Deerfawn, who just as surely had opened his house to the public to help pay his taxes, it might turn out to be of more interest than some of the shabby great houses we'd seen. For one thing, there were two authenticated paintings by Rubens and six family portraits by Van Dyck.

There was the usual sign pointing to the west basement where would be found the usual tearoom and curio and postcard counter. This was our first stop—as Jix demanded, to insure his life, coffee with a lacing of aspirin. Dorian chafed and wrote two postcards to her two best friends at home, until Jix could navigate again. She then insisted that we return outdoors and make a proper entrance.

Jix said, "I'll shuck my coat and follow you." From where we'd parked the car we could look down the avenue and see if the coach tour was approaching. I wrote off Jix and his delaying tactics for the rest of the morning.

All in all, Deerfawn Manor House wasn't bad. It wasn't great like Warwick Castle—ah, Warwick! where I'd learned what the Biblical word "covet" truly means—but it wasn't impossibly tawdry like some attractions which shall remain nameless. We went unguided, yet not unobserved. There were guardians of the treasures stationed in each room to make sure filching was out of style.

It was past one o'clock when we again descended the carved staircase to the entrance hall.

"Now we'll do the gardens," Dorian announced.

"Hadn't we better have a bite to eat first?" I'd become as English as the English; despite the breakfast spread, I was ready for another meal.

"Later," Dorian stated.

The English are absolutely mad for gardens. As most of the tours this time of year were overwhelmingly composed of English-speakers, the formal layout surrounding the manor was already overpopulated with ritual flower-print dresses and flat tweed caps.

One look and Dorian decided, "We'll come back. After we visit the Folly."

She headed for the footpath into the deep woods, just past the handmade wooden sign: *To the Folly*. Almost immediately the path became a narrow aperture leading into far deeper woods, the kind where the sun never penetrates the undergrowth of fern. The trees actually were as tall as cathedrals.

After a more than sufficient spell of stumbling and edging onward, I ventured, "I think we took the wrong path."

"How could we?" Dorian asked, but not with her usual assurance. "The sign pointed this way. You saw it."

"It could have been turned the wrong way," I suggested half-heartedly.

At that moment a strangled cry rose from somewhere in the

density. Dorian bashed up quick against my quaking shoulder. And then I remembered. "Those damn peacocks!"

She managed a shaky grin and was herself again. She crashed on and before long called back to my plodding rearguard, "There's daylight ahead. This must be it."

Hopelessly, I hoped so. I was so hungry I was ready to turn poacher at sight of game. One thing came clear in our meandering: the reason Cromwell hadn't destroyed the Folly. He couldn't find it.

Ahead there was indication of a clearing of some sort. Dorian had disappeared off the path into it. I heard her cry out and I picked up speed. The cry hadn't been of delight but of disaster.

The open space was hardly bigger than a table top. Standing in it, facing each other, were Dorian and Brummel. He wasn't the young aristocrat of the Oak and Swan. He wore the leather apron and the mudsplattered boots of the Manor's outdoor staff.

His face was the color of rain and absolutely vacant of any expression. It took me that long to see what was at his feet. An oversized black sweater, dirty rose-colored pants, and flowing yellow hair. In Brummel's right hand there was a big rock. Its smooth surface was discolored.

"Oh, no," Dorian was whimpering.

My entrance released Brummel from shock. "You, too?"

Dorian also came to life. But she didn't run away. She ran toward him. "Come on. We've got to get you out of here."

He half stumbled as she tugged at him, then stoutly released himself and stood away. "Wait," he said. "I must—"

We all heard the suspicious rustle of leaves. It could have been some Cromwellian spy creeping up on us.

"One moment," Brummel whispered. He actually knelt and with quick fingers explored the crumpled body. He took something from beneath the sweater, palming the object into his apron pocket before we could see what it was. "This way," he said under his breath, absently picking up the weapon before he moved.

He set off into what looked like impenetrable forest but which shortly emerged into a path leading up a hill. Don't ask my why, like a dumb sheep, I followed a red-handed killer. Perhaps at the time it seemed better than being lost in the woods with no chocolate bar. As for Dorian, she doubtless had absolved him from guilt the moment she recognized the victim.

Like most women, Dorian has a bloodthirsty streak where rivals are concerned.

When the going was easier, I suggested, "Hadn't you better get rid of that rock?" It was making me nervous.

"What rock?" he said, puzzled, and then realized he was still holding it. "Oh, the rock," he said vaguely. "Yes. Yes, I should, I presume."

He gestured us off the path, then advanced a few yards, pondered, and selected a tree no different from any other of the hundred trees in the forest. Carefully he tucked the rock under the ferns there. It didn't seem my place to point out that his fingerprints might be all over it. Possibly it wouldn't turn up for some three hundred years, and the Dorians of that day would believe the bloodstains were made in the first Danish invasion.

Brummel seemed quite relieved to be rid of it. "Come along now," he said. "We must hurry." He was leading us not back to our hillside path but through and around the woods in what seemed a circular pattern. If Dorian wasn't uneasy, I was ashamed to be. And shortly, there lay the enormous Manor House below.

Brummel paused only for a few breaths, looking down on the back court where the cars and coaches were parked. In sight were only a couple of drivers having a gossip over their cigarettes. The red shine of our Triumph was like a beacon.

Brummel said to Dorian, "You and Kell won't have any difficulty getting away. Don't talk to anyone—just go."

"But you're the one who has to get away," Dorian cried out, remembering to keep it a muted cry.

He shook his head. "I can't."

Of course he couldn't: he'd have to hide the body first.

Dorian thought quickly. "We can't either. We can't go off and leave Jix without a ride."

"I'll take care of Jix! Please. Hurry."

I was the practical one. "How do we get to the car? Make like birds or toboggans?"

"I'll lead you down," Brummel said, "but once we're in the court, walk over, get in your car, and take off. Fast." He didn't wait for Dorian to give him further argument. He set off on a transverse, and somehow or other we all managed to get down to the ditch below and start clambering up its slope into the courtyard.

We almost had it made when what can only be described as a hue-and-cry began. There were uniformed attendants legging out of every door and it didn't take someone of normal I.Q. to realize that the body had been discovered.

Under his breath, Brummel muttered, "That's torn it. Come on."

We fled to the Triumph and he squeezed in without the usual preliminary of ladies first. Dorian said, "You drive, Kell," and slid in beside him. The engine caught and we were headed down the drive before anyone could stop us. Not that anyone tried.

"Take off that silly costume," Dorian ordered, "and put on Jix's coat."

Brummel ducked out of the leather apron and stuffed it under the seat while Dorian helped envelop him in Jix's coat of too many colors. As a disguise it wasn't what I'd have chosen.

I kept a nice pace to the gate, not too fast, and returned the gatehouse attendant's friendly salute. The word hadn't reached him yet.

In the lane I picked up speed. "To Stratford?"

"Yes," Brummel said.

By this time we were approaching the turn into the Stratford road—approaching it, I suddenly observed, much too rapidly. I removed my foot entirely from the gas pedal. I didn't want to compound our troubles by crashing into the police car which was blocking the intersection.

Brummel sighed and Dorian, for once, said nothing. I braked, and a young constable strolled over to my side of the car. The bobbies in their helmets and dark formal uniforms somehow look unreal in the country; they belong in London.

"Good afternoon," he said pleasantly. "You've come from Deerfawn Manor?"

There was no other place we could have come from unless we'd been haring across the meadows, and he knew it.

I said meekly, "Yes, sir."

"I'm afraid I'll have to ask you to go back."

"But why?" Dorian asked with outraged innocence.

"There's been a bit of trouble, Miss," he said. "No one is to leave until the Chief Constable arrives."

There was no point to arguing, particularly with Brummel sitting there trying to look unperturbed and, in that dreadful coat, succeeding in looking like some ghastly Teddy boy. Back

306

we crawled to Deerfawn Manor to join the now thronged court-yard.

We didn't need a guide to identify the nationalities of the tourists. The Americans were the indignant ones, the Continentals the wary, and the British the ones who accepted matters as if nothing untoward had happened. The only exceptions were Jix and his South Carolinian babe—they didn't mind the delay a bit. I noted that all of Clara's tour were on hand, including her special boy friend. He was trying to find the reason for this procedure in his guide book.

Brummel took off Jix's coat, placed it on the seat, and got out of the car. A member of the Manor staff was trotting toward him. He tried to cut away but the man planted himself head on. "I'm terribly sorry, your Lordship. It seems a girl's body has been found in our woods." The words came out distinctly in spite of the strong country accent.

Your Lordship. Our Brummel was the Marquis of Deerfawn! With my mouth dropped witlessly, I looked toward Dorian. Her mouth was also cavernous, but mercifully silent.

Brummel simulated astonishment. "A girl's body?"

"Yes, your Lordship." The servitor volunteered, "It would seem to be one of the trippers, sir."

"Is Colonel Whitten in charge?"

"He has been notified. He hasn't yet arrived."

Brummel gave some inaudible directions and the man took off at a brisk pace, away from the stone steps where the constabulary were gathered. Still ignoring us, Brummel strode toward them.

"Well," I uttered.

"Well what?" Dorian bristled. "Don't just stand there. Come on." She followed Brummel and I followed her.

By then he was listening with gravity to what the police had to tell him. Meantime, his eyes were searching frantically, or as near to frantically as a Marquis' eyes could, the sinuous mass in the court. His frenzy changed to resignation as the police parted the crowd to permit the entrance of a large black Humber. From it dismounted what had to be Colonel Whitten, Chief Constable of the shire. His mustaches were as long as a soliloquy. But he was as deferent to Brummel as the old retainer had been.

An inspection post was being set up and the English, sure enough, formed the inevitable queue. The foreigners had no

307

choice but to join it. When in Rome. As Dorian and I were up front, our turn came quickly. However, before I could give name, address, and passport number to the officer at the table, Brummel was saying, "These are friends of mine, Colonel Whitten. I can assure you they know nothing about this affair."

"All we know," said Dorian in a sweet, clear voice, "is that Brummel—his Lordship—couldn't possibly have killed Clara."

If she'd said she was carrying a nuclear warhead in her handbag, she couldn't have caused more consternation. I wasn't the only one whose mouth could drop witlessly—every policeman in the vicinity was doing it. Brummel looked as if he wanted to weep.

"Because," Dorian appeared not to notice any reaction, "she was already dead when he got there."

"You saw the body? You know who this girl was?" It wasn't the speechless Colonel Whitten but an intelligent-looking bobby who put the question.

"Of course we knew her. She was the German girl who's been in Stratford all week."

"I can explain," Brummel said without conviction, eyeing the crowd as if trying to find an escape route through it.

"My cousin and I heard her death cry," Dorian orated melodramatically, dragging me into it, "before his Lordship found her."

The Germans who understood some English were falling to pieces. Loudly and tearfully.

"The reason he had that bloody rock—excuse me, but it was bloody—in his hands," Dorian carried on with simple devastation, "was that he knew it must be the murder weapon and he wanted to preserve the evidence for—"

At that moment I heard Jix's voice above all other sounds. A good loud indignant American voice. "What's that guy doing in my coat?"

The queue swayed in the direction of Jix's bellow. We all saw a figure in German shorts and Jix's hound's tooth jacket racing toward the woods.

"He mustn't get away," Brummel warned as he started after him. The police followed like Keystone Cops. Need I say that I, following Dorian, brought up the usual rear?"

But Jix was well ahead in the chase. It was he who brought down the man before the others caught up, and wrestled the jacket off of him.

The thief, shouting and gesticulating in outraged German, was none other than Clara's dour friend, the black-notebook writer. Brummel waited until the German gulped for breath, then said in his most quiet way, "It's no good, Lengel. And it wasn't hidden in that coat."

On the outskirts of our panting group a rather tall man in a gray suit asked calmly, "What's going on here?"

Brummel's expression melted into enormous relief. "What took you so long, Freddie?" He indicated the captive. "This is your man. He gave himself away."

The police recognized Freddie as important. They parted to let him into the inner circle.

Distaste touched Freddie's mouth as he regarded the prisoner. "He didn't get away with anything?"

"With your men on guard? Not likely," Brummel assured him. "Besides, he's only an advance man, Freddie. Clara was always sure of that. She nipped the notebook, gave me the nod—" His look saddened. "Evidently he missed it before I could get to her. He got to her first."

Freddie took a step toward the struggling Lengel.

"He doesn't have it," Brummel said. "It seems these Americans—" So much for the earlier friendship he'd protested for us. "—blundered on the meeting place before he had a chance to search the body."

"You have it?" Freddie relaxed.

"I found it." Brummel couldn't resist a gibe at the German. "He thought I'd hidden it in that coat I was wearing."

"You were wearing—" Freddie's calm faltered at sight of the coat on Jix's arm.

"As a disguise," Brummel said quickly. "I wanted to get the notebook to you before it became police property. Colonel Whitten—"

Colonel Whitten hadn't made the run. He could be seen in the distance at stone-step headquarters, puffing nonchalantly on his pipe.

"He does rather talk to reporters," Brummel regretted. "I was hoping we could continue to keep our plans private."

Freddie nodded agreement. "Let me have it."

"It's wedged under the seat of their car." Brummel gave our group the faintest nod. "The little red one."

Freddie took off at a sprint. Brummel loped behind. All strangers, and that included us, were thereupon herded down the hill by the police and pointed to the Manor gates. Dorian was determined not to leave but she had stupidly destroyed whatever influence she might have had with the Marquis of Deerfawn. Without so much as a backward glance, the Marquis and Freddie were now moving away from our car, the notebook retrieved.

We drove single file back to Stratford. Even Dorian had no stomach for St. Orlgwulf's eighth-century disasters after first-hand exposure to twentieth-century violence. She spent the remainder of the afternoon on the banks of the Avon with me, inventing one far-fetched spy thriller after another to explain what had happened. Jix was again off somewhere with his fancy jacket and southern accent.

Dorian continued to fantasticate at the Mace and Swan that night until unexpectedly Brummel appeared at our table.

"May I sit down with you?" he asked. If he hadn't, Dorian would have yanked him into the empty chair. "I do want to apologize for any inconvenience I may have caused you today."

"They were spies, weren't they?" Dorian burst out.

"Oh, no," Brummel said, for a moment giving her that faintly alarmed glance which Britons reserve for nutty Americans. "They were after the paintings."

This was the summer of increasing thievery of art master-pieces. Dorian was disappointed. The stories she'd dreamed up in her own little head were much wilder and much more exciting.

"Freddie is head of the London branch of Interpol. They had a tip that Deerfawn was the next target. He asked me to help out. Working with Clara."

"Clara was an operative?" I goggled.

"She was good, wasn't she?" His somber face lighted. "The way she got herself up like a grisette."

"You mean—she wasn't really—" Dorian stammered.

"She was a lovely girl," Brummel said. Defendingly, not romantically. "A very clever girl. She got on the student tour that the gang was using as a cover and attached herself to Lengel." He shook his head. "We don't know if someone informed or if he suddenly realized that she wasn't as stupid as he thought her. But when she found out he was going to Deerfawn after telling her he was going to Leamington Spa, she knew she had to get the notebook as soon as she could. It has the plans for all the robbings in the Midlands. It's my fault she was killed." His emotion was too deep for display. "I didn't arrange carefully enough."

Dorian, possibly therapeutically, broke the silence. "I knew you didn't kill her."

Brummel came out of his shadows. "I'm afraid I panicked a bit when I saw you and Kell there. I'm rather new at this sort of thing. And I had to find that notebook." He turned and looked into Dorian's eyes, not half shy. "And I must say I wanted to get you away from there before you found out my connection with Deerfawn. I was afraid it might spoil things between us."

It didn't. During our last days in the Stratford country, Dorian and Brummel were as inseparable as Jix and South Carolina. This was a happy breather for me. I read Shakespeare by day and watched it by night. I'm as much of a nut on Shakespeare as Dorian is on ancient monuments. Oh, yes, the Folly sign had a habit of veering. Most people had sense enough to take the pebbled path to the right, not wander into untrammeled woods.

I also had plenty of time for thought those days. But I wasn't able to discuss certain peculiar aspects of the Deerfawn day until we were off on the road again, headed toward Shropshire. Without Jix—he would join us after South Carolina moved on.

I asked Dorian flatly, "What were you trying to do to Brummel, hang him? Telling the police all that stuff."

"Of course not!" she replied with indignation. "I knew he wasn't a killer, not even when I first saw him bending over the body with that bloody rock. Before you got there. He isn't the type."

A lecture on criminal types would have made no dent at that moment. She was on her high white horse with banners flying. "But if he was guilty," she proclaimed, "I wasn't going to let him get away with doing Clara in, just because of all that bow-and-scrape-your-Lordship stuff."

For one split second I believed Dorian had recovered from Anglophilia.

And then she was blasting in my ear, "Stop the car! Stop the car!"

I wondered if in the side mirror she'd noted Brummel catching up with us a day early. No, it wasn't that. It was only another ragged clump of rocks rising out of the rolling green.

With a silent sigh I wheeled into the nearest lay-by and stopped the car.

THE OLD MAN

BY DAPHNE DU MAURIER

Daphne du Maurier was born in London in 1907, the granddaughter of artist and writer George du Maurier (*Peter Ibbetson, Trilby*) and the daughter of a noted actress and actor. *Rebecca* (1938) is one of the most popular novels ever written. Among her other suspense works are *Jamaica Inn, My Cousin Rachel, The House on the Strand,* and *Don't Look Now.* She has also written romantic historical fiction such as *Frenchman's Creek* and *Hungry Hill.* One of her short stories became the basis for Hitchcock's film, *The Birds.* She received the Grand Master Award in 1978.

DID I HEAR YOU ASKING about the Old Man? I thought so. You're a newcomer to the district, here on holiday. We get plenty these days, during the summer months. Somehow they always find their way eventually over the cliffs down to this beach, and then they pause and look from the sea back to the lake; just as you did.

It's a lovely spot, isn't it? Quiet and remote. You can't wonder at the Old Man choosing to live here.

I don't remember when he first came. Nobody can. Many years ago, it must have been; he was here when I arrived, long before the war.

Perhaps he came to escape from civilization, much as I did myself. Or maybe where he lived before, the folks around made things too hot for him. It's hard to say. I had the feeling, from the very first, that he had done something, or something had been done to him, that gave him a grudge against the world.

I remember the first time I set eyes on him, I said to myself, "I bet that old fellow is one hell of a character."

Yes, he was living here beside the lake, along with his missus; funny sort of lash-up they had, exposed to all the weather, but they didn't seem to mind.

I had been warned about him by one of the fellows from the farm, who advised me, with a grin, to give the Old Man who lives down by the lake a wide berth, he didn't care for strangers.

So I went warily. I didn't stay to pass the time of day. Nor would it have been any use if I had, not knowing a word of his lingo. He was standing by the edge of the lake, looking out to sea, and from tact I avoided the piece of planking over the stream which meant passing close to him, and crossed to the other side of the lake by the beach instead.

Then, with an awkward feeling I was trespassing and had no business to be here, I bobbed down behind a clump of gorse, and took out my spyglass, and had a peep at him.

He was a big fellow, broad and strong—he's aged of course lately, I'm speaking of several years back—but even now, you can see what he must have been once. Such power and drive behind him, and that fine head, which he carried like a king. There's an idea in that too. No, I'm not joking.

Who knows what royal blood he carried inside him, harking back to some remote ancestor, and now and again, surging in him, not through his own fault, it gets the better of him and drives him fighting mad?

I didn't think about that at the time. I just looked at him, and ducked behind the gorse when I saw him turn, and I wondered to myself what went on in his mind, and whether he knew I was there, watching him.

If he should decide to come up the lake after me, I should look pretty foolish.

He must have thought better of it, though, or perhaps he did not care. He went on staring out to sea, watching the gulls, and the incoming tide, and presently he ambled off his side of the lake, heading for the missus, and home, and maybe supper.

I didn't catch a glimpse of her that first day. She just wasn't around. Living, as they do, close in by the left bank of the lake, with no proper track to the place, I hardly had the nerve to venture close, and come upon her face to face.

When I did see her, though, I was disappointed. She wasn't much to look at after all. What I mean is, she hadn't got anything like his character. A placid, mild-tempered creature, I judged her.

They had both come back from fishing when I saw them, and were making their way up from the beach to the lake.

He was in front, of course. She tagged along behind. They neither of them took the slightest notice of me, and I was glad because the Old Man might have paused, and waited, and told her to get on back home; and then come down towards the rocks where I was sitting.

You ask what I would have said, had he done so? I'm damned if I know. Maybe I would have got up, whistling, and seeming unconcerned, and then with a nod and a smile—useless, really, but instinctive if you know what I mean—said good day, and pottered off. I don't think he would have done anything. He'd just have stared after me, with those strange narrow eyes of his, and let me go.

After that, winter and summer, I was always down on the beach, or on the rocks, and they went on living their curious remote existence, sometimes fishing in the lake, sometimes at sea, and occasionally I'd come across them in the harbor, on the estuary, taking a look at the yachts anchored there, and the shipping. I used to wonder which of them made the suggestion,

314

she or him. Perhaps suddenly he would be lured by the thought of the bustle and life of the harbor, and all the things he had either wantonly given up, or never known, and he would say to her, "Today, we are going into town."

And she, happy to do whatever pleased him best, followed along.

You see, one thing that stood out, and you couldn't help noticing it, was that the pair of them were devoted to one another.

I've seen her greet him when he came back from a day's fishing, and had left her back home, and towards evening she'd come down the lake and onto the beach and down to the sea, to wait for him.

She'd see him coming from a long way off, and I would see him too, rounding the corner of the bay.

He'd come straight onto the beach, and she would go to meet him, and they would embrace each other, not caring a damn who saw them. Which, I don't know, was somehow touching. You felt there was something lovable about the Old Man, if that's how things were between them. He might be a devil to outsiders, but he was all the world to her. It gave me a warm feeling for him, when I saw them together, like that. You asked if they had any family. I was coming to that. It's about the family I really wanted to tell you. Because there was a tragedy, you see. And nobody knows anything about it except me.

I suppose I could have told someone, but if I had, I don't know. They might have taken the Old Man away, and she'd have broken her heart without him, and anyway, when all's said and done, it wasn't my business. I know the evidence against the Old Man was strong, but I hadn't positive proof—it might have been some sort of accident—and anyway, nobody made any inquiries at the time the boy disappeared, so who was I to turn busybody and informer?

I'll try and explain what happened. But you must understand that all this happened over quite a time, and sometimes I was away from home, or busy, and didn't go near the lake, and nobody seemed to take any interest in the couple living there but myself, so that it was only what I observed with my own eyes that makes this story, and it was nothing I heard from anybody else. No scraps of gossip, or tales told about them behind their backs.

Yes, they weren't always alone, like they are now. They had

315

four kids. Three girls and a boy. They brought up the four of them in that ramshackle old place by the lake, and it was always a wonder to me how they did it.

I've known days when the rain lashed that lake into little waves that burst and broke on the muddy shore near their place, and turned the marsh into a swamp, and the wind driving straight in; you'd have thought anyone with a grain of sense would have taken his missus and his kids out of it, and gone off somewhere where they could get some creature comforts at least.

Not the Old Man. If he could stick it, I guess he decided she could too, and the kids as well.

Maybe he wanted to bring them up the hard way.

Mark you, they were attractive youngsters. Especially the youngest girl. I never knew her name, but I called her Tiny; she had so much "go" to her. Chip off the old block, in spite of her size.

I can see her now, as a little thing, the first to venture paddling in the lake, on a fine morning; 'way ahead of her sisters and her brother. The brother I nicknamed Boy. He was the oldest. And between you and me, a bit of a fool. He hadn't the looks of his sisters, and was a clumsy sort of fellow. The girls would play around on their own, and go fishing, and he'd hang about in the background, not knowing what to do with himself.

If he possibly could, he'd stay around home, near his mother.

Proper mother's boy. That's why I gave him the name.

Not that she seemed to fuss over him any more than she did the others—she treated the four alike, as far as I could tell. Her thoughts were always for the Old Man, rather than for them.

But Boy was just a great baby, and I have an idea he was simple.

Like their parents, the youngsters kept themselves to themselves. Been dinned into them, I daresay, by the Old Man. They never came down to the beach on their own, and it must have been a temptation, I thought, in full summer, when people came walking over the cliffs down to the beach to bathe and picnic.

I suppose, for those strange reasons best known to himself, the Old Man had warned them to have no truck with strangers.

They were used to me, pottering, day in, day out, fetching driftwood and that; and often I used to pause and watch the kids playing by the lake. I didn't talk to them, though. They might have gone back and told the Old Man. They used to look up, when I passed by, then glance away again, sort of shy; all but Tiny.

Tiny would toss her head and do a somersault, just to show off.

I sometimes watched them go off, the six of them—the Old Man, the missus, Boy, and the three girls—for a day's fishing out to sea. The Old Man, of course, in charge, Tiny eager to help, close to her Dad, the missus looking about her to see if the weather was going to keep fine, the two other girls alongside, and Boy, poor simple Boy, always the last to leave home.

I never knew what sport they had. They used to stay out late, and I'd have left the beach by the time they came back again.

But I guess they did well. They must have lived almost entirely on what they caught. Well, fish is said to be full of vitamins, isn't it? Perhaps the Old Man was a food faddist in his way.

Well, time passed; and the youngsters began to grow up.

Tiny lost something of her individuality then, it seemed to me. She grew more like her sisters. They were a nice-looking trio, all the same. Quiet, you know, well-behaved. As for Boy, he was enormous. Almost as big as the Old Man, but with what a difference!

He had none of his father's looks, or strength, or personality; he was nothing but a great clumsy lout.

And the trouble was, I believe, the Old Man was ashamed of him. He didn't pull his weight in the home, I'm certain of that. And out fishing he was perfectly useless. The girls would work away like beetles, and Boy, always in the background, making a mess of things.

And if his mother was there, he just stayed by her side.

I could see it rattled the Old Man to have such an oaf of a son. Irritated him too, because Boy was so big. It probably didn't make sense to his intolerant mind. Strength and stupidity didn't go together. In any normal family, of course, Boy would have left home by now and gone out on his own. I used to wonder if they argued about it back in the evenings, the missus and the Old Man.

Or whether it was something never admitted between them but tacitly understood—that Boy was no good.

Well, they did leave home at last. At least, the girls did.

I'll tell you how it happened.

317

It was a day in late autumn, and I happened to be over doing some shopping in the little town overlooking the harbor, three miles from this place, and suddenly I saw the Old Man, the missus, and the three girls, and Boy, all making their way up to the Pont; that's the head of a creek, going eastwards, from the harbor.

There are a few cottages at Pont, and a farm and a church up behind. The family looked washed, and spruced up, and so did the Old Man, and the missus, and I wondered if they were going visiting.

If they were, it was an unusual thing for them to do. But it's possible they had friends, or acquaintances, up there, of whom I knew nothing. Anyway, that was the last I saw of them, on that fine Saturday afternoon, making for Pont.

It blew hard over the weekend—a proper easterly gale.

I kept indoors, and didn't go out at all. I knew the seas would be breaking good and hard on the beach. I wondered if the Old Man and the family had been able to get back. They would have been wise to have stayed with their friends, if they had friends there.

It was Tuesday before the wind dropped, and I went down to the beach again. Seaweed, driftwood, tar and oil all over the place. It's always the same after an easterly blow.

I looked up the lake, towards the Old Man's shack, and I saw him there, with the missus, just by the edge of the lake; but there was no sign of the youngsters.

I thought it a bit funny, and waited around, in case they should appear. They never did. I walked right round the lake and from the opposite bank I had a good view of their place, and even took out my old spyglass to have a closer look.

They just weren't there. The Old Man was pottering about, the way he often did when he wasn't fishing, and the missus had settled herself down to bask in the sun.

There was only one explanation. They had left the family with friends in Pont. They had sent the family off to have a holiday.

I can't help admitting I was relieved, because for one frightful moment I thought maybe they had started off back home on the Saturday night and got struck by the gale; and that the Old Man and his missus had got back safely, but not the kids.

It couldn't be that though. I should have heard. Someone would have said something. The Old Man wouldn't be pottering there in his usual unconcerned fashion, and the missus basking in the sun.

No, that must have been it. They had left the family with friends.

Or maybe the girls and Boy had gone up country, gone out on their own at last.

Somehow, it left a gap. I felt sad. So long now I had been used to seeing them all around, Tiny and the others.

I had a strange sort of feeling that they had gone for good.

Silly, wasn't it? To mind, I mean. There was the Old Man and his missus and the four youngsters, and I'd more or less watched them grow up, and now, for no reason, they had gone.

I wished then I knew even a word or two of his language. So that I could have called out to him, neighborlike, and said, "I see you and the missus are alone. Nothing wrong, I hope?"

But there, it wasn't any use. He'd have looked at me with his strange eyes and not said a word.

I never saw the girls again. No, never. They just didn't come back. Once I thought I saw Tiny, somewhere up the estuary, with a group of friends, but I couldn't be sure. If it was, she'd grown, she looked different. I tell you what I think. I think the Old Man and the missus took them with a definite end in view, that last weekend, and either settled them with friends they knew, or told them to shift for themselves.

I know it sounds hard, not what you'd do for your own son and daughters, but you have to remember the Old Man was a tough customer, a law unto himself.

No doubt he thought it would be for the best, and so it probably was, and if only I could know for certain what happened to the girls, especially Tiny, I wouldn't worry.

But I do worry sometimes, because of what did happen to Boy.

You see, Boy was fool enough to come back.

He came back about three weeks after that final weekend.

I had walked down through the woods, not my usual way, but reached the lake by the stream that feeds it from a higher level. I rounded the lake by the marshes to the north, some distance from the Old Man's place; and the first thing I saw was Boy.

He wasn't doing anything. He was just standing by the marsh.

He looked dazed. He was too far off for me to hail him; besides, I didn't have the nerve. But I watched him, and he stood there, in his clumsy loutish way, and I saw him staring at

319

the far end of the lake. He was staring in the direction of the Old Man.

The Old Man, and the missus with him, took not the slightest notice of Boy. They were close to the beach, by the plank bridge, and were either just going out to fish, or coming back; and here was Boy, with his dazed, stupid face, but not only stupid—frightened.

I wanted to say, "Is anything the matter?"—but I didn't know how to say it. I stood there, like Boy, staring at the Old Man.

Then, what we both must have feared would happen, did happen.

The Old Man lifted his head and saw Boy.

He must have said a word to his missus, because she didn't move. She stayed where she was, by the bridge, but the Old Man turned like a flash of lightning, and came down the other side of the lake towards the marshes, towards Boy.

He looked terrible. I shall never forget his appearance. That magnificent head I had always admired, now angry, evil; and he was cursing Boy as he came; I tell you, I heard him.

Boy, bewildered, scared, looked hopelessly about him for cover. There was none. Only the thin reeds that grew beside the marsh. But the poor fellow was so dumb he'd have gone in there and crouched, and believed himself safe.

It was a horrible sight.

I was just getting my own courage up to interfere when the Old Man stopped suddenly in his tracks, pulled up short as it were, and then, still cursing, muttering, turned back again: and returned to the bridge. Boy watched him, from his cover of reeds; then, poor clot that he was, he came out onto the marsh again, with some idea, I suppose, of striking for home.

I looked about me. There was no one to call. No one to give any help. And if I went and tried to get someone from the farm they would tell me not to interfere, that the Old Man was best left alone when he got in one of his rages, and anyway, that Boy was old enough to take care of himself.

He was as big as the Old Man. He could give as good as he got.

But I knew different. Boy was no fighter. He didn't know how.

I waited quite a time beside the lake, but nothing happened.

It began to grow dark. It was no use my waiting there. The Old Man and the missus left the bridge and went on home. Boy was still standing there on the marsh, by the lake's edge. I called to him, softly.

"It's no use. He won't let you in. Go back to Pont, or wherever it is you've been. Go some place, anywhere, but get away from here."

He looked up, that same queer dazed expression on his face; and I could tell he hadn't understood a word I said.

I felt powerless to do any more. I went home myself. But I thought about Boy all evening, and in the morning I went down to the lake again and I took a great stick with me to give me courage.

Not that it would have been much good. Not against the Old Man. Well . . . I suppose they had come to some sort of agreement, during the night. There was Boy, by his mother's side, and the Old Man was pottering on his own.

I must say, it was a great relief. Because, after all, what could I have said or done? If the Old Man didn't want Boy home, it was really his affair. And if Boy was too stupid to go, that was Boy's affair.

But I blamed the mother a good deal.

After all, it was up to her to tell Boy he was in the way, and the Old Man was in one of his moods, and Boy had best get out while the going was good.

But I never did think she had great intelligence. She did not seem to show much spirit at any time.

However, what arrangement they had come to worked for a time.

Boy stuck close to his mother—I suppose he helped her at home, I don't know—and the Old Man left them alone and was more and more by himself.

He took to sitting humped, down by the bridge, staring out to sea, with a queer brooding look on him.

He seemed strange, and lonely. I didn't like it.

I don't know what his thoughts were, but I'm sure they were evil. It suddenly seemed a very long time since he and the missus and the whole family had gone fishing, a happy, contented party.

Now everything had changed for him. He was thrust out in the cold, and the missus and Boy stayed together.

I felt sorry for him, but I felt frightened too. Because I felt it could not go on like this; something would happen.

One day I went down to the beach for driftwood—it had

been blowing in the night—and when I glanced towards the lake I saw that Boy wasn't with his mother; he was back where I had seen him that first day, on the edge of the marsh.

He was as big as his father, and if he'd known how to use his strength he'd have been a match for him any day; but he hadn't the brains.

There he was, back on the marsh, a great big frightened foolish fellow, and there was the Old Man, outside his home, staring down towards his son with murder in his eyes.

I said to myself, "He's going to kill him."

But I didn't know how, or when, or where; whether by night, when they were sleeping, or by day, when they were fishing.

The mother was useless, she would not prevent it.

It was no use appealing to the mother. If only Boy would use one little grain of sense, and go away . . .

I watched and waited until nightfall. Nothing happened.

It rained in the night. It was gray, and cold, and dim.

December was everywhere, trees all bare and bleak.

I couldn't get down to the lake until late afternoon, and then the skies had cleared and the sun was shining in that watery way it does in winter—a burst of it, just before setting below the sea.

I saw the Old Man. And the missus too. They were close together, by the old shack, and they saw me coming, for they looked toward me.

Boy wasn't there.

He wasn't on the marsh either. Nor by the side of the lake.

I crossed the bridge and went along the right bank of the lake, and I had my spyglass with me, but I couldn't see Boy.

Yet, all the time, I was aware of the Old Man watching me.

Then I saw him. I scrambled down the bank, and crossed the marsh, and went to the thing I saw lying there, behind the reeds.

He was dead. There was a great gash on his body. Dried blood on his back. He had lain there all night. His body was sodden with the rain.

Maybe you'll think I'm a fool, but I began to cry, like an idiot, and I shouted across to the Old Man, "You murderer, you bloody murderer!"

He did not answer. He did not move. He just stood there, outside his shack with the missus, watching me.

You'll want to know what I did. I went back and got a spade and I dug a grave for Boy, in the reeds behind the marsh, and I

322

said one of my own prayers for him, being uncertain of his religion.

When I had finished I looked across the lake to the Old Man, and do you know what I saw?

I saw him lower his great head and bend towards his missus and embrace her. And she lifted her head to him and embraced him too.

It was both a requiem and a benediction. An atonement and a giving of praise. In their strange way, they knew they had done evil, but now it was over, because I had buried Boy, and he was gone.

They were free to be together again and there was no longer a third to come between them.

They came out into the middle of the lake and suddenly I saw the Old Man stretch his neck, and beat his wings, and he took off from the water, full of power, and she followed him, and I watched the two swans fly out to sea right into the face of the setting sun, and I tell you it was one of the most beautiful sights I ever saw in my life—the two swans flying there, alone, in winter. . . .

DEATH ON THE AIR

By NGAIO MARSH

Dame Ngaio Marsh was born April 23, 1899, in Christ-
church, New Zealand, and attended the Canterbury
University School of Art, intending to become a painter,
but changed her mind and decided to write plays. She
toured as an actress with the English Shakespeare Company, and wrote, produced, and directed plays for
various amateur theatrical groups until she went to England in 1929. Her first mystery novel, *A Man Lay Dead*,
was published in 1934 and introduced Superintendent
Roderick Alleyn, who has appeared in all her sub-
sequent books. Dame Ngaio received the Grand Master
Award in 1978.

ON THE 25TH OF DECEMBER at 7:30 a.m. Mr. Septimus Tonks was found dead beside his wireless set.

It was Emily Parks, an under-housemaid, who discovered him. She butted open the door and entered, carrying mop, duster, and carpet-sweeper. At that precise moment she was greatly startled by a voice that spoke out of the darkness.

"Good morning, everybody," said the voice in superbly inflected syllables, "and a Merry Christmas!"

Emily yelped, but not loudly, as she immediately realized what had happened. Mr. Tonks had omitted to turn off his wireless before going to bed. She drew back the curtains, revealing a kind of pale murk which was a London Christmas dawn, switched on the light, and saw Septimus.

He was seated in front of the radio. It was a small but expensive set, specially built for him. Septimus sat in an armchair, his back to Emily and his body tilted towards the wireless.

His hands, the fingers curiously bunched, were on the ledge of the cabinet under the tuning and volume knobs. His chest rested against the shelf below and his head leaned on the front panel.

He looked rather as though he was listening intently to the interior secrets of the wireless. His head was bent so that Emily could see the bald top with its trail of oiled hairs. He did not move.

"Beg pardon, sir," gasped Emily. She was again greatly startled. Mr. Tonks' enthusiasm for radio had never before induced him to tune in at seven-thirty in the morning.

"Special Christmas service," the cultured voice was saying. Mr. Tonks sat very still. Emily, in common with the other servants, was terrified of her master. She did not know whether to go or to stay. She gazed wildly at Septimus and realized that he wore a dinner-jacket. The room was now filled with the clamor of pealing bells.

Emily opened her mouth as wide as it would go and screamed and screamed and screamed. . . .

Chase, the butler, was the first to arrive. He was a pale, flabby man but authoritative. He said: "What's the meaning of this outrage?" and then saw Septimus. He went to the armchair, bent down, and looked into his master's face.

He did not lose his head, but said in a loud voice: "My Gawd!" And then to Emily: "Shut your face." By this vulgarism he betrayed his agitation. He seized Emily by the shoulders and thrust her towards the door, where they were met by Mr. Hislop, the secretary, in his dressing-gown. Mr. Hislop said: "Good heavens, Chase, what is the meaning—" and then his voice too was drowned in the clamor of bells and renewed screams.

Chase put his fat white hand over Emily's mouth.

"In the study if you please, sir. An accident. Go to your room, will you, and stop that noise or I'll give you something to make you." This to Emily, who bolted down the hall, where she was received by the rest of the staff who had congregated there.

Chase returned to the study with Mr. Hislop and locked the door. They both looked down at the body of Septimus Tonks. The secretary was the first to speak.

"But—but—he's dead," said little Mr. Hislop.

"I suppose there can't be any doubt," whispered Chase.

"Look at the face. Any doubt! My God!"

Mr. Hislop put out a delicate hand towards the bent head and then drew it back. Chase, less fastidious, touched one of the hard wrists, gripped, and then lifted it. The body at once tipped backwards as if it was made of wood. One of the hands knocked against the butler's face. He sprang back with an oath.

There lay Septimus, his knees and his hands in the air, his terrible face turned up to the light. Chase pointed to the right hand. Two fingers and the thumb were slightly blackened.

Ding, dong, dang, ding.

"For God's sake stop those bells," cried Mr. Hislop. Chase turned off the wall switch. Into the sudden silence came the sound of the door-handle being rattled and Guy Tonks' voice on the other side.

"Hislop! Mr. Hislop! Chase! What's the matter?"

"Just a moment, Mr. Guy." Chase looked at the secretary. "You go, sir."

So, it was left to Mr. Hislop to break the news to the family. They listened to his stammering revelation in stupefied silence. It was not until Guy, the eldest of the three children, stood in the study that any practical suggestion was made.

"What has killed him?" asked Guy.

"It's extraordinary," burbled Hislop. "Extraordinary. He looks as if he'd been—"

"Galvanized," said Guy.

"We ought to send for a doctor," suggested Hislop timidly.

"Of course. Will you, Mr. Hislop? Dr. Meadows."

Hislop went to the telephone and Guy returned to his family. Dr. Meadows lived on the other side of the square and arrived in five minutes. He examined the body without moving it. He questioned Chase and Hislop. Chase was very voluble about the burns on the hand. He uttered the word "electrocution" over and over again.

"I had a cousin, sir, that was struck by lightning. As soon as I saw the hand—"

"Yes, yes," said Dr. Meadows. "So you said. I can see the burns for myself."

"Electrocution," repeated Chase. "There'll have to be an inquest."

Dr. Meadows snapped at him, summoned Emily, and then saw the rest of the family—Guy, Arthur, Phillipa, and their mother. They were clustered round a cold grate in the drawing-room. Phillipa was on her knees, trying to light the fire.

"What was it?" asked Arthur as soon as the doctor came in.

"Looks like electric shock. Guy, I'll have a word with you if you please. Phillipa, look after your mother, there's a good child. Coffee with a dash of brandy. Where are those damn maids? Come on, Guy."

Alone with Guy, he said they'd have to send for the police.

"The police!" Guy's dark face turned very pale. "Why? What's it got to do with them?"

"Nothing, as like as not, but they'll have to be notified. I can't give a certificate as things are. If it's electrocution, how did it happen?"

"But the police!" said Guy. "That's simply ghastly. Dr. Meadows, for God's sake, couldn't you—?"

"No," said Dr. Meadows, "I couldn't. Sorry, Guy, but there it is."

"But can't we wait a moment? Look at him again. You haven't examined him properly."

"I don't want to move him, that's why. Pull yourself together, boy. Look here. I've got a pal in the C.I.D.—Alleyn. He's a gentleman and all that. He'll curse me like a fury, but he'll come if he's in London, and he'll make things easier for you. Go back to your mother. I'll ring Alleyn up."

That was how it came about that Chief Detective-Inspector Roderick Alleyn spent his Christmas Day in harness. As a matter of fact he was on duty, and as he pointed out to Dr. Meadows, would have had to turn out and visit his miserable Tonkses in any case. When he did arrive it was with his usual air of remote courtesy. He was accompanied by a tall, thick-set officer—Inspector Fox—and by the divisional police-surgeon. Dr. Meadows took them into the study. Alleyn, in his turn, looked at the horror that had been Septimus.

"Was he like this when he was found?"

"No. I understand he was leaning forward with his hands on the ledge of the cabinet. He must have slumped forward and been propped up by the chair arms and the cabinet."

"Who moved him?"

"Chase, the butler. He said he only meant to raise the arm. Rigor is well established."

Alleyn put his hand behind the rigid neck and pushed. The body fell forward into its original position.

"There you are, Curtis," said Alleyn to the divisional surgeon. He turned to Fox. "Get the cameraman, will you, Fox?"

The photographer took four shots and departed. Alleyn marked the position of the hands and feet with chalk, made a careful plan of the room and then turned to the doctors.

"Is it electrocution, do you think?"

"Looks like it," said Curtis. "Have to be a p.m. of course."

"Of course. Still, look at the hands. Burns. Thumb and two fingers bunched together and exactly the distance between the two knobs apart. He'd been tuning his hurdy-gurdy."

"By gum," said Inspector Fox, speaking for the first time.

"D'you mean he got a lethal shock from his radio?" asked Dr. Meadows.

"I don't know. I merely conclude he had his hands on the knobs when he died."

"It was still going when the housemaid found him. Chase turned it off and got no shock."

"Yours, partner," said Alleyn, turning to Fox. Fox stooped down to the wall switch.

"Careful," said Alleyn.

"I've got rubber soles," said Fox, and switched it on. The radio hummed, gathered volume, and found itself.

"No-oel, No-o-el," it roared. Fox cut it off and pulled out the wall plug.

"I'd like to have a look inside this set," he said.

"So you shall, old boy, so you shall," rejoined Alleyn. "Before you begin, I think we'd better move the body. Will you see to

328

that, Meadows? Fox, get Bailey, will you? He's out in the car."

Curtis, Hislop, and Meadows carried Septimus Tonks into a spare downstairs room. It was a difficult and horrible business with that contorted body. Dr. Meadows came back alone, mopping his brow, to find Detective-Sergeant Bailey, a fingerprint expert, at work on the wireless cabinet.

"What's all this?" asked Dr. Meadows. "Do you want to find out if he'd been fooling round with the innards?"

"He," said Alleyn, "or—somebody else."

"Umph!" Dr. Meadows looked at the Inspector. "You agree with me, it seems. Do you suspect—?"

"Suspect? I'm the least suspicious man alive. I'm merely being tidy. Well, Bailey?"

"I've got a good one off the chair arm. That'll be the deceased's, won't it, sir?"

"No doubt. We'll check up later. What about the wireless?"

Fox, wearing a glove, pulled off the knob of the volume control.

"Seems to be O.K." said Bailey. "It's a sweet bit of work. Not too bad at all, sir." He turned his torch into the back of the radio, undid a couple of screws underneath the set, and lifted out the works.

"What's the little hole for?" asked Alleyn.

"What's that, sir?" said Fox.

"There's a hole bored through the panel above the knob. About an eighth of an inch in diameter. The rim of the knob hides it. One might easily miss it. Move your torch, Bailey. Yes. There, do you see?"

Fox bent down and uttered a bass growl. A fine needle of light came through the front of the radio.

"That's peculiar, sir," said Bailey from the other side. "I don't get the idea at all."

Alleyn pulled out the tuning knob.

"There's another one there," he murmured. "Yes. Nice clean little holes. Newly bored. Unusual, I take it?"

"Unusual's the word, sir," said Fox.

"Run away, Meadows," said Alleyn.

"Why the devil?" asked Dr. Meadows indignantly. "What are you driving at? Why shouldn't I be here?"

"You ought to be with the sorrowing relatives. Where's your corpseside manner?"

"I've settled them. What are you up to?"

"Who's being suspicious now?" asked Alleyn mildly. "You

may stay for a moment. Tell me about the Tonkses. Who are they? What are they? What sort of a man was Septimus?"

"If you must know, he was a damned unpleasant sort of a man."

"Tell me about him."

Dr. Meadows sat down and lit a cigarette.

"He was a self-made bloke," he said, "as hard as nails and—well, coarse rather than vulgar."

"Like Dr. Johnson perhaps?"

"Not in the least. Don't interrupt. I've known him for twenty-five years. His wife was a neighbor of ours in Dorset. Isabel Foreston. I brought the children into this vale of tears and, by jove, in many ways it's been one for them. It's an extraordinary household. For the last ten years Isabel's condition has been the sort that sends these psycho-jokers dizzy with rapture. I'm only an out-of-date G.P., and I'd just say she is in an advanced stage of hysterical neurosis. Frightened into fits of her husband."

"I can't understand these holes," grumbled Fox to Bailey.

"Go on, Meadows," said Alleyn.

"I tackled Sep about her eighteen months ago. Told him the trouble was in her mind. He eyed me with a sort of grin on his face and said: 'I'm surprised to learn that my wife has enough mentality to—' But look here, Alleyn, I can't talk about my patients like this. What the devil am I thinking about?"

"You know perfectly well it'll go no further unless—"

"Unless what?"

"Unless it has to. Do go on."

But Dr. Meadows hurriedly withdrew behind his professional rectitude. All he would say was that Mr. Tonks had suffered from high blood pressure and a weak heart, that Guy was in his father's city office, that Arthur had wanted to study art and had been told to read for law, and that Phillipa wanted to go on the stage and had been told to do nothing of the sort.

"Bullied his children," commented Alleyn.

"Find out for yourself. I'm off." Dr. Meadows got as far as the door and came back.

"Look here," he said, "I'll tell you one thing. There was a row here last night. I'd asked Hislop, who's a sensible little beggar, to let me know if anything happened to upset Mrs. Sep. Upset her badly, you know. To be indiscreet again, I said he'd better let me know if Sep cut up rough because Isabel and the young had had about as much of that as they could stand. He was

330

drinking pretty heavily. Hislop rang me up at ten-twenty last night to say there'd been a hell of a row; Sep bullying Phips—Phillipa, you know; always called her Phips—in her room. He said Isabel—Mrs. Sep—had gone to bed. I'd had a big day and I didn't want to turn out. I told him to ring again in half an hour if things hadn't quieted down. I told him to keep out of Sep's way and stay in his own room, which is next to Phips', and see if she was all right when Sep cleared out. Hislop was involved. I won't tell you how. The servants were all out. I said that if I didn't hear from him in half an hour I'd ring again and if there was no answer I'd know they were all in bed and quiet. I did ring, got no answer, and went to bed myself. That's all. I'm off. Curtis knows where to find me. You'll want me for the inquest, I suppose. Goodbye."

When he had gone Alleyn embarked on a systematic prowl round the room. Fox and Bailey were still deeply engrossed with the wireless.

"I don't see how the gentleman could have got a bump-off from the instrument," grumbled Fox. "These control knobs are quite in order. Everything's as it should be. Look here, sir."

He turned on the wall switch and tuned in. There was a prolonged humming.

". . . concludes the program of Christmas carols," said the radio.

"A very nice tone," said Fox approvingly.

"Here's something sir," announced Bailey suddenly.

"Found the sawdust, have you?" said Alleyn.

"Got it in one," said the startled Bailey.

Alleyn peered into the instrument, using the torch. He scooped up two tiny traces of sawdust from under the holes.

" 'Vantage number one," said Alleyn. He bent down to the wall plug. "Hullo! A two-way adapter. Serves the radio and the radiator. Thought they were illegal. This is a rum business. Let's have another look at those knobs."

He had his look. They were the usual wireless fitments, bakelite knobs fitting snugly to the steel shafts that projected from the front panel.

"As you say," he murmured, "quite in order. Wait a bit." He produced a pocket lens and squinted at one of the shafts. "Ye-es. Do they ever wrap blotting-paper round these objects, Fox?"

"Blotting-paper!" ejaculated Fox. "They do not."

Alleyn scraped at both the shafts with his penknife, holding an envelope underneath. He rose, groaning, and crossed to the desk. "A corner torn off the bottom bit of blotch," he said presently. "No prints on the wireless, I think you said, Bailey?"

"That's right," agreed Bailey morosely.

"There'll be none, or too many, on the blotter, but try, Bailey, try," said Alleyn. He wandered about the room, his eyes on the floor; got as far as the window and stopped.

"Fox!" he said. "A clue. A very palpable clue."

"What is it?" said Fox.

"The odd wisp of blotting-paper, no less." Alleyn's gaze traveled up the side of the window curtain. "Can I believe my eyes?"

He got a chair, stood on the seat, and with his gloved hand pulled the buttons from the ends of the curtain rod.

"Look at this." He turned to the radio, detached the control knobs, and laid them beside the ones he had removed from the curtain rod.

Ten minutes later Inspector Fox knocked on the drawing-room door and was admitted by Guy Tonks. Phillipa had got the fire going and the family was gathered round it. They looked as though they had not moved or spoken to one another for a long time.

It was Phillipa who spoke first to Fox. "Do you want one of us?" she asked.

"If you please, miss," said Fox. "Inspector Alleyn would like to see Mr. Guy Tonks for a moment, if convenient."

"I'll come," said Guy, and led the way to the study. At the door he paused. "Is he—my father—still—?"

"No, no, sir," said Fox comfortably. "It's all shipshape in there again."

With a lift of his chin Guy opened the door and went in, followed by Fox. Alleyn was alone, seated at the desk. He rose to his feet.

"You want to speak to me?" asked Guy.

"Yes, if I may. This has all been a great shock to you, of course. Won't you sit down?"

Guy sat in the chair farthest away from the radio.

"What killed my father? Was it a stroke?"

"The doctors are not quite certain. There will have to be a postmortem."

"Good God! And an inquest?"

"I'm afraid so."

"Horrible!" said Guy violently. "What do they think was the

matter? Why the devil do these quacks have to be so mysterious? What killed him?"

"They think an electric shock."

"How did it happen?"

"We don't know. It looks as if he got it from the wireless."

"Surely that's impossible. I thought they were foolproof."

"I believe they are, if left to themselves."

For a second undoubtedly Guy was startled. Then a look of relief came into his eyes. He seemed to relax all over.

"Of course," he said, "he was always monkeying about with it. What had he done?"

"Nothing."

"But you said—if it killed him he must have done something to it."

"If anyone interfered with the set it was put right afterwards."

Guy's lips parted but he did not speak. He had gone very white.

"So you see," said Alleyn, "your father could not have done anything."

"Then it was not the radio that killed him."

"That we hope will be determined by the postmortem."

"I don't know anything about wireless," said Guy suddenly. "I don't understand. This doesn't seem to make sense. Nobody ever touched the thing except my father. He was most particular about it. Nobody went near the wireless."

"I see. He was an enthusiast?"

"Yes, it was his only enthusiasm except—except his business."

"One of my men is a bit of an expert," Alleyn said. "He says this is a remarkably good set. You are not an expert, you say. Is there anyone in the house who is?"

"My younger brother was interested at one time. He's given it up. My father wouldn't allow another radio in the house."

"Perhaps he may be able to suggest something."

"But if the thing's all right now—"

"We've got to explore every possibility."

"You speak as if—as—if—"

"I speak as I am bound to speak before there has been an inquest," said Alleyn. "Had anyone a grudge against your father, Mr. Tonks?"

Up went Guy's chin again. He looked Alleyn squarely in the eyes.

"Almost everyone who knew him," said Guy.

"Is that an exaggeration?"

"No. You think he was murdered, don't you?"

Alleyn suddenly pointed to the desk beside him.

"Have you ever seen those before?" he asked abruptly. Guy stared at two black knobs that lay side by side on an ashtray.

"Those?" he said. "No. What are they?"

"I believe they are the agents of your father's death."

The study door opened and Arthur Tonks came in.

"Guy," he said, "what's happening? We can't stay cooped up together all day. I can't stand it. For God's sake what happened to him?"

"They think those things killed him," said Guy.

"Those?" For a split second Arthur's glance slewed to the curtain-rods. Then, with a characteristic flicker of his eyelids, he looked away again.

"What do you mean?" he asked Alleyn.

"Will you try one of those knobs on the shaft of the volume control?"

"But," said Arthur, "they're metal."

"It's disconnected," said Alleyn.

Arthur picked one of the knobs from the tray, turned to the radio, and fitted the knob over one of the exposed shafts.

"It's too loose," he said quickly, "it would fall off."

"Not if it was packed—with blotting-paper, for instance."

"Where did you find these things?" demanded Arthur.

"I think you recognized them, didn't you? I saw you glance at the curtain-rod."

"Of course I recognized them. I did a portrait of Phillipa against those curtains when—he—was away last year. I've painted the damn things."

"Look here," interrupted Guy, "exactly what are you driving at, Mr. Alleyn? If you mean to suggest that my brother—"

"I!" cried Arthur. "What's it got to do with me? Why should you suppose—"

"I found traces of blotting-paper on the shafts and inside the metal knobs," said Alleyn. "It suggested a substitution of the metal knobs for the bakelite ones. It is remarkable, don't you think, that they should so closely resemble one another? If you examine them, of course, you find they are not identical. Still, the difference is scarcely perceptible."

Arthur did not answer this. He was still looking at the wireless. "I've always wanted to have a look at this set," he said surprisingly.

"You are free to do so now," said Alleyn politely. "We have finished with it for the time being."

"Look here," said Arthur suddenly, "suppose metal knobs were substituted for bakelite ones, it couldn't kill him. He wouldn't get a shock at all. Both the controls are grounded."

"Have you noticed those very small holes drilled through the panel?" asked Alleyn. "Should they be there, do you think?"

Arthur peered at the little steel shafts. "By God, he's right, Guy," he said. "That's how it was done."

"Inspector Fox," said Alleyn, "tells me those holes could be used for conducting wires and that a lead could be taken from the—the transformer, is it?—to one of the knobs."

"And the other connected to earth," said Fox. "It's a job for an expert. He could get three hundred volts or so that way."

"That's not good enough," said Arthur quickly; "there wouldn't be enough current to do any damage—only a few hundredths of an amp."

"I'm not an expert," said Alleyn, "but I'm sure you're right. Why were the holes drilled then? Do you imagine someone wanted to play a practical joke on your father?"

"A practical joke? On *him?*" Arthur gave an unpleasant screech of laughter. "Do you hear that, Guy?"

"Shut up," said Guy. "After all, he is dead."

"It seems almost too good to be true, doesn't it?"

"Don't be a bloody fool, Arthur. Pull yourself together. Can't you see what this means? They think he's been murdered."

"Murdered! They're wrong. None of us had the nerve for that, Mr. Inspector. Look at me. My hands are so shaky they told me I'd never be able to paint. That dates from when I was a kid and he shut me up in the cellars for a night. Look at me. Look at Guy. He's not so vulnerable, but he caved in like the rest of us. We were conditioned to surrender. Do you know—"

"Wait a moment," said Alleyn quietly. "Your brother is quite right, you know. You'd better think before you speak. This may be a case of homicide."

"Thank you, sir," said Guy quickly. "That's extraordinarily decent of you. Arthur's a bit above himself. It's a shock."

"The relief, you mean," said Arthur. "Don't be such an ass. I didn't kill him and they'll find it out soon enough. Nobody killed him. There must be some explanation."

"I suggest that you listen to me," said Alleyn. "I'm going to put several questions to both of you. You need not answer them, but it will be more sensible to do so. I understand no one

335

but your father touched this radio. Did any of you ever come into this room while it was in use?"

"Not unless he wanted to vary the program with a little bullying," said Arthur.

Alleyn turned to Guy, who was glaring at his brother.

"I want to know exactly what happened in this house last night. As far as the doctors can tell us, your father died not less than three and not more than eight hours before he was found. We must try to fix the time as accurately as possible."

"I saw him at about a quarter to nine," began Guy slowly. "I was going out to a supper-party at the Savoy and had come downstairs. He was crossing the hall from the drawing-room to his room."

"Did you see him after a quarter to nine, Mr. Arthur?"

"No. I heard him, though. He was working in here with Hislop. Hislop had asked to go away for Christmas. Quite enough. My father discovered some urgent correspondence. Really, Guy, you know, he was pathological. I'm sure Dr. Meadows thinks so."

"When did you hear him?" asked Alleyn.

"Some time after Guy had gone. I was working on a drawing in my room upstairs. It's above his. I heard him bawling at little Hislop. It must have been before ten o'clock, because I went out to a studio party at ten. I heard him bawling as I crossed the hall."

"And when," said Alleyn, "did you both return?"

"I came home at about twenty past twelve," said Guy immediately. "I can fix the time because we had gone on to Chez Carlo, and they had a midnight stunt there. We left immediately afterwards. I came home in a taxi. The radio was on full blast."

"You heard no voices?"

"None. Just the wireless."

"And you, Mr. Arthur?"

"Lord knows when I got in. After one. The house was in darkness. Not a sound."

"You had your own key?"

"Yes," said Guy. "Each of us has one. They're always left on a hook in the lobby. When I came in I noticed Arthur's was gone."

"What about the others? How did you know it was your brother's?"

"Mother hasn't got one and Phips lost her weeks ago.

336

Anyway, I knew they were staying in and that it must be Arthur who was out."

"Thank you," said Arthur ironically.

"You didn't look in the study when you came in," Alleyn asked him.

"Good Lord, no," said Arthur as if the suggestion was fantastic. "I say," he said suddenly, "I suppose he was sitting here—dead. That's a queer thought." He laughed nervously. "Just sitting here, behind the door in the dark."

"How do you know it was in the dark?"

"What d'you mean? Of course it was. There was no light under the door."

"I see. Now do you two mind joining your mother again? Perhaps your sister will be kind enough to come in here for a moment. Fox, ask her, will you?"

Fox returned to the drawing-room with Guy and Arthur and remained there, blandly unconscious of any embarrassment his presence might cause the Tonkses. Bailey was already there, ostensibly examining the electric points.

Phillipa went to the study at once. Her first remark was characteristic. "Can I be of any help?" asked Phillipa.

"It's extremely nice of you to put it like that," said Alleyn. "I don't want to worry you for long. I'm sure this discovery has been a shock to you."

"Probably," said Phillipa. Alleyn glanced quickly at her. "I mean," she explained, "that I suppose I must be shocked but I can't feel anything much. I just want to get it all over as soon as possible. And then think. Please tell me what has happened."

Alleyn told her they believed her father had been electrocuted and that the circumstances were unusual and puzzling. He said nothing to suggest that the police suspected murder.

"I don't think I'll be much help," said Phillipa, "but go ahead."

"I want to try to discover who was the last person to see your father or speak to him."

"I should think very likely I was," said Phillipa composedly. "I had a row with him before I went to bed."

"What about?"

"I don't see that it matters."

Alleyn considered this. When he spoke again it was with deliberation.

"Look here," he said, "I think there is very little doubt that your father was killed by an electric shock from his wireless set.

337

As far as I know the circumstances are unique. Radios are normally incapable of giving a lethal shock to anyone. We have examined the cabinet and are inclined to think that its internal arrangements were disturbed last night. Very radically disturbed. Your father may have experimented with it. If anything happened to interrupt or upset him, it is possible that in the excitement of the moment he made some dangerous readjustment."

"You don't believe that, do you?" asked Phillipa calmly.

"Since you ask me," said Alleyn, "no."

"I see,"'said Phillipa; "you think he was murdered, but you're not sure." She had gone very white, but she spoke crisply. "Naturally you want to find out about my row."

"About everything that happened last evening," amended Alleyn.

"What happened was this," said Phillipa; "I came into the hall some time after ten. I'd heard Arthur go out and had looked at the clock at five past. I ran into my father's secretary, Richard Hislop. He turned aside, but not before I saw . . . not quickly enough. I blurted out: 'You're crying.' We looked at each other. I asked him why he stood it. None of the other secretaries could. He said he had to. He's a widower with two children. There have been doctor's bills and things. I needn't tell you about his . . . about his damnable servitude to my father nor about the refinements of cruelty he'd had to put up with. I think my father was mad, really mad, I mean. Richard gabbled it all out to me higgledy-piggledy in a sort of horrified whisper. He's been here two years, but I'd never realized until that moment that we . . . that . . ." A faint flush came into her cheeks. "He's such a funny little man. Not at all the sort I've always thought . . . not good-looking or exciting or anything."

She stopped, looking bewildered.

"Yes?" said Alleyn.

"Well, you see—I suddenly realized I was in love with him. He realized it too. He said: 'Of course, it's quite hopeless, you know. Us, I mean. Laughable, almost.' Then I put my arms round his neck and kissed him. It was very odd, but it seemed quite natural. The point is my father came out of this room into the hall and saw us."

"That was bad luck," said Alleyn.

"Yes, it was. My father really seemed delighted. He almost licked his lips. Richard's efficiency had irritated my father for a long time. It was difficult to find excuses for being beastly to

338

him. Now, of course . . . He ordered Richard to the study and me to my room. He followed me upstairs. Richard tried to come too, but I asked him not to. My father . . . I needn't tell you what he said. He put the worst possible construction on what he'd seen. He was absolutely foul, screaming at me like a madman. He was insane. Perhaps it was D.T.s. He drank terribly, you know. I dare say it's silly of me to tell you all this."

"No," said Alleyn.

"I can't feel anything at all. Not even relief. The boys are frankly relieved. I can't feel afraid either." She stared meditatively at Alleyn. "Innocent people needn't feel afraid, need they?"

"It's an axiom of police investigation," said Alleyn and wondered if indeed she was innocent.

"It just *can't* be murder," said Phillipa. "We were all too much afraid to kill him. I believe he'd win even if you murdered him. He'd hit back somehow." She put her hands to her eyes. "I'm all muddled," she said.

"I think you are more upset than you realize. I'll be as quick as I can. Your father made this scene in your room. You say he screamed. Did anyone hear him?"

"Yes. Mummy did. She came in."

"What happened?"

"I said: 'Go away, darling, it's all right.' I didn't want her to be involved. He nearly killed her with the things he did. Sometimes he'd . . . we never knew what happened between them. It was all secret, like a door shutting quietly as you walk along a passage."

"Did she go away?"

"Not at once. He told her he'd found out that Richard and I were lovers. He said . . . it doesn't matter. I don't want to tell you. She was terrified. He was stabbing at her in some way I couldn't understand. Then, quite suddenly, he told her to go to her own room. She went at once and he followed her. He locked me in. That's the last I saw of him, but I heard him go downstairs later."

"Were you locked in all night?"

"No. Richard Hislop's room is next to mine. He came up and spoke through the wall to me. He wanted to unlock the door, but I said better not in case—he—came back. Then, much later, Guy came home. As he passed my door I tapped on it. The key was in the lock and he turned it."

"Did you tell him what had happened?"

"Just that there'd been a row. He only stayed a moment."

"Can you hear the radio from your room?"

She seemed surprised.

"The wireless? Why, yes. Faintly."

"Did you hear it after your father returned to the study?"

"I don't remember."

"Think. While you lay awake all that long time until your brother came home?"

"I'll try. When he came out and found Richard and me, it was not going. They had been working, you see. No, I can't remember hearing it at all unless—wait a moment. Yes. After he had gone back to the study from mother's room I remember there was a loud crash of static. Very loud. Then I think it was quiet for some time. I fancy I heard it again later. Oh, I've remembered something else. After the static my bedside radiator went out. I suppose there was something wrong with the electric supply. That would account for both, wouldn't it? The heater went on again about ten minutes later."

"And did the radio begin again then, do you think?"

"I don't know. I'm very vague about that. It started again sometime before I went to sleep."

"Thank you very much indeed. I won't bother you any longer now."

"All right," said Phillipa calmly, and went away.

Alleyn sent for Chase and questioned him about the rest of the staff and about the discovery of the body. Emily was summoned and dealt with. When she departed, awestruck but complacent, Alleyn turned to the butler.

"Chase," he said, "had your master any peculiar habits?"

"Yes, sir."

"In regard to his use of the wireless?"

"I beg pardon, sir. I thought you meant generally speaking."

"Well, then, generally speaking."

"If I may say so, sir, he was a mass of them."

"How long have you been with him?"

"Two months, sir, and due to leave at the end of this week."

"Oh. Why are you leaving?"

Chase produced the classic remark of his kind.

"There are some things," he said, "that flesh and blood will not stand, sir. One of them's being spoke to like Mr. Tonks spoke to his staff."

"Ah. His peculiar habits, in fact?"

"It's my opinion, sir, he was mad. Stark, staring."

340

"With regard to the radio. Did he tinker with it?"

"I can't say I've ever noticed, sir. I believe he knew quite a lot about wireless."

"When he tuned the thing, had he any particular method? Any characteristic attitude or gesture?"

"I don't think so, sir. I never noticed, and yet I've often come into the room when he was at it. I can seem to see him now, sir."

"Yes, yes," said Alleyn swiftly. "That's what we want. A clear mental picture. How was it now? Like this?"

In a moment he was across the room and seated in Septimus's chair. He swung round to the cabinet and raised his right hand to the tuning control.

"Like this?"

"No, sir," said Chase promptly, "that's not him at all. Both hands it should be."

"Ah." Up went Alleyn's left hand to the volume control. "More like this?"

"Yes, sir," said Chase slowly. "But there's something else and I can't recollect what it was. Something he was always doing. It's in the back of my head. You know, sir. Just on the edge of my memory, as you might say."

"I know."

"It's a kind—something—to do with irritation," said Chase slowly.

"Irritation? His?"

"No. It's no good, sir. I can't get it."

"Perhaps later. Now look here, Chase, what happened to all of you last night? All the servants, I mean."

"We were all out, sir. It being Christmas Eve. The mistress sent for me yesterday morning. She said we could take the evening off as soon as I had taken in Mr. Tonks's grog tray at nine o'clock. So we went," ended Chase simply.

"When?"

"The rest of the staff got away about nine. I left at ten past, sir, and returned about eleven twenty. The others were back then, and all in bed. I went straight to bed myself sir."

"You came in by a back door, I suppose?"

"Yes, sir. We've been talking it over. None of us noticed anything unusual."

"Can you hear the wireless in your part of the house?"

"No, sir."

"Well," said Alleyn, looking up from his notes, "that'll do, thank you."

Before Chase reached the door Fox came in.

"Beg pardon, sir," said Fox, "I just want to take a look at the *Radio Times* on the desk."

He bent over the paper, wetted a gigantic thumb, and turned a page.

"That's it, sir," shouted Chase suddenly. "That's what I tried to think of. That's what he was always doing."

"But what?"

"Licking his fingers, sir. It was a habit," said Chase. "That's what he always did when he sat down to the radio. I heard Mr. Hislop tell the doctor it nearly drove him demented, the way the master couldn't touch a thing without first licking his fingers."

"Quite so," said Alleyn. "In about ten minutes, ask Mr. Hislop if he will be good enough to come in for a moment. That will be all, thank you, Chase."

"Well, sir," remarked Fox when Chase had gone, "if that's the case and what I think's right, it'd certainly make matters worse."

"Good heavens, Fox, what an elaborate remark. What does it mean?"

"If metal knobs were substituted for bakelite ones and fine wires brought through those holes to make contact, then he'd get a bigger bump if he tuned in with *damp* fingers."

"Yes. And he always used both hands. Fox!"

"Sir."

"Approach the Tonkses again. You haven't left them alone, of course?"

"Bailey's in there making out he's interested in the light switches. He's found the main switchboard under the stairs. There's signs of a blown fuse having been fixed recently. In a cupboard underneath there are odd lengths of flex and so on. Same brand as this on the wireless and the heater."

"Ah, yes. Could the cord from the adapter to the radiator be brought into play?"

"By gum," said Fox, "you're right! That's how it was done, Chief. The heavier flex was cut away from the radiator and shoved through. There was a fire, so he wouldn't want the radiator and wouldn't notice."

"It might have been done that way, certainly, but there's little to prove it. Return to the bereaved Tonkses, my Fox, and ask prettily if any of them remember Septimus's peculiarities when tuning his wireless."

Fox met little Mr. Hislop at the door and left him alone with

342

Alleyn. Phillipa had been right, reflected the Inspector, when she said Richard Hislop was not a noticeable man. He was non-descript. Gray eyes, drab hair; rather pale, rather short, rather insignificant; and yet last night there had flashed up between those two the realization of love. Romantic but rum, thought Alleyn.

"Do sit down," he said. "I want you, if you will, to tell me what happened between you and Mr. Tonks last evening."

"What happened?"

"Yes. You all dined at eight, I understand. Then you and Mr. Tonks came in here?"

"Yes."

"What did you do?"

"He dictated several letters."

"Anything unusual take place?"

"Oh, no."

"Why did you quarrel?"

"Quarrel!" The quiet voice jumped a tone. "We did not quarrel, Mr. Alleyn."

"Perhaps that was the wrong word. What upset you?"

"Phillipa has told you?"

"Yes. She was wise to do so. What was the matter, Mr. Hislop?"

"Apart from the . . . what she told you . . . Mr. Tonks was a difficult man to please. I often irritated him. I did so last night."

"In what way?"

"In almost every way. He shouted at me. I was startled and nervous, clumsy with papers, and making mistakes. I wasn't well. I blundered and then . . . I . . . I broke down. I have always irritated him. My very mannerisms—"

"Had he no irritating mannerisms, himself?"

"He! My God!"

"What were they?"

"I can't think of anything in particular. It doesn't matter, does it?"

"Anything to do with the wireless, for instance?"

There was a short silence.

"No," said Hislop.

"Was the radio on in here last night, after dinner?"

"For a little while. Not after—after the incident in the hall. At least, I don't think so. I don't remember."

"What did you do after Miss Phillipa and her father had gone upstairs?"

343

"I followed and listened outside the door for a moment." He had gone very white and had backed away from the desk.

"And then?"

"I heard someone coming. I remembered Dr. Meadows had told me to ring him up if there was one of the scenes. I returned here and rang him up. He told me to go to my room and listen. If things got any worse I was to telephone again. Otherwise I was to stay in my room. It is next to hers."

"And you did this?" He nodded. "Could you hear what Mr. Tonks said to her?"

"A—a good deal of it."

"What did you hear?"

"He insulted her. Mrs. Tonks was there. I was just thinking of ringing Dr. Meadows up again when she and Mr. Tonks came out and went along the passage. I stayed in my room."

"You did not try to speak to Miss Phillipa?"

"We spoke through the wall. She asked me not to ring Dr. Meadows, but to stay in my room. In a little while, perhaps it was as much as twenty minutes—I really don't know—I heard him come back and go downstairs. I again spoke to Phillipa. She implored me not to do anything and said that she herself would speak to Dr. Meadows in the morning. So I waited a little longer and then went to bed."

"And to sleep?"

"My God, no!"

"Did you hear the wireless again?"

"Yes. At least I heard static."

"Are you an expert on wireless?"

"No. I know the ordinary things. Nothing much."

"How did you come to take this job, Mr. Hislop?"

"I answered an advertisement."

"You are sure you don't remember any particular mannerism of Mr. Tonks's in connection with the radio?"

"No."

"And you can tell me no more about your interview in the study that led to the scene in the hall?"

"No."

"Will you please ask Mrs. Tonks if she will be kind enough to speak to me for a moment?"

"Certainly," said Hislop, and went away.

Septimus's wife came in looking like death. Alleyn got her to sit down and asked her about her movements on the preceding evening. She said she was feeling unwell and dined in her room. She went to bed immediately afterwards. She heard Septimus yelling at Phillipa and went to Phillipa's room. Septimus accused Mr. Hislop and her daughter of "terrible things." She got as far as this and then broke down quietly. Alleyn was very gentle with her. After a little while he learned that Septimus had gone to her room with her and had continued to speak of "terrible things."

"What sort of things?" asked Alleyn.

"He was not responsible," said Isabel. "He did not know what he was saying. I think he had been drinking."

She thought he had remained with her for perhaps a quarter of an hour. Possibly longer. He left her abruptly and she heard him go along the passage, past Phillipa's door, and presumably downstairs. She had stayed awake for a long time. The wireless could not be heard from her room. Alleyn showed her the curtain knobs, but she seemed quite unable to take in their significance. He let her go, summoned Fox, and went over the whole case.

"What's your idea on the show?" he asked when he had finished.

"Well, sir," said Fox, in his stolid way, "on the face of it the young gentlemen have got alibis. We'll have to check them up, of course, and I don't see we can go much further until we have done so."

"For the moment," said Alleyn, "let us suppose Masters Guy and Arthur to be safely established behind cast-iron alibis. What then?"

"Then we've got the young lady, the old lady, the secretary, and the servants."

"Let us parade them. But first let us go over the wireless game. You'll have to watch me here. I gather that the only way in which the radio could be fixed to give Mr. Tonks his quietus is like this: Control knobs removed. Holes bored in front panel with fine drill. Metal knobs substituted and packed with blotting paper to insulate them from metal shafts and make them stay put. Heavier flex from adapter to radiator cut and the ends of the wires pushed through the drilled holes to make contact with the new knobs. Thus we have a positive and negative pole. Mr. Tonks bridges the gap, gets a mighty wallop as the current passes through him to the earth. The switchboard fuse is blown almost immediately. All this is rigged by murderer while Sep was upstairs bullying wife and daughter. Sep revisited study some time after ten twenty. Whole thing was made ready be-

345

tween ten, when Arthur went out, and the time Sep returned—say, about ten forty-five. The murderer reappeared, connected radiator with flex, removed wires, changed back knobs, and left the thing tuned in. Now I take it that the burst of static described by Phillipa and Hislop would be caused by the short-circuit that killed our Septimus?"

"That's right."

"It also affected all the heaters in the house. *Vide* Miss Tonks's radiator." Alleyn nodded slowly and went on.

"Yes. He put all that right again. It would be a simple enough matter for anyone who knew how. He'd just have to fix the fuse on the main switchboard. How long do you say it would take to—what's the horrible word?—to recondition the whole show?"

"M'm," said Fox deeply. "At a guess, sir, fifteen minutes. He'd have to be nippy."

"Yes," agreed Alleyn. "He or she."

"I don't see a female making a success of it," grunted Fox. "Look here, Chief, you know what I'm thinking. Why did Mr. Hislop lie about deceased's habit of licking his thumbs? You say Hislop told you he remembered nothing and Chase says he overheard him saying the trick nearly drove him dippy."

"Exactly," said Alleyn. He was silent for so long that Fox felt moved to utter a discreet cough.

"Eh?" said Alleyn. "Yes, Fox, yes. It'll have to be done." He consulted the telephone directory and dialed a number.

"May I speak to Dr. Meadows? Oh, it's you, is it? Do you remember Mr. Hislop telling you that Septimus Tonks's trick of wetting his fingers nearly drove Hislop demented. Are you there? You don't? Sure? All right. All right. Hislop rang you up at ten twenty, you said? And you telephoned him? At eleven. Sure of the times? I see. I'd be glad if you'd come round. Can you? Well, do if you can."

He hung up the receiver.

"Get Chase again, will you, Fox?"

Chase, recalled, was most insistent that Mr. Hislop had spoken about it to Dr. Meadows.

"It was when Mr. Hislop had flu, sir. I went up with the doctor. Mr. Hislop had a high temperature and was talking very excited. He kept on and on, saying the master had guessed his ways had driven him crazy and that the master kept on purposely to aggravate. He said if it went on much longer he'd . . . he didn't know what he was talking about, sir, really."

"What did he say he'd do?"

"Well, sir, he said he'd—he'd do something desperate to the master. But it was only his rambling, sir. I daresay he wouldn't remember anything about it."

"No," said Alleyn, "I daresay he wouldn't." When Chase had gone he said to Fox: "Go and find out about those boys and their alibis. See if they can put you on to a quick means of checking up. Get Master Guy to corroborate Miss Phillipa's statement that she was locked in her room."

Fox had been gone for some time and Alleyn was still busy with his notes when the study door burst open and in came Dr. Meadows.

"Look here, my giddy sleuth-hound," he shouted, "what's all this about Hislop? Who says he disliked Sep's abominable habits?"

"Chase does. And don't bawl at me like that. I'm worried."

"So am I, blast you. What are you driving at? You can't imagine that . . . that poor little broken-down hack is capable of electrocuting anybody, let alone Sep?"

"I have no imagination." said Alleyn wearily.

"I wish to God I hadn't called you in. If the wireless killed Sep, it was because he monkeyed with it."

"And put it right after it had killed him?"

Dr. Meadows stared at Alleyn in silence.

"Now," said Alleyn, "you've got to give me a straight answer, Meadows. Did Hislop, while he was semi-delirious, say that this habit of Tonks's made him feel like murdering him?"

"I'd forgotten Chase was there," said Dr. Meadows.

"Yes, you'd forgotten that."

"But even if he did talk wildly, Alleyn, what of it? Damn it, you can't arrest a man on the strength of a remark made in delirium."

"I don't propose to do so." Alleyn paused. "Another motive has come to light."

"You mean—Phips—last night?"

"Did he tell you about that?"

"She whispered something to me this morning. I'm very fond of Phips. My God, are you sure of your grounds?"

"Yes," said Alleyn. "I'm sorry. I think you'd better go, Meadows."

"Are you going to arrest him?"

"I have to do my job."

There was a long silence.

"Yes," said Dr. Meadows at last. "You have to do your job. Goodbye, Alleyn."

Fox returned to say that Guy and Arthur had never left their parties. He had got hold of two of their friends. Guy and Mrs. Tonks confirmed the story of the locked door.

"It's a process of elimination," said Fox. "It must be the secretary. He fixed the radio while deceased was upstairs. He must have dodged back to whisper through the door to Miss Tonks. I suppose he waited somewhere down here until he heard deceased blow himself to blazes and then put everything straight again, leaving the radio turned on."

Alleyn was silent.

"What do we do now, sir?" asked Fox.

"I want to see the hook inside the front door where they hang their keys."

Fox, looking dazed, followed his superior to the little entrance hall.

"Yes, there they are," said Alleyn. He pointed to a hook with two latchkeys hanging from it. "You could scarcely miss them. Come on, Fox."

Back in the study they found Hislop with Bailey in attendance.

Hislop looked from one Yard man to another.

"I want to know if it's murder."

"We think so," said Alleyn.

"I want you to realize that Phillipa—Miss Tonks—was locked in her room all last night."

"Until her brother came home and unlocked the door," said Alleyn.

"That was too late. He was dead by then."

"How do you know when he died?"

"It must have been when there was that crash of static."

"Mr. Hislop," said Alleyn, "why would you not tell me how much that trick of licking his fingers exasperated you?"

"But—how do you know! I never told anyone."

"You told Dr. Meadows when you were ill."

"I don't remember." He stopped short. His lips trembled. Then, suddenly he began to speak.

"Very well. It's true. For two years he's tortured me. You see, he knew something about me. Two years ago when my wife was dying, I took money from the cash-box in that desk. I paid it back and thought he hadn't noticed. He knew all the time. From then on he had me where he wanted me. He used to sit there like a spider. I'd hand him a paper. He'd wet his thumbs

348

with a clicking noise and a sort of complacent grimace. Click, click. Then he'd thumb the papers. He knew it drove me crazy. He'd look at me and then . . . click, click. And then he'd say something about the cash. He never quite accused me, just hinted. And I was impotent. You think I'm insane. I'm not. I could have murdered him. Often and often I've thought how I'd do it. Now you think I've done it. I haven't. There's the joke of it. I hadn't the pluck. And last night when Phillipa showed me she cared, it was like Heaven—unbelievable. For the first time since I've been here I *didn't* feel like killing him. And last night someone else *did!*"

He stood there trembling and vehement. Fox and Bailey, who had watched him with bewildered concern, turned to Alleyn. He was about to speak when Chase came in. "A note for you, sir," he said to Alleyn. "It came by hand."

Alleyn opened it and glanced at the first few words. He looked up.

"You may go, Mr. Hislop. Now I've got what I expected—what I fished for."

When Hislop had gone they read the letter.

Dear Alleyn,

Don't arrest Hislop. I did it. Let him go at once if you've arrested him and don't tell Phips you ever suspected him. I was in love with Isabel before she met Sep. I've tried to get her to divorce him, but she wouldn't because of the kids. Damned nonsense, but there's no time to discuss it now. I've got to be quick. He suspected us. He reduced her to a nervous wreck. I was afraid she'd go under altogether. I thought it all out. Some weeks ago I took Phip's key from the hook inside the front door. I had the tools and the flex and wire all ready. I knew where the main switchboard was and the cupboard. I meant to wait until they all went away at the New Year, but last night when Hislop rang me I made up my mind to act at once. He said the boys and servants were out and Phips locked in her room. I told him to stay in his room and to ring me up in half an hour if things hadn't quieted down. He didn't ring up. I did. No answer, so I knew Sep wasn't in his study.

I came round, let myself in, and listened. All quiet upstairs, but the lamp still on in the study, so I knew he would come down again. He'd said he wanted to get the midnight broadcast from somewhere.

I locked myself in and got to work. When Sep was away last

year, Arthur did one of his modern monstrosities of paintings in the study. He talked about the knobs making good pattern. I noticed then that they were very like the ones on the radio and later on I tried one and saw that it would fit if I packed it up a bit. Well, I did the job just as you worked it out, and it only took twelve minutes. Then I went into the drawing-room and waited.

He came down from Isabel's room and evidently went straight to the radio. I hadn't thought it would make such a row, and half expected someone would come down. No one came. I went back, switched off the wireless, mended the fuse in the main switchboard, using my torch. Then I put everything right in the study.

There was no particular hurry. No one would come in while he was there and I got the radio going as soon as possible to suggest he was at it. I knew I'd be called in when they found him. My idea was to tell them he had died of a stroke. I'd been warning Isabel it might happen at any time. As soon as I saw the burned hand I knew that cat wouldn't jump. I'd have tried to get away with it if Chase hadn't gone round bleating about electrocution and burned fingers. Hislop saw the hand. I daren't do anything but report the case to the police, but I thought you'd never twig the knobs. One up to you.

I might have bluffed through if you hadn't suspected Hislop. Can't let you hang the blighter. I'm enclosing a note to Isabel, who won't forgive me, and an official one for you to use. You'll find me in my bedroom upstairs. I'm using cyanide. It's quick.

I'm sorry, Alleyn. I think you knew, didn't you? I've bungled the whole game, but if you will be a super-sleuth . . . Goodbye.

Henry Meadows